COLOURS IN HER HANDS

COLOURS IN HER HANDS

A NOVEL

ALICE ZORN

Freehand Books gratefully acknowledges the financial support for its publishing program provided by the Canada Council for the Arts and the Alberta Media Fund, and by the Government of Canada through the Canada Book Fund.

This book is available in print and Global Certified Accessible™ EPUB formats.

Freehand Books is located in Moh'kinsstis, Calgary, Alberta, within Treaty 7 territory and Métis Nation of Alberta Region 3, and on the traditional territories of the Siksika, the Kainai, and the Piikani, as well as the Iyarhe Nakoda and Tsuut'ina nations.

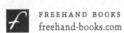

FREEHAND BOOKS
freehand-books.com

Library and Archives Canada Cataloguing in Publication
Title: Colours in her hands : a novel / Alice Zorn.
Names: Zorn, Alice, author.
Identifiers:
Canadiana (print) 20240410629
Canadiana (ebook) 20240410637
ISBN 9781990601774 (softcover)
ISBN 9781990601781 (EPUB)
ISBN 9781990601798 (PDF)
Subjects: LCGFT: Novels.
Classification: LCC PS8649.O67 C65 2024 | DDC C813/.6—dc23

Edited by Deborah Willis
Design by Natalie Olsen
Author photo by Michel Dubreuil
Printed and bound in Canada

FIRST PRINTING

FOR JOANN AUBÉ (1958–2013)

"Normal, qu'est-ce que ça veut dire, Caroline? C'est un cycle de lavage."

—Pascale Quiviger, *Si tu m'entends*

"Normal, what does that mean, Caroline? It's a wash cycle."

(Translated by Alice Zorn)

"Every heart I ever met
Is a work in progress."

—Sheree Gilchrist, Facebook, December 29, 2021

1

Bruno peered over the top of his glasses at the shaver he'd bought only a few weeks ago. Mina had called to say it didn't work anymore. The depilatory cream she'd used for years had started giving her a rash, and if she didn't do anything about her facial hair, she soon grew a wispy moustache and beard. She'd asked him for an electric shaver, a lady's, she insisted. As far as he could tell, a lady's worked the same as a man's, only it was pink and it cost more.

"Hyundai!" boomed from the TV in the corner. The TV in the bedroom trumpeted a theme song. Mina got offended if a person raised their voice, but she adored the noise of competing TVs. Loud visuals too. The walls, armrests, and tables were draped with tangerine swirls, leaf-green zigzags, violet mandalas, scarlet clouds.

Mina sat in the corner of the small sofa, buoyed by the cushions she'd stuffed under, around, and behind her. Since she'd been a child, the corner of the sofa was her spot. That was where she stitched, did hidden word puzzles, practised her letters. She kept the shelves next to her crammed with balls of yarn, notebooks, framed photos, knitting needles, calculators in different sizes, pen holders stuffed with markers — everything she might at any moment need. Their dad used to tease her by pretending to sit there himself. And oh boy, what a scene she made then.

Bruno clicked the shaver on and off. The motor whirred but nothing happened when he ran it down his cheek. "What did you do with this?"

"T-t-told you. It's broken."

He blew along the shaver head. "You're supposed to use it on your face, Mina. What's this red stuff?" He pinched a speck he held out, but proof wasn't a concept she'd ever acknowledged. On the carpet was the small toolbox he kept at her place because something always needed to be fixed. The plug torn off the toaster, a jammed DVD player, a fan with an inexplicably twisted blade. Mina was a force destined to sunder parts from their whole.

She waved a regal hand. "Take it back."

"What do you mean, take it back?"

"Like the camera."

Last summer she'd asked for a digital camera for her birthday. He showed her how to attach the strap to her wrist while she was taking a picture so she wouldn't drop it. She slid the strap over her wrist, snapped a picture, slid the strap off, and dropped the camera on the sidewalk.

"The camera was still new. You used this — and on something that wasn't your face."

"No!"

"Okay, then you started growing red specks on your face."

She glared at him, insulted.

"So what did you use it on? You might as well tell me."

She jutted her lips. He waited. Laughter cackled from the TV. Finally she pushed herself off the sofa and toddled to the kitchen. She was so big all around and had such tiny feet. He hated to think of her walking on icy sidewalks, but it wasn't possible to keep her indoors as long as the paradise aisles of the dollar store beckoned.

He heard her open a drawer and rummage inside, shoving and clanking objects. Something hard dropped to the floor.

Brushing past his chair again, she tossed a spongy red place mat on his lap. One edge looked chewed.

"Why did you shave a place mat?"

"Egg!" A sharp accusation.

Ah ... the fault lay with the egg that had slopped off the plate, with the place mat she couldn't clean with a dishrag, with the shaver that should have worked but didn't. Perhaps she even blamed him for not having told her the shaver wouldn't clean a place mat.

He sighed. Maybe a brush would get out all the red bits.

He got up to return the place mat to the kitchen. Picked up the ladle from the floor and tried to angle it into the overstuffed drawer she'd left open. He decided not to mention the dirty dishes crowded along the counter. Their mother had shown Mina how to keep a kitchen neat, but for ten years their mother hadn't been there to check. Now Mina had someone who came to clean, and although Bruno had told her that was no excuse for making a mess, she ignored him.

Stacked unevenly against the wall were the week's accumulation of empty TV dinner packaging. Up until a year ago she'd still been able to prepare simple meals for herself. Bake a chicken leg, brown hamburger meat, add sauce, boil pasta. Then she started to complain that it was too hard to open jars and cans. She made a couple of spectacular microwave messes. She didn't always remember to turn off the stove. Her social worker arranged for Meals on Wheels, but Mina didn't want them, even when Bruno tried to tempt her by reading out the menus. Cream of celery soup and chicken pot pie! Beef bouillon and cheese lasagna! She wouldn't answer the door when meals were delivered, and if the trays were left on the floor in the hallway, she kicked them aside. Then someone else began taking them and he cancelled the service. Mina wanted Skinny Cuisine TV dinners because she'd seen on TV that they made you lose weight. Only if you ate only one, he said. He knew she would eat two. They were the most expensive option, ridiculous for someone on a limited income, but they ensured that she was getting a full, supposedly nutritious meal.

She'd taken up her embroidery hoop and was watching TV again. He pushed his toolbox onto the top shelf of the closet where he hoped she couldn't reach even if she climbed on a chair. She did enough damage without recourse to a hammer.

"Bye, Mina."

"Bye." But she kept her eyes on the TV.

The row of beige doors in the hallway were stark after the caco-phony of noise and colour in her apartment. Before he reached the lobby, he heard the click of her lock followed by the rattle of the chain. She liked to be barricaded inside her fortress.

He pulled his chin into his jacket collar as he stepped outside. For days now, it had been cold enough to snow and he wished it would, but the air stayed dry, the sky blue. Except for the newer apartment building where Mina lived, row houses over a century old lined the street. Brick boxes with flat roofs, side by side. Simply carved wooden cornices, the same design often several houses along. Thick stone foundations. Three steps up from the sidewalk to the front door. Typical architecture for Pointe Saint Charles in southwest Montreal.

Bruno lived a few blocks away on a street that looked the same. The Pointe had been settled by workers employed in the railyards and the factories along the Lachine Canal. The factories had since been closed, but to Bruno the Pointe still looked like an obdurate work-ing-class neighbourhood—even as the old houses were sold, had their brick sandblasted and windows replaced with thermal panes.

A few years earlier when Val, the choreographer with whom he worked, was looking for a new rehearsal space for their small dance ensemble, he suggested they move to the Pointe. For a third of the rent they'd been paying, they could get a large studio in an old tex-tile factory. There were storage closets along one end and space for his carpenter's workbench behind a dividing wall. He'd sanded the original pine planks and laid Marley flooring. When he'd heard of a hair salon being renovated, he rescued the old mirrors and installed them along one wall. The reflection wasn't seamless but it was continuous.

Their group—Val, Tandi, Mathieu, and himself—had just taken almost a month off, following an extravaganza sixteen-dancer per-formance with Chair Vive that had been billed as the highlight of the 2010 fall dance season. There had been no talk yet of what they would be working on next, but Bruno knew Val's brain could never rest long. He hadn't been surprised to get an email summoning them to a meeting next week.

He had a few noisy, dirty jobs he wanted to finish first. At the factory he jogged up the metal stairs to the second floor. As he walked down the hallway, he could hear the grumble of industrial sewing machines from the small futon enterprise across from them.

He hadn't expected to find their door ajar and gently pushed it wider. Val stood, legs braced as if against a strong wind, at the edge of the dance floor. Bruno couldn't see her face but didn't have to. He knew her tense-abstracted look. She still wore her street shoes but had dropped her coat on a canvas camping chair. She had wide hips with long thighs and such an astounding ability to spring that Jean-Pierre Perreault had famously asked if she was part Alpine goat. That was more than twenty years ago but old friends still teased her about it.

Bruno didn't think he'd made a sound but she pivoted. "Bruno, what are you doing here?"

"I need to dismantle that star-shaped platform. It's not easy to store and we might not use it again."

"But if we do?"

"I'll build another — maybe a better one. Remember how we said the angles should be less regular?"

"More asymmetrical, yes." She walked to the camping chair and scooped up her shawl and coat.

"I don't have to do it now, if you need to be here."

"I need to go, I'm already late. Places to go, people to see … Isn't that a line from a song? I'll see you next week." And whirling her shawl around her shoulders, she strode out.

He debated crossing the hallway to see if the futon seamstresses had any coffee on the go, but it would cost him half an hour of chit-chat. Maybe later. He pulled aside the tarp covering the plywood star that was propped against the wall and tipped it flat onto the floor. His tools were in the long cupboard and hooked along the wall next to his workbench. He blew sawdust off his safety glasses, wiped the lenses with the bottom of his sweater, and fit them over his glasses. Grabbed the crowbar, his hand comfortable with its familiar shape and heft.

*

Mina poked her needle into the fabric and reached underneath to pull the thread snug. It was getting too short. Time to change, the colours said.

She had lots of colours now that Iris was bringing them. They screamed and throbbed. Tingly, sleek, creamy, shimmering colours. Go crazy, Iris said. Use whatever colours you want. Iris was the crazy one. Who wanted to go crazy?

Mina squinted at the crimson she'd already stitched, and then at her tray of threads. Me! cried the pale pink. She lifted a strand, wet her fingers with spit, pinched the thread flat. Aimed it at the long eye of the needle. "D-d-do it," she said and it did.

On TV, bells gonged wildly as a woman shrieked, "Harrison Ford! Harrison Ford!"

"I knew that," Mina said. Harrison Ford was beau. She would let him kiss her. She would kiss him too.

The woman on TV won a lot of money with her shrieking. The numbers flashed by too quickly for Mina to fasten on, except for the many os. If she had that much money, she could buy everything she wanted. Now all she had was the twenty dollars the bank machine gave her. Other people got more. She kept trying to get more but it never worked for her. She knew why. Because stupid Bruno had a way of stopping the machine.

She stitched pink into the slits she'd left along the edge of crimson. The colours pulsed so she saw where to go. Up through here, down here.

Today's story she was telling the colours was about the seven little animals. Seven was important. Numbers were always important. She couldn't remember the name for the animals, but in her head she could see the pictures in the book. The animals had ears like a dog and were brown and white. Some wore dresses, some shorts. Their mama told them to be careful and not open the door. Doors, keys, and locks were important too. Who you let in, who you kept out.

On TV the bells gonged again and she wanted to look, but the colours were impatient to hear the rest of the story.

Yeah … the little animals were trying to be good. They stayed inside with the door locked. The way their mama had told them. A voice called, Open up! It's your mama come home again. But they could hear how the voice was growly and they knew it was the wolf! They told him to go away. But the wolf kept trying to fool them. He was smart and finally —

Mina stopped stitching. This part was sad. He tricked them and they opened the door. And then you know what. "He gobbled them."

The colours hummed. No, no, no, no …

Just wait, she thought, as she pulled the pink thread up through the cloth. I'll tell you what happened next. He didn't get the littlest who hid in a cupboard. Then, when their mama came home and she saw the chairs and table knocked upside-down, she started crying. All her darlings gone! From inside the cupboard the littlest called, Mama, I'm here!

"Mama," Mina said out loud because that was the best word.

Mama and the littlest went outside and found the wolf sleeping under a tree with his hairy black snout in the air. That was another picture in the book, the wolf asleep and Mama with her apron. In her apron pocket she had sharp scissors she took out to cut his belly open. And out jumped all her children!

"Rocks," she told them. Seven rocks for seven children. "In his belly." Then flick, flick, flick, Mama's needle sewed him up fast.

Mina stabbed her own needle into the cloth. Needles were magic too. Good magic.

With seven rocks in his belly, you bet the wolf died. No more big bad wolf!

Under her hand the colours vibrated. That was a good story.

*

Bruno had several antique dealers for whom he did odd jobs, repairing or replacing broken parts, doing deliveries. Since the dance studio was still empty, he'd gone there to work on a leg he was building for a Morris settee. On his work bench he had one of the original legs he was using as a guide.

He'd been there for a few hours and decided to cross the hallway for that piece of cake Liliane, one of the futon seamstresses, had told him she'd made. She'd even brought a bowl of whipped cream. *Real* whipped cream. She cut him a generous piece with a big dollop. He had a bite and said it reminded him of Austrian cake his mother used to make. Not Austrian! she cried. This is Slovenian and it's better! He didn't argue, but to him the buttery cake topped with cherries and whipped cream tasted like childhood.

Now, as he walked home, he felt tiny frozen pinpricks dissolving on his face. By the time he reached his street, snow was falling. The lights at his place were on. The upstairs tenants were home too, an older couple whose grandkids came once a month for Sunday supper. For an afternoon there was running and shouting, but otherwise he rarely heard anything from upstairs. The couple were clean and their rent paid his mortgage. He was glad to have them there.

He unlocked his door onto music with a blues beat and the smell of garlic frying, but when he came down the hallway, Gabriela was on the phone. She worked as a physiotherapist and still wore her leggings and had her dark curls twisted up. He hung back, waiting to hear what she was saying.

"A what? … Can you say that again?"

Mina. The more excited she got, the more she lisped and stammered. The skewed bounce of her logic didn't help.

"Pierre wants a dress?" Again Gabriela listened. "I'm sorry, sweetie,
I don't understand. I'll tell Bruno to call you when he gets home."
Turning, she saw him, but he'd already lifted his palms and was
shaking his head.

"Yes, he'll call you. Bye!" She put the phone on the counter. And,
all lightness gone from her voice, "You could have talked to her since
you were right there."

"I'm covered in sawdust. I need to shower. Do I have time?"

"Twenty minutes." She jabbed the wooden spatula through strips
of chicken that were browning. A heap of mushrooms waited on the
chopping board.

He slid the ice tray from the freezer. The gin was with the tamari,
vinegar, and Worcestershire sauce — more a bottle than a liquor cupboard. "What did she want?"

"Something about Pierre and a dress. It sounds like she wants you
to get him one. I couldn't figure it out."

He set her G&T by the stove and took his to the bedroom where
he emptied his pockets. His wallet, a receipt he read and crumpled, a
few coins. The stub of pencil he always carried because when his dad
taught him carpentry, he said a pencil to mark where you wanted to
cut was as important as the saw.

Bruno didn't like Mina's latest boyfriend, Pierre, but she was
an adult and he respected her right to choose her own boyfriends.
At least they never lasted long, her heart didn't seem to get broken,
and eventually she found another. There was the one with the curly
blond hair of a rock star; the one who was a champion bowler — a
champion among the Down Syndrome crowd; the one who kept notebooks where he printed numbers, beginning with 1 on the first line,
2 on the next, and on through the numbers until he reached the last
page. He began each new notebook with 1 again. The jump from 99
to 100 was always a conundrum. Mina had been as proud of him

as if he were elucidating quantum physics. It didn't seem to matter that she knew what followed 99 and could have told him. But whatever a boyfriend's charms, as soon as he did something to displease her — which didn't have to be much — she pushed him out the door. Sometimes literally.

Bruno had towelled off and was pulling a sweatshirt over his head when the phone began ringing.

"Answer that!" Gabriela called.

He still took his time walking to the living room. He didn't like Mina leaving a message, only to call again when she thought he was home. It made him feel stalked.

"Allô?"

"S-s-something to tell you." It was how Mina began every call.

"Is it what you told Gabriela?"

She hesitated. She had no problem lying but wasn't sure if Gabriela was nearby to contradict her.

"Yeah."

"So why are you calling again?"

"I want to know."

"Okay, so tell me why Pierre wants a dress."

"Not Pierre, me!"

"What happened to that nice dress Kris made for you?" Kris was an old girlfriend of his who had sewn a dress wide enough to accommodate Mina's round shape and high-hipped bum, while also proportioned for her short arms and legs.

Mina huffed into the phone.

"What?"

"Six years."

Had it been that long? Since he and Kris had broken up, okay, but he'd assumed the dress would last forever.

"I want a n-n-new one."

"It's impossible to find a dress to fit you."

"Gabriela can —"

"You know Gabriela doesn't sew."

The story came out in spurts and stumbles. He had to ask questions and hazard guesses.

Pierre was going to his cousin's wedding in January, had invited Mina, but told her to get a new dress. Pierre was a spoiled lug of a fellow who lived with his mother. She was probably the one who'd suggested the new dress. Thanks a lot, Bruno thought. He told Mina he would have to think what to do. He lifted his glass to his mouth before realizing he'd finished his drink.

Gabriela was spooning chicken and mushrooms over plates of pasta. On the table was a bowl of green salad.

He got the pitcher of water from the refrigerator and poured them glasses. "Mina wants a new dress to go to a wedding with Pierre."

"With Pierre. That makes more sense."

"It's hard enough to find a T-shirt to fit her. Where am I going to find a dress?"

Gabriela brought the plates to the table and sat across from him. "A new dress to go to a wedding is a perfectly normal thing to want."

"Wanting a new dress might be normal. It's her body that's the problem."

"Mina and I always find something when we go shopping. We have fun."

"Not everyone's idea of fun. Especially before Christmas with the whole city in the stores."

Gabriela was pushing her fork through her pasta. The thick lids of her deep-set eyes were lowered. "I'll take her if you don't want to."

"I didn't mean that. Of course, I'll take her. She's my sister."

"Then why are you complaining?"

"I'm not complaining. I'm stating a fact. It won't be easy to find a dress to fit her."

She looked up. "Why do you decide everything is hard before you even start?"

"In this case, my decision is based on many years of experience. Trying to find clothes to fit Mina ..."

"Do you ever listen to yourself? You make life sound like an obstacle course."

"That's not fair."

"All you think is how much work something will be. Or how difficult. You don't open yourself to the possibility —"

"No." He knew where she was heading now. "Don't start again."

For months they'd been arguing. And why? He'd told her when they first met that he didn't want children. He already had Mina, who every year got more demanding. He was stretched to the limit and had no more to give. It wasn't as if having a baby was something where they could compromise — only a half a baby or only half the time. He resented her suggesting they speak with a counsellor. He liked their life the way it was. He thought Gabriela liked it too. But all of a sudden having a baby was important. It turned out she'd been waiting for him to change his mind; she was almost thirty-nine, and couldn't wait any longer. He couldn't help that. She didn't need to look so imploring and hurt and accusing — by now it all looked the same — as if he'd let her down. He hadn't changed. She had. He was the person he'd always been.

The room was silent now, the CD finished. She pushed back her chair and walked to the living room where she turned on the TV. He cleared the table, and as he passed the doorway saw how she sat in the armchair with her legs tucked tight.

While he did the dishes, he boiled water for tea and brought her a mug. He took his tea to the computer in the nook off the kitchen to scroll through the news and watch some hockey.

She usually told him when she was going to bed, but when he closed the laptop, the house was silent and the light in the living room was off. From the hallway he saw that she was already asleep, her back and the curve of her hip turned away from his side of the bed.

*

Snow softened the gritty edges of the city. Stray flakes twirled from the trees, glittering in the sunlight like diamond sugar in the air. The backstreets where Iris walked hadn't been cleared yet, and she hummed as she kicked through the ankle-high fluff.

Yesterday, when she'd been shopping for sewing supplies, she'd picked up some new colours for Mina. Embroidery floss wasn't that expensive and she was always curious to see what Mina would make. The stitching itself was simple, a backstitch that sometimes morphed into a running or a stem stitch, but Mina's certainty about choosing colours and how to blend them never erred. If anything, the slight messiness of the needlework leant an impetuous energy that was unexpected in the slow work of embroidery.

She'd met Mina last summer in the park. She'd been out walking when a splash of discordant colour caught her eye. A short, round woman on a bench — so short that her feet dangled and her maroon Bermuda shorts covered her knees. A yellow dotted shirt and a vivid green beret. And was she sewing? The gesture of pulling thread through fabric wasn't one you saw often, certainly not outside. But she wasn't just sewing. She held an embroidery hoop and was so absorbed in her stitching that she didn't notice Iris, who had slowed and then stopped.

"Hi," Iris said.

The woman looked up, mouth still open. Her facial features were slack and behind her thick glasses, her eyes tilted upward. Iris had gone to school with a girl whose brother had Down Syndrome. He always stayed inside the fence that enclosed their yard and would never have dared go farther by himself. This woman looked as if she planned to spend the afternoon in the park. Her enormous turquoise bag yawned with magazines, knitting needles, a melon of white yarn, notebooks, and coloured pens. Did she expect to use all these today or did she carry all her options so she could satisfy whatever fancy took her?

"Can I see what you're making?" Iris asked.

"Wh-wh-what?"

Even through the stammer, Iris heard the sharpness. She tried again, more cautiously. "I'd like to see, please. I —" She touched her breastbone. "I sew."

"I'm knitting."

Maybe she didn't know the word for embroidery. Iris had said sew because she thought it was simpler. But she mustn't underestimate. Look how skillfully the colours were blended. Separate strands of red and purple thread gleamed with an electric lick of blue. DANNY PLO with the dip of another letter in the making. The letters hadn't even been pencilled on the cloth. She was stitching freeform — in itself a feat.

Iris sat carefully at the end of the bench. "Is that for Danny?"

"C'est pour moi." It's for me.

"Is Danny a friend?"

"No!"

With every guess Iris got wrong, the woman looked more disgusted. Iris probably had only one more chance to say something right. "Danny's lucky that you like him so much."

"He c-c-calls me. For my birthday!"

"Is your birthday soon?"

"Quat' juin."

"That's next week."

"Friday."

"What else are you doing for your birthday?"

"I go out with Bruno — and Gabriela."

"And how old will you be?"

"Thirty-eight." Said with pride. Two years older than Iris. Then, as if it were equally important, "Bruno is forty-six."

"And how old is Danny?"

She frowned. "Don't know."

"Do you embroider Bruno's name too?"

A disdainful slide of the eyes.

Iris had been stupid again, though she had no idea why. She didn't dare ask who Gabriela was. Quick, quick, what might save her? "Maybe I can take you out for your birthday too — for coffee."

The woman pushed up her glasses, considering. The button on her hat said CAESAR'S PALACE. Had she been to Vegas? Anything seemed possible. "Thé," she announced.

"Okay, tea." Someone who didn't speak both English and French wouldn't be able to keep up with her.

"With a muffin."

"Okay, with a muffin."

"But no chocolate! I'm dibète."

"All right, but when? It should be next week if it's for your birthday."

The woman pursed her mouth as if mentally flipping through a fat list of social engagements. And finally, "Mercredi."

"So we'll go out for tea and a muffin — that *isn't* chocolate — on Wednesday for your birthday which is on Friday." Iris wanted to show she had all the facts straight. "My name's Iris."

She got a long look and then, "Mina."

"Your name is Mina?"

"Oui, c'est ça."

They made a date to meet in the park next Wednesday. "Same time, same place," Iris said. And glancing at her watch, "Two o'clock?"

Mina considered her own watch. It was so tightly clamped on her wrist that the flesh bulged. Did she believe time would escape if it wasn't securely harnessed? She tapped her finger on the watch face, showing Iris.

"1:53. You mean, you want to meet at 1:53?"

A single decisive nod.

"Perfect," Iris said hastily. She took a pen and notebook from her bag, wrote *Mina Wed 1:53*, and underlined the time.

Mina was watching so intently that Iris wondered if she should explain. "I write notes to remind myself, see? Today at six, I'm having a bolt of satin delivered." She heard how chirpy she sounded, as if talking to a child, and lowered her voice to a normal register. "Do you know what satin is?"

Mina was still staring at her notebook.

"Do you want to see what I draw?" Iris flipped through a few sketches. Some were her own designs, some clothes she'd seen on people or in shops. Trousers with wide, flared legs. A sheath dress cut on the bias. "I design clothes." Maybe design was too complicated a concept. "I make these."

"For you?"

"Oh, geez." Iris laughed. "Not for me. I'm more casual." She patted the simple cotton dress she was wearing. Although, even simple, it had welt pockets and a cowl neckline. The world wouldn't believe you were a couturière unless you looked the part. "I design clothes for people who go to fancy suppers and parties. But what I really want is to make clothes for performers." How to explain so that Mina understood? "Like ... for people on TV."

"TV?" A full-on, if unbalanced stare. One of her eyes was slightly crossed.

"What I'd really love is to design an outfit for Madonna. Do you know who that is?"

Mina looked away, already less interested.

"Who's your favourite singer?"

"Elvis. And Théline."

"That's what I mean. I want to make a dress for Céline to wear when she's singing. Except that the singer I want to make a dress for, her name is Madonna." A dress was easier to explain than the pink cone brassiere corset Jean Paul Gaultier had made famous. "I make clothes, and here in this notebook is where I draw them. Just like you. I sew. You embroider."

"Knit," Mina corrected her but with less asperity.

"Right," Iris agreed. "Your knitting is amazing. I'd love to see more of it. Do you have more?"

Hand flapped high in the air.

"Maybe one day you'll show me."

Mina opened a small plastic tub next to her on the bench. Inside was a pincushion where she poked her needle. She snapped shut the tub and tucked it in a pocket in her shoulder bag. She folded DANNY PLO into another pocket, zipped shut the bag, and wrestled the strap over her head. With effort she began to inch and wiggle her weight forward off the bench. Was she leaving without a word of goodbye or explanation? Shit! Iris shouldn't have asked to see more embroidery. "Are we still on for tea and a muffin next week?"

"For my b-b-birthday."

"But you're leaving now."

"To show you."

Just like that? Iris sprang to her feet. She wasn't tall but Mina was more than a head shorter. "Do you live far? Do you need help?"

Mina hugged her bag closer and didn't speak. Her pace was slow yet determined. Turquoise bag, maroon shorts, yellow dotted shirt, crème-de-menthe beret. Whatever colour smarts dictated her co-mmingling of threads didn't extend to her wardrobe. Though who knew? Maybe painted large on a canvas her clothes would look like a Miró.

Iris assumed that Mina lived with her family or in a group home, but she stopped before a low apartment building, faced the three steps with the grim resolution of an athlete, grabbed the railing, and yanked herself up. In the lobby she tapped her finger on the name printed in crooked letters on a mailbox. *Philomena Corneau.* "C'est moi."

Iris liked how she distinguished between Mina for everyday use and Philomena for officialdom. Mina had thrust her hand into another pocket in her bag and now flourished a large pink key fob. She unlocked the door and marched down the hallway, holding the second key ready like a pistol.

Iris followed her into a small living room crammed with furniture. There was such a surfeit of colour and objects — small tables, shelves, notebooks, balls of yarn, figurines, jars of marker pens, notebooks — that it took her a moment to focus on the resplendence of embroidery draped across every horizontal surface and hung from the walls. Speckled ovals, zigzags, balloons of paisley, labyrinthine whorls. And colours? Colours! She gaped as she turned a slow circle. "You did all this?"

Mina had snatched off her hat and heaved herself onto the sofa. She gave Iris a smug look. This was her queendom. Who else but her?

The colours were a kaleidoscope of contrasts. Lime green and lavender. Canary, rust, and pink. Couplings unlike anything Iris had ever thought of trying. Yet it all worked so gorgeously. And there was so much of it! In the park she'd wondered if Mina's use of colours was a happy accident, but now she saw the certainty of choice, purpose, and commitment.

Embroidery here, embroidery there. Even on the wall behind the sofa where decals were crowded, each stitched with a name like the one Mina was embroidering in the park. BOBBY MONAHAN, PAUL POULIN, JACK ANTOINE, HENRI DUHAMEL, BUTCH SCHMIDT, MARC VALLIERE. The cloth had been cut into approximate ovals, pasted on cardboard, and stuck to the wall.

Above the names hung a carved angel head that didn't look like a made-in-China ornament. The flesh tones were too delicate. The gilding on the wings gleamed like real gold.

How had she gotten it? One day Iris would ask her — because she knew she was going to see Mina again, and not just for tea and a muffin on her birthday.

Mina watched her take in the wealth of her world with a satisfied air.

"This emb — I mean, knitting is unbelievable."

"Je sais." I know.

Iris began stopping by to see Mina every few days. Her studio in Verdun was only a half-hour walk away. She brought Mina a better quality of embroidery floss than Mina had been buying for herself at the dollar store. She'd tried silk thread once, because the colours were more lustrous, but Mina complained the silk caught on her fingers. She seemed to embroider on whatever fabric she could find — cloth napkins, tea towels, even clothes she cut up. Iris brought her neat squares of cotton and linen.

She'd met Mina's brother, Bruno, but hadn't liked how abruptly he asked what she was doing with Mina. She said she wasn't doing anything, she was bringing her thread. He quirked his mouth and said, Yeah, how much does that cost? Nothing, she said stiffly. Later he apologized, saying he had to be careful. People had gotten Mina to sign contracts and her signature was binding. It wasn't always easy to untangle her messes. He was a nice-looking man — nice enough that the gap between his top teeth was cute — but he could have learned a few manners. Iris told him that she was a couturière and she knew textiles. The thread Mina was buying for herself was crap. Her embroidery was stunning and she should have better material to work with. He said Mina had always stitched at something or other. He didn't think it mattered to her what she used. Their mother had taught her to keep her busy.

Bruno thought Mina was just keeping busy? Couldn't he see how creative she was? Wasn't it just like family, she thought, to not be able to see what a person could do? Especially when it didn't fit into their expectations. Her parents and siblings were the same. They'd gotten educations so they could get nice, clean desk jobs. They couldn't believe that Iris wanted to sew clothes like her grandmother. They understood nothing about the work she did — the designing, the cutting, tailoring techniques, sourcing the right fabrics, and marketing. And starting her own business? Taking out loans and the risk? They thought she was crazy. That was because they had no idea how much she charged for a jacket with hand-tailored buttonholes. Or how much her ladies in Outremont and Westmount were willing to pay for home visits for fittings.

She knocked the snow off her boots, waiting for Mina to answer the intercom. As she walked down the hallway, she heard the rattle of the chain. Mina had told her she wanted a deadbolt too, but stupid Bruno said no.

She'd already returned to the sofa and was picking up a pair of fat knitting needles — real knitting needles. For the last while she'd been knitting a length of garter stitch in fiery pink and orange yarn. This, which *was* knitting, she called knitting too. When Iris had asked what it was going to be, Mina flicked her a look that didn't need words to convey that a thing didn't have to be anything.

The TV blared the sonorous notes of soap opera doom. Iris unbuttoned her coat and sat in the armchair. She was only allowed in during a soap opera if she didn't speak until a commercial.

When men in white jumpsuits deployed a high-alert to clean up a juice spill, she set her flat paper package on the sofa. "I brought you some new thread."

Mina glanced but that was all. Now was when she knit. She would look in the bag when it was next time to embroider.

"Are you working tomorrow?"

Two days a week Mina sorted paper at a recycling plant. She blinked, as if the days might have shifted since she'd last thought of them. "Yeah," she said finally.

"What do you do again?" Iris asked because Mina liked to explain.

"White paper here." She patted an invisible table. "Other paper here."

"What's the other paper?"

"Red. Yellow. B-b-blue. Orange. Green."

Once Iris had said coloured paper but Mina hadn't liked her simplifying a complex procedure that required judgment and precision.

The soap opera started again, the camera zooming on an anguished face.

Iris would wait for the next commercial before leaving. She'd left the pieces for the cape a client had commissioned stabbed with pins on the cutting table. The pieces still needed to be traced with chalk and cut. Yesterday she'd found Norwegian pewter buttons that would be perfect. One good thing about her ladies: cost was never a hindrance.

*

Gabriela sat waiting for the salesclerk to bring boots in her size. Near the shoe racks two teenagers were trying to decide on gym shoes. He was skinny but his feet were enormous and she was teasing him in that rough way that Gabriela knew was clumsy flirting.

She and Bruno were already adults with a few scars and disappointments when they met. Even so, everything had felt new. So much fun they'd had in those first years, walking and cycling around Montreal, trips to different cities to watch dance performances, taking Mina on outings, visits with her parents in Toronto. Bruno had come with her to Guanajuato for her abuela's ninetieth birthday celebration, danced with her mamá and tías, gone for a daredevil ride in the hills with her cousins. They'd made love on a rooftop under a starry indigo sky. She thought she'd found the man she would love and grow old with. And though it was true, he'd always said he didn't want children, she hadn't believed that a man who was so responsible and family-oriented, who cared for his sister as he did, wouldn't eventually want the fulfillment and joy of a child. Having a child wouldn't be the same as overseeing Mina's affairs. A child would grow with them. A child would complete them, would continue who they were. A child would bring so much into their lives. But he didn't see, didn't want to keep discussing it, and it didn't seem to matter to him what she wanted. Time was passing and her ovaries were ageing and her hormones must be off-kilter after years of being on the pill. Even if she could still conceive, at this point she would be a *geriatric pregnancy* — a sobering label — at risk for miscarriage, diabetes, and high blood pressure. With every month the chance of getting pregnant decreased and the risks increased. How much longer could she keep waiting for Bruno? And what if he never agreed? She could live with not having a child. But if she faced a future where they had never even tried? She didn't know if she would be able to forgive him for having so deliberately closed that door.

"Madame?" A hesitant voice.

Her expression must have startled the salesclerk and she forced a smile.

*

The lights were bright, the aisles broad. Lots of room to walk slowly. Mina could feel her fingers sizzling, ready to jump. She'd taken off her mitts and stuffed them in her shoulder bag. Her coat had big, deep pockets.

The thing she was going to buy was facecloths. That was what she would say if anyone asked. Facecloths were in the bathroom aisle, she knew exactly where. That was why facecloths were a good thing to say. If she stayed away from where they were, then she was still looking. Nobody could tell you not to be in the store if you were looking.

The times she got caught, they always asked what she was doing in the store. Now she had a what. Facecloths. That was what she would say.

She didn't walk down the Christmas aisle because there was nothing she wanted there. Red and silver ribbons, shiny balls to hang on trees, pretend green branches, candy canes she wasn't allowed to eat. Stupid things.

When she was little, Christmas was special because Daddy sang "White Christmas" like Elvis and Mama made Christmas tree cookies with green icing and silver balls. But with Daddy and Mama gone … She squeezed her eyes shut to make the tears stop. Not now in the store.

In a minute she was okay and turned into another aisle. Screws and big rolls of tape and electrical cords. Maybe a roll of tape?

A man in a green apron walked up to her, not even pretending to be nice. Not polite. "What are you looking for?"

"F-f-facecloths."

"Two aisles left. That way." He pointed — as if she didn't know where left was!

"D'okay," she said but still took her time, waiting for him to go wherever he was going. He had a job to do. She had all day.

Swaying from step to step, walking slowly, she saw ... what? *That.* But no stopping! Not yet. She walked to the end of the aisle, turned, and walked back. She didn't know what it was but she could tell right away when a thing was hers, and if it was hers, she could take it. She'd tried explaining to Bruno but stupid Bruno didn't understand. He shouted about stealing. She knew what stealing was. It was taking something that wasn't yours. But when a thing said I'm yours, then it was.

She didn't know what this thing was or what to do with it, but whup! Her fingers fast-fast into her pocket, and once in her pocket, it was definitely hers. She would keep saying that even if she was caught and they called Bruno and he made his big bad wolf head. Too bad! Tit for tat.

Today was a good day. No one would catch her today, she could tell. A package of noodles you only had to pour hot water on. A tiny flashlight. A striped toque. A few erasers. She snickered a little. Grinned. Didn't leave the store yet because it gave her an excited, tickly feeling to keep walking up and down the aisles, looking for facecloths.

*

Bruno stood staring at his reflection in the train window. Ghost forehead, the squarish black frames of his glasses, the holes of his eyes, the straight line of his mouth. Would the skeletal mirroring work as a stage effect or would the dancer have to stand too close to the glass? He backed up a step to see, backed up again, and bumped into a woman. "Sorry."

She raised her eyebrows. The clean lines of her blue-black skin, the haughty disdain of her look. Then, unexpectedly, she smiled. A real smile too, her mouth, her eyes, her face. He smiled in return. The train slowed, the doors opened, and she walked off. A brief bloom of contact in a crowd of strangers. The memory of their shared smile was still on his lips when he got off at the next stop.

The Pointe was only four métro stops from the concrete, lights, and bustle of downtown, but he came up the escalator into a more modest world of brick and silence. Long before he reached the outdoor hockey rink, he heard the scrape and swirl of skates, the whack of the puck against boards, and from behind the new condos, the rumble of freight trains. Trees, twice as high as the flat-roofed houses, arched over alleys and backyard fences.

It was his night to cook but first he had to stop to see Mina. The social worker had called about a complaint that Mina was taking the plastic bags of flyers and grocery store specials from the entrance of her building. Weren't the Publisacs there to take? he asked. Apparently she was taking all of them. Next question: had anyone seen her? Mina's neighbour had seen her take more than one. More than one wasn't all of them. No, but overnight they were all gone. So why blame Mina? Was that the same neighbour she was always fighting with? Last summer Mina had started calling swear words out the window when the neighbour walked past on the sidewalk. Mina thought that since she was hidden behind the curtain, no one knew it was her. When Bruno confronted her, she said the neighbour had slapped her purse on the window screen. The window was above shoulder level. Slapping a purse up that high definitely was no accident. But who had done which first? As Bruno had discovered, so-called normal people could behave very badly. Since the woman lived next to Mina, opportunities for the two of them to aggravate each other were endless.

There wasn't a single Publisac left in the entrance of Mina's building. Maybe the janitor had already cleared them away? Though usually they stayed in a messy pile all week. Bruno debated knocking on his door, but it was suppertime and he didn't want to disturb him. The janitor had always been kind to Mina, who liked him too.

She didn't answer the intercom the first time Bruno buzzed. He buzzed again.

And finally, "Yeah?"

"It's me."

"What?"

"Just let me in, okay?"

By the time he reached her door, she'd returned to her meal of Skinny Cuisine macaroni and cheese at the small table in the kitchen. Though she couldn't see the TV from where she sat, she stared at the wall in its direction. She forked up noodles and ignored him. She didn't like being interrupted while she was eating. She also knew unexpected visits could mean a scolding.

He looked around for the Publisacs, but if she'd taken them, she would have hidden them, and there was such a jumble of crowded furniture and heaped belongings in her apartment that they could have been anywhere. He decided to make his life easier and not ask about the Publisacs until the social worker had proof. "Guess what?" he said.

Another bite of noodles.

"We're going to take you shopping for a dress."

Even with her one slightly crossed eye, her look could skewer him. "W-w-with Gabriela?"

"You think *I'm* coming in the change room with you?"

She broke into a laugh, delight suffusing her face. Her moods could change so quickly.

"I thought you would like that."

"Gabriela est ma belle-coeur!"

She'd never called any of his previous girlfriends her belle-coeur. Her beautiful heart. The French was grammatically incorrect and Mina didn't usually mess up gender. Was it an accident or a deliberate play on belle-soeur or sister-in-law? He knew she would have liked him and Gabriela to be married.

"Not this coming Sunday. Next Sunday."

"When?"

"At noon."

With a flourish she reached for a pen and with deliberate if uneven letters printed the time on the calendar that was on the table in the kitchen. He watched to make sure she had the right Sunday, though she never made a mistake with dates. She slid off her chair to go mark the calendar on the wall by the sofa, maneuvering around the armchair and its end table on light feet. Returning to her meal, she snuffled happily.

"Life's good now?"

"Yeah."

"I can go?"

"Yeah." And dismissing him properly, she added, "Bye."

He threw a last look at the carved angel head over the sofa. Its benign gaze and glimmering, gold-leafed wings. He had so often told Mina that the angel was their mother watching over her that he'd half-started to believe it. He hoped that if she were watching, she would see that he was doing his best.

Their mother had upended her own life to ensure that Mina was properly settled. After her husband's sudden death, she realized that she too might not always be there. Several years after Bruno moved to Montreal to go to technical college, she sold the house with its large garden that she loved in order to bring Mina, who was now eighteen, to Montreal where there was a comprehensive network of social services. In the small town where they'd lived, the school hadn't even had a special ed teacher. Mina had been kept at home, where their mother taught her letters and numbers, but not how to read. She didn't think Mina could learn. Even as a boy, Bruno hadn't believed that. He knew that sometimes, when Mina pretended not to understand, she was only being stubborn. She was crafty and she kept secrets. She had her own way of explaining the world.

In Montreal their mother moved into an apartment with Mina and got her enrolled in programs where she was taught how to manage a weekly allowance, take the subway, make a shopping list with picture cards, and work within a supervised group. When Mina turned twenty, their mother said it was time for her to live by herself. Mina had sulked and cried, but their mother insisted that Mina learn how to be independent. It was a carefully curated independence overseen by their mother and a social worker, but Mina wasn't aware of that. Once she'd adjusted, she gloried in having her own apartment, a job, belonging to a social club that went to movies and bowling, having a best friend and often a boyfriend. She was happy.

Bruno wasn't sure their mother was. She didn't like being in the city where the air was foul and food bought in grocery stores didn't taste of anything. She missed her house, her garden, and her fruit trees. She missed having Mina with her. He supposed she took comfort in believing she'd done the right thing — as it turned out she had when she was diagnosed with stage 4 stomach cancer. Now, at least, there would be no question of placement or how Mina would manage on her own. She could cook and do laundry. She had a job, friends, and hobbies. There was already a social worker assigned and Bruno would always watch out for her.

Their mother never asked him to become Mina's legal guardian. She didn't expect that of a man, and he didn't know that a legal guardian was needed until Social Services called a family meeting. Two social workers, a supervisor, Mina, their mother, and himself. There's no one else? the supervisor asked. Didn't she already know? Bruno thought. There had been only minimal contact with his dad's family in the Gaspé after he died, and that had slowly petered out. His mother's relatives were far away in Austria. Himself, Mina, and their mother were their family. Soon it would be only himself and Mina. He was thirty-five years old, Mina twenty-seven.

He listened to the social workers' incomprehensible legalese, not sure what the purpose of the meeting was. When he finally understood that Mina was going to be made a ward of the state, he said no. Their mother objected. She didn't want to burden him. Mina wasn't a burden, he said. She's my sister.

Since then more than ten years had passed. Mina had slowly

become more instead of less demanding. Arranging her life as she
felt it should be wasn't always easy.

He was late getting home, but not too late. Gabriela knew he often
stopped to see Mina. He kicked the snow off his boots, unlocked the
door, and was still in the entrance when he heard a cupboard door
bang. He walked down the hallway to the kitchen where Gabriela
stood at the counter, chopping.

"What are you doing? I'm cooking tonight."

She swivelled her head to glare at the clock on the stove.

"It's only ten after six. I had to see Mina. The social worker had a
complaint from the neighbour."

Gabriela set the knife on the cutting board and rinsed her hands
at the sink.

"Supper will be ready at seven," he said. "When we usually eat."

"I'm hungry," she muttered as she stepped past him.

He opened the refrigerator to get the salmon, snatched a baking
sheet from the cupboard, then realized he should start the rice.
No, he'd make basmati. It would be faster. Wild rice would be nicer,
but it seemed Madame couldn't wait.

*

Stabbing her needle into the cloth and pulling it through. Stabbing
her needle into the cloth and pulling it through. Over and over, a
movement graceful as a dance. The crimson and pink she'd started
with were finished. Now she was making stems. Or fingers. Or
maybe bones. She didn't know what the shapes were. She didn't need
to. The colours told her what to do and where to go.

On TV people were talking and laughing. Bruno always complained that she listened to TV too loud but she had to hear it over
the TV in the bedroom — and yeah, that TV had to be on too! TV was
like people who came to visit, except better because TV people stayed
in their boxes. She could change the channel when they were stupid.
She could turn them off.

It was easier to breathe with her mouth open, her tongue relaxed on her lower lip. Because her tongue was too long. Mama told her. But when someone else was there, she was supposed to put her tongue away and keep her mouth closed. Mama used to tap her to remind her. Close your mouth. Like picking your nose. Things you only did alone.

She looked at her watch and checked the time against the clock on the wall. 1:06. The clock had hands, her watch had numbers. She could tell time on both, but her watch was better because of the numbers.

What was missing on her hand since last Thursday was her green birthstone ring. Her ring winked and made her feel happy, but Bruno had to take it to be made bigger because she was getting fatter. He told her she shouldn't be getting fatter but what was she supposed to do? Her belly was her belly. And grinning now, thinking about her nice belly, she patted it.

Which colour wanted to come next? She looked at her tray and waited. Me, boomed black. Her threads were neatly arranged, each in their own slot. Not messy like the apartment.

Evita should clean more often, but she only came on Fridays, clattering the dirty dishes into the sink and kneeling on the floor to scrub at the crusted drips. She pushed the bucket around, mouth tight like it was too heavy, but Mina knew the mean eyes and tight mouth were for her. Too bad! Tit for tat. Evita was supposed to clean, not talk on the phone to her children. Mina knew it was her children because she couldn't understand what Evita said, the way Mama used to say words that only Mina and Bruno understood.

Liebes Engelchen, Mama would croon, cuddling her close and stroking her hair. She could hear Mama's voice in her head as clearly as if she were beside her. The sudden hurt of knowing that Mama wasn't there made the pain come alive, bulging hard in her chest. "Mama," she moaned. A broken word. A lost word.

Bruno said the angel on the wall was like Mama watching her, but she didn't want Mama watching. She wanted her gentle hands and strong arms holding her.

Eyes wet, she blinked at the TV until the noise of a lady screaming in disbelief grew big enough to fill the room.

Mina groped under the hoop for the tip of the needle. Her colours quivered and hummed, the red bristling, the pinks cool and slick, the black slicing sharp. Black had a bad-man, scary feeling, but when the colours said black, she had to use black. That was how it was.

The stories she told them were sometimes scary too. The witch who wanted to cook and eat the boy. The stone head that growled, frightening the girl so much that her braids stood straight up off her head. Having to cut off your finger to save your brother. How to trick the giant. She remembered the stories — the words and the pictures — from the book in the secret language that only she and Bruno and Mama knew.

When the intercom buzzed, she stopped stitching and listened. Nobody was supposed to be coming. You had to be careful with strangers. They could trick you. The buzzer sounded again. She frowned, suspicious. But curious too, so she answered. "Yeah?"

"It's me!"

Pierre? But today was Wednesday. He should be at his job at Canadian Tire.

"Come on, Mina, let me in!"

That could only be Pierre. She pressed the buzzer, got up to unlock her door, and returned to the sofa where she heaved herself up again. Bruno had told her she should stay at the door until she saw who it was, but she had her own deep-down sense that she should be sitting when people walked in. She didn't pick up her hoop again because she couldn't knit with Pierre there. He moved too much and wanted her to listen.

He banged through the door, slammed it shut, and let his parka fall to the floor. "Guess what?" He threw himself into the armchair. "I'm going to drive a car, my dad said so. In summer when we go to my uncle's. There's an old car in a field. I'm going to drive it, I am!"

She didn't believe him. People like them couldn't drive. "Why aren't you at w-w-work?"

"Blood test." He thrust his arm out to show her the gauze and tape. "I want a cigarette!"

"No."

"Bitch.".

She wrinkled her nose at the bad word but didn't change her mind. No was no. She counted her cigarettes when she bought a pack. That number got marked in green ink on the calendar that hung in the bedroom next to her Elvis poster. Every day was minus one until the number was zero. Whenever she removed a cigarette from the pack, she counted the cigarettes that were still left and checked the number against the number on the calendar. If Pierre had a cigarette, her numbers would be wrong. Also: the cigarettes were hers. He got more money from his mom and dad than she got from the bank machine. He could buy his own cigarettes, except his mom wouldn't let him. Huh. She wrinkled her nose again. He did other things his mom didn't know about. He could buy cigarettes too if he really wanted. His mom was easy to fool.

"Just one," he grumbled, kicking a foot in the air.

She didn't answer because she'd already told him. She knew he wouldn't dare take one or she would punch him. They'd found that out one day when the blow of her fist made him stagger. She was shorter than he was but she was strong.

He lunged to grab the remote off the armrest next to her and changed the station. He made a stupid barking sound, thinking she would be upset, but she wasn't. Her program only started at 2:00. She checked her watch and the clock on the wall. 1:34. At 2:00 she was getting the remote back or he would be in trouble.

"Don't touch the tape," she said. Bruno had covered some of the buttons on the remote so the picture wouldn't keep changing into squares.

He pouted. "Not drinking anything?"

She counted her cans of pop too. That number got marked in red ink on the calendar in the kitchen. That morning, when she'd checked, there was still a can for every day until she got her groceries again, plus three extra. So Pierre could have one.

In the kitchen she poured them both a glass but she could only carry one at a time. With careful steps she brought him his. As she set it on the table beside him, he smacked her bum.

"Don't." She didn't like when he was rough. Although depending on how she felt, she let him touch her. Some of her princes wanted to touch and do things. Others didn't. She didn't mind them sucking her titties but didn't like when they shoved down there or wanted her to rub their cocks until white stuff squirted out. The white stuff smelled. That smell was sex.

Since Pierre had walked in, jittery and excited about having a day off work, she knew he was going to want sex.

*

Gabriela stood by the table where Mr. Lavoie lay with his knees bent. "Okay," she said. "Press your lower back into the mattress and at the same time clench your stomach muscles." She opened her hand over his waist, almost but not touching it, as if to guide him. "Now lift one leg, keeping the knee bent. Hold it. Keep your stomach muscles clenched. Now put it down and lift the other."

"That's not so hard," he said.

"The hard part is that twice a day you have to stop what you're doing, get on a mat, and do it."

He made an acknowledging sound in his throat, lifting one leg and then the other.

She was aware of his son who was sitting behind her. He'd wheeled his dad into the room and helped Gabriela get him onto the table. She'd felt the firmness of his arm against hers. Smelled the tang of his aftershave. His suede jacket hung open on a turtleneck sweater. His short hair, cut close to his skull, was lightly silvered.

Mr. Lavoie was having a hard time maintaining his balance for the quadruped arm and leg raise. "It gets easier with practice," she said. "You'll see."

From behind her she heard, "You're very patient."

"It's my work." She turned to the son and saw how he glanced at her name tag and again at her face.

"May I ask if you're from Central America?"

"Mexico."

"That's where you always go, Daniel," his dad said.

She expected she would now hear a story about vacationing in Acapulco or visiting an Aztec pyramid, but instead he asked, "Do you still have family living there?"

"My grandparents, aunts, uncles, and cousins."

"Not your parents?"

He'd been listening. Even when people asked about background, they often didn't pay attention. They only wanted a general idea. "My parents are in Toronto. I was born in Canada."

"And the family in Mexico? Where are they?"

"In or near Guanajuato."

"Me encanta esa ciudad." His Spanish was accented but practised. "The way the streets climb the slopes, the hills all around, hiking up the Cerro de la Bufa, eating at the market ..."

"You've been there."

"Muchas veces." His face seemed lit with happy memories. He also made it sound as if he'd gone alone. Did that mean he was single?

At her computer she chose and printed a list of exercises that she gave to Mr. Lavoie. "Come back to see me in two weeks. Show me how well you're doing these."

At the door Daniel held out his hand. "Hasta la próxima."

The warm pressure of his palm against hers. The grip of his

fingers. The words were no more than a polite formula, but the sound of Spanish — the language of her childhood, the language of affection — curled around her.

Past him, in the waiting room, she saw her next patient, Mrs. Androssian, but she didn't call her in. She closed her door and returned to her desk. What was happening to her that a stranger could stir her pulse with possibility in a way that rarely happened with Bruno anymore?

She straightened in her chair and took a long breath. She always told her patients to pay attention to how they breathed. She focussed on the computer screen, closed Lavoie Ernest's file, and opened Androssian Marta.

*

It had to be a blue pen. That was one rule for doing hidden word puzzles. Another was to always start a fresh puzzle. It didn't matter if Mina hadn't finished the last one. When it was time to do word puzzles, she opened the magazine to a new page. She couldn't do them in the kitchen either. She had to be sitting on the sofa with the rolling table pulled up close.

Gripping a blue pen, she stared at the grid of letters that were supposed to be words. She didn't know words but she didn't need to. She knew her letters. A then B then C then D. In hidden word puzzles the letters were jumbled and scattered in the grid. She had to find how the jumbles in the grid matched the words on the list beside it. It was a hard game and she had to concentrate. She couldn't look at the TV, even if there was screaming and gongs. She had to keep her eyes fixed on the letters, fingers on her blue pen, ready to lasso them.

There! J and U and M and P. A sneaky one because the word went at an angle, but she found it because she knew how. And this was very important too: when she found the letters that made a word in the grid, she had to cross the word off the list because those letters were done.

She was good at puzzles because she'd been doing them since

a long time ago when Mama showed her. Books and books of them. Packages of blue pens.

Mama had shown her another trick too. Some letters were easier to spot because there weren't many of them. X and K and J and V and Z. So she always looked for those first.

Here, she found a word on the list with a V in the middle. She scanned the grid across each line, so intent on finding a V that she jerked when the intercom buzzed. She glared at the metal plate on the wall. No one was supposed to come when she did her hidden word puzzles. Everyone knew she was busy and they were supposed to stay away.

She bent to the page again, staring hard to put the letters back in her head, but the buzzer had scattered them. It didn't ring again but she knew who it was because she heard the neighbour's door closing. That stupid old lady was always bothering her!

She squinted at the page, determined to make the puzzle work, but now the letters stayed hidden. She waited and waited, but nothing happened. Nothing! She shoved the table away so hard that it crashed into the TV, the book fell off, and the pen skittered behind some-where. She pushed herself off the sofa to get the book because there were lots of pages she hadn't done yet, but the pen could stay lost.

That old lady … She could just wait, she would find out. Mina was going to get her yet, oh yes.

*

Mathieu and Tandi were already at the studio when Bruno walked in, both on the floor in their leotards, Mathieu still wearing his hoodie and yellow leg warmers. "Hey," he said when he saw Bruno. "Didn't you get my text about bringing coffee?"

Bruno ignored him. One, he didn't text — he didn't have a cell phone, as everyone knew — and two, he did not fetch coffee.

"Hiya Bruno," Tandi said. She had a robust build, and although Mathieu who was slender could lift her, they usually choreographed moves where she took him by the hips. Val liked to subvert gender expectations and play with contrast in body shape and colour. His extreme fairness, her deep rich brown.

Bruno opened a canvas camping chair for himself. The turquoise chair that was already open was Val's, though she was more likely to warm up with the dancers than to sit. He grabbed the clipboard from his workbench, tossed it onto his chair, and went to the cupboard for the tripod. He was responsible for lighting, sound, set, props, costumes, and whatever else Val wanted in a production — from mixing a 45-minute sound loop of goats bleating to shopping for nipple pasties. He set up the camera that he would turn on once the meeting started. Improv and workshop ideas were the prompts they built on to create the choreography.

Behind him Tandi and Mathieu gossiped about a dancer from another ensemble who had apparently received a call from a scout for Hubbard Street Dance in Chicago.

"Chicago ..." Mathieu moaned.

"I'm holding out for NYC," Tandi said. "Anyhow, is that even true? Who told you?"

"A friend of a friend who knows someone —"

"*Someone?*" Tandi cut him off. "Sounds like a really good source."

"Don't be such a cynic! I want to believe this. Everyone needs to dream."

Bruno heard the tock of heels coming down the hallway and Val walked in. She slipped off her boots and shrugged free of her coat that she hung on a peg. "Am I late or are you all early? What have you been doing this past month? Let me hear." As she spoke, she dropped the straps of the overalls she wore over her leotard and stepped out of them.

"I had to work double shifts bartending," Mathieu grumbled.

Tandi said, "I did a workshop with teens. They were so enthusiastic, I wanted to adopt them. And before that I went to Magog for a week."

Val approved with a nod, still standing over them.

"And you?" she asked Bruno. "Did you and the lovely Gabriela have that holiday?"

He didn't know what she meant.

"That's what she was telling me at the party. She said you were going to leave the city for a while, just the two of you."

He remembered now. Gabriela had mentioned going away but they hadn't made plans. He'd replaced his tenants' toilet and painted their bathroom. "We stayed in the city. I had things to do."

"Aren't you Mr. Fun Times?" Mathieu said.

Maybe, Bruno thought, Mathieu wouldn't have to work double shifts if he was a little less Mr. Fun Times.

"What did you do?" Tandi asked Val.

Val had grown very still. Not fixed — more like gathering her energy all the better to combust. They were instantly alert, Tandi and Mathieu rising to their feet, Bruno leaning forward to turn on the camera.

Val began to pace, head erect, her path swerving. Mathieu fell in step beside her, Tandi beside him. To the far end of the studio and whipping around. When Val stopped, they all stopped. Val shuffled her feet. They all shuffled. They were a snake of three sideways bodies, their copied movement the livewire that joined them.

"I walked," Val called as if across a distance.

"Walked?" Mathieu began stepping backwards, knees lifted high, and they followed him now.

"Walked," Val repeated.

Bruno wrote *walked* on his clipboard.

"Walked where?"

"The city." Val swung an arm, pointing in one direction and then another. The dancers swung as if yanked by her arm.

"And what did I see?" she demanded as she began a tiptoe zigzag route that they followed.

Bruno wrote *city*.

"Buildings."

"Buildings." Mathieu bobbed his head.

"Cars."

"People." Tandi hunched her back and began creeping. Ditto Mathieu and Val.

"Garbage."

"Sunsets."

"Not enough trees."

"Too many cars."

"Too many buildings."

"Why so many buildings?" Val beseeched them.

Bruno wrote *buildings*. He couldn't yet tell where they were going but Val had brought them back to buildings.

Mathieu began to lunge-step, taking the snake with him. "For people to work."

"And live," Tandi said. "My home."

"My home," Mathieu echoed.

"Right." Val jabbed a finger. "Your home and your home and your home and your home and your home." She included an unseen crowd who were all, Bruno could hear in her voice, the lucky ones who had a home. "A condo, an apartment, a house, a room, a flat. But—" she whirled away, "what about everyone in this great big city—where there are sooooo many buildings—and still people without a home? Doesn't everyone need a home? Isn't that what we long for? Think about having nothing more than a flattened box to sleep on! What does that say about us that we just keep walking past—that we don't see that?"

Bruno wrote *home / homeless*.

Tandi began looking around and scooping her arms toward her.

Val scooped too, both women gathering nothing—but nothing was all they had. A desperate but necessary gesture.

Mathieu had begun stomping a circle around himself. Tandi's arms stretched ever farther, her grasping more erratic, until the fingers of one hand scraped across Mathieu's arm and he wheeled around as if to defend his territory, albeit no larger than his feet.

They sensed and reacted to each other, each twist, each leap, each crouch, each roll across the floor shaping a sequence of movement that might become a dance.

*

The sewing machine whirred as Iris folded fuchsia bias tape around piping cord with one hand. With the other, she kept the silk bias tape aligned with the edge of grey linen she was feeding under the bite of the needle.

Her friend Jenny sat on a high stool, twisting from side to side. She was waiting for Iris to finish so they could head uptown for a bite and to see *The Girl with the Dragon Tattoo*. Jenny had read the novel. Iris hadn't but she liked the title.

"I can't even think about sleeveless in the winter!" Jenny raised her voice over the machine. "Just watching you work on that dress is making me shiver!"

Iris stopped sewing to shake a curl out of the bias tape that trailed onto the floor. "The client isn't going to wear the dress to go skiing." She reached behind the machine to examine what she'd sewn. A thin gleam of deep pink against the weave of grey linen. She pressed her foot on the pedal again.

The friends had known each other since college where Iris studied fashion and Jenny graphic design. Jenny worked at a small advertising firm now. Her parents had paid for her condo and she had an on-again, off-again lawyer boyfriend. Iris sometimes wondered if Jenny's life might have been too easy and that was why her ambition didn't stretch farther. She had a good eye, a sense of composition, and could draw. At college she'd always told Iris which of her fashion designs were the best, and those were the ones that got the highest marks. Jenny could easily have put together a portfolio and applied to a fine arts program, but she had an uncle who was an artist and she didn't want that uncertain boho kind of life.

She'd abandoned the stool and was pacing around the studio now. In one corner was a bamboo screen where clients could change, next to it a coat stand and a three-way mirror. There were two large tables for sewing and cutting, another table topped with a sleeve ironing board on sturdy wooden feet, a wall unit of fashion textbooks and binders filled with drawings and clippings, shelves of fabric samples, bins filled with interfacing and lining, skeins of waxed silk thread pinned to a corkboard, fabric scissors hanging from hooks on the wall, a cabinet of many tiny drawers filled with spools of thread, zippers, and other notions.

Jenny picked up one of the fabric hams that were used for pressing curved seams open, hefted it like a football, and mimed throwing it.

Iris, who caught the movement, stopped sewing. "The more you distract me, the longer this will take."

Jenny made a deferential show of returning the plaid ham to the ironing table. She approached the four headless cloth dummies and straightened the mock-up shell for a dress that one wore.

During another lull in the noise of the machine she asked, "How's your little friend, the one who does embroidery?"

"Hardly little," Iris murmured as she pressed the pedal again. Not in size nor how she used a needle.

"What did you say?"

Iris stopped. "She's working on ... I don't know how to describe it. The last piece she did looks like blue and green cucumbers on acid. Or maybe they're giant rain worms that got poisoned. I don't know where she gets her ideas. Her stuff is wild."

"So you keep telling me. It'd be nice if I could see something she's done."

"I told you. She won't let anything out of her apartment. She's territorial about what she makes. It's hers and that's that."

"But you bring her the thread she's using, right?"

"Doesn't matter. She assumes that's what I do. She's not big on thank yous."

Jenny sucked her teeth with resonance worthy of her Bajan grandmother. "Didn't anyone teach her how to share?"

Iris smoothed the next length of silk tape around the piping cord and pressed the pedal again. That was the kind of thing you would say about a child. Though she understood what Jenny meant. Trying to reason with Mina could be frustrating.

Jenny had stopped at the cutting table where Iris had laid strips of different colours across a length of ochre pea-spotted silk. "You know what I've noticed?" Jenny shouted over the noise of the machine. "Your colours have gotten more interesting since you've known her."

Iris heard but didn't answer. She'd studied design and colour theory. She had skills and expertise. What was Jenny implying? Although … she had sometimes wondered if Mina's very ignorance of colour theory and psychology was the secret. The way she paired and mixed colours was unique and unpredictable.

Behind her now, Jenny ran her fingers up Iris's nape through her hair. "This is good. You should do it again."

Usually Iris had her hair cut in a bob, but this time she'd had it cut very short up the back, longer on the sides and permed. Loose curls twirled in soft ringlets to her cheeks. "You like it?"

"It suits you. Your face is thin. Curls fill it out."

"Curls cost, let me tell you."

Jenny puffed out air. "You can't begin to compare to what I have to spend." She circled her arm high in the air around her weave.

"And my face isn't thin. It's perfectly normal."

"Yeah, yeah, keep your freckles on."

Iris stepped on the pedal again. She knew how to see her face and body critically. She had to. A couturière was a living, 3-D model for her work. The proof that she knew how to dress a body to advantage.

She reached the end of the seam and snipped the threads. With the whole dress on her lap, she ran the piping she'd sewn through her fingers. Touch could feel imperfections the eye couldn't see.

The seam was smooth and even. Deep pink silk and grey linen: a good choice.

"That's it for today." She got up from the machine and lay the dress on the ironing board.

"About time," Jenny said, though she was the one who'd suggested coming to the studio to wait for Iris. She lifted her duvet coat off the stand, zipped it, and pulled up the enormous hood. "Look at me." She posed before a mirror. "I'm a walking sleeping bag."

Iris took longer, winding herself in layers. A snug cloche hat that bundled her new curls close to her cheeks, a wool cardigan over the cashmere pull she already wore, a pashmina scarf. Over that, the wide-shouldered coat she'd designed to match the 1950s glass buttons she'd cut off a thrift-store find.

She held the door open for Jenny, who flounced out as only she could inside a sleeping bag and in heavy heels.

*

Tuesday evenings Gabriela worked late at the clinic and Bruno was usually alone at home. He sat on the sofa with a heap of laundry still warm from the dryer. The Tragically Hip played from the stereo in the dining room. His hands moved mechanically, folding T-shirts and matching socks, turning them into flat oblongs the way his mother had. He'd never thought that the way he made sock packages was unusual, but over the years different girlfriends had commented on his orderly Teutonic habits. He had no idea if all Austrians or only his mother folded socks like this. People were so ready to generalize.

He'd only been to Austria once, with his parents when he was seven. Grandparents, aunts, and uncles had examined him from head to toe, pinched his cheeks, shouted at him to eat more, grasped him to their full bosoms. The relationship they so boisterously claimed made him feel strange and shy. His cousins were either much older or much younger. There was no one to play with. He got lost in his uncle's enormous house with its marble floors and broad echoing hallways. His grandparents lived in one corner, his uncle, aunt, and cousins in another. The largest part of the house were the workshops where statues lay on their backs on tables, their beckoning hands paralyzed mid-motion, and crucifixes with sorrowful faces leaned against the walls. There were so many that they crowded into the hallway. To go to the bathroom meant walking a gauntlet of men with drooped heads hanging from nails stabbed through their hands and feet. No one ever explained, and he only pieced together later that the family business was church restoration.

One time his uncle saw him staring at the burlap sheets of paintings that hung from the ceiling to the floor. A man on a horse slaying a dragon. A woman holding a bloody head aloft.

His uncle said the paintings were frescos that had been painted on church walls. They'd been removed to expose an older fresco beneath. He knew the technique for how to peel them off intact. It was a secret passed down from his father, who had it from his father, who had it from his. The knell of ancestors and the mystery of what he was describing had stayed with Bruno, so that even now, forty years later, he recalled the suspense of hoping his uncle might tell him.

Another equally magical memory was of going with his mother to the workshop where her sister was gilding a wooden statue. Feel, his aunt said, holding out the leather pad she had strapped on her palm. On the pad lay a tiny glistening square of gold leaf. He'd been careful, understanding it was delicate, but before he even thought he'd touched it, the square crumbled into weightless flakes. Eat them, she said, nodding at the specks on his finger. Gold is good luck. On his tongue he tasted and felt nothing, but after he returned to Canada and his teacher asked him to tell the class about his trip, he didn't talk about his family, the large house and the statues, or swimming in a lake ringed by snow-capped mountains. He said he ate gold leaf. The teacher thought he meant paint. Not paint, but he didn't know how to explain the ephemeral squares of real gold.

The only hard proof he had of a connection to that time and place were the two Baroque angel heads — one in his bedroom, the other in Mina's living room. Their mother had realized she was pregnant while in Austria and she'd wanted angels for her two children. She said it was their birthright, by which she didn't mean religion but connection to the family business. For herself, she'd brought back the doll that had belonged to her grandmother. She said her brother and sister had twelfth-century Venetian glass, silver coins stamped with the Crusaders' cross, thousand-year-old Etruscan drinking bowls. They wouldn't miss an old doll and two cherubim.

While he was there, Bruno's opa had also given him a book of Grimms' fairy tales. Their fatalistic tone reflected the dark postwar years when the book was published. In these stories the wicked stepmother was forced to step into red-hot iron shoes. The evil sister was drenched in tar. Rumpelstiltskin stomped his leg so deeply into the ground that he ripped himself in two when he tried to pull it out again. Bruno's mother had helped him read the German, and later he read out loud to Mina, her leaning so far over the drawings that he had to keep nudging her aside so he could see the print. The scratchy ink illustrations were as frightening as the stories. Sagging jowls and bulbous eyes. Hairy warts and crooked toes. Bruno could still recall the snaggle-toothed devil snoring. Rumpelstiltskin whirling in a rage.

He flapped out a tea towel as he peered across the room at the bookshelves. There: he made out the glimmer of the tooled gold letters on the spine, and dropping the towel on the folded pile, he got up.

The cover was worn, the edges rubbed soft. A book much read and loved. It fell open on a page with a puckered mark where Mina used to plant a wet kiss on an elderly woman whose cartoonish jaw was shaped like two bony hills, one trailing a long wiry hair. The German was dense and old-fashioned, but he could still half-understand it. He flipped ahead to a drawing of a woman with greedy, fleshy lips, stooped to drink from a pond where a duck swam. She planned to cook and eat her two stepchildren. To outwit her, they'd turned themselves into a pond and a duck. When she bent to drink, the duck pulled her into the water and she drowned. She was bad and deserved to die. The logic of a Grimms' story was implacable. He kept leafing through the pages. A wolf with his belly distended with the little goats he'd gobbled. A girl who had to cut off her finger to use as a key because she'd lost the key to open a door. He recalled being a boy, with Mina beside him, reading the stories with a horror that felt delicious.

When he heard the front door open, he returned the book to the shelf. With her coat still on, Gabriela hurried past down the hallway to the bathroom.

The phone began ringing and he picked it up. "Allô?"

"S-s-something to tell you." Although this was how Mina started every phone conversation, today the words sounded like an echo from a fairy tale.

"I'm listening."

"My groceries."

"What about them?" The latest person Social Services was sending to do Mina's groceries either lacked common sense, was stealing, or both. He'd questioned why there was a box of a hundred teabags and a jumbo tub of margarine on *every* bill. Social Services said they would look into it but they hadn't yet.

"She got cookies. I'm dibète!"

"So don't eat them."

"Mais sont ici!"

"I'll take them away the next time I come."

"When?"

"I don't know. But not now."

"I can't eat cookies!"

"So don't eat them. Just. Don't. Eat. Them."

"They're here!"

"How about you put them in the bathroom?"

"Salle de bain?" She sounded horrified.

Gabriela had quietly come into the room and sat in the armchair. She'd changed from her work clothes into a loose sweater, pyjama bottoms, and fuzzy socks. Her hair, released from its bun, tumbled onto her shoulders.

"You don't eat in the bathroom, do you?" he said.

A snort of disgust.

"So put them in the bathroom and you won't eat them."

Mina was quiet for a moment.

"I'll stop in after I finish work tomorrow and get them."

"Quand?"

"I don't know when, but you can go out if you have to. I'll find them in the bathroom."

"I'm n-n-not going out."

"*In case* you're going out. *In case* something comes up. Don't stay there waiting for me." He could have told her that he would be there by five, but then she would be in a snit if he was a few minutes late.

Finally she sighed. "D'okay."

He didn't know if she thought d'okay was a word or if she knew their dad had made it up, crisscrossing English *okay* with French *d'accord*. She'd deliberately adopted a few of his habits. Only Pepsi, never Coke. For breakfast one piece of toast with Cheez Whiz, another with peanut butter. And once she moved into her own apartment, she announced that she was going to start smoking. Their mother told her it was a dirty habit and that cigarettes were expensive. She was going to have to pay for them out of her weekly spending money. Mina said she wanted to smoke because Daddy did. She was also only going to smoke one a day. When their mother told Bruno, he was surprised by such willful nostalgia. Mina was only ten when their dad died.

When he hung up, Gabriela said, "What is she not going to eat in the bathroom?"

He explained and she gave a soft laugh. "At least she knows she can't resist cookies."

"She cheats often enough. I don't even think that was about the cookies. She wanted me to know the woman who does the shopping is making mistakes."

Another soft laugh. "She's the CEO of her little world."

"And wants me to play henchman."

Gabriela smiled. The evening clinic was always busy and she looked tired, but also more relaxed than she'd seemed lately. "Work okay?" he asked.

"This guy. How he ended up ..." She swung her head in disbelief.

"Klutz of the year?" But he said it gently, not sure if he was presuming too far by making fun of her patients.

"His desk job was giving him a stiff back, so he decided to start jumping rope. Why jumping rope and not stretching, I have no idea. He grabs his skipping rope, except he's also still trying to read his screen. His rope hooks his screen, he tries to save it, gets tangled in the skipping rope, falls over his chair, and ends up in a neck brace and with a sprained ankle. He's actually pretty lucky that's all that happened."

"I don't even think you could choreograph that."

She sniffed, agreeing. "What about you? Your gang met today? You know what you'll be working on next?"

"A new idea, yeah ..."

"Wait. I put water on to boil. Let me get tea."

He carried the folded laundry to the closet in the hallway and into the bedroom. He'd meant to talk with her about telling Val that they were going away when they hadn't even made plans. She'd made him look like a fool. But they were having a quiet evening. Why start an argument?

She'd put on Yolandita Monga — slow, soulful music — one of her favourite singers. There were two mugs on the coffee table and she'd moved to the sofa. He sat close enough that she could put her feet on his lap and she did. He began to massage them as he told her about Val's idea to intimate the horrendous disparity in a city, where there were buildings as far as the eye could see, and still there were people in the street who had no home. Val wanted to focus on their plight, really try to understand it. Not having a home, how desperate that could make a person. How they would fight for whatever they could still call their own.

Now and then Bruno wheeled a hand in the air to help him find the words. Talking about dance wasn't his forte. He preferred to stay in the background, doing just about anything but talk. Gabriela nudged him with her foot to remind him to keep massaging. Her dark eyes watched him, her round cheeks dimpling even when she asked a serious question. This was how they used to talk, understanding each other, no bristle of conflict between them. Relaxing together in the evening.

He tugged off her fuzzy socks to squeeze her arches and pull her toes. For a few moments there was only music in the room. His hands on her skin, feeling the bones, rotating her ankles. Her heavy-lidded eyes almost closed. "Bruno ..."

"Mmm?"

"Ditch your glasses. Come here."

*

An ugly room in old bread colours. Nothing on the wall but the clock. Mina checked her watch but she already knew the clock was wrong by three minutes. It was always wrong! But she would still sooner look at the wrong time than watch the rest of the group who were poking and pinching each other. She always sat farther down the table by herself. She turned her head not to see François stretching his long tongue to touch the bottom of his glass. She could do that too, but you just didn't. Nobody wanted to see that. Mama told her.

She was waiting for her sandwich and hoping it was egg. That was one good thing about work. She didn't have to get her lunch ready. But: she couldn't smoke a cigarette after lunch. She had to wait till she was home again.

The others thought they were being funny. They weren't. She didn't like any of them, and especially not Henri who used to be her prince once upon a time. She had to throw him out after what he said about *Swing Time*. *Swing Time* was her and Daddy's special movie that they used to watch together. Bruno gave it to her on DVD so she could still watch it. She put it on one day when Henri was visiting. He said he didn't like the dancing. She told him he was stupid. He said to turn it off. She said no and kept the remote clutched in her fist. He got up to stop the player and she bolted off the sofa to shove him away. She kept shoving him right out the door and slammed it. She wouldn't open it again even to throw out his coat. Too bad! Tit for tat. She didn't care if he bawled and screamed in the hallway and the neighbours got upset. It was her apartment and her TV and she said what to watch.

The sandwich wasn't egg but tuna. She wrinkled her nose at the smell. She *could* eat tuna but she *wanted* egg. She knocked the pickle off her plate onto the table. Didn't want that either.

Even in the factory when they sorted paper, she sat as far from the others as she could. She didn't want her work to get mixed up with theirs. They made mistakes, but she never did. She was the best! The supervisor always said so. You're my star, Mina. She knew she was!

Before, she always used to work with Joanie. It didn't matter what kind of job it was — in a store or in a factory. Joanie was her friend. They did everything together. But then Joanie fell into a hole and she never saw her again. It made her sad when she remembered and sometimes she cried, but not as much as for Mama. She cried about Albert too. He was another friend — not a prince, a friend — but then he started yelling all the time and he wasn't Albert anymore.

Bruno told her that was how things were. He said she would make new friends, but you had to know people for a long time before they were your friends. Friends weren't like princes who were easy come, easy go. When you lost your friends, that was that. You didn't have friends anymore.

She was starting the second half of her sandwich when the supervisor walked into the room. "Listen, everyone! Il faut écouter maintenant!" Two of the guys wouldn't stop clowning until the supervisor called their names and told them to stop. "Are you all listening now? You can finish eating but I need to tell you something important."

Mina couldn't eat if she was listening, so she didn't listen. But even though she tried not to hear, words still came through. "Factory … recycling …" She already knew that! That was the work they did. And then, "automated." That meant machines. She didn't want to do anything with machines and stopped listening even more, humming a little as she chewed. But she heard, "pas besoin" and "une autre job" and "we might not be able to keep you together as a group."

Another job? She didn't want another job. She was good at this one! "D-d-don't want …" she began, not sure where to go from there except to say it as loudly as she could.

"I'm sorry, Mina. We don't have any choice. It's not just our group. The other employees are being laid off too. The factory is installing a fully automated system."

But she loved this job! She didn't want to do work where you had to put things on shelves. Her feet hurt too much. Her belly was too big. She couldn't!

Through the blur of her tears she saw that one of the guys down the table was making a haw-haw-haw face at her. She roared at him, "S-s-stop!"

He didn't so she picked up her plate and threw it at him — but it was only a paper plate and it flopped onto the table.

*

After a few hours of sewing, Iris needed to get out of the studio. Jiggle her hips, swing her arms, realign her spine. Some days she had errands in the city and she set off with her knapsack. Today, bundled in a long coat, toque, and scarf, she headed to the river — not any old,

no-name river. This was the St. Lawrence, the waterway that connected the Great Lakes with the Atlantic, as vital a waterway as the
Mississippi, the Yangtze, the Thames, the Nile, the Amazon. It looked
narrow here, because it was bisected by an island. The island, too, was
studded with condo towers that blocked the horizon. But even here,
the water was powerful and moved swiftly.

From her studio it was only a ten-minute walk to the bike path
that followed the bluff overlooking the river. There was also a footpath lower down by the shore. In winter, most people stayed on the
bike path that was more or less cleared of snow, but Iris watched
between the bare, twiggy trees until she spied footsteps, pocked in
the knee-high snow, angled down the slope.

The air was cold on her cheeks, the cattails golden in the sun,
the snow white, the late-afternoon sky blue. What a day! A woman
trudging toward her shared a delighted look. The spaniel with her
snuffled a zigzag through the snow and dry grass.

As Iris walked, she stretched her neck. She'd sat too long in one
position, hand-hemming a three-metre-long ruffle that would border
the opening of a wraparound blouse. The extravagant ruffle was its
own statement. She hadn't needed to play with colours. But she'd
urged the client to choose lime green silk for the ruffle on the ochre
pea-spotted blouse.

Would she have done that two years ago? Maybe not, but she had
more experience now. Her sense of what could be done was growing.
She was ready to take more risks.

And maybe Jenny was right. Maybe her colours were more interesting since she'd gotten to know Mina. So what, if there was some
give and take, some colour intuition she was channeling? It wasn't
as if Mina wanted to design clothes and Iris was taking something
from her. If anything, Iris was helping her, bringing her a richer
variety of colours to work with.

On the frozen edge of the river were tracks where people had
walked or skied. They'd still stayed close to land. Farther out, an

artery of water cleft the ice. Iris was watching its cold black gleam —
and so saw when the rays from the setting sun turned the glassy
wetness a searing, incandescent emerald. She stopped. In all the
times she'd walked here, she'd never before witnessed anything like
this. No doubt there was an explanation. Light refracting, water
temperature, angles, whatever. But at that instant it felt like a sign.
The elements aligning. A benediction even.

The light shifted infinitesimally and the water gleamed black
again. Iris glanced behind her. There was no one else on the path.
She was the only one who'd seen. Because the glimpse was *meant for
her*. Ever more she'd become convinced that the day she met Mina in
the park was no coincidence. It couldn't be.

*

Only six p.m. but it could have been deepest night. Gabriela, walking home from the métro, looked up into the black winter sky — and
saw the two bicycles strapped to the balcony of a triplex, wheels in
the air as if the building might cycle off.

Yesterday evening with Bruno had been fabulous. The way they'd
used to be. She hung her breasts over his mouth and straddled him.
How long since they'd last made love? And why? Didn't they both
need this? But as their hips rocked together, a thought flicked at her
that this was another opportunity lost. She had to force herself back
into the moment. The swelling ribbons of sensation.

Her friend Marie-Paule had told her she should just stop taking
birth control. When she got pregnant, Bruno would have to accept
it. But Gabriela couldn't do that — not to Bruno, not to a child. She
wanted a loving father who wanted to be a dad, not someone forced
into an impasse.

The Christmas decorations people had hung in their windows
were brilliant in the darkness. A string of coloured lights trans-
formed a straggly, leafless bush into a hedgehog bristling with gems.
On their street the neighbour, who swept the sidewalk after the

garbage and recycling trucks passed, had rigged a speaker to play tinny Christmas jingles.

Their lights were on. Good. Bruno was home. He wasn't in the living room or kitchen, but there was a bowl on the counter. Yam fingers tossed with olive oil and spices. She loved his baked yam fries.

"Bruno?" she called.

"In the basement!" he hollered through the floor.

She opened the refrigerator and saw the large pottery bowl of spinach salad. Another of her favourites.

When the phone began ringing, she reached for it but he was already bounding up the stairs. "It'll be Mina. I didn't —" He snatched the phone. "Allô? ... Yes, I know, I didn't get the cookies but they're in your bathroom, right? So you won't —" He was listening, his brow furrowed.

Gabriela could hear the sputtering, loud and distressed, but that didn't mean something was wrong, only that Mina was upset. Bruno stood with his head bent into the phone. Thready cobwebs from the cellar floated from his jeans. She would have brushed them away, except that his intent expression stopped her.

"No more what? No more paper? There'll always be paper — for a while yet at least ... Do you mean no, that's not right, or no, there's no more paper?" As he kept listening, the lines on either side of his mouth deepened. "They can't stop your work without telling me. ... No, I ... I don't know. I'll call your social worker and find out what's going on."

Mina protested for a while longer but finally he hung up. Instead of putting down the phone, he called someone else. He still hadn't looked at Gabriela. He must have gotten an answering machine. He grimaced and left a message — for the social worker, Gabriela guessed.

"Assuming she takes her messages," he muttered as he stooped to the cupboard for a baking sheet. "Something's going on where Mina works. I don't know what. I have to find out."

"Where she works?"

"That's what I just said."

Gabriela straightened. He might be annoyed but that was no reason to snap at her.

"From what I can understand, it sounds like there's no more work."

"If this is about where she works, that's the social worker's purview."

He upended the bowl of yam fingers on the baking sheet and was spreading them. "I'm aware of that."

"So why don't you let her take care of it? You say you're overwhelmed with everything you have to do, but now, when there's nothing you can even do —"

"I need to find out. She's upset."

Gabriela knew it wasn't Mina's fault. Mina simply called Bruno as she always did. The problem was with how he reacted. As evenly as she could, she said, "Why do you always feel you have to intervene?"

Even though his hand was oily, he shoved his glasses up his nose. "I'm responsible for her."

"Social Services are too — and this is something you can't do anything about."

"I can still find out."

"Why?"

"What's the matter with you? She's my sister. I thought you understood that."

"You know I do. But that doesn't mean your whole life has to revolve around her needs."

"That's crazy. I can't believe you even said that."

"Maybe you should think about it."

"I'm taking care of Mina. It's what I always do."

She waited a beat. "You hop, skip, and jump at Mina's least little wish and you won't even consider what I want."

"You're an adult. You can do whatever you want. Mina can't."

"Whatever I want?" Her voice trembled. "You know what I want."

He flung his hand at the phone, saw his oily fingers, and went to the sink where he turned the tap on full.

She waited until the kitchen was quiet again. "You always use Mina as an excuse. You don't know where to draw the line."

"You want to talk about lines? How about you telling Val we're taking a vacation when we never even made plans? I looked like an idiot when she asked me. I appreciated that, thanks!"

Gabriela gave a slow nod. "I thought we were going to."

"Sure." His tone was trenchant. "You could have told me."

"I told you a few times. I suggested that inn we stayed in once in St. Jovite."

"Right. But that's as far as it went—a suggestion. Talk." The oven pinged and he slammed the baking sheet inside.

"Exactly, Bruno. That's what I mean. Mina calls with one of a zillion possible things she's upset about and you immediately make calls to find out what's going on and stir up a fuss, even if it's something you can't do anything about. But I suggest a few days away and—" She had to stop. It hurt too much that he wasn't even trying to understand.

He stood with his hands braced on the edge of the counter, not looking at her.

"Bruno," she said.

"What?"

"This isn't working anymore."

A bitter laugh. "Because we didn't go to St. Jovite? Because I'm trying to find out what's going on with Mina? Can't you wait a few extra minutes for your supper?"

"Stop that. You know what I'm talking about. I want a baby."

"You want to talk about this now?" His voice rose in disbelief. "I already told you, no. I don't—"

"No!" she shot back. "You don't get to decide for me."

"So what are you saying? Are we breaking up? Are you going to find someone else to have a baby with?"

He was angry. She could see on his face that he hadn't meant to
say it. But he had.

Eyes burning, not trusting her voice, she walked blindly down
the hallway to the bedroom.

Half an hour later, when she smelled that the sausages were
frying and supper must be ready, he didn't call her and she didn't
go. She stayed curled on her side of the bed.

*

What was the word? Mina knew she must know it because the story
was in her head. A story about a sister and a brother. The daddy got
angry and said awful words that turned the brother into a big black
bird that flapped away. Far away. A black bird, a big one. "A crow!"
she remembered.

She wasn't worried about her job anymore because Bruno would
fix that. He had to. Mama said so. Everything everything everything
that was wrong: tell Bruno.

She pulled free another strand of creamy grey thread. When she
held it up, it looked grey, but when she started to stitch it turned a
little pink.

Iris wanted to know what the knitting was going to be but Mina
didn't know. She didn't have to. She only had to pay attention to
the colours. Iris also wanted her to promise to keep everything. But
Mina's knitting was her knitting. Some she kept, some she hid, some
she threw away. Iris was always talking. Blah blah blah blah. She
still sometimes forgot and called knitting *broderie*, but broderie was
flowers and silly things. The colours Mina knit were big and strong.
They didn't want to be flowers. This up-and-down that she did with
thread into cloth wasn't the same as when she hooked a fat needle
through loops of wool — but it was the same too. All stuff she did
with needles. Iris didn't understand.

On TV three friends were hugging after climbing out of a balloon-
boat that raced through rocks and foaming water. People on TV did

crazy things. "See?" she told her new pincushion. It used to live in the dollar store but it wanted to come home with her, so she brought it.

Mama gave Mina her first pincushion made out of smooth green velvet. She had it for a long long time and it got so full of holes that her needles got lost in it. She still loved it. Then one day it was gone and there was a new pincushion beside her knitting. Mama said to stop crying. Nobody cried for a pincushion. But it was *hers!* Remembering made her unhappy. She didn't want to remember the times Mama wasn't nice.

Better to tell the story about the boy who became a crow and flew away. There was nothing his daddy or mama could do. "Only his sister." She had to run past the moon who wanted to eat her. In the book the moon was a mean gnarly head with big teeth. The sun was mean too. "Wanted to b-b-burn her." But the stars were nice. They were ladies in long dresses. They gave her a key to get into the glass mountain where her brother lived as a crow.

A key, the colours hummed. Keys were important! Mina never let anyone have hers. Bruno had one because he was Bruno, but he wasn't allowed to use it. He had to buzz the intercom and wait till she opened the door.

The little sister wanted to save her brother but she lost the key!

No, no, the colours didn't like that but what could Mina do? That was the story. When the little sister got to the glass mountain, she couldn't get in. She had to —

What? the colours demanded.

Mina had stopped stitching because this was so horrible. "C-c-cut off her finger."

Why? the colours cried.

To use as a key. Those were the rules. Witches ate children. The wolf tried to trick you. Riddles came one, two, three. And you should never never never never never lose a key! Or else.

Mina sucked in her lips. It wasn't a happy story. Because even when the little sister unlocked the door and the crow turned into

her brother again, the finger didn't come back. Mina didn't like this
story, but it was the story that came today and once she started, she
had to finish.

She opened and closed her fingers. She wouldn't be able to knit
without them. She spread her hand on the stack of knitting beside
her and felt how the colours pulsed and thrummed into her palm
and her bones. She could never lose a key. She needed her fingers.

*

In the morning when Bruno woke, Gabriela was gone, but she often
had to go to work early. She'd left the thermos carafe half full of
coffee as usual. He assumed that meant everything was all right.

Last night, after they'd argued and she'd stormed to the bedroom,
he'd still prepared two plates of food and set them on the table. He
waited but didn't call her. She knew he'd made supper. When she still
didn't come, he began to eat, but he was too angry to do more than
masticate and swallow. At that point, if she'd come to the table, he
was ready to tell her that maybe she shouldn't stay with him if what
she needed so badly was a child. By the time he finished the food
on his plate, the feeling of aloneness had settled and pooled around
him. They'd had fights before, obviously, but never one that ended
in what sounded like an ultimatum. Her meal was cold by now, the
yam fries limp. He went to the kitchen to reheat the sausage and
fries. He carried the food to the bedroom and tapped on the door.
The room was dim except for her bedside lamp that lined the curve
of her shoulder and hip with light. You have to eat, he said. When
she pushed away her hair and he saw how swollen her eyes were, he
sat on the bed by her legs. I'm sorry, Gabriela. He meant for having
asked if they were breaking up. She sat up against the head of the
bed and took the plate from him. He'd forgotten cutlery but she said
it didn't matter. She ate a few yam fries and said thank you. And
then: I know you're not going to change your mind. He hoped that
meant the argument was over. He asked if she was going to come to

the living room to have tea. She said she wanted a long bath. That night they slept curled close, two animals needing comfort.

It was too early to go to the studio and he decided to try to reach the social worker. At least now, in the daytime, he could talk to the receptionist. The receptionist said the social worker was dealing with an emergency, but social workers were always dealing with emergencies. At night their dreams must be crisscrossed with hazard tape. Bruno said he would wait.

By now he had over a decade of experience with social workers. Every year or two Mina was assigned to a new one. With each, he had to re-explain her habits, likes, and dislikes. Didn't they keep files they could pass along? Or were they testing *him* each time? He wished Mina could keep the same worker for more than a year, but Social Services probably knew that clients who grew too familiar could become demanding, even abusive. He could definitely see it happening with Mina.

Mina's first apartment was in Park Ex so that was where her file was. When Bruno became her guardian, he could still easily get to the social worker's office if he had to. Their mother was keeping close tabs on Mina too. But after she passed away and when he bought a house in the Pointe, he asked to have Mina moved closer to where he lived. Social Services said that transferring her file from Park Ex to the Pointe would be too complicated. She didn't want to move either and she had the right to decide where she lived. He countered that she would adapt to a new neighbourhood as she'd adapted to moving to Montreal. As Social Services continued to buck, he told Mina to call her social worker every time she needed something. The social worker couldn't take Mina shopping for a new pair of sandals that very day no matter how hot it was. The social worker couldn't fix a tap that dripped and didn't appreciate getting serial messages on her answering machine about it. Mina's move didn't happen quickly — nothing involved with her care ever did — but finally she was assigned a subsidized apartment in the Pointe.

Her all-time favourite social worker had been Danny Plourde, who'd distinguished himself by going bowling with Mina's social group and being on her team, which she took as a personal compliment. Even when she was no longer his client, he still called her on her birthday. Bruno had found him smug and sometimes wrong about Mina, but his life had been easier during Danny's tenure.

The worst social worker was the one who'd kept trying to make Mina say her name, Jacinthe. Bruno had repeatedly pointed out that Mina had a lisp and she stammered. It wasn't fair to expect her to say Jacinthe. Jacinthe still tried, showing Mina where to put her tongue and how to hold her teeth. Jacinthe also tried to stop Mina from wearing polka dots with stripes. Bruno said that so-called normal people slouched around in jeans with the waists under their bums and nobody stopped them. Why couldn't Mina wear what she wanted? Jacinthe said Mina needed to normalize her appearance. Bruno said Mina was short, obese, and cross-eyed. What did polka dots and stripes matter? Jacinthe was horrified by his derogatory language and unhealthy attitude. He groaned. I love her however she looks. She's my sister. But I can also see how she looks. Leave her be! But Jacinthe insisted. When Mina didn't dress *correctly*, she barred her from bowling and birthday suppers. Bruno called her superior and discovered that the social worker was allowed to curtail Mina's activities to make her behave. He and Mina were both happy when Jacinthe moved to another department.

Her current worker, Faiza, had a shrill voice that electrified rather than helped issues. However, she usually notified Bruno of upcoming changes and he was surprised that she hadn't told him what was happening at the paper recycling plant. Or perhaps — he still hoped — maybe Mina had misunderstood.

He heard a click on the phone and then Faiza's pencil-sharpener voice. "Monsieur Corneau?"

"What's this Mina tells me about her job?"

"They only just told me! I wasn't even notified! I—"

"Okay," he said calmly, hoping to stop the effusion of exclamation marks. "So my next question is, do you have another job lined up? I don't want Mina staying home."

"Yes! Of course, there are other places where Mina can work! I'm going to visit her very soon to discuss them!"

"Because the longer she doesn't have a job, the more likely she'll resist starting a new one. Once she gets used to not going out, there's no way she'll budge. Like what happened with the social group." After a month-long hiatus when the two volunteers who supervised the group returned from vacation, Mina no longer wanted to go on outings. She'd readjusted her schedule and had new routines.

"The more her life is circumscribed," Bruno said, "the more inflexible she gets, the less healthy it is for her physically and mentally."

"As is the case for each of the clients who've been let go from the recycling plant, Monsieur Corneau, not just your sister!"

"Actually, no. Mina is the only one who lives alone. The others are in group homes or with their families. So she's more isolated. She should be prioritized."

"Yes! I agree. Hm ... There is another matter I wanted to bring to your attention. The superintendent in her building is retiring."

"I'm sorry to hear that," Bruno said. "Mina liked him and he kept an eye on her."

"He's not being replaced. The tenants will be given a number they can call."

Bruno gave a disbelieving laugh.

"She can call—"

"Oh, I know she can call. Believe me, I know. Do they have the least inkling of how often she can call when she thinks she needs something? The managers of that building have no idea."

"Perhaps Mina shouldn't have the number then. She could call you and you could—"

"No way. If her toilet won't flush, I do not want to be on the front line. It's their building. If they won't pay for a janitor, let them deal with their tenants."

"There's also the problem with the Publisacs."

"We've already discussed this. No one has seen her take them and I haven't seen any in her apartment. Why are the neighbours accusing my sister without any proof? Would they do that with someone who could defend and explain themselves? What is it with people?"

There it was. Mina versus the world — and himself her only advocate, because even if she was in the wrong, who else would defend her?

*

Today was Mina's day to buy cigarettes. She still had three left in the freezer but it was very important never to run out. When Daddy used to run out, he said câlisse! and grabbed his car keys. But she counted her cigarettes and marked down the number, so she never ran out.

She got them in the dép two streets away. It had dirty windows and smelled like old food, but the man at the cash was nice. "Hi Mina. You came out in the cold to see me?"

"Cigarettes," she said. Then added, "S'il vous plaît." He knew what kind she wanted. Export A, like Daddy.

Another man walked up behind her, holding a case of beer on his hip. "Smoking's no good for you, you know that?"

She wrinkled her nose. None of his business. But she said, "Yeah."

He gave a laugh. "That's the way. Fuck 'em!" He was skinny with a shaved head. His jacket was open and on his T-shirt there was a shape that made her hold her breath.

"Hey," he said. "You okay?"

She didn't answer. She looked hard at the shape so she wouldn't forget it.

The man at the cash said, "She's fine. She doesn't always have a lot to say."

She walked home as fast as she could, but she had to be careful because of the ice and snow. Her head was bursting with the power of these new blunt lines.

At home she struggled out of her coat and flung off her hat. She had to knit that shape! She unscrewed her hoop and pulled off the grey knitting she'd been doing. Her squares of cloth, she needed a white one. The man's t-shirt was white. His shape was black but it wasn't his shape anymore. It was in her head now and she liked purple better. As long as it was dark. The shape told her it had to be dark.

She began stitching. Yeah, this was good, so good! A couple of times, when she reached for more purple, dark red or dark green called, Me, take me! Thin lines that made the purple stronger.

When the phone rang it was Iris who wanted to bring her some new thread.

The shape wasn't finished but already it was so good that Mina wanted to show her. She kept stitching, stitching. She had to be careful to keep the lines even and straight with no curves. This shape did not want curves!

When the intercom buzzed, she unlocked the door and heaved back up onto the sofa, grinning with expectation. Iris always liked her knitting, but wait until she saw this!

Iris walked in, all energy and loud talk. "Wait till you see, Mina, I got you this thread that's a wool-silk blend. I know you don't like silk but—" She saw the knitting on the hoop.

Mina waited for her to get excited, but Iris said slowly, "Where did you see this?"

Mina gaped. How had she known? "N-n-nowhere!"

"You didn't make this up. It's not your idea."

"C'est moi." She clenched a fist to her chest.

"This is … I don't know how to explain, but if anyone sees this, it will make them angry. It's not a good design. Don't show it to anyone, okay?"

Mina knew it was good! She could feel the shape's punch. Iris was stupid! Mina wanted her to go!

"I'm your friend, right? I wouldn't tell you something if it wasn't true. Maybe I'll call your brother and he can explain it better."

Bruno didn't know anything about knitting! Mina knew this was good!

"Do you want to look at this new thread I got you?"

She kept her eyes on the TV where people were standing around cars and talking.

"I'm sorry, Mina. You know I love what you do. It's just that this ..."

She kept not looking at Iris and finally Iris said, "I guess I'd better go."

Go! Yes, get out! Mina thought as hard as she could. When the door closed, she pushed off the sofa to lock it and put on the chain.

Mouth set, she picked up her hoop to keep knitting. What she was making was good! Iris could go fart in the flowers!

*

When the phone rang, Bruno slid it a resentful, sidelong look. Mina was going to make a scene when he told her about the paper recycling plant. Make that two scenes because of the janitor leaving. All beyond his control but she would still blame him.

"Hi, is that Bruno? It's Iris. You've met me at Mina's. I bring her embroidery —"

Immediately alert, he cut her off. "Is something wrong?"

"With her, no, but ... do you know she's embroidering a swastika?"

"*What?*"

"Right. I was surprised because I thought everything she did was original."

"She must have seen one somewhere."

"Probably. But you know, it's not just the Nazis who used it. It's a symbol that's been around for thousands of years. It represents the power of life."

He barked a laugh. "That's Mina, all right. The power of life."

"I tried to explain to her that it's a bad sign, but I don't think she understood."

"Explanations are dicey. She has a sense of logic but it's not one that's obvious. And she can be pretty stubborn about not understanding what she doesn't want to understand."

"She didn't like that I told her not to make it."

"Did she hit you?"

"Does she hit people?" Iris sounded surprised.

"If she gets angry enough. Back when she still did her own groceries, she clobbered a guy who tried to steal her cart."

"Served him right, don't you think?"

"I would sooner she control her temper."

"I didn't know she had one."

"Then you'd better hope you don't find out the hard way."

"Has she ever hit you?"

"She used to when we were kids, but only once since I've become her guardian. She hit me hard, straight in the stomach too."

"Wow."

"The risks of being in charge. I had to take away her spending money for a month. It's the only form of discipline that works with her."

"So she's never hit you again."

"No, ma'am."

"Sounds like you know what you're doing. But how will you stop her embroidering swastikas?"

"I'll talk to her, but I know it'll go in one ear and out the other — with no telling what spin she'll put on it in transit."

"But what if someone sees her with a swastika and gets upset?"

"If someone believes that Mina is a neo-Nazi, then they understand even less than she does. Which I'm not saying won't happen," he added.

He was smiling when he hung up. Iris was more sensible than he'd expected. He appreciated that she'd called to tell him. Nice, too, to have someone acknowledge that he knew what he was doing. To get some positive input for a change.

He hadn't meant to go out again today, but he should look into this swastika business. He had to tell Mina about her job too. Might as well get it over with.

The hard-packed snow squeaked with each step. Cold seeped through his toque. The air was so frigid his eyes watered. At Mina's he had to buzz the intercom twice.

She was already back on the sofa, her mouth set, her profile stubborn. Her embroidery hoop was next to her on a cushion. A grey and pink design fanned out like wings.

He leaned across her for the remote to turn down the TV. She objected with a huff.

"What, don't you want to hear? I talked to Faiza."

Now she looked at him, face expectant.

"But listen, it's not good news. The paper recycling factory is closing." That was easier to explain than that they were going to replace people with machines.

"My job!"

"You can't have a job there if there's no factory."

"B-b-but—"

"Faiza will find you another job." All the while he talked, he scanned the shelves and her furniture, but he saw only the usual colourful paisleys and zigzags.

"I want—"

"That job doesn't exist anymore. It just doesn't."

Her breath started hitching and he looked around for tissue. How could there be such a jumble of stuff, but not a single box of tissue? In the bathroom he spun a wad of toilet paper off the roll. "Here." He'd never known how to comfort her when she wept. Her sorrow was so deep, each small loss seeming to hook into every other loss. Or maybe she had no filter. No protection. He couldn't tell her now about the janitor leaving.

Inane dialogue continued to chirp from the TV. From where he sat, he still looked around the room but no longer expected to find the swastika. She must have hidden it, and hidden, he would never find it.

Mina had stopped crying but she looked miserable. Her glasses sat crookedly and the lenses were smeared. "I'm going to clean your glasses, okay?" She let him lift them from her face. There was dish detergent in the kitchen but the tea towels looked dirty. He dried the lenses with the bottom of his T-shirt.

He set them on her nose again, and though she still sniffled, the worst seemed to have passed. "Mina, Mina," he sighed. "Where do you come from?"

Her face brightened. It was a question he used to ask when they were kids — partly teasing her and partly believing that she was different because maybe she'd come from a mysterious place — while also knowing without a doubt that she was his sister.

And more gently now, "What were you stitching earlier today? What you showed Iris."

Her mouth smacked shut. Her look slid away.

He took a notebook from the end table and on a blank page drew a swastika. She gaped. "This —" he began.

"That's m-m-mine!"

"Other people used it before you. It's a bad sign."

She was stammering and protesting. He still had the remote next to him and he turned the TV off, which always shocked her into silence. "Listen to me, Mina. This is important. This sign means bad things. It's for hating people and killing them. Next time you're at my place, I'll show you on the computer. People used to put it on flags they hung on buildings. Maybe you saw it on TV or in a movie, but it's a bad sign."

She was staring at him but he couldn't tell what she understood.

"People with guns," he said. "You don't like guns, do you? The people who used this sign carried guns. They would have —" But telling her what the Nazis did to people like her would make even less sense.

"Don't stitch this, okay? There are a lot of other things you can stitch, but not this. I'll show you on the computer — soldiers with guns marching and holding up this sign. Also — are you listening to me? Mama didn't like this sign. She told people she was Swiss so they didn't associate her with it." He hoped that invoking their mother would have some weight. He ripped the page out of the notebook and balled it.

But what had she done with the swastika she'd made? In the doorway of her bedroom, he looked right and left. Elvis fixed him with his trademark smile from the poster on the wall. The bed was heaped with stuffed animals and clothes that might or might not be dirty. Years ago she'd asked for and he'd bought her a clothes hamper, but it stood empty in the corner. No sign of the disappeared Publisacs either.

*

Mina slammed the fridge door and thunked the juice on the counter. Too many dishes in the way so she swiped with her arm, crashing them into the sink. Did that glass break? Tit for tat! Too bad! Bruno was supposed to fix her job. She didn't *want* another one. He was supposed to make things right! Mama promised her. You can always tell Bruno. He'll always be there for you. Huh! Mama didn't know how stupid he was!

She was enraged that Iris told Bruno and Bruno thought he could tell her what she could knit. Her shape was good, she knew it was. Strong with arms that wheeled. She didn't believe about the marching soldiers and guns. Mama never told her and Mama told her everything.

She rammed her shoulder against the fridge — stopping in surprise when it rocked. She hadn't known she could do that. She rammed it again but there was nowhere for it to go, stuck between the stove and the counter.

She had to do something bad, she had to! She fished out the bag of chocolate caramels she kept tucked away where no one could find it. She was good at hiding. Better than Bruno was at finding. When she was little, she took his things and hid them. He never found them.

Only when Mama asked, did she put things back. Not right away, not so anyone saw, but she did it. She moaned softly, sucking the deliciousness of forbidden chocolate and missing how deeply good it had felt doing what Mama asked.

*

Val had asked Bruno to set out a chair and small table as physical barriers for Tandi and Mathieu to creep around and bump against in their frustration. They had nowhere that was their own but still they were hemmed in.

From his workbench where Bruno was doing surgery on dolls, he could hear wooden legs being shoved across the floor.

"Bump into each other too! No, don't just clip him. Crash into him. Good! And you, Mathieu, what now? You're out in the street and this other person has invaded the little space you've got."

Bruno heard the thud of a foot and Tandi yelped, "Hey!"

"You knew I was coming."

"That doesn't mean you have to kick me."

Val had decided there should be one small object that Tandi would guard viciously and Mathieu would destroy. Light enough to be flung about, an object the audience would immediately recognize as having value. A knapsack? Shoes? No, no, too obvious, too literal. Then Tandi said, how about a doll? A doll ... Val paced. Precious to a child, invested with history, shaped like a human but inanimate. The dancers, too, could morph into and out of being dolls. Locked knees, frozen faces. A doll was a great idea.

Bruno had found dolls at the thrift store for fifty cents apiece, well within their budget. Tandi had one tucked under her arm as she whirled in a circle. Mathieu snatched it from her, Tandi dove after him, and he spun around and smashed the doll to the floor.

If they were headed in that direction, Bruno saw he would need more dolls. For now, how about they use cushions?

Val kept urging the dancers to feel the desperation of needing a place, however small, that they could claim as their own. Wasn't that what everyone needed? Not just humans, but animals of all species. Basic, rock-bottom survival. How would you feel if what little you'd scraped out of the nothing that was still yours was threatened? The rage that would burst! And what if the doll was the last and only thing left from when you still had a home and a family? How invested would it be with your very identity? Val always got impassioned, talking through her ideas. Revving herself up, as Bruno thought. And of course, she needed the words for grant applications and funding, not to mention the programme notes for people who needed to be told what a dance meant.

By now, Bruno had collected a box full of dolls, but a few days earlier, as he was watching Mathieu pummel and fling the cushion across the floor, he realized that a doll with a cloth body and a solid head would be more visually dramatic. The floppy limbs, the wobble of the neck, the hard bounce of the head. When he suggested it, he got an enthusiastic thumbs up. Go for it!

Easier said than done. He had only one cloth doll in his box. He visited more thrift stores but cloth dolls were rare, and the ones he found had cloth heads. Okay, then, time for some head transplants.

On his workbench he had four cloth bodies he'd beheaded, waiting for their new plastic heads. Beside them, four plastic dolls to decapitate. Those, too, he had to choose. Plastic heads that popped off were useless because he needed a head with a neck to attach to the cloth body.

Now he was considering which tools to use as surgical instruments. A utility knife or a hacksaw?

*

Gabriela was leaving work when she saw the oversized T-shirts in a boutique window. Mina would love the one with the big-eyed puppy on the front. Although they would be seeing each other on the weekend to go dress-shopping, Gabriela decided to give it to her now.

When she pressed the intercom, there was crackling and a pause before Mina shouted, "Don't want to s-s-see you!"

"Mina? It's Gabriela."

There was another pause before Mina buzzed her in, and when Gabriela opened the lobby door, she wondered to see Mina at the end of the hallway, glaring as if she suspected a trick.

"It's just me," Gabriela called. "Who don't you want to see?"

Mina flapped her arms against her hips. "Bruno. He w-w-won't —"

Gabriela held out the package. She didn't want to hear what Mina expected that Bruno hadn't done.

An unexpected present! Mina beamed. She still waited until they were inside her apartment and she was on the sofa again before accepting it from Gabriela. And although the plastic was open at one end, she bunched it in her fists and ripped, spilling out the T-shirt. When she saw the puppy, her fingers became delicate, tracing the outline softly. "Que t'es beau," she crooned.

"Do you like it?"

"Yeah …"

"So what have you been doing today?"

Mina was upset about something to do with margarine. Gabriela understood that much but not what the problem was. She asked if Mina needed margarine, but that wasn't it. There was something about the margarine. Did it not taste right? No! Mina was getting exasperated. Was it … Gabriela couldn't think what might be wrong with margarine.

On the shelf was a photo of Bruno and Mina taken when they were younger and Mina was still only chubby. She stood in front of him with her head leaned back on his chest. He had his hands on her shoulders and was smiling at the camera. Gabriela had always liked that he hadn't had the gap between his two top teeth fixed. It made him look boyish. But seeing it now hurt her.

"Where's Bruno?" Mina demanded.

"Probably still at work. But you know, if you need something, you don't always have to call Bruno. You can call your social worker too."

"Her!" Mina batted a contemptuous hand.

"There are some things Bruno can't do, only she can. Like finding you a new job."

"That's why."

"That's why what?"

"I have Bruno."

So much for that. Mina's go-to device was permanently set.

Gabriela had sat on the sofa with Mina and was leafing through the stack of embroidery between them. Each was wild and fancifully coloured. Sometimes Mina tacked one on the wall or lay it across an armrest or a table, but she always kept a pile next to her.

Vivid green nubbled with pink streaks. Blue squiggles and white oblongs. Gabriela flipped back the next one and gave a start. A large purple swastika. "Mina ..."

"It's mine!"

"Of course," Gabriela said gently, understanding that she needed to be cautious.

Mina sniffed self-righteously.

"Did you make more like this?"

"No!"

"So this is special because it's the only one."

"Yeah."

"Hm ... I know it's yours — and it will always be yours because you made it — but I would really love to have it. It will make me think of you even when I'm not with you."

It was a gamble to ask. Mina never gave things away. Whatever was in her apartment was hers. She was watching Gabriela now with wide eyes.

Gabriela hesitated. She'd never before tried to play her trump card. "I thought you might let me have it because I'm your belle-coeur."

Mina lifted her chin. "D'okay," she said gravely. And added, "Ma belle-coeur."

"Thank you so much." Gabriela leaned across the stack of swirling, zigzagged, and ballooning colours to kiss Mina on the cheek. She folded the swastika, letting Mina see how respectfully she handled it, and tucked it in her purse.

Once she was outside again, she would thrust it deep into a city garbage can. She didn't know why Mina had stitched a swastika, but if Bruno saw it, it would be yet another thing for him to go on a rampage about. Another Mina crisis.

*

Yesterday Mina wouldn't let Iris in. Iris guessed she was still upset about the swastika. The question was: how long could she hold a grudge?

That morning Iris called, and as soon as Mina picked up the phone, before she'd even said a word, Iris sang, "Frîtes, frîtes frîtes!" Mina wasn't supposed to eat French fries because she was dibète, as she liked to vaunt, but she also loved frîtes and delighted in cheating.

Mina was waiting on the sidewalk, short and squat in her purple parka, when Iris turned down the street. They headed to the small diner around the corner, which wasn't Mina's favourite but it was the closest. The sidewalk had been scraped and spread with gravel, but they still didn't talk while they walked because Mina wanted to pay attention.

Once in the diner, she barrelled to a booth as if someone might elbow her aside and get there first. She'd told Iris that this diner wasn't as good because it didn't have menus. Iris had offered to read from the black pegboard on the wall, but that wasn't the point. Mina already knew what she wanted. She still liked to look at the pictures in a menu.

She ordered frîtes and a diet Pepsi. Iris asked for tea.

She waited for the waitress to leave before asking, "Aren't you having any beans?"

"No," Mina said with decision. But she looked happy, she loved this game.

"Maybe you'll change your mind?"

Mina pursed her mouth. "No."

"They're supposed to be very good here."

"No."

"Look at the man at the next table, he's having beans. They look delicious."

"No."

"You don't even want to try?" Iris wheedled.

"No!"

The climax of the joke was to ask why she didn't want beans. Mina gave a toss of the head. "They make me fart!"

The waitress brought the frîtes and Iris tore open a packet of ketchup. Mina could do it herself but there was no telling where the ketchup would land. She'd already snatched up a fry and was waiting, lips wet with impatience, for Iris to squeeze ketchup on her plate.

She still wore her hat. It didn't matter that they were indoors. When Mina wasn't home, her hat stayed on her head — and every hat sported a button or two. Today's hat was a plaid deerstalker with ear flaps hanging down her cheeks. One button proclaimed I LOVE MY CANOE DOG in orange and green letters. The other announced that Céline Dion loved René Angélil with a photo of the couple smiling.

"Can I have a frîte?" Iris asked.

Mina poked a finger in the air. One.

Iris hovered her hand over the plate, making a show of choosing. She wasn't sure if she'd been forgiven yet for not having admired the swastika or if this outing was an interlude of grace for the sake of the fries. For the moment it seemed they were on good terms.

"That was tasty. Can I have just one more?"

Again the single finger. Ah, the glory of routines and rituals.

*

That morning, when Gabriela looked at the list of patients for the day, she immediately spotted Lavoie Ernest, slotted for 11:15. Mr. Lavoie with his interesting son who spoke Spanish and had been to Guanajuato. *His son?* Why was she being so coy? His father had called him Daniel. Daniel Lavoie. She knew his name.

When she called in her 11:00 patient, she scanned the waiting room and saw Mr. Lavoie, but he was accompanied by a woman. Probably his daughter. Gabriela couldn't help it. She felt disappointed.

Mr. Lavoie showed her how he could hold a plank pose for a full minute. He was determined never to have a sciatica attack again.

His daughter had stayed in the waiting room and they were alone. Gabriela told herself she couldn't ask. But then she did. "You don't have your son with you today?"

"He's teaching." Mr. Lavoie said he taught history at high school. He said it proudly.

She waited for him to tell her more but he didn't.

*

12:09 on the car clock. Bruno was late. The problem was that Mina would be waiting outside, as she always did, determined not to miss a single instant of an outing. He'd picked up the car a little earlier, thinking that would give him time to buy a lamp. Mina said she needed one to see her knitting better. He'd chosen quickly, paying no attention to the design, only clicking the switches to test how solid they were.

He parked in front of his house and left the car running as he bounded up the steps and flung open the door. "Gabriela, we're late!"

She stood in the hallway, coat and boots already on, long hair tucked under her hat. "I've been ready for the last twenty minutes."

The way she said it made him not explain about the lamp. What was the point? She'd already put him in the wrong. It would take only minutes to drive to Mina's.

12:16 on the car clock as he turned onto Mina's street and there she was, bundled inside the bell of her purple parka, swaying slightly in her stubby orthopedic boots. He sprang out to help her into the back, but Gabriela was already settling her in the front where it was warmer.

He turned the heat and fan on full blast. "Why do you stand outside, especially today when it's so cold? You should have stayed in your apartment. Or in the lobby. I've told you, Mina, I've told you."

Her scarf was knotted tight. She wore a red and white toque with a giant red pompom. From what he could see of her nose and mouth, he was getting her I-don't-like-you profile.

"What do you think about this new job you'll be doing? You'll be by yourself in a church. Did Faiza tell you?" He knew Faiza had because she'd told him.

No response.

"And guess what? I bought you a new lamp. That's why I'm late." Her pout softened a little.

"It's sturdy. I don't think you'll break it. Right away," he added.

"What's that?" Gabriela leaned forward between the seats. During winter she didn't get mushroom pale like he and Mina did. She was lucky with her brown skin.

Mina tugged off her mitt to cup Gabriela's cheek. "Ma belle-coeur," she murmured.

"Are you warm, little Mina?"

"Yeah," she said dreamily as she stroked Gabriela's cheek.

Glancing, Bruno saw the ring he'd had enlarged. "Does your ring fit better now?"

"My b-b-birthstone." She held out her hand and straightened the ring so the green stone was centered. She'd bought it herself. A cheap ring but she loved it.

"Ah oui." She looked at Bruno now. "Y a un problème."

"Where's this?"

"At the bank. People sh-sh-shout."

"Shout at you?"

"Yeah!"

"At the banking machine or in the bank?" He controlled her online account and knew that she went to the machine to withdraw her weekly $20 but to a teller to make tiny deposits of $4.20 or $2.55. He wasn't sure why she deposited the small change. Maybe she hoped the coins would sprout nickels and multiply in the bank. It wasn't a crazy idea. People who had large amounts of money did the same.

"The bank," she said indignantly.

"You mean the tellers?"

"The people."

"Why?"

"D-d-don't know." She was always innocent.

"What do you do?"

"Go in."

"What do you do when you go in?"

She frowned, not understanding.

"Do you get in line?"

She turned her head to stare at him, affronted. "No time!"

"You go right to a teller."

"Yeah."

"But all those other people have been waiting in line ahead of you."

Gabriela began to try to explain. Good luck, he thought. If Mina had ignored queuing up all these years, she wasn't likely to change now.

He let the women out at the entrance to Sears and parked the car. When he got inside, he found them among the racks of lingerie.

"Mina needs underwear," Gabriela said.

"Fine, where are the granny bloomers?"

"Bruno!"

"What?"

"*Granny bloomers?*"

"You," he asked Mina. "Do you want bikini panties?"

"No!"

"Okay, then we need underpants that will stretch around your ginormous bum, but let's not call them granny bloomers."

Mina started blinking, the corners of her mouth turning down.

"What's wrong?" he asked. She didn't usually mind when he talked about her size. If anything, she seemed proud of her girth.

"You. You're n-n-not nice to Gabriela."

He glanced between the two women. Gabriela's face was stiff, ignoring him as she sorted through piles of underwear. He grabbed a hanger with a clutch of large underpants. "What about these?"

Mina's eyes widened with shock.

"What's wrong now?" He looked to Gabriela for an explanation. She seemed puzzled too. "Why not, Mina? I think they'll fit."

He held them over Mina's bum but she swatted his hand away. "Too s-s-sexy."

"These?"

"The holes."

The fabric had a miniscule eyelet pattern. "You think someone will see through the holes?" He held the panties up to his face to show her how unlikely that was, but she refused to look.

"How about these?" Gabriela had found some equally roomy panties in plain cotton.

Bruno was the only man in the lineup at the lingerie counter. The women who were waiting held their scant handfuls close as if to hide them from his voyeuristic eyes. He dangled Mina's huge panties with insouciance, rocking the hanger on his finger.

As he waited he kept an eye on the red pompom. Gabriela and Mina had made their way as far as the sweaters. He couldn't hear but he could see how Mina stuttered with yearning. Walking with her through a store was like trailing flypaper. In any direction she would see something she wanted with all her heart.

At least she wouldn't be able to steal a sweater. People were fooled by her slow walk, but her hands were quick and her pockets deep.

She'd been caught shoplifting several times, and each time Bruno had to convince the store management not to bring charges. Legally, they could. He'd even wondered if it might not be a good lesson for her to spend an afternoon in jail — except would she understand that it was the consequence of taking without paying? Cause and effect never seemed to register with her. He couldn't tell if she truly didn't understand or didn't want to. The threat that she might get caught again was too abstract, whereas all those delightful small items she could snatch were so real. Her shelves, cupboards, and dresser were packed with notebooks, soaps, batteries, ankle socks.

By the time Bruno had paid for the underpants, Gabriela and Mina had moved along to the racks of plus-size dresses. Now and then Gabriela held one up. The neckline had to be high. Mina wouldn't wear anything below her collarbone. Sleeves had to be short because long ones flopped past her hands.

When Gabriela finally had a few possibilities, she and Mina went to the change room. He could hear Mina's voice raised in complaint, then hooting with laughter. After a very long time she reappeared, face red from exertion, hair swiped aside, the frayed edges of her long johns under the sagging hem of a navy blue dress.

"Does it fit?" he asked because he couldn't tell.

"She can get into it and the waistline sort of sits on her waist, except we're not really sure where that is, are we?" Gabriela smiled at Mina, who was gazing up at her happily.

"Good! We've got a dress." He gave a thumbs-up, though they weren't even looking at him. Great, he thought. I guess I'm just here to pay and carry.

The afternoon wasn't over yet, because shopping trips with Mina included tea and a muffin. Slowly they crept in the direction of the food court, Mina mesmerized by every store they passed. She came to dead stop before a kitchen display.

"What do you see?" he asked warily.

She pointed at a bright yellow mixing bowl.

"But you have lots of bowls and you don't cook anymore."

Her lips puckered until the word burst. "Splool!"

He considered the bowls and utensils. "The spatula?"

"Yeah!"

"What are you going to do with it?"

She didn't answer but her eyes were attached to it as if with strings.

"Go ahead then," he said. "Buy it. We'll wait for you." All the money he was spending today came from her account, but he'd allotted it for clothing. If she really wanted a yellow spatula at designer store prices, she could pay for it. That was why she had spending money.

"Didn't b-b-bring money."

"You never leave your apartment without your wallet. You know you're not supposed to. All your important information is in your wallet."

She squinted at the contradictions she was going to have to navigate to keep up the masquerade. "My wallet," she admitted. "Mais pas d'argent."

"Ah … there's no money in your wallet."

"Yeah." She looked relieved she'd outwitted him.

"Stop teasing her," Gabriela said.

"I'm not teasing her. She's teasing me. Let me see your wallet, Mina."

Reluctantly she fiddled with the snaps and compartments of her bag and tugged out the wallet. Gabriela muttered something in Spanish that could have been lord-give-us-mercy or what-an-asshole. But he knew Mina was lying. He wasn't even surprised to find the bill section empty. "You knew we were going shopping and you didn't bring any money. What if you saw something you wanted?"

"You pay."

"I pay, eh?" He slid a finger into the inside pockets of the wallet until he found the folded square. Three twenty-dollar bills and a ten.

"Th-th-th-th—"

"Look at this! You can even contribute toward your dress." He didn't expect her to but he couldn't resist the dig.

"M-m-my money!"

"The dress is for you, isn't it? I'm not going to wear it."

"Stop it!" Gabriela snapped. "Give her back her wallet. I'll buy the spatula."

"She should buy it herself."

"Why?" Gabriela turned on him. "Give me one good reason why."

"I'll give you a few reasons. Because it makes no sense to buy her something she'll never use. Because her apartment is stuffed to the ceiling already. Because that spatula will cost more here than just about anywhere else. Because if she absolutely wants something stupid, she has her own money to buy it. Because —" Mina had started sniffling. "Stop that," he told her. "Gabriela's got her wallet out. Looks like she doesn't mind being a sucker."

"Come." Gabriela slid her arm across Mina's shoulders to bring her into the store.

And Gabriela had the nerve to accuse him of not knowing where to draw the line. At least he could tell the difference between a legitimate and a ridiculous grief.

Mina reappeared with a beatific face, her new yellow ergonomic spatula in a paper bag that sprouted ears of tissue paper. Brightly Gabriela said, "Are we ready for muffins and tea?"

He walked ahead. Why even pretend to walk with them, since he was the big bad meanie who'd been excluded. Though he forced himself to keep the pace slow, knowing that Mina didn't move fast. He wasn't going to argue now in front of her, but boy oh boy, he and Gabriela were going to have a talk about this, oh yes.

There was enough bustle around them at their table that Mina didn't notice his silence. Gabriela was asking her about the wedding she was going to. Did she know Pierre's cousin? No. Then why was she going? For the dancing! Mina loved dancing. Back when she still belonged to a social group, Bruno had asked if they could be taken dancing instead of bowling for a change, but Social Services had decreed that bowling was more beneficial.

"What about you?" Gabriela asked Mina. "Have you ever wanted to get married?"

Mina shook her head.

"Why not?"

"How about we leave well enough alone?" he said. "It would be very complicated for Mina to get married, so it's fine that she —"

"Dishes," Mina said. "Clothes. W-w-washing ..."

"That's housework, sweetie. That's not the same as being married."

"That's what she saw our mother do," Bruno said. "Anyhow, can we drop it?"

"Maybe someone should explain to her what marriage is."

"Okay," he said. "Mina, do you want Pierre to live in your apartment?"

"No!"

"Being married is when someone lives with you and you share everything."

Her eyes fixed him with cross-eyed intensity. "You're not married."

"Not everyone who lives together gets married. Gabriela and I are fine the way we are." But he didn't look at Gabriela.

Mina wrinkled her nose, either not understanding or getting bored with the talk.

"How's your new shaver?" he asked. He hadn't been able to return the one she'd broken but he'd found another model reduced by fifty percent.

"D'okay." She touched her jaw as if making sure, but he could see she'd shaved for the outing.

"Do you put cream on your skin after you shave?" Gabriela asked.

"What?"

Gabriela explained. Didn't she understand this would now be another thing Mina would decide she absolutely had to have? "Any old cream will do," he interrupted. "The one you already use for your hands and face."

Mina looked to Gabriela for confirmation, not at him.

She finally finished her muffin and they shuffled through the shopping mall again, Bruno trying to herd them toward the middle of the concourse, as far as possible from the stores. At the closest exit he escaped to fetch the car.

Gabriela got in the back with Mina and the two whispered and giggled as he drove. So Gabriela could still have a good time. Only not with him.

At Mina's, he carried in her bags and the box with the new lamp which he forbade her to open. He would come very soon to put it together. No, he didn't know when. For now, how about she be happy with her new underpants, her new dress, and her new yellow spatula?

When he returned to the car, Gabriela had moved to the front but she didn't speak until he signalled to turn at the head of the street. "Where are you going?"

"To return the car."

"Can't you take me home first?"

"You can walk home with me."

"I'm not wearing boots for walking in snow."

It was only a few blocks. A few blocks she could walk.

She said nothing but as soon as he parked the car, she got out, slammed the door, and strode across the lot. "Wait!" he called but had to run after her. "I thought you couldn't walk in those boots. And tell me, what was that good cop/bad cop stunt you pulled with the spatula? One day you accuse me of being too involved in her life, the next you're playing fairy godmother."

"A spatula, Bruno. Get some perspective."

"I have the gobsmacking advantage of a 360-degree perspective! She's my sister. I watch out for her."

"She's her own person."

"Believe me, I know that better than anyone. But she'd be flat-out broke if I didn't handle her money, and who knows how Social Services would do it if I didn't."

"At least they wouldn't give her a big guilt trip every time she wanted a treat."

"She gets lots of treats. Today she got a new lamp, a new dress and —"

"Underpants!" Gabriela clapped her gloved hands. "Aren't you generous? I was in the change room with her and let me tell you, she needed new underpants!"

"So I'm supposed to check the state of her underpants too? I thought I was doing too much for Mina — but now you're implying it's not enough?"

Mouths bitter, jaws clenched, they marched along the street, turning down theirs.

But when he unlocked the door, leaving it open behind him, she didn't follow. She stayed on the sidewalk, three steps down, framed by the wood-panelled entrance.

"Aren't you coming in and closing the door? Or are we heating the street now?"

She looked up at him. "I can't anymore, Bruno. I just can't." She hadn't shouted. She'd simply said it.

He didn't ask what she meant. The sadness on her face drained his anger. He didn't know either. How could they continue like this? His hands hung.

She lowered her eyes and walked out of the frame.

He nearly called after her but didn't. What could he say if she was ready to walk away from what they had because she wanted something else?

He shut the door gently, pulled off his boots, and went to the living room where he collapsed on the sofa.

*

The toilet lid dropped with a loud clap. One of these days it would break. Everything was waiting to break. That was how things were.

Mina sat carefully on the lid, a pair of the new underpants in hand, her stretchy bellbottoms beside her on the vanity. She lifted one foot and aimed it into one leg hole. Got balanced with her foot on the floor again. Stretched the underpants so she could see the other hole. Lifted the other foot.

Juliette was coming at 11:00 to do her feet. Mina liked Juliette, who had a soft voice and strong hands. In her satchel she carried all kinds of pretty things to snip and to rub with. Not long ago, when Juliette left the room to wash her hands, Mina slipped a pair of little scissors with red handles under her cushion. Later she tucked the scissors in the top pocket of the raincoat she didn't wear anymore because the snaps were broken. Also in the pocket were Bruno's striped blue socks. She'd been at his house and the socks were in a pile of folded laundry on his bed. She couldn't wear them because they were too big and Bruno would see them. But that didn't matter. What mattered was that she had them. They were hers now.

She had to stand to pull up her underpants and now had to sit again — carefully! — to put on her bellbottoms. They were harder because the legs were long and her feet had farther to go. She hoped the bellbottoms weren't twisted around with the bum part over her belly. That was almost funny when it happened, except it was so much work to get them off and start again. She knew the tag was supposed to be at the back. Mama had showed her a long long time ago when she was little. The problem was that no matter how she started, the pants could twist around.

She grunted as she stood to yank them up over her belly. Her elbow knocked hard against the sink. "Taberouette!" The bad word jumped from her mouth. It used to jump from Daddy's too. You weren't supposed to say bad words but her princes sometimes did. Pierre shouted cunt and bitch and fuck-you when he was doing sex.

She patted around her hips and belly. The bellbottoms were on the right way. Good. She looked again. Yeah, they were.

She squeezed her eyes shut for pulling on her T-shirt. This was harder because things could happen. Her arms getting stuck or her glasses crooked or she could get dizzy. The bathroom was too small. She'd told Bruno and he said, Too small for what? She couldn't explain. Why couldn't he see? The handle on her toilet broke and had to be changed. The shampoo spilled outside of the tub and Evita got angry about having to wipe it away. It wasn't her fault! It happened because the bathroom was too small.

Once her arms were in the sleeves and the T-shirt was over her head, she pulled it straight. Gabriela's puppy was on the front. She patted its head and laughed because she was patting her titty too. Good puppy, good titty.

Getting dressed was a big task and she only did it every few days. It was easier to keep the clothes on. In the mirror she saw that her hair was messy from pulling on her T-shirt but she'd already brushed it and wasn't going to brush it again. She didn't have to shave because it was Tuesday. She only shaved on Wednesday and on Sunday. She still needed to put on her fleece to stay warm but it was on the sofa. She didn't have to go into the bathroom and close the door to put on a fleece or a sweater.

By the wall was the box with the new lamp. She hadn't opened it, but she wrote MiNA with heavy purple marker on the top and all the sides. Bruno better come today and set up the lamp because she needed it.

She squirmed her bum up onto the sofa and got settled with a pad of paper and marker pens to print letters. Different letters got different colours. B was red. N was orange. That was why she needed a whole package of markers. It was okay if Juliette came and she had to stop doing letters, because later she could look hard at the letter and tell what it was. An A had a point at the top. Both T and J had hats and sticks. That was harder. An S curved. But if she really couldn't figure it out, she could throw away the paper because it wasn't in a notebook. That was why, when she made letters, she used a pad with pages that tore off.

On TV a big hairy dog was gobbling a bowl of food. She patted the puppy on her T-shirt. "Look." The puppy saw but it didn't need food because it was on her T-shirt.

The phone began ringing while she was in the middle of a P. P, she thought, P, P, P, P. That would help her remember. Then she grabbed the phone. "Oui?"

"Mina, it's Juliette. Listen, I'm sorry but I've got a problem with my car." She kept talking fast.

"Wh-what?" Something about a car. Cars always made people late.

"Are you going out this afternoon?" Juliette spoke more slowly. "Can I come at 2:00?"

"Leven," Mina said. They already had an appointment and it was for 11:00.

"No, I can't. I'm sorry. My car broke."

Mina was impressed. A car was a big thing to break.

"Can I come at 2:00? Will you be home?"

"My program —"

"Your program, of course. Don't worry, you can watch TV and I won't talk to you."

"D'okay." Except it wasn't. Mina liked to watch Juliette do her feet. She felt she was being cheated of something. She wasn't sure what, but all of a sudden the whole day was upset.

She pushed away the pad and markers. She didn't want to do letters anymore. Even the pictures on the shelf beside her didn't make her feel better. Herself and Bruno in a restaurant. Bruno and Gabriela. Youpi, their dog from when she and Bruno were little. Even the cigarette she'd taken from the freezer and set next to her pencil holder so it would be ready after lunch. None of it was any good now. And there, on the bedroom door, hung the dress from the store. She hadn't wanted to say no because Gabriela liked it, but she couldn't dance in a dark blue dress. She wore a dark blue dress when Daddy died. She could never wear it again and Mama didn't make her.

The intercom buzzed and she looked at her watch. 11:05. Juliette was only five minutes late! She pushed the intercom button and went to unlock the door. She was already back on the sofa again when she heard, "Mina! You didn't even ask who it was."

Iris? What was she doing here?

"Since when do you let people in like that?"

"I d-d-don't."

"You just did. Anyhow, what are you up to today?"

Mina lifted a foot in the air and waggled it. "Mes pieds."

"Is that today? Well, don't worry, I'm not staying." Iris unzipped her knapsack. "This linen was on sale so I got a few metres for you. I left you one complete metre in case you want to do a larger piece, but I cut the rest into the size you normally like."

Mina rubbed the cloth between her fingers. Iris had brought her some like this before. A little slippery but her needle liked it. Except why this boring porridge colour?

"What have you been working on?" Iris tilted her head to see, but Mina remembered how Iris didn't like the shape she'd made the other day and she'd already flipped the hoop over. All that could be seen now were the tails and crisscrossed threads underneath.

"You're not going to let me see?" Iris made a sad face. "That's not very nice. I just brought you stuff."

Too bad! Tit for tat.

Then Iris noticed the dress hanging on the bedroom door. "Is that new?"

Mina regarded it balefully. She'd already told Iris about going to the wedding with Pierre.

"Did your brother get you this?"

"Yeah."

"I suppose it's nice he got you a dress, but … do you like it?"

The feeling was too strong. "No," she admitted.

"It's not right for your body shape. Oh you know, why didn't I think of this? *I* can make you one. I'll get a brighter fabric too."

Make her one like Kris did long ago? Iris was talking too fast and digging through her knapsack. "What kind of couturière am I? Don't even have a measuring tape on me. Do you have one?"

Mina didn't know what that was.

"That's okay. I can use yarn if I can find some that doesn't stretch." She started to look in the bin of yarn beside the sofa.

"To kn-kn-knit?"

"No, to measure you. So *you* are going to have to stand up, milady. Move it, my dear! Bouger les fesses!"

Mina didn't know why Iris was being so funny but she wiggled off the sofa.

"Take off your fleece. You can keep the rest on. I'll factor that in with the measurements. Don't worry, I won't be designing anything too form-fitting." Iris was on her knees on the floor, waving her hands and a long string of yarn.

"Okay, lift your arm. No, just … yes, like that." She poked an end of yarn in Mina's armpit which tickled and made her giggle.

"Hush!" Iris ordered but Mina saw her wink. Iris stretched the length of yarn from Mina's armpit to her wrist. Then she snipped it.

"You're m-m-making a dress?" Mina wanted to be sure.

"That's what I do, right?" Iris had snatched a roll of Scotch tape off the shelf to stick the yarn in her notebook where she wrote a number beside it. "This is your underarm sleeve length, which is important to bear in mind, as it's so extraordinary in proportion to the rest of you." Mina didn't know what that meant but Iris was grinning, so she grinned too.

"You're a little wide for your height. You know that, don't you?" Iris held more yarn across Mina's back to each of her shoulders. "You just wait and see. I'll make you look nice for Pierre."

Mina didn't care about looking nice for Pierre, but there would be dancing at the wedding and she loved dancing. She wanted a dress to dance in.

2

Mina reached under her hoop to pull the needle with its snake of thread. "One, two, three, four …" She paused. Not because she didn't know what came next but to make sure the colours were listening. "Five, s-s-s-six, seven …" She paused again. "Eight, nine, ten … leven, twelve!" Twelve princesses in pretty dresses dancing all night long!

On TV people were standing in an old barn crowded with old things. Chairs and plates and tools. Daddy used to go to barns like that. Sometimes he took her along. She liked to be with Daddy. In the car he sang "Blue Sway Shoes," sounding just like Elvis. Remembering made her eyes wet and she had to blink hard.

What about the dancing? the colours asked. Tell us about dancing!

She stabbed her needle into the cloth again and reached under for the tip. The princesses had a bad daddy. He didn't want them dancing and he locked the door. "With a key." But the princesses were smarter. Mina nodded. She would find a way to get out too if it meant getting out to go dancing.

Then — a mystery! In the morning the princesses' shoes had holes. That, she didn't understand. She had shoes she didn't want to wear anymore because they slipped when she walked or they were too hard to put on. But there were never holes in her shoes. How did shoes get holes in them? But holes were part of the story, so she said it.

What mattered was the dancing. All night long! Even now, sitting on the sofa, Mina could feel dancing in her legs and her belly and her arms. It made her want to dip and sway. The colours wiggled and shimmered with her. Me! said the orange. Me! said another. The colours jumped, wanting to dance.

Mina would have danced all night like the princesses. The music was still loud and everyone was dancing. But Pierre's mom made them go. Time to go, she said. But it wasn't! Pierre's mom said it was. And Pierre standing there with his big stupid face because he didn't know how to dance. Why didn't he? What a stupid prince! He didn't have his own cigarettes or spending money and didn't even try to dance. She didn't want him to be her prince anymore and she was going to tell him, but in the car his mom wouldn't stop talking. Blahblahblah Pierre blahblah Pierre blahblahblahblah.

Dancing! the colours shouted. Me! cried the orange.

Mina pulled free a strand, wet the tip between her lips and aimed it at the needle. "D-d-do it."

Thisaway! Over here! Crisscross crisscross! The colours were so happy, but she had to watch the time because she had to go to work today. She wasn't sure yet if she liked the new job. The nun who showed her what to do was nice, but the church was big and there were stairs. She'd told Bruno she wanted a job sitting down.

Right now her watch said 11:28 but on the wall clock it was past 11:25 but not yet 11:30. That was the problem with hands on the clock. They were never as right as numbers. She set aside her knitting and got off the sofa. Bruno had put the clock high on the wall but she could reach it with the broom. She jabbed and poked until it crashed to the floor. Last time there was a glass covering that broke but this clock didn't have one.

It was easy to break the hand off because she was strong. Better no hand than a wrong hand. But how to get the clock back up on the wall? It didn't want to go. There was nowhere she could reach where she could hook it. Stupid clock. Bruno would have to do it.

The intercom buzzed but she wasn't expecting anyone. Maybe Iris? Then it buzzed again — very long — so she knew it wasn't Iris.

"Yeah?"

"Let me in!"

She groaned. She didn't want to see Pierre! She'd told him in the car. No more! Go away! Why were some princes so stupid that she had to tell them again and again?

She unlocked her door but stayed in the doorway to stop him from coming in. "Go," she said when he got close enough to hear.

He kept lumbering down the hallway.

"G-g-go. C'est fini."

"No!"

"Yeah."

He clenched a fist to his chest. "I love you!"

She scrunched her face. She hated when princes were like that.

"One more," he whined.

"No! No more!"

He banged the door open hard and she stumbled and nearly fell except that he grabbed her arm and dragged her to the living room. "Ow! No!" she screamed but he smashed her face-first over the arm of the sofa. Her feet didn't touch the floor and her arms were pinned. He yanked at her pants, tugging them down from behind. She tried to kick but her belly was pressed too hard, her feet flailing. He was slapping her bare bum. "Bad girl! Bad! Dancing, you you — you cunt! You bitch!" He kept shoving her down, her face in the cushions, slapping her harder. But he had to stop to pull his thing out. She pushed and squirmed. She knew she was stronger, twisting herself enough to knock him away and struggling to get upright. On her feet again, she punched as hard as she could where Bruno had told her to punch if a man was hurting her. Don't be nice, Mina, let him have it for all you're worth. You punch as hard as you can. So she did and Pierre buckled over, yowling, but she kept punching. On his head, his arms, his back. She punched him all the way to the hallway, slammed her door, and locked it.

*

Tandi and Mathieu were working through a sequence that would propel her collision with the table into a roll across it. Bruno was watching them — and past them, their doppelganger reflection in the mirror, the bright scarlet shorts Tandi wore over her black leotards an energetic balloon of colour among the movement of their limbs, the geometric shape of the table.

When Val called for a break, Mathieu slipped away to beg a coffee from across the hallway. Bruno said, "We haven't talked about costumes yet."

Val was rooting through her deep shoulder bag. "Tattered and ripped?"

"What about historical?"

She shook a cough drop from a packet. "Such as?"

"Doublets and tights?" Tandi quipped.

But he wasn't joking. "More like peasants. It wouldn't take much to suggest it — an apron, britches." In his mind he saw the ink illustrations in his book of Grimms' fairy tales. If, as Val kept saying, home was an existential need, then not having a home was an existential fear that was always there. He was still trying to explain when Val interrupted.

"Yes, that's interesting. Convey universality by referencing time. Homelessness is and always was terrifying. And what did you say, an apron? That's a symbol of home."

"Let's let Mathieu wear the apron," Tandi said, looking over her shoulder as if to make sure he wasn't there to object. "I want the britches."

"No." Val waved a dismissive hand. "We're not making this about gender."

Tandi glanced at Bruno. They both knew that when Val used that tone, the discussion was closed. "Where are you going to get britches?" she asked.

"Bruno can find anything," Val said.

Not anything, he thought, but he had an idea. The dress Iris had made Mina not only fit her, it suited her. He wondered if Iris had ever considered making costumes.

"Okay, people," Val said, as Mathieu walked in flourishing a mug. "Back to work!"

Bruno stayed where he was, watching. He had no particular reason to be there, but here he at least belonged to the team. He was appreciated for what he could do.

Since the trip to the shopping mall with Mina, life at home was disintegrating. When Gabriela had returned that night, she'd taken her pillow from their bed and the duvet from the closet and slept on the sofa. For almost a month now she avoided him in the evening. She either worked the late shift at the clinic or she went to her sister's where she ostensibly helped with the boys. Christmas had been a farce. Gabriela's sister, Claudia, had invited them for supper, including Mina as she usually did, but Gabriela sat at the other end of the table with her nephews who clamoured to have her between them. She must have confided in Claudia, who was politely cool to him. The men seemed not to know that he was persona non grata, but they talked mostly in Spanish and his Spanish was too grade-school to follow. He had Mina beside him, her head mostly bent to her food. They were a silent twosome at a table where everyone else laughed and chattered. On New Year's Eve Gabriela didn't come with him to Tandi's party and he'd been relieved. He didn't want his friends to see how she ignored him. Last week she came home, and with her coat still on, walked into the living room where he sat. Do you still have feelings for me at all? The blunt demand made him pause. Before he could answer — even knew what to answer — she turned on her heel. He thought she was leaving again but she hung up her coat and went to the bedroom where she closed the door. He heard rummaging in the closet. Was she packing? When his girlfriend Kris decided to take a job promotion in Toronto, even though she knew he had to stay in Montreal because of Mina, there had been nothing he could say or do to make her stay. How did other couples bridge impossible decisions? That night, when he left his computer to go to bed and saw how Gabriela lay on the sofa with the duvet pulled high around her shoulders, he imagined walking to the sofa and nudging her hip to make room for him. Whispering to remind her how they'd made love on her mother's rooftop. The tiles still warm from the day's sunlight, the glimmer of stars bright in the clean mountain air. Her skin so soft and faintly redolent of chocolate. But was she still that woman?

Val had stopped the dancers to walk to the chair where her phone was ringing. She frowned at it, answered, and still frowning held it out to Bruno.

He'd given Social Services her number in the event of an emergency, but this was the first time anyone had ever called. Already knowing that this could not be good news, he took the phone, didn't know where the speaker was, but held the flat surface to his face as he'd seen other people do. "Yes?"

"Monsieur Corneau? C'est vous?" Faiza's tight, shrill voice.

"Yes, what is it?"

"You must come to the hospital immediately!"

"What? What happened?"

"Mina isn't hurt, but you need to come now! The police are here and she wants you."

*

Gabriela let Marie-Paule cajole her into coming for lunch at the Vietnamese restaurant across the street from the clinic. She ordered soup but wasn't even hungry for that.

Marie-Paule tapped her chopsticks on the plate of spring rolls the waitress had set between them. "I'm not eating these by myself."

"Bring them back to work. Some resident will scarf them down." The voracious and indiscriminate appetite of doctors who'd been on call all night in the ER was legend.

"You're having at least one. You're losing weight. Your dimples are starting to look like they're carved on your face."

"I can't. I'm not hungry."

"You're not happy."

"Food isn't going to make me happy."

"I never said it would. But upsetting your biochemical balance will land you in a psych ward — and that's not happening on my watch."

Gabriela gave a weak smile. She appreciated Marie-Paule's concern, but her balance sheet of caloric intake and mental health wasn't motivational.

"Hey," Marie-Paule said gently. "I saw the boxes in your office. You've decided?"

Gabriela had asked the satellite pharmacy in the surgical department where she once worked if they could save her a few boxes. This morning the orderly who used to weigh patients for her tapped on her door. He'd flattened a dozen sturdy boxes and tied them with string.

"I might already be too old to have a baby. It might never happen. But if I stay with Bruno, it definitely won't." She tried to say it calmly but the last words scraped up her throat.

Marie-Paule reached across the table to squeeze her arm. "You're strong, Gaby. Really strong. You'll come through this. And one day — I'm sure of it — I'll hold your baby."

*

Iris darted around a man in a wheelchair being pushed into the ER. She hadn't understood what Mina had bellowed and stuttered into the phone, but she'd grabbed her coat, ran to Wellington, and hailed a taxi. Outside Mina's building there were police cars, but all the police would confirm was that the ambulance had just left. *Ambulance?* Where? Which hospital?

"Mina Corneau? Philomena Corneau?" she asked the receptionist who sat behind glass so thick it must be proof against every variety of super-bug and machine gun.

"Are you family? We're trying to find the family."

"Yes," she said, because otherwise they wouldn't tell her anything.

The woman leaned back in her chair to snag an orderly's tunic and nodded at Iris who couldn't hear what she said. The orderly waved Iris to come to the sliding door where he met her. "Is she your sister?" he asked as they walked down one hallway and another.

"Yes, what happened to her?"

"I don't know what happened to her but she did a real number on her boyfriend."

"Then he deserved it."

Stretchers lined the hallway. Doctors in surgical greens strode past. Unseen equipment beeped. The orderly seemed to think she wanted a tour of the whole ER. "Some people get violent all on their own," he said. "We see some pretty crazy things in here."

"She's not violent." But then Iris remembered Bruno said she could be.

The orderly opened a door and there was Mina in a blue hospital gown, propped against cushions on a stretcher. She looked strangely composed. Her belly, a soft mound under the thin blue fabric, gave her a Buddha-like presence. She didn't react on seeing Iris.

"What happened, Mina? Are you okay?"

"Yeah," she said gravely. She seemed either medicated or awed by the high seriousness of being in the hospital.

"But what happened? Was it Pierre?"

"He hit me." Mina whacked her hand through the air. "Comme ça."

"Mina!" A petite woman with a piercing voice bolted into the room. "I've just spoken to the doctor! The important thing is you're not hurt."

"My b-b-bum hurts."

"But nothing's broken. You're not bleeding." She was looking at Iris. "I'm her social worker, Faiza. You're …?"

"I'm Iris, I'm a friend. Mina called me."

"Iris," the social worker enunciated. "I could never make out your name. I always thought she was saying Arse—which didn't make sense. But she's told me about you. You bring her thread."

Iris was pleased to hear that she figured in Mina's hierarchy of people. "Can you tell me what happened?"

Again the door was flung wide and there was Bruno, looking haggard. A man who'd crossed deserts and scaled mountains to get there as fast as he could.

Mina's face distorted. "Pierre h-h-hit me!" And now she began to cry.

Bruno turned to the social worker who quickly gave him the details. A neighbour had called the police. Pierre was in the ER too. "She hit him very hard in the groin."

"What did he do to you?" Bruno asked Mina.

"He —" Her mouth worked, lips trying to shape sounds but nothing articulate came out.

"Tell me slowly," he said. "Calm down."

From her stammering he understood words that he repeated back at her, fishing out the details. Pierre had attacked her from behind and pulled down her pants. He hit her bum and pulled out his — Mina scrunched her mouth with revulsion, flapping a hand at her crotch.

Even through Iris's alarm at the story unfolding, she noticed how well Bruno understood Mina and how completely she trusted him. She hadn't told Iris or the social worker how she felt; only Bruno when he arrived. Mina always scoffed and said Bruno was stupid, but she clearly knew he wasn't.

"And you punched him the way I showed you?"

"Yeah."

"You told her to punch him?" the social worker shrieked.

"Not him specifically. Anyone who attacked her. Sounds to me like this was an attack. She has to know how to defend herself."

"But she really hurt him!"

"Too bad. Let him keep his pants zipped and his hands to himself." To Mina he said, "Is this the first time he tried to have sex with you?"

She scowled but didn't answer.

"The truth, Mina. It's important. I know you've had sex with other boyfriends."

She still didn't want to speak but he persisted. "I mean ordinary sex. Did you have ordinary sex with Pierre?"

Iris felt a readjusting inside herself. How was it that she knew Mina — who was an adult — had a boyfriend, but it never occurred to her that she had sex?

Mina was wrinkling her nose. "White stuff. I don't like ..."

"I know," Bruno said. "You've told me. But did you have sex like that with Pierre?"

"Yeah."

"And usually, when you had sex with him, did he hit you?"

Mina's eyes widened with indignation. She might put up with sperm but definitely not with hitting.

Most people wouldn't have known where to begin, Iris thought, but Bruno cut right to the chase. He knew what questions to ask. She remembered how quickly he'd responded when she called him about the swastika. He must have dealt with it too, because she'd never seen it again.

"So what happened today?" the social worker asked Mina. "Did you argue with him? Did something—"

"What are you saying?" Bruno cut her off. "She nearly got raped — sodomized against her will — and you're trying to figure out how *she's* responsible?"

The social worker drew herself up. "I'm trying to see the whole picture!"

"I don't give a damn about the whole picture. She's my sister and I'm concerned about her — even if she started out wanting to have sex, which I gather is not the case here." He looked at Mina. "Who took his penis out of his pants, you or him?"

She gave him an affronted stare.

"Just say it, okay? You or him?"

"Him."

"And after this, you're not going to have anything more to do with him, I hope."

She jutted her lips and with a regal hand knocked the mere idea of Pierre to oblivion.

Iris was quietly astonished and impressed. Bruno was really good with Mina. They were obviously closer than Mina made it sound when she complained about him. He was also more good-looking than she remembered. The gap between his top teeth was even sort of sexy. An oddity that lent interest to his otherwise regular features. His hair was dark brown like Mina's, though his was edged with grey.

"How much longer do we have to wait around here?" he asked the social worker.

"We're waiting for a sexual trauma therapist to be assigned to her."

"To what end?" He raised a palm as she puffed herself up to object. "She doesn't know the therapist and won't listen to her, and is the therapist going to understand anything she does say? You know how long it takes for her to trust a new social worker. By the time she *might* agree to trust the therapist, she won't be thinking about Pierre anymore. She'll already have a new boyfriend. It would make more sense to sign her up for boxing lessons."

"The therapists are trained —"

"To help women, yes. I agree, I agree. But Mina is a unique case. Aren't you, sweetie?" He squeezed her foot through the sheet. "I'm going to find a doctor to get us out of here."

In the silence after he left the room, Iris sat forward to take Mina's hand.

"Ouch!"

"Is your hand hurt?"

"P-p-punching."

"But you can move your fingers? Let me see." Iris would personally castrate Pierre if he had in any way damaged Mina's hands.

Mina wiggled her fingers well enough, though her mouth tightened as if with pain.

When Bruno returned with a nurse, Iris said, "Mina's hand hurts."

"She's had x-rays," the nurse said. "Nothing's broken." And to Bruno, "There's no bruising on her buttocks yet, but there might be later. You're sure you don't want to bring charges?"

"Useless. Her word against his, and even if a judge can understand what she's saying and believes her version over his, how will they sentence him?" And with a shrug, "Sorry if I sound cynical. I haven't dealt with this particular kind of situation before but with lots of others. The world doesn't make much effort to understand people like Mina."

The nurse didn't argue. "All right," she said to Mina, "let's get you dressed."

Bruno left the room and the social worker followed. Iris stayed to help the nurse. Mina snuffled at the treat of having two people dress her. She made a game of poking her hands into her sleeves and dangling her feet over the edge of the stretcher, bunching her toes so her socks wouldn't slip on. No one watching would think that she had just been assaulted.

When Bruno opened the door again, he had a wheelchair. He helped Mina get into it. To Iris he said, "Thanks for coming. I guess she had your number. There's probably a message on my answering machine at home."

"You don't have a cell phone?"

"I know. The social worker is scandalized."

He was pushing Mina down the hallway when a woman standing at the nursing station began shouting. "You, you tramp! What did you do to my boy?"

"Hey!" Bruno stepped in front of the wheelchair. "You back off or I'll bring rape charges against your brute of a son."

"He's a good boy! I brought him up right. But she has a dirty mind." Arm rigid, pointing at Mina. "What do you expect — not even living in a proper home, all on her own the way she is. It's irresponsible!"

"*He* attacked her."

An orderly moved forward. "Okay, okay, let's calm down here."

"I saw how she behaved at the wedding! It was indecent!"

More orderlies had materialized, stepping between Bruno and the woman.

"Cutting in on couples, wagging her big gut at everyone — thought she was dancing, did she? And Pierre, she left him by himself at the table. She was his date!" She shook a fist, but an orderly pulled it down and firmly led her away. She kept shouting over her shoulder. Another orderly was at her side, trying to quieten her.

"You should go," an orderly told Bruno.

He stepped behind Mina's chair again when a patient being wheeled past on a stretcher began shouting. "You cunt! You bitch!"

Mina flinched against Iris, who was walking beside her.

"I'm gonna fuck you so bad!" The stretcher had already been pushed around a corner but Pierre was still shouting.

Iris turned to see what the mother thought of this proof of her good boy's manners, but she was no longer there.

*

The sleeves of Bruno's coat were too long and it wouldn't zip over her belly, but Mina was warm inside it. He'd snugged his toque over her head, almost down to her eyes. He sat in the back of the taxi with her. He never did that.

But where, she wondered ... "Wh-wh-where's Gabriela?"

"She doesn't know you were at the hospital. I'll tell her. How are you feeling?"

"D'okay," she said, even though everything was strange.

At her apartment door she hung back. Even from the hallway she could see that inside looked different. The cushions from the sofa were on the floor. The table wasn't where it was supposed to be.

Bruno put his hand on her shoulder and brought her in. He began picking things up and putting them where he thought they belonged. She went to the kitchen table and sat. She could see what he was doing but didn't want to help. She felt tired, very tired.

"Do you want the TV on? You always have it on." He switched it on but didn't make it loud enough. "Your stitching … Is it still okay?" He'd lifted the hoop from the floor, the thread hanging. The green with the orange she was zigzagging across it.

"G-g-garbage."

"You want me to throw it away?"

She pointed at the garbage can.

He took the knitting, hoop and all, to the garbage.

"No, the —"

He didn't know what she meant and she held out her hand for the hoop, unscrewed the ring, pinched the knitting off, and held it out with the tips of her fingers.

He took it from her and dropped it in the garbage. "Gone," he said.

But it wasn't gone. It was still there. She could feel it.

He kept picking things up, but he was only making a different kind of mess, putting her hidden word puzzles in a stack so she didn't know which one she'd been working on.

"Do you want a cup of tea?" he asked.

"Yeah."

"Why don't you make yourself comfortable on the sofa?"

From where she sat at the kitchen table, she considered the sofa. That was where it happened. But the sofa was also her place to sit. Under the angel. That made her mouth tremble. Mama saw what happened and didn't stop it.

"I think I have to get you a new kettle," Bruno said at the counter. "The cord on this one looks like someone played a game with a knife."

A new kettle was good. She wanted a new kettle.

She pushed herself up from the table and walked to the sofa, staring at it hard, making a grim mouth. My sofa. Mine. My place to sit.

Bruno brought her a mug of tea and set it next to her. He knew to put in one Splenda and enough milk that it didn't burn her mouth. She sipped it to check he did it right.

"Why is your clock on the floor?"

"F-f-fell."

He stooped to pick it up. "The minute hand fell off too?"

She had another swallow of tea.

"I can stay and watch TV with you if you want."

She held out her hand for the remote that he'd put on a shelf. He gave it to her and she turned the volume up. She would turn the other TV on and play an Elvis CD. She would lock the door and never ever ever ever let Pierre in again.

Bruno still stood, watching her.

"Go," she told him.

"Are you sure?"

"Yeah." Once he was gone, she could put the chain on the door.

He put on his coat. "Call if you need something. I'll come right away."

"Bye." She wouldn't be safe until the door was locked with the chain on.

But even with the chain on, she didn't feel safe. She finished her tea with both TVs on loud. Even Elvis was too far away.

She wished she had someone who sat close and held her and stroked her head. But the only one who had ever held her close like that was Mama.

And now she began to cry. Great, wet, aching breaths sobbing from deep inside her.

*

The air thundered with the roar of snow removal. First, the enormous plough that scraped the road so savagely that the houses trembled. Then the industrial snow blower that churned up the ploughed snow to shoot into dump trucks that rumbled alongside. Bruno usually appreciated the choreography of the monstrous machinery, but this evening the lumbering procession sounded like enemy tanks invading. He'd never liked Pierre but had never expected anything like this.

Perhaps more surprising was that nothing like this had happened before. He'd followed their mother's lead in not interfering with Mina's boyfriends. She'd said Mina should be allowed to like whom she liked. She couldn't get pregnant because she'd had a hysterectomy at eleven years old — as the doctor had advised and their mother had agreed. Bruno had been too young at the time, barely an adult, to fully comprehend that Mina was being sterilized while still a child and too young to give her own consent. Later, he told their mother he didn't think it was right. It would never have been allowed for a 'normal' child. Although he had to admit he was glad now that he didn't have to deal with sanitary napkins or pregnancy.

Except that pregnancy clearly wasn't the only possible conse- quence of Mina having a boyfriend. Her judgment wasn't reliable and she was vulnerable. How was Bruno supposed to protect her right to make her own decisions while also protecting her from those decisions? That was the ongoing question with no absolute answer. With Mina every situation posed its own ethical maze.

He wished he could tell what she was feeling now, but he had never known how to get her to talk about her feelings. As well as he could remember, not even their mother had tried. When Mina was sad or agitated, their mother cuddled her, murmuring assurance until the upset passed. But that didn't mean it was forgotten or had left no trace.

The lights were on at his house but Gabriela wasn't in the living room. He found her in the bedroom with open boxes on the floor and the bed. She was shaking out a sweater and refolding it. Her hair was twisted up. Her normally soft, round features looked stern.

"I have to leave," she said. "For myself."

In that instant, confronted with the fact of her packing — seeing that she truly meant what she said — he didn't know what he felt. Too much had happened today already. He leaned against the door- frame, fingers squeezing the bridge of his nose, pushing his glasses to his eyebrows.

"It's not just that I want a child. I want to be a mom."

"And I don't—"

"Yes, I know. You've made it clear you will not even consider having a child."

She spoke evenly, but he could hear the edge of resentment. "It wasn't me who changed," he said. "It was you."

From an open drawer she grabbed socks he'd folded into neat oblongs. "I never said it wasn't me."

"You know that I already have—"

"Stop that! Stop using Mina as an excuse." Her voice trembled. "Taking care of her is not the same. I want to feel what your mother felt for Mina—not what you feel as her brother. Being a parent is not the same, Bruno, it's just not."

He exhaled. "I guess you don't know that she was in the hospital today."

Her eyes, large with concern, shot to him. "Is she all right?"

"She's home again. Pierre attacked her but she fought him off."

"Attacked her sexually?"

"Tried to but she socked him in the groin."

Gabriela dropped the skirt she was holding onto the bed. "I'll call her."

"She's not upset, so don't upset her."

"How can you say that?" she said sharply. "Of course she's upset." She strode past him to the living room. In a moment he heard the murmur of her voice.

Inside the closest box were scarves, summer dresses, her jewellery box. She was taking everything then. She really was leaving. He'd guessed this could happen and part of him was relieved the tension was finally broken, but it also hurt that she'd chosen what she wanted over their life together.

Gazing around the room, he met the eyes of the angel on the wall. Gilt wings and a mysterious four-hundred-year-old smile. No, he thought, only wood and paint.

When he heard the tap running in the kitchen, he made himself move. She stood waiting for the water to boil with a mug on the counter. "Do you want tea?" she asked.

"No. Yes."

She looked at him.

"Yes."

She reached into the cupboard for another mug. "I'll go see her tomorrow. You're right, she sounds okay — but she also kept repeating that the front door is locked, her apartment door is locked, and she has the chain on. If she has to keep reminding herself that she's safe, then I don't know how safe she feels. What if Pierre comes back?"

"I'm pretty sure his mother won't let him." He told Gabriela about the scene in the ER and what Pierre had shouted. As he talked, he wondered how they could be discussing Mina so calmly, yet Gabriela was leaving.

They stood holding their mugs. Neither moved to the living room or to sit at the table. Finally he said, "Have you been seeing someone else?"

She looked startled. "No. Why do you say that?"

"Who are you going to have a baby with?" Even as he said it, he heard how crude it sounded. But that wasn't how he meant it. He truly didn't understand.

She set her mug hard on the counter. "The one person I'm not going to be having a baby with is you."

"But you can't just —"

"That's not your business."

"Am I allowed to ask where you're going?"

"I can stay at my sister's for a while."

"They don't have enough space."

"The boys said they'd share a room. It'll just be till I find a place." Her eyelashes fluttered. She seemed about to start crying.

He wanted to move toward her but he was pretty sure she would push him away.

Not looking at him, she grasped her mug again. "I'm going to pack a few more things."

Suddenly he thought of how this would affect Mina. "Can we not tell Mina, at least not yet?"

Her full lips tightened.

"I don't want her even more upset after what happened today."

She gave a single nod and walked to the bedroom.

Still standing by the counter he could hear the slide of dresser drawers. Her steps around the bed. Dragging a box across the floor.

He didn't want her to come out of the bedroom and see him listening to the sounds of her leaving. Taking herself away, out of his life. He went to the nook off the kitchen and opened his laptop. Val and Tandi had sent emails to ask about Mina.

That afternoon at the studio when he got the phone call felt so long ago. He wrote to Tandi first because she always talked to him about Mina. As he was sending Val a note, Tandi answered. *Mina rocks! She gets attacked and she fights back.*

That almost made him smile. Almost.

*

With two fat needles she was knitting a blue square. When it was done, she would knit it to other blue squares to make a bigger square. On the table was the bag with the banana muffin Gabriela had brought her. She would have it with tea after lunch. Before her cigarette.

Gabriela had said Pierre *wouldn't* come again. But: *if he did*, she shouldn't open the door, she should call 911. Gabriela printed the number for her in heavy black marker but Mina didn't need to have 911 printed. It was in her head like birthdays and the PIN for her banking card. Gabriela had lifted the pile of knitting away from the middle of the sofa, so that she could sit close and put her arm around her. Cuddled together made Mina feel happy. With her finger she stroked under Gabriela's chin. The skin was soft because Gabriela didn't shave like she did. But finally Gabriela gave her a tighter hug

and said she had to get to work. She would come again, she promised she would. Gabriela was her belle-coeur.

Now, when the intercom buzzed, Mina's hands froze and she sat
very still. If it was Pierre, he would keep buzzing till she opened.
She waited and there was another buzz, but only short. That wasn't
Pierre. But what if it was Pierre trying to trick her? Or maybe it was
Gabriela again. Or Bruno or Iris. She wanted to see all those people,
but not Pierre!

When the phone rang, she grabbed it. "Oui?"

"You're there!" Faiza's sharp voice. "I'm at the door."

"H-h-here?"

The buzzer sounded again. "That's me."

Mina put down her knitting carefully because this was the kind
that could slip off the needles. By the time she got off the sofa and
to the door, Faiza was already there.

"How are you feeling today?" Her sharp voice filled the room,
piercing even through the TVs. She perched in the armchair, her
briefcase flat on her lap.

"D'okay."

"Did you sleep last night?"

"Yeah."

"No bad dreams?"

Dreams were in the night. Why would she think about dreams
in the daytime? Faiza asked crazy questions.

"Because you know, what happened yesterday isn't the way men
are supposed to behave. I don't want this to make you frightened.
You shouldn't feel ashamed about what happened! Do you understand what I mean by shame?"

Mina stopped listening. Too much blahblahblah. She lay her hand
on the stack of knitting Gabriela had put back, close to her. Turquoise
glimmered. Red looped around to catch it. With her fingers she felt
how the colours moved with each other, calming her. She pressed her
palm flat, absorbing the hum.

"Are you feeling badly today because of what happened with Pierre?"

Mina looked up, shocked. She hated what happened! She didn't want it ever to happen again! That was why she punched him! What was Faiza asking?

"Because it's not your fault."

"I know!" Pierre was the bad one!

"And his behaviour wasn't acceptable. Do you understand that? This is the only time this has ever happened to you in … how many years? How old are you now?"

Finally a good question. "Thirty-eight."

"Only one Pierre in thirty-eight years!"

Why did Faiza keep talking about him? Why wouldn't she stop?

"Nobody will ever do that to you again." Faiza leaned forward with her elbows on her briefcase, head angled like a cartoon bird. Why was she acting like that? But finally she sat back again. "You're a survivor, Mina. You're resilient. But you know you can talk to me at any time. And if you need therapy, there are resources. I can refer you." She waited. "Is there anything I can do for you right now?"

"Yeah." She'd asked Gabriela but Gabriela didn't know. Faiza would. She took a notebook from her shelf and opened it. "Name."

"Whose name?"

"Pierre. Nom de famille aussi."

Faiza sat up straight. "Why do you want his name?"

It was too hard to explain. Mina always got a prince's name right at the start, because it was hard to get it when they were gone. Pierre couldn't write so she asked his mom to write his name. But she didn't like his mom and didn't want her writing in her notebook and she'd ripped it out.

She held up the notebook, open to a clean page. "I n-n-need it."

A prince wasn't gone from her life till she knit his name. She also couldn't start another knitting until she did his name. Those were the rules. She didn't want to knit Pierre's name but she had to.

*

A man coming out of Mina's building held the door for Iris so she didn't buzz the intercom, but when she knocked on Mina's door no one answered, even though she could hear the TVs. She knocked again. "Mina, it's Iris!"

The next door opened and an elderly woman peered out. "The police were here yesterday because of her. It's not the first time either."

"Aren't people supposed to call the police when they need help?"

"*I* called them." The woman's face puckered with indignation. "People like her don't belong in this building."

"What do you mean, people like her?" Iris demanded, but the woman was already backing away, closing her door, and Mina had opened hers but kept the chain on.

"It's me." Iris gave a cheery little wave. "Aren't you going to let me in?"

Mina unhooked the chain and walked back to the sofa where she got herself settled and took up her hoop. She seemed her usual placid self, but Iris recalled how she'd been quiet at the hospital until Bruno arrived.

When Iris had last come, Mina was embroidering an orange, green, and lavender design. Now she had white cotton on the hoop and was stitching letters. "Did you finish what you were doing the other day?"

No answer.

Iris got up from the armchair to see. P I E R . . . And on the shelf next to Mina, an open notebook with Pierre's name printed across the page.

"Mina! You're not embroidering Pierre's name after what he did to you?"

Mina pointed at the names on the wall above her.

"But isn't that to remember your boyfriends? Why would you want to remember Pierre?"

Mina looked past her at the TV. Without thinking, Iris turned to look too. A woman was beaming at her office colleagues because she'd had probiotic yogurt that morning.

"Listen," Iris tried again. "It makes no sense to commemorate him after what he did. And it's such a waste of your time and your talent. You could be making something new with the Italian Bella Lusso I got you. I didn't think you'd be able to resist those gorgeous colours, but you haven't even tried them yet, have you? Where's the knitting you were working on the other day, the green and orange one?"

Mouth set, Mina poked her needle into the fabric, rounding the top of the second R.

"Or the grey one before that? It was stupendous, what you were doing." Mina had spliced dashes of pale aqua and rose that brought out the hidden tones in the grey. She'd created a shape like a splash that she edged with a darker rose and turquoise aura. "It was beautiful. I was looking forward to seeing it finished and you never showed me."

Mina considered the notebook next to her and began to stitch another letter.

From her manner, no one would know what had happened yesterday.

The room looked the same as ever. No sign that there had even been a struggle. Except for the clock on the floor. "Did your clock get knocked down?"

"Bruno," Mina said. "He can f-f-fix it."

"Oh, is he coming?"

"Il est au travail." Mina kept stitching.

"He works with a dance company, right?"

"Yeah."

"Do you ever go see his shows?"

"Yeah."

"Maybe I can come with you some time."

"I g-g-go with Gabriela." And with a proud sniff, "Ma belle-coeur."

"Is that … Do you mean belle-soeur? Are they married?"

Mina frowned. "No."

Iris made her own deductions. Gabriela and Bruno weren't married and she hadn't been at the hospital yesterday. Mina might claim her but Bruno seemed less attached.

Mina pushed up her glasses and turned to stare at her tray of threads. This was the moment Iris always hoped to catch. Mina's attention seemed to hover, as if the colours were a freeform blur that suddenly sharpened. Then, with no hesitation, she reached for a new thread.

So far, Pierre's name was embroidered in deep brown that now veered into cold lemon yellow. Iris would never have chosen yellow, but the effect was startling, poisonous, and perfect.

*

Even though Gabriela had been sleeping on the sofa since Christmas, she had still been there. In the morning he could hear the murmur of the radio. The gush of water in the sink. He smelled her toast. Her pumice stone hung off a hook in the shower. Her lotions and creams were in the bathroom cabinet. Even with the tension between them, when he got up after she left for work, there was coffee in the carafe for him. The radio might still be on.

This morning he woke to the resounding non-sound of absence. He lay in bed knowing that he was alone. Gabriela had left boxes stacked in the hallway, but she'd taken her toiletries and a couple of suitcases. She hadn't wanted any furniture, and in any case, he already had the furniture when she moved in. The only large piece they'd bought together was the refrigerator.

Over the few days it had taken her to pack, he'd come home to the space on the hutch where the Mexican fruit bowl had been. The gaps on the shelves where she'd taken her books. He still couldn't fathom it. He'd been so busy with Mina and with work. He hadn't begun to think what it meant that he would be alone again. He'd confided in Tandi that Gabriela was leaving. She asked him why. But instead of sympathy she said, what choice did you give her?

He heard a soft creak through the ceiling. One of the upstairs tenants. Was he going to become an old man listening for sounds in the house and pretending that he wasn't alone?

Come on, he told himself. You've been on your own before. It's not like … He remembered his mother's face, rigid and not crying when the two policemen sat in their living room and told her.

He sat up and reached for his glasses, bringing into focus how the open closet door gaped on his few shirts. It used to be crowded with Gabriela's clothes.

The kitchen was still and empty. No carafe on the counter. He took the jar of coffee from the freezer. The filters were in a drawer — only a few left, he had to buy more. He poured water in the coffeemaker and stabbed the on/off button.

Get real, he thought. Feeling sorry for yourself because you have to make your own coffee.

*

Mina squirted glue across the back of the cloth where she'd knit Pierre's name, smushed the glue around with her finger, and then pressed the fabric onto cardboard that she'd cut into a long circle shape.

The colours were impatient for her to finish and start telling them a story.

"G-g-grass house," she began. A grass house made no sense but that was the story. What a stupid pig! No wonder the wolf came and huffed-and-puffed it away.

The next pig made a wood house. Mama and Daddy's house was wood, but Mama said they were safe because the wolf didn't know where they lived. When the wolf huffed-and-puffed the pig's wooden house, the pig had to run fast, all the way to the market …

No. She stopped. The pig running to the market was a song Mama used to play on her toes. It was about piggies too, but there was no wolf in the song. The wolf was bad, very dangerous, but he wasn't everywhere. He hadn't been where she and Bruno lived with Mama and Daddy.

With her scissors she trimmed the cloth where it was too big for the cardboard. She'd knit Pierre's name as fast as she could. She didn't want to have to think about him ever again.

The smartest pig made a house from brick. The wolf couldn't huff-and-puff brick. When he tried to climb down the chimney, he fell into a big pot of ... boiling water! And a boiled wolf was a ... "dead wolf!"

The colours liked that story. It said she was safe here. Her walls were brick. She had an intercom to find out who was there. And her door locked with a key *and* a chain.

She walked to the kitchen to hide the cardboard with Pierre's name behind the kettle so she didn't have to see it. When it was dry, she would tack it on the wall. Once the names were on the wall, she didn't look at them again. They just had to be there.

She didn't know who the next prince would be, but there was always another.

Except. The colours shivered. What if the next prince turned into a wolf too?

*

When Gabriela visited her sister and it was the boys' bedtime, the youngest, Diego, always wanted her to read to them. She loved to feel their excitement about the narrative unfolding, their laughter at silly outcomes, their stillness when it was suspenseful.

That evening at supper Diego asked if she was going to read to them every night now that she was living with them.

"I'm not living here," she tried to say lightly. "I'm only here until I find my own place."

"Why don't you stay?"

"You know you're welcome for as long as you need to," Claudia said.

"I can't impose too long on Manny's generosity." The older boy had relinquished his bedroom, saying he could do his homework downstairs, but she'd seen the longing look he threw at it when he walked down the hallway.

She loaded the dishwasher and cleaned the kitchen as Claudia took the boys upstairs for their baths. Through the ceiling she could hear the thump of running feet.

Claudia came downstairs again. "They're ready for you. Only one chapter, okay? School tomorrow."

Diego was crouched on the carpet, twisting a block puzzle he dropped when she walked into the bedroom. She hadn't heard Manny's soft tread but he slipped into the room behind her. The book they were reading now was an adventure with men in medieval costume on the paperback cover.

Diego cuddled next to her on the bed, hair wet from his bath. Manny, a long-legged nine-year-old, sat on a stool. Against the wall was the air mattress where he would sleep. The book was geared more to his age. When Diego didn't know a word, he interrupted to ask. Before she could answer, Manny did — which was just as well since she didn't know what a pole arm was.

Diego's warm, small body next to her was solace. Even the jut of his sharp elbows and knees. Both boys listened intently and she would have happily kept reading, but she didn't want to disobey their mom. At the end of the chapter she said, "To be continued tomorrow."

Manny rose from his stool. He was allowed to stay up for another half hour downstairs.

She touched her finger to Diego's nose. "Scoot under your blanket and I'll give you a hug."

He did but informed her primly, "It's not a blanket, it's a duvet." And without a pause, "Why aren't you with Bruno anymore?"

She tucked the duvet around him. Claudia had said to tell the kids the truth if they asked.

"We realized we don't want the same things."

"Why not?"

Her eyes smarted as she bent to kiss him. "Sometimes things just happen this way."

*

Bruno unlocked the door onto his dark house and flicked on the light in the entrance. He dropped his coat on the peg and took off his boots, pretending not to see Gabriela's boxes in the hallway. In the kitchen he grabbed a beer and went to the living room. He'd eaten a falafel on the way home.

A small plus, he thought cynically. With Gabriela gone, he could watch hockey on TV instead of on a small computer screen.

He groaned at the game. The Habs were playing like all they wanted was to collect their salary. After another stupid miss and his beer was finished, he decided to go to bed.

In the bedroom he was about to bat the closet door shut so his few shirts didn't mock him, when he noticed the box on the shelf that had been hidden by Gabriela's clothes. The old shoebox. He'd found it in his mother's closet when he was packing up her apartment. Inside was the doll she'd brought back with her from Austria. It had belonged to her grandmother who was called Philomena. Mina had been named after her and he supposed he should have given the doll to Mina, but that was as good as asking for it to be broken.

He sat on the bed with the box and eased off the lid. Folded back the white tissue paper. The porcelain face was painted cream and pink with the doll's lips parted on small teeth. She seemed about to start speaking. She had blue eyes and a braided crown of dark hair. A blue dress gathered with a wide yellow cummerbund. Tiny hand-stitched leather boots. But all the details paled next to the unnerving gesture of speech arrested. He covered her mouth with his hand. Without her teeth showing, her expression was cold and fixed.

The dolls he'd found to use as props for the dance had peachy, surfer-girl tans. He supposed the colour made them look friendlier to a child living in the twenty-first century. But this doll, despite the hard cream and pink tones, looked infinitely more bewitching.

3

Mina had had a good day. First, the #61 bus to the dollar store, then she walked to the video shop where she got an Indiana Jones movie. She'd seen it many times already but she wanted to watch it again. She'd walked so far that she needed a rest before getting on the bus to go home, so she went into Lafleur to have an order of frîtes. Each golden brown fry dipped into a happy blob of ketchup!

When she got home, the man from down the hallway with the little dog held the door for her. She said hello to the dog, who was very smart. He only ever barked once to let you know he was there. That was enough. Dogs who barked and barked were stupid.

She locked her door and put the chain on. Took off her hat and emptied her pockets to examine her loot. A long skinny tube of peanuts from the video shop. A package of erasers. Dishrags in blue and pink for the sink. An oblong piece of plastic. She didn't know what it was for, but it had a dial with numbers on it and numbers were always good.

She had to use her scissors to get the cardboard off. Too much cardboard! A job she'd had once was stapling cardboard onto hangers. That was all it was: stapling the same size of cardboard to the same kind of hanger, one after the other. Cardboard and hanger, cardboard and hanger, cardboard and hanger, cardboard and hanger, cardboard and hanger. At night she started dreaming about cardboard and hangers. But when she tried to tell Bruno, he didn't understand.

Her stapler had to fall in the toilet and wouldn't flush down before they let her stop doing that job.

After supper she made a cup of tea to get ready to watch Indiana Jones, but when she put the movie into the player, it didn't work. She pressed every button. She punched the top. If she poked with a knife in the front to fix it like last time, Bruno would make his angry stone head. She grumbled at the angel. Why did Mama give her Bruno and not someone nicer?

But. She had no choice. With a grim face she dialled.

"Allô?"

"Something to tell you."

"I'm sure you do."

"My D-D-D-D—" She exhaled, too annoyed. "For watching movies!"

"Minaaaaaaah! You didn't break your DVD player again, did you?"

"No!"

"Right. It broke all on its own."

"Yeah."

"How often do you even use your player? Whenever I come you're watching TV."

"Movies too."

"Like what? Tell me."

"*Swing Time*." He should know that. He gave it to her.

"Is that the only one?"

"No."

"So what else?"

Movies were movies. What did he mean?

"Movies about what? What happens in these movies?"

She sighed. "Y a un homme. Pis une femme."

"A man and a woman," he said slowly. "Are they dressed?"

"Yeah." And then she added, "No." Because sometimes they were and sometimes they weren't. Didn't Bruno watch movies?

"What's going on in these movies? Are they doing things?"

How could it be a movie if they did nothing?

"Are they driving? Do they have guns? Are they talking?... Are they having sex?"

All those things happened in movies! Why was Bruno always trying to trick her with questions? "It's b-b-broken!"

"Okay, okay, I'll come over."

"Quand?"

"Now. I want to see what kind of movie you've got."

Was Bruno going to watch a movie with her? They hadn't done that for a long while. What a great day!

But as she waited, glancing at her watch to see how much longer he would be, she wondered why he was coming now when he should be having supper with Gabriela.

*

Iris sat in an alcove of the bar with a glass of Merlot. Techno music pulsed softly. Jenny was coming when she finished work and Iris had her notebook out to show her. Bruno had seen the sketches and said they were perfect.

At first Bruno had only asked if Iris could make britches. Easy, she said. They're no different from trousers, only they have a cuff below the knee. Why, are they for you? No, he said, surprised. It's a costume for a dance. So the fabric has to be stretchy, she said. Exactly, he nodded. Stretchy and quick-drying since it might have to be washed after every performance. They'd kept talking about costumes for dance in general and he seemed impressed with her ideas. He said he wished they had a budget for costumes because he would hire her. She offered to make them pro bono if her name was on the program as costume designer.

An upright sleeping bag loomed over the table. Jenny threw back her hood, unzipped her coat, stuffed it on the bench, and slid into the booth. "My coat doubles as a pillow."

"Quadruples," Iris said.

A slender figure who might have been waitstaff paused at their table. "Mojito," Jenny said. And to Iris, "What's up with you? You look like you're going to pop out of your shirt."

Iris flipped her notebook open to a page with two quickly pencilled bodies. One wore a tiny apron — a triangular flap that barely covered the groin, more a suggestion than a functional apron. The other had knee-length britches.

A tall glass with a clear drink where mint leaves and lime slices floated was set near Jenny's hand. "Merci, cher," she said. And waving a hand across the drawings, "These are …?"

"Costumes for Bruno's dance company."

"Mmmm." Jenny hummed as she took a sip. "Are they paying you?"

"Not yet, but I get my name on the program."

Jenny raised her glass in the air. "You always said you wanted to do costumes. You go, girl! Just don't forget me when you're famous. Remember who your friends are."

"I'm not going to get famous from this. It's only a mini-apron and britches."

"It's a start. *And* …" Jenny singsonged. "Did you say Bruno's dance company, as in you'll be seeing more of him?"

"He has a girlfriend. I told you."

Jenny shrugged. Whenever Iris mentioned a man, Jenny imagined possibilities. She thought it was too long that Iris had been single.

Iris didn't understand why people always thought that being single was a failing. It wasn't as if she'd never been in a relationship. But everyday life with Josh had been frankly boring and Renée had wounded her too deeply when she decided to return to her ex. Iris didn't ever want to be hurt like that again. Casual arrangements were more practical and suited her. The neighbour, Xavier, who sometimes tapped on her door. Xavier had a wife and a kid and no claim on Iris. Or the nights she put on a dress and went to a bar. If a woman stood in a certain way, or had Renée's eyes, Iris might follow her home. There had even been the odd client who arrived for a fitting in suggestive lingerie, though that felt more risky because it could impinge on her professional reputation. She didn't tell Jenny about the one-off escapades. Or about Xavier. No more than she would have shown her the lipstick vibrator in her bedside table. The official party line was that running her own business took up all her time. She had neither the energy nor the patience for the strategies and compromises that coupledom required.

Yet Jenny persisted in believing that having someone else's toothbrush in your bathroom was a universal ambition. "I think you like this Bruno." She clinked her glass against Iris's. "The way you talk about him."

"Sure," Iris agreed. "I appreciate that he asked me to make costumes."

"And you're nice to his sister."

"That's got nothing to do with him."

"Don't be so sure."

Irish shook her head. She'd met Mina first.

Jenny ordered another drink and asked if Iris was having another too. Sure, why not?

Then Iris said, "There is something strange about the girlfriend. He's never mentioned her but Mina talks about her, so I assume he has one. But yesterday when I went to the studio, one of the dancers said something that made it sound like he's on his own. She told him not to turn into a hermit, he should come over for supper."

"Uh oh, you've got competition already."

"She's got a boyfriend. And besides ..." Iris tapped her notebook. "This is what interests me."

Jenny leered over her straw. "It's not *all* that interests you."

*

The queen had locked the girl in a stone room that was full of straw. "She was c-c-crying." Because the queen said she had to knit the straw into gold. Straw was old and dry. Gold was shiny like the wings on Mama's angel.

How? The colours asked.

Mina didn't know. She could knit but she couldn't knit straw into gold. She poked her needle into the cloth but didn't pull it through. She was remembering the scary part and she squinted, not wanting to remember.

The story! the colours shouted. They already knew about the little man. They'd heard the story before. But Mina still had to tell it.

"D'okay," she said. The little man came. He didn't need a key because he was magic. All night he knit and in the morning the queen unlocked the door. The man was gone and the straw was gold. Shining piles of it all over the floor and heaped against the stone walls. Mina remembered the picture in the book.

Now the girl married the prince. That was good. "And she had a baby." But that wasn't good because the little man was going to come take her baby. That was the deal.

Mina would never make a deal like that with her colours. They were hers! She lay her hand on the stack of knitting beside her on the sofa. In her fingers and in her palm she could feel how the colours throbbed, the outlines of the shapes, the energy mingling.

Go on, the colours said. Finish the story.

"His n-n-name." The girl had to guess his name. That was the tricky part of the deal. There were always tricks when you made a deal. The name was long and hard but the girl remembered it. "Stiltskin!" A hard name but Mina remembered it too.

The little man was so angry that he stomped on the ground. He stomped so hard that his leg got stuck. When he tried to pull it out, he ripped in two. No more mean little man! That was a good story.

*

Mathieu was prancing about the studio in the mock-up britches Iris had sewn from remaindered purple paisley broadcloth. When she'd taken them from her knapsack, Bruno said, We can't use that, it's too heavy for dance. I know, she said, this is only for the pattern. To give me an idea. Don't worry, for the costume I'll get spandex.

He flushed, embarrassed that he'd been so quick to criticize. Why had he done that? But she seemed not to notice. She laughed at Mathieu's enthusiasm. He'd already peeled off his tights and was waiting in his boxers to try on the britches.

Val and Tandi made faces as Mathieu preened and posed, pointing his ankles and bulging his calves. "We try not to flatter him," Tandi told Iris. "As you can see ..."

"I love the button-up flap!" Mathieu swivelled his hips.

Iris was attaching a wrist strap, topped with a pincushion that was bristling with straight pins. "I would have sewed a few pompoms on if I knew you were going to move like that. But you know, the flap is just for now, right? For the real costume, I'm going to draw the lines."

"Can I still have buttons?" he pleaded.

Iris looked over her shoulder at Bruno who said, "We can't risk a button getting ripped off and rolling across the stage."

"I'll draw the buttons," she said. "That'll still be cool. Come." She beckoned Mathieu toward her.

He executed a neat demi-plié and skipped across to where she waited on her knees.

"You'd better be still now." She held up a straight pin. "Or you know who will get pricked — not me." As she began to pin the inside leg seam, Mathieu looked as if he'd even stopped breathing.

"Now we know how to threaten him when we want him to shut up," Val said.

"Injury to his precious kiwis," Tandi droned.

Mathieu slit eyes at them but took care not to move.

Bruno saw how Iris's hands, so practical and assured, moved on Mathieu's body, and imagined her touching him like that. Her competent hands smoothing his thighs.

She sat back on her heels, appraising the fit. "Good," she nodded. "But they're full of pins. Hold still, I'll get them off you." She unbuttoned the flap over his crotch and gently eased the tight britches down his legs.

Boogie was crossing the room on soft feet, returning from his smoke break. He lifted the neck and body of his cello from the floor and settled himself on a chair that would correspond to downstage right. Boogie — real name Bogdan — had only started coming last week. He sat with his eyes half-closed, listening to the dancers' movements, now and then plucking strings. He was composing a soundscape, which wasn't meant as an accompaniment but an aural environment for the choreography. He would play onstage during the Montreal performances, and Bruno would record him for when they took the show on tour.

Val clapped once. "Thank you, Iris, the britches are fabulous. Now let's get back to work, people! Let's try that last sequence again."

Bruno moved to turn the videocam on but saw now that he'd forgotten to turn it off when Iris arrived. It had been recording the whole time. Val wouldn't be amused when she reviewed the day's work.

Tandi and Mathieu windmilled their arms and stretched their necks, limbering up. Iris had squatted against the wall to watch.

"Can we go back to that leap over the head?" Val called. "I need you to swing your leg higher." Val always wanted higher, deeper, more intense, more powerful.

Bruno, heading back to his workbench, stole a last glance at Iris. He liked seeing how absorbed she was. He would be meeting her more often if she kept making costumes for them. A prospect he realized he liked.

He had four dolls on whom he'd performed successful head transplants. The trick was to pull the fabric shoulders of the cloth doll up around the plastic neck and use crazy glue. Anything less wouldn't withstand being smashed on the floor.

Now he had another idea. He'd braced one doll in c-clamps. On the cupboard door next to him he'd tacked an enlarged photo of his mother's doll. He got out his paints and the lid of an old tub that he used as a palette. He squished out a thick swirl of white and a separate tiny dab of ochre, touched only the tip of his brush into the ochre and mixed that into the white. He looked from the paint he'd mixed to the photo, back to the paint again, back to the photo. Close.

He could hear Val telling Tandi to stoop lower. There was silence, then audibly expelled breath, and a thump on the floor. "No," Val said. "Let's rethink this."

He felt movement beside him and was surprised to see Iris. He would have thought watching the dancers was more interesting than him painting a doll's head.

"You want to match the colour." Iris was looking from the photo to the doll in the c-clamps.

"Same timeframe as the britches."

"She's beautiful but she's creepy. The way it looks like she's going to start talking."

"I can't change the mouths on these dolls, but the complexion ..."

"Porcelain, yeah," she said. "I like that. It looks cold. And hard."

He was conscious of how close she stood. Curls loose around her face but short on her nape. The delicacy of her pale skin. He wasn't usually attracted to blonds.

"I have another costume idea I wanted to tell you about," she said. "You know how Val talks about frustration bursting out as viciousness?"

He made a sound in his throat he hadn't meant for her to hear but she said, "What?"

He shrugged.

"Tell me." She nudged his arm.

"Just something ..." He could smell the faint scent of her soap.

"Yeah?"

"Val spins a lot of words and ideas around the dances."

"You don't like the dance?"

"I always love the dance," he said quickly. "I work in dance because I admire what dancers do. The way the body moves. But I could do with less talking about what a dance means and why it's relevant. Movement should speak for itself, don't you think?" Even as he said it, he knew he wasn't being fair to Val.

"But the talk is necessary too, isn't it? People want it."

"People want it, you're right. In fact, if you don't know how to spin words, forget getting funding. We're actually lucky that Val knows how to play the game." He couldn't believe that he'd almost betrayed Val. Like a kid showing off how much he knew. But instead of coaxing him to say more, Iris had snatched him back onto safe ground. She was okay.

"Can I tell you my idea?" she asked. "I thought I could sew a few strips of fur to the britches. Nothing that would get in the way, just a wee subliminal hint to the audience."

"You're good at this, aren't you?"

She smiled up at him, pleased, and he felt how he was smiling back.

Then Val was calling, "Bruno? We need you!"

*

Twice now, when Gabriela called in the evening, Bruno was with Mina. Mina was confused that Gabriela was calling while Bruno was there — but Gabriela hadn't known he was there, and as long as he didn't tell Mina that they'd separated, it wasn't possible to explain.

Gabriela decided to start calling Mina in the morning on her coffee break. How about, she suggested, they have a chat every Monday and Thursday at ten a.m.? She knew Mina loved having a specific appointment she could write on her calendar.

Today Mina was recounting a meandering tale about Cheez Whiz. For breakfast she always had one piece of toast with Cheez Whiz, another with peanut butter. If peanut butter or Cheez Whiz ever became obsolete, Mina's world would tip off its axis. Gabriela was trying to understand what Mina was telling her about Cheez Whiz but couldn't untangle the words.

So far, Mina hadn't questioned why they were now talking in the morning. She never needed an explanation for what she liked. Gabriela still wished Bruno would tell her. The ongoing charade that they were a couple was ridiculous — and painful. Mina often gave her messages for Bruno. None had been important, and in any case she knew Mina would tell him again.

"What else have you been doing since Monday?"

"My D-D-D-D —! For movies!"

"Your DVD player?"

"Yeah."

"Is it ... broken?" That was a fair guess if Mina used that complaining tone.

She huffed with disdain. "Bruno didn't fix it."

"I don't think they're easy to fix. He does his best, you know. He —" Why was she defending Bruno? More quietly she continued, "I'm sure he'll get you a new DVD player if yours can't be fixed."

"When?" Mina's expectation that her wishes be fulfilled promptly would be funny if it weren't so exasperating.

Claudia had cautioned her about these conversations with Mina. Didn't that only keep reminding her of Bruno? Was that a good idea? Maybe not, but Mina was her belle-coeur as she was Mina's. Why should Mina be penalized because she and Bruno couldn't agree?

*

Mina had to be careful on the snowy sidewalk but the métro wasn't far. When she got to the station she checked the time on her two watches. Perfect! They both said the same time.

Even though she'd told Bruno and told him that she needed a new watch, she'd finally had to buy it herself. He said there was nothing wrong with her watch. Wasn't it enough that he'd just bought a new clock for her wall? No, it wasn't! She needed a second watch for times like now when she couldn't see the clock on the wall. Bruno never understood.

She'd gone to the pharmacy where she knew they had watches. She needed one that had numbers, not a face, because numbers were better. She saw a big watch with numbers she liked, but it was inside a cage so it couldn't jump into her pocket. It was $34.99. That was a lot, but she had a lot of money — twelve $20 bills in different hiding places in her apartment. Next week when she went to the bank she would have another $20. That would be thirteen $20. The watch would cost two of the $20. Having money hidden was important but knowing the right time was important too. She decided to buy it. The nice woman behind the counter fixed the time and put the new watch on her wrist. No, she didn't want the other one off. She wanted both of them.

It was very good that she had two watches now because she was going to the dentist and shouldn't be late. The dentist was only two métro stops. She took her métro card from the outside pocket of her bag where she had it ready, and with a flourish slapped it on the scanner to make the turnstile work. Bruno had told her she didn't need to smack it like that, but it worked better when you did. She held onto the railing when she took the escalator down down down. Waiting for the train didn't matter because someone always gave her a seat. She only had to step on and someone would get up and sometimes even help her sit.

She was on the métro and already sitting when her head felt woozy and she fell over. People caught her before she landed all the way on the floor. They helped her sit again and asked if she was all right. Yeah. Was she sure? Yeah.

But getting woozy made her miss the stop for the dentist and she didn't know the stop where she got off. She told a lady where she needed to go and the lady took her up an escalator, down again, and said to go three stops on this train. Do you know what three stops are? Of course she knew! "Un, deux, trois," she counted on her fingers, showing the lady.

She couldn't tell Bruno about falling over because he already didn't

want her going places by herself. He wanted her to call Transport
Adapté, but that always took too long because the van kept stopping
for people in wheelchairs who took too long to get on and off. She
didn't have time for that! She knew how to take the métro by herself.

At the dentist, *she* wasn't late for her appointment, but he was.
With her two watches she could see the time and check it too. She
didn't want to have to get up from her chair, so she called across the
waiting room that her appointment was late. The lady who cleaned
her teeth came and led her inside. She didn't like having to keep her
mouth open to have her teeth cleaned, but Mama told her that she
had to, and she liked the dentist who had gentle hands and was beau.
Très beau.

He said her teeth were perfect. He asked how often she brushed
and she said after breakfast and before bed. "Good girl!"

Because he was beau, she didn't correct him. She wasn't a girl
anymore, not for a long time.

*

Bruno was walking down Parc, heading to the métro. To one side
were trees, a winter-desolate soccer field, and greystone buildings;
to the other, the humped black silhouette of the mountain. The stone
angel hailed him with a lifted arm. Hers was a daredevil, balancing
act — high atop a monument, one foot on a ball, wings spread. She
was an adult angel. His and Mina's were baby angels, their wings no
larger than a gold-leafed frill hugged close to their shoulders.

On the métro he thought he saw Iris, and without thinking he
began stepping around and past people to get closer when he realized that the only similarity were the blond curls that edged her
hat. The woman wore a camouflage parka that looked bought in a
discount store. Even when Iris dressed casually, her clothes looked
designed and hand-tailored.

His disappointment that it wasn't Iris made him pause. The rush
of adrenalin when he'd thought it was. Yesterday too. He actually

asked Mina if Iris had a boyfriend. Mina said no. How about a girl-friend? Mina only looked at him. Then he said, Sorry, he was just ... But what was he doing?

This evening he didn't turn down Mina's street. He was hungry and with no one else to share the cooking, he was making every meal. They'd gotten very simple. No fine dining when your only compan-ion was the TV.

The house was cold because he'd turned down the thermostat. Why heat rooms when no one was there? He opened a jar of tomato sauce and put water on to boil for pasta.

When the phone rang, he moaned. Who would it be but Mina with a complaint, a dilemma, a resentment, something broken, a grievance — maybe an itch she expected him to come scratch. Did he have to be on call *every* night? But who was he kidding? He was alone except for Mina who needed him.

"Let me guess," he said. "You have something to tell me."

"Bruno ... it's Gabriela."

The familiarity of her voice — that was already no longer as fam-iliar — pressed on a bruise. She'd recently moved into an apartment and had called him with the address to forward her mail. It was in Mile Ex, nowhere near the Pointe, which meant they weren't likely to cross paths, but also felt like a rebuff.

"I want to come get my bike from the basement, do you mind?"

"Now? There's still snow."

"There's a shop with an Early Bird Special. Tune-up costs half price if I bring it in now."

He used to do her tune-up. But why was he even thinking that? They hadn't split up over her bike. He still felt a brief flare of pique that he'd been replaced so easily.

"You don't have to be home when I come. I didn't realize it but I still have the key. I'll drop it through the mail slot after I lock up."

He didn't want her walking through the house and seeing the single plate and mug in the dishrack. Feel how empty the air was without her. But he didn't want to see her either. "I'll carry the bike up from the cellar."

"You don't have to."

"I will."

"Okay, thanks."

He didn't ask what she'd been doing. He didn't want to know. Probably already seeing someone new to make that baby she so desperately wanted. She was an attractive woman and well-liked where she worked. When he'd met her, she'd come home with him that first night. She wasn't a woman who wasted time.

She cleared her throat. "Can I ask when you intend to tell Mina? It's getting complicated."

"Why would it be complicated for you? You're not the one who sees her every day."

"I call her twice a week. She keeps talking about her birthday—"

"That's not till June."

"You know how she looks forward to it. She loved that we took her on a boat last year."

"That's obviously not going to happen this year."

"She's hoping it will."

"I'll talk to her before her birthday." He appreciated that Gabriela stayed in touch with Mina, but he didn't need her telling him what to do.

"There are other things too. She's noticed I never answer the phone anymore. There's only so often I can say I must have been cooking or I was out with friends. She's not stupid."

"She's not. But she's like most people who are perfectly happy to believe what they want to believe."

"Don't you see that you're putting me in an uncomfortable position always having to make up stories?"

He didn't answer. Her comfort wasn't his concern anymore, was it? She'd made that perfectly clear when she'd decided to break them up.

When he hung up, he swore softly. He knew he had to tell Mina.

*

Mina giggled at the funny way the pink and green feathers flopped and swished along the balustrade. This was better than the way Mama used to wipe with a cloth. If the nun had told her to dust with a cloth, she wouldn't have done it.

She wore yellow kitchen gloves because people on TV wore gloves to clean, but these were too big and kept twisting. *Again* she had to stop to fix them! She put the feathers on the handrail, but even though she told them to stay, they tipped and fell all the way to the floor. She would have to walk down the stairs to get them. She didn't like stairs. They were dangerous. Last summer she saw an ambulance come and strap an old lady lying in the street onto a stretcher. Everyone who was standing there said she fell down her stairs. Maybe the neighbour who always bothered Mina would fall down the stairs. That would be good.

She held the railing going down the stairs and walked along the pews until she saw the pink and green feathers. She tried to reach them but her arm was too short. "Crisse de tabernac!" The bad words helped.

But she wasn't climbing those stairs again. She'd been up there already. Sister Marguerite wouldn't know because she was cleaning the priest's room. The priest must be a very dirty man. Mina could dust the whole church and Sister Marguerite was still cleaning the priest's room.

Swiping feathers across the tops of the pews was easy, but she had to stand the whole time and her feet hurt. She'd told Bruno that a job where she could sit was better, but he didn't listen. He never did.

"Philomena!" Sister called. "Are you already down here? Did you finish upstairs?"

Mina jabbed around with the feathers, showing Sister how busy she was. She pulled aside a red curtain over a closet. On the bench to sit ... Her eyes widened. The cushion wasn't there the last time she dusted. It was a good cushion — only a flat square — but the knitting on it swirled with blue flowers and gold and silver leaves. She'd never seen knitting like this. It wanted to be hers, but it couldn't with Sister watching.

"Do you know …" Sister was all smiles. "We've worked so hard today that I think we deserve a special treat. Why don't we go to the café for our tea?"

"With a m-m-muffin?" Last time Sister took her to the café she sat beside her and held her hand. Sister said she was one of God's innocents. Mina didn't know what that meant but Sister was happy to say it.

"Yes, my dear. I believe that's what we'll do. But only when you're finished. And don't rush now. Remember, this is God's house."

Tea and a muffin and sitting close with Sister was good, but right now it was more important that Sister go. Go! She thought at her. Bouge-toi! Move!

Sister turned away but then stopped to drop to her knee before the altar. Even when she was finally gone, Mina waited until she heard the roar of the vacuum cleaner in the priest's room.

Now! Mina snatched the cushion and walked to the pew where she'd left her bag and coat. Fast-fast she pulled out pens and a ball of yarn, punched the cushion down deep, fit the pens and yarn over it, strapped the bag shut again. Hers now!

*

Iris switched off the iron and fit the dress on a hanger. An old-style, belted linen shirtdress. She didn't usually work so late but the client was coming tomorrow morning to pick it up.

Yesterday, instead of working on the dress, she'd gone to the fabric stores on St. Hubert to look for the right shade and texture of short-haired fur to match the fabric for the britches. As she'd told Bruno, nothing too obvious. In fact, it would be even better if the audience thought the fur was a trick of the light. After she'd sewn a few strips to the britches, she was so pleased with the effect that she couldn't resist taking them to the studio. Val proclaimed the idea brilliant, Mathieu loved it, and even though Bruno was less voluble, she could see he was impressed. She'd ended up staying longer than she'd expected. She liked the companionable vibe and felt she belonged there — and this was only the beginning. Who knew who might come to the performance and see her name on the program. Other choreographers, maybe even a theatre or opera producer.

And although she wasn't about to admit it to Jenny yet, the more she saw of Bruno, the more she liked him. His shy but pleased look when she joined him at his workbench. There didn't seem to be a girlfriend anymore either. Iris had overheard Tandi and one of the futon seamstresses talking. Tandi had noticed Iris listening and said, You like him, eh? He's a deep one, our Bruno. Have you met his sister yet? Iris said it was through Mina that she met Bruno. Tandi began telling her stories about Mina — the time she stole a bus driver's keys; how she refused to see her social worker when he grew a moustache that she thought made him ugly. Mina was a woman who knew her own mind and what she wanted.

Iris agreed — but what Tandi didn't mention was Mina's embroidery, which was what Iris found most extraordinary about her. Her intuitive mastery of colour and wildly freeform designs. Not even Bruno, who saw Mina's embroidery all the time, recognized it for what it was. Were they all blind? Was it because she had Down Syndrome?

Iris wished she could get Jenny's opinion, but when she asked Mina if she could bring a friend to visit, Mina said no. Categorically no. Iris asked if she could borrow an embroidery for a night. Again, no. Iris couldn't even sneak one out because Mina was always there. And what if Mina counted her embroidery the way she counted her cans of Pepsi and her cigarettes? Iris had to come up with a plan for Jenny to see one of these astounding embroideries. Have her stand on the sidewalk while Iris held one up in the window? That would mean convincing Jenny to come to Mina's address but stay outside. Not likely.

Iris had finished tidying her studio, sweeping the floor, and knotting the bag of garbage to take downstairs. It was already past nine and she wanted to get home, have a glass of wine, and relax. But for a few days now she'd been meaning to look up ...

She crossed the room to her laptop. Quickly she typed, *Down Syndrome*, paused and then added *artist*.

What??? Almost half a million search results! She let out the breath she hadn't realized she was holding. Most were the same names repeated. Many were painters. Vivid abstracts, cartoon graphics, thickly layered strokes, huge landscapes. A few ceramicists. All were in the US — though that said more about how Americans liked to toot their horn than demographics.

The name that appeared most often was Judith Scott, a fibre sculptor. She wrapped objects in yarn, cord, rope, thread, twine — whatever she could get her hands on. The fibres twisted, knotted, and crisscrossed, forming an intricate, visually dense sculpture that begged the mystery of what it hid. And the colours! Like Mina, she mingled and juxtaposed colours that most people would say didn't belong together — only look at the marvellous effect.

Iris clicked on one image after another, each rich, colourful, and textural. Judith had had exhibitions around the world, with sculptures in permanent collections in the MOMA, San Francisco, Dublin, Paris. Her biography was amazing too. She was deaf and had lived for thirty-six years in a state institution where she was considered to be severely handicapped. Her twin sister had rescued her, advocated on her behalf, and, recognizing that she loved to draw, enrolled her in an arts centre where her creativity burgeoned.

Judith had passed in 2005, but happily there were videos of her making sculptures: wrapping objects with twine, yarn, plastic tubing, cord, leather strips, a man's orange tie. The core might be an umbrella, a skateboard, a coat hanger, a chair. x-rays revealed that even smaller objects were hidden inside the dense fibre constructs. As Judith worked, she changed angle, tension, colour, material. She

had the same tactile sureness that Iris recognized from watching
Mina. In one video, though Judith seemed to be working without
pause, she suddenly stopped, eyed the piece all around, and with a
regal flip of the hand gestured to take it away. It was finished.

Judith had the same passion as Mina for hats, though Judith's
tastes were bolder. She wore period hats and ropes of chunky costume
jewellery. Maybe Mina had been constrained by what was available
at the dollar store. Iris could imagine her in a wide-brimmed cloche
or a velvet accordion hat. Wouldn't it be fun to jazz up Mina's artistic persona? And as an artist, she would be Philomena! Wasn't that
a born artist's name?

Iris kept clicking and scrolling. Museum curators and other
artists discussed Judith Scott's art—not once hesitating to call it
art. Also asking what art was when people whom society labelled as
intellectually deficient were making it. Judith Scott's work was clearly
the outpouring of a startling artistic intelligence. Iris grabbed a
pencil and began taking notes.

*

Bruno was reaching for his jacket when the phone rang. He had to
get to work. It was probably only Mina. But what if it wasn't and what
if it was important? He headed back down the hallway.

"Monsieur Corneau!" Shrill enough to make a dog whine.

Cautiously, "Yes?"

"Do you know that Mina is wearing a pro-choice button on
her hat?"

"You're calling me about the buttons on her hat?"

The nun where Mina worked had made a complaint about the
button on Mina's hat. She'd asked Mina to remove it and Mina had
refused.

"Her buttons are her buttons. Leave them alone."

"But Monsieur Corneau, if your mother had had an abortion,
where would Mina be?"

"I'm not sure what that has to do with anything, but isn't the point about pro-choice that you have the choice? Mina is all about choice."

"The nun won't have her coming to the church with that button on her hat."

"Why don't you suggest that Mina wear a different hat? She's got a bag full of them and each one has buttons. Though you never know, there might be one that's pro-life too. Tell the nun that Mina's buttons aren't her affair."

"But —"

"You tell the nun or I'll tell the nun, but if *I* tell her, it won't be polite."

He had to get to the studio. He was ready to help if Mina had a problem, but he didn't see why a pro-choice button should be a problem. Although as he zipped his jacket and stepped outside, he remembered the swastika. A person didn't need to know how to read or write to seem to belong to an ideological camp.

*

Mina shoved her arm between the mattress and the box spring, groped with her hand, grunted and stretched as far as she could. From the wall Elvis watched but didn't help.

Exhausted, she dropped back onto her bum on the floor. Yesterday she'd examined the gold and silver cushion and then pushed it between the mattress and box spring to hide it. But where did it go if she couldn't find it now? No one had been in her apartment since then, except for Evita to clean that morning, and Mina had watched from the armchair as Evita scooped clothes off the bed and tugged at the comforter. Evita always complained about having to make the bed. Huh. She only straightened the top. She knew Mina slept on the sofa. Only Bruno didn't. After he bought the new bed he kept asking if she liked sleeping there, but the sofa was closer to all her favourite things. It was better to sleep there. She only needed a bed because she had a bedroom.

Evita couldn't have taken the cushion, so *where was it?* Too many
strange things happening around here lately. The pan that started
smoking on the stove. The margarine she'd put in the fridge but she'd
found in the cupboard. And now the bed swallowing her new pillow!

"G-g-give me—" She thrust her hand under the mattress again.
And right away she touched the cushion. Good! She needed to look at
it again. Not the colour of the knitting but the ... She didn't know the
word. She stroked the gold and silver with her finger, feeling how it
was stiff. How to explain that to Iris? She couldn't show her the cushion because it was a secret that it was hers now. That was the rule.

Leaning against the mattress, she heaved herself up from the
floor. On a shelf in the living room she had a plush kitten with a
ribbon around its neck. She ran her finger along it. The ribbon was
green but the colour didn't matter. It was the stiff part along the
edge she meant.

As she pressed the numbers on her phone, she said them out loud.
At Iris's end it rang for a long time. If people weren't there, why did
it take so long for the answering machine to start? She groaned, listening to the message which she'd heard so often already. "Exclusive,
custom-fitted designs ..." All fancy and silly. Iris said it all in French
and then again in English. Why? Stupid to say it twice.

Finally it was over! "S-s-s-something to tell you." Mina paused
because that was how you talked on the phone. "I need thread." She
paused again. "D'okay? Bye."

She looked around the living room, trying to remember what
she had to do next. Something important ... The cushion! She'd left
it on the bed. She bent to shove it as far as she could under the mattress and pulled down the comforter. She didn't want Bruno to see
it. Or Iris.

Or even Gabriela. She didn't come often but you never know,
she could.

Something was different about Gabriela. She was never home anymore. She called at 10:00 in the morning on Monday and Thursday—

which was good — but that was the only time they talked. For a long time now there hadn't been any trips to the restaurant or to go shopping.

Mina had been trying to think what would make Bruno and Gabriela take her. It couldn't be the new toaster she wanted because Bruno could buy that on his own. She had to go to the store with both of them. So yesterday she took her two bras and her biggest scissors. It wasn't easy to cut through the elastic but she was strong. She tore the fabric too. She bundled the mangled bras into a bag that she dropped in a bin outside. She knew not to choose a bin near her building but farther away. This morning, when Gabriela called, she told her she needed bras. The ones she had were gone and you had to wear a bra. Mama told her. But Gabriela didn't say anything, so she told her again. I n-n-need a bra. Gabriela said to tell Bruno, but that was crazy! She couldn't go shopping for bras with Bruno! Gabriela had to go into the change room with her.

Settled on the sofa again, she stroked her finger along the cloth where she wanted to knit with stiff, glittery thread. She huffed with impatience. Why didn't Iris call back? She needed that thread and she needed it now!

She held the hoop, tipping it so the colours she'd already knit caught the light. She always knit with the flow of the colours, but what if... She stared at the swirl shape she was making, unscrewed the hoop, and moved the fabric to a new place. From her tray of threads a creamy lavender called, Me! As she stitched, she could feel how she was going against the flow and how it throbbed differently. A new kind of dance. The colours liked it too.

But hey! they cried. What about our story? Before she went to find the pillow, she'd been telling them the story about the princess who was sleeping. Trees with thorns and branches made a thick wall around her. When the prince came, he had to get past so he could kiss her. No sex! Just a kiss. Kisses were best. Princes in stories only ever kissed. "A k-k-kiss." In all the stories. The glass slipper. Or when he climbed the high tower. Too high but the princess hung her long hair down the wall.

Mina stopped knitting to say the rhyme. "Ponzel, P-P-Ponzel! Let down your hair! So I can climb! The g-g-golden stair!" Bruno used to sing the words.

In all the stories, the prince kissed the princess and they lived happily ever after. That was what was supposed to happen. Bruno should know that. He knew the stories. What was wrong between him and Gabriela?

*

Gabriela loved Claudia's chiles rellenos de tinga but didn't appreciate finding out that she'd been invited for supper in order to meet this Victor who'd been sat next to her at the table.

No doubt, he was a nice man, apparently single, and nobody had to translate for him or be puzzled about his odd job or what he was saying. Victor had grown up in Canada with Mexican parents like herself, Claudia, and their brothers. Victor belonged in a way that Bruno hadn't—which wasn't fair to Bruno, nor to her who had chosen him.

From across the table, Claudia was sending her looks she ignored.

Victor asked if she would like more wine, the bottle of red he held already poised over her glass.

"Sí. Gracias." If this was going to continue all evening, she needed more wine.

He seemed to stiffen, drawing back a little, and she heard how cold she sounded. Poor man. What had they told him? That she was single, pretty, had a good job, could cook, and loved children. Maybe, too, that she needed to be rescued before she ended up with another weird white boyfriend. He wouldn't have been told that her heart was still bruised and she wasn't ready to start dating or mating or however people worded it.

She took a swallow of wine and asked Victor about his job. Didn't men like to talk about what they did? She'd never liked setups. She was more intuitive — but only when a man stirred her intuition, which Victor, nice, single, and handsome though he was, didn't.

She would much sooner have been sitting at the other end of the table with her nephews.

*

These last few days, the air had been mild and the sky was a soft blue. There was still snow on the ground but sun warmed the brick housefronts.

Bruno had left the studio early and decided to see Mina on the way home. As he walked down her hallway, he could hear the noise of her TV coming out the door she'd opened when she buzzed him in. For a while, after Pierre, she'd waited until she saw a visitor before taking the chain off, but routine was finally stronger than caution.

She was already back on the sofa. On her small rolling table she had a notebook open, a half-finished row of capital Bs in green marker across one page, the facing page filled with rows of Ks in orange. Years ago he asked if she wanted to learn words. No. Then why was she printing letters? To practise.

"You know?" she said now. More a challenge than a question.

"Not yet, but I guess you'll tell me."

"N-n-n-need to go shopping."

"Looks to me like you have everything — and in surplus."

She fixed him in her misaligned sights. "With Gabriela."

He glanced at the angel for help.

"I need —" She slapped both hands on her chest.

"A T-shirt? You have lots."

She smacked her chest again.

"I don't know what you mean if you don't say."

"I told Gabriela."

"And what did she say?"

Her lips curved downward as if she might start crying and quickly he said, "She's very busy these days. She probably doesn't have time right now. But I have an idea. How about I take you out for supper next week?"

"With Gabriela!"

"Just you and me. She's too busy right now. She won't be able to come." He saw that Mina knew something wasn't right. He had to tell her. But not right now, not this minute. "We'll go to your favourite place in St. Henri."

She looked trapped, not getting what she wanted but also not wanting to miss the chance of supper out. As he waited for her to decide, he noticed the wispy hair on her chin. "What's happening on your face?"

"Nothing." She looked away.

"Exactly, nothing. When's the last time you shaved? Isn't your shaver working?"

"Yeah."

"So why aren't you using it? You broke the one I got you —"

"Didn't!"

"— and I got you another one because it was apparently such a big deal, and now you're not even using it. Did you decide you want a stubble beard because all your favourite actors have one? I've got news for you. Your hair is too thin, it won't work."

He could see she wasn't listening. What was he even saying? How was he going to tell her about Gabriela? "Go ahead then," he said. "Grow a beard, do what you want since that's what you always do. But don't expect me to hop, skip, and jump next time —"

The intercom buzzed and she snatched the phone as at a rope to escape him. He heard a woman's voice and Mina was grinning. Could it be Gabriela? He rose from the chair.

"Who is it?" he asked as Mina wiggled off the sofa but she didn't answer.

There was a tap on the door and Mina opened it. Iris was standing there. His shoulders relaxed — and did he imagine it or did her smile broaden when she saw him?

She waved a flat paper bag at Mina. "Got the goods." To Bruno she said, "Mina asked for gold thread. Not just gold-coloured but metallic texture. And when Mina asks …"

Iris knocked aside cushions and sat on the other end of the small sofa to upend the bag. Out tumbled sleek, glinting loops of gold, silver, and copper thread. Mina seemed to watch with great suspense as Iris pulled an end of thread free from the skein and handed it across. Mina rubbed it between her fingers.

"Metal thread is stiffer than what you're used to. You might have to make bigger stitches. You should practise on some scrap fabric first."

Bruno had never seen Mina with such a focussed expression. She was like a professional handling tools. He'd known she liked to stitch but hadn't realized it meant so much to her. Wasn't it nice for her, then, to have met Iris who understood about thread and textiles?

Nice of Iris too. Very nice of her. She was explaining about using a needle with a larger eye for sewing with metal thread. She'd brought a package that she now showed Mina. Lamplight shone on her curls. Her face.

He suddenly realized he'd been sitting, doing nothing but watching her, and what must she think? He stood. "I'm off, okay? I'll see you at the studio, Iris. You know how to reach me, Mina, right?"

"Bye," she said absently but Iris looked up at him, smiling.

He'd already opened the door when he had an idea. "Can I ask you a favour, Iris?"

She followed him into the hallway. "What's up?"

"Mina says she needs something but she won't tell me what. I think it's personal, something female. Can you find out?"

"No problem. I'm glad I can help. I'll call you later."

At home, he moved around the kitchen, reaching for the chopping board, the knife, an onion, oil, a saucepan. He sipped his G&T. The house didn't feel as empty. He was waiting for the phone to ring.

*

Slowly Iris scrolled through the images on her computer. Beside her, Jenny hadn't spoken yet.

A shape that might have been a baseball was bound over and over and over again with coloured strings. The frenetic thickness of the mesh was impressive, even as one noticed the individual strands, their colour, texture, and direction. The next object was ... a hat box? A small drum? It was wrapped in pink and red wool and twine. On closer examination there were yellow and grey strings too — not colours you would expect with pink and red, but they worked.

"And you're telling me," Jenny said slowly, "that Mina's embroidery is as good as this? Because this is big, Iris, really big. This is stupendous. If Mina's embroidery is as complex as this ..."

"It is. And I can —" Iris hesitated. What if Jenny thought what she'd done was wrong? Or what if she didn't agree that Mina's embroidery was as good as Iris thought? Maybe the magic of Mina's colours could only be experienced in the realm of her apartment.

"You can what?" Jenny eyed her.

Iris crossed the room to the chest of shallow drawers where she kept spools of thread and notions. Yesterday, when Mina went to the bathroom, Iris darted to the stack of embroidery on the sofa, pulled one out, straightened the pile as best she could, and shoved the one she'd snatched in her knapsack. She hadn't known she was going to do it until she did. She didn't even know which one she'd taken.

Now she slid open the bottom drawer to lift out the roll she'd wrapped in tissue paper.

"Hey, you've got one!" Jenny gaped at her. "Why didn't you tell me?"

"It's not one of her best but I didn't have time to choose. I just grabbed it."

"You mean you *stole* it? You are bad!" But Jenny sounded more delighted than shocked.

"She didn't give me any choice. She wouldn't even lend me one for a few hours."

"So show me." Jenny slapped her arm. "Let's see it!"

Inside the tissue paper, the roll of cotton was floppy with tails of thread and bunched knots. The backs of Mina's embroideries were always messy, but if they were framed and on a wall, no one would see the back. Carefully Iris unrolled the cloth, revealing a cave of orange and red stalactites edged in cobalt. Even this, one of Mina's simpler pieces, had that jolt of visual tension, the rush of colour that leapt.

"You're saying this isn't one of her best?"

"Usually there's more energy. But this is how she uses colours and this is how she works with thread and —"

"It's wild," Jenny said quietly.

"You think so?" Iris said equally quietly, though inside herself she was yowling.

"Wild," Jenny repeated as she lightly touched the stitches and spread her fingers to lay her hand flat.

"But how … how am I going to get more to show to —" Iris gestured at the computer.

"You want to take them to an art gallery?"

"I guess. I don't know. How do you do that?"

"I can ask my uncle."

"That would be great. But … how am I going to get more? It was hard enough to get just one. I can't keep taking them."

"You'll figure out something — you have to."

Both stood, enthralled by the jagged orange and red shapes edged in brilliant blue.

"You know what," Jenny said. "When all this starts to happen, she's going to need a manager. Someone who's been there from the start and who knows her work. You know who I mean? You."

"Don't exaggerate. I'm not a manager." Although ever since Iris read about Judith Scott, she'd been imagining interviews and how she would tell the story of meeting Philomena in the park, how Philomena had embroidered for years with dollar-store thread, but Iris, recognizing her gift, brought her better materials to work with. That would make a funny detail too, how she called her embroidery knitting. Philomena would be present during the interviews too, of course, maybe not saying much, just being herself. Like Judith Scott, she had presence. Iris would get her some funky hats and make her a few outfits.

"And Bruno?" Jenny asked. "What about him? Where does he fit in all this?"

"He doesn't care about her embroidery. He doesn't think it's anything special. He was there when I brought Mina some metallic thread she'd asked for and he hardly even noticed."

She didn't add that she and Bruno had spent an hour on the phone later that evening. She'd told him that what Mina wanted was bras. She offered to take her shopping, but he said he would ask the social worker to do it. They kept talking, at first about costumes and dance, then circling closer to their lives. Finally he told her that his girlfriend had left. But he didn't say it as if he expected sympathy. He wanted her to know he was single.

"I'm not talking about the embroidery," Jenny said. "If he's Mina's guardian, you have to get his permission to approach a gallery."

"It's her work so it should be up to her, not him. She has the legal right to make decisions for herself. He told me so."

"She might have the legal right but is it ethical?"

"What do you mean, ethical? What's wrong with giving her the chance to be recognized as an artist?"

"I still think you should tell him."

Iris didn't want to talk about Bruno. She went to the cutting table to unpin the pattern pieces for a lapel neck blazer she'd traced. Over her shoulder she asked when Jenny had last talked to her uncle and could they call him.

*

Gabriela dragged the back of her hand across her mouth. Her sister had called to scold her for being rude to Victor. Gabriela said she hadn't been rude. She wasn't interested. Why not? Claudia demanded. Gabriela sighed. Nothing there. No click. He was just … I don't believe it, Claudia said. You sound like a teenager. Are you expecting fireworks too? Yes, Gabriela said. Don't you?

She was curled in her new armchair. It had seemed comfortable in the store, but she'd only sat on it to feel how firm it was. She hadn't taken off her boots and tucked her legs up. Now that she was sitting as she liked, she could feel how it didn't fit her body like Bruno's armchair had. But you don't stay with a man for his armchair. She would get used to this one. Or it would to her. Wasn't a chair like a shoe you had to break in?

The apartment was small but large enough for her. For now, the front room had one chair, a coffee table and two lamps she'd got at a second-hand store, and a TV. She'd angled her chair so she had a view onto the tree that grew high above the houses across the street. She ignored the satellite dishes, antennae, and wires in the lower part of the window. She kept her eyes on the tree.

She was thinking about Daniel who'd talked to her about Guana-juato. Had they even exchanged ten sentences? But how much or how long they'd talked didn't matter. Guanajuato was a place special to both of them. The warmth of his hand in hers. The Spanish that he spoke with an accent that charmed her in a way that Victor's easy Mexican colloquialisms hadn't.

Late at night, after a glass of wine, alone in her new apartment, she'd tried to find Daniel Lavoie online. Acting like a giddy teen-ager tracking down the tall, dark stranger. So what? she thought. Unfortunately — bad luck for her — Montreal was full of Lavoies, including fourteen listed on LinkedIn who were teachers. Daniel's dad hadn't said where he taught.

She even had the crazy idea to call his dad for a follow-up ques-tionnaire — which did not exist. That was probably illegal, abuse of privacy, or some such issue that could put her license at risk. And how was she supposed to turn questions about exercise regimes into information about his son?

For that matter, was Daniel Lavoie even single? He'd made it sound like he was travelling on his own through Mexico, but that didn't mean he didn't have a partner waiting at home or off on an adventure.

Tomorrow Marie-Paule had invited her to a Singles Valentine's Day cocktail party. *Really?* Gabriela said. Really, Marie-Paule said. A little romance with testosterone. Who knows what will happen? We can go dancing after.

*

Mina pored over the plasticized menu with its glossy photos. She always ordered a club sandwich with frîtes but still liked to revel in temptation. Pizza dotted with pepperoni, fat smoked meat sandwiches, poutines drenched in gravy.

Bruno let her take her time. They sat in booths upholstered in red vinyl. A radio station played seventies rock and traffic reports. A full meal, including soup, a choice of drink, and a bowl of red Jell-O cost $7.99. He'd tried taking her to a more upscale resto but she didn't like pesto or grilled fish. She wanted a club with frîtes and Jell-O for dessert.

With a sound between a sniffle and a moan, she tapped a photo of layered pasta oozing tomato sauce and melted cheese.

"You want lasagna?" Pretending that she might choose something other than a club was a game she liked.

She squinted hard with the force of considering. "M-m-maybe."

Today she wore a brimless pillbox hat with a yellow button announcing that Every Day Is A Good Day For Golfing! Next to it, a pink Madonna button. Her trademark long legs in hot pants.

Mina closed the menu with a decisive slap. The waitress, who'd served them on previous outings, had been waiting patiently. Mina ordered a club with frîtes, a Pepsi, and Jell-O. Bruno said he would have the same but no Jell-O.

"How's the new job?" he asked Mina when they were alone again.

"D'okay."

"Any problems with the nun?"

"No."

"Did she say anything to you about the buttons on your hats?"

"No."

Was that a real no or an I-don't-want-to-talk-about-it no? "I see you've got a Madonna button. Do you like her music now?"

Mina only looked at him.

"Madonna is on one of your buttons. She's a musician."

Still blank.

And tilting his head at her, he asked the old question. "Mina, Mina, where do you come from?"

Her mouth relaxed in a smile. Even when she was a baby, he knew she was different. Always placid, gazing at him with slanted eyes, never fussing or crying like the neighbour's baby. She arrived in his life at almost the same time as the book of fairy tales he was learning to read, and in his child's mind they seemed connected. A doorway that could rain gold or tar. Dwarves who spoke in riddles. A boy who ran along the top of a rolling coin. In these stories the biggest wasn't necessarily the best nor the smartest. Logic didn't always rule. Good things came in threes. Their mother taught him how to read German, and when he was older he read to Mina. She cuddled next to him, transfixed by the stories and the drawings. She giggled at the nonsense jingles that weren't German or English or French. *Rucke di gu. Manntje, manntje, timpe te.* Is this what you say? he used to ask her. Is this where you come from? When their mother heard him, she said not to tease. She explained about the extra chromosome that made Mina the way she was. But when he and Mina were alone, he would sometimes whisper, Mina, Mina, where do you come from? She always smiled.

Now he asked, "Do you remember those fairy tales I used to read to you? The little girl who had to run past the moon? The woman in the sky shaking feathers from her duvet to make snow?"

"Mama's stories," Mina said promptly.

My stories, he almost said but then wondered if Mina wasn't right. They belonged to their mother's language and culture.

The waitress set plates heaped with golden frîtes before them. Mina immediately snatched one but still waited for Bruno to squirt a puddle of ketchup on her plate. She swiped the fry through the ketchup and popped it in her mouth. Such utter pleasure in a piece of potato. If only every minute of every day would be so easy.

She eyed the thick sandwich triangles before grasping one, aimed it at her mouth and bit. Because they were in a diner, and even though she was eating with her hands, she tried to be dainty. She didn't lean her elbows on the table. She took small sips with her straw.

He let her finish one triangle before saying, "Listen, there's something you won't like that I need to tell you."

She stopped mid-chew, eyes wide with alarm.

"Don't worry, it's not a tragedy. No one's hurt."

Still she stared at him.

"Finish what you've got in your mouth." He ate a few of his fries to demonstrate that all was well. See?

She swallowed, still watching him.

"It's Gabriela."

"Wh-wh-wh —"

"Nothing happened to her. She's fine. Truly, Mina, she's fine."

Even with crossed eyes, she could skewer him. He should have led up to it. She already expected the worst. He might as well say it. "Gabriela and I aren't together anymore."

Mina's bottom lip trembled. Her emotions were always huge, enveloping, and unrestrained.

"She's going to stay in touch with you. You know how she's been calling you? She'll keep doing that. Gabriela loves you, you know she does. Maybe she'll even take you shopping. You know what fun you always have with her. I used to feel like I was just tagging along. The two of you don't need me there." He had no idea if Gabriela would take Mina shopping. He was promising what he had no right to predict. He didn't even know what he was saying anymore. The tears streaming down Mina's cheeks were making his own eyes wet. He reached across the table with his napkin to wipe snot off her lips, needed more napkins, and stood to take them from another table. "Move over," he said but she didn't, so he squeezed onto the bit of bench beside her. He eased her glasses off and set them on the table so he could wipe her cheeks. "I'm sorry, Mina. I'm sorry. Stop crying, please."

A woman eating at another table glared at him. Fuck off, he thought.

"We weren't getting along so well anymore. There were things we didn't agree on. You should understand, Mina. You've broken up with lots of boyfriends —"

"N-n-not Gabriela!"

"Us breaking up is like when you and Butch or you and Henri broke up. It sometimes —"

"No!" She twisted on the bench to face him, cheeks smeared with tears, eyes even more accusing without the mask of her glasses. "You're stupid!"

"Why me? Why do you think it's my fault?"

She shoved him so hard that he would have fallen if he hadn't grabbed the tabletop.

The waitress strode across the restaurant. "Qu'est-ce qui se passe ici?"

"Nothing. My sister's upset by some bad news." He'd moved to the opposite bench again.

"So it's very nice that you give her bad news here where she has so much privacy." She bent to Mina who was trying to put her glasses on again with greasy fingers. "Ça va, ma chère? Are you all right?"

"Bruno can g-g-go fart in the flowers!" Mina said loudly enough that people from nearby tables turned their heads.

"Mina!" That was her worst curse. To the waitress he said, "That's fine. I'll talk to her."

"Do you want him to talk to you?" she asked Mina.

Mina looked at her plate of food. Their mother had used to close herself off with the same flat expression, set mouth, and lowered eyes.

"I said I'll talk to her," Bruno repeated. "She's my sister."

The waitress still didn't leave, but with Mina not answering her and a man at another table lifting his hand to get her attention, she had no reason to stay.

"Eat some frîtes," Bruno said. Mina picked one up, dragged it through ketchup, chomped down on it.

"You know, I'm upset too. It's not just you who's losing her. I lost her too. And she said she would still see you. She didn't say she would see me."

Mina gave a snort.

"What?"

She kept eating fries.

"If you know something I don't, I wish you would tell me." Not that he expected Mina to have insight on his relationship.

"You!"

"Me what?"

She threw him a look that, from anyone else, would have been contemptuous. "No ring!" She balled a fist, showing him her birth-stone ring.

"You think we split up because I didn't give her a ring?"

Mina seemed to feel she'd made her point. She picked up another triangle of sandwich and took a vicious bite. A slice of bacon squished from the bread onto her plate. Pinching her fingers with the finesse of a gourmand, she poked it in her mouth.

A couple of years ago he'd asked Gabriela if she wanted to get married. She said it was complicated because he wasn't Catholic and her family was. It didn't seem to matter to her and he let it drop. To him it was only a piece of paper.

He definitely wasn't going to tell Mina the breakup was about a baby. What would she make of that? Easiest was to let her believe he'd failed Gabriela by not giving her a ring.

*

Mina woke on the sofa with her face smushed against the cushions and her arms clenched in anger. In a rush she remembered why. Bruno was so stupid stupid stupid stupid stupid! Why did he let Gabriela go? They were supposed to stay together. Why didn't Gabriela do something so Bruno would behave? It was so ... But she couldn't make herself call Gabriela stupid.

She stomped to the kitchen, gushed water into the kettle, and banged it on the counter. Ripped open the box of tea and slammed the cupboard door. She growled at the dirty dishes on the counter and swiped her arm, crashing them into the sink. Did a plate break? Good!

She punched the bathroom door so hard that it whacked the toilet. And there, by the door, was the stupid cart stuffed with dirty clothes that needed to be washed. Stupid câlisse de merde Bruno! Everything was his fault, dirty clothes too! She grabbed her key and two coins from the roll of loonies in the yellow duck dish, and dragged her cart down the hallway.

The three washing machines in the basement were all washing. She jabbed the button on one to make it stop. She waited for the water to drain and slopped the wet clothes out and onto the floor so she could shove hers in, stuffing them down. She never used two machines for light and for dark. It cost too many loonies. She made all the clothes fit in one. The wet heap on the floor oozed a puddle across the concrete. Too bad. Tit for tat. She left her cart by the machine to show it was hers now.

Back in her apartment she locked the door and put the chain

on. The kettle had boiled and she poured water over the teabag in
her mug.

She was eating peanut butter on toast when someone started
banging on her door. Banging didn't matter. Huffing and puffing
didn't matter. She lived in a brick house.

"I know that was you, you fat slob! I know that's your cart. You
did it on purpose. You can't fool me with that retarded act. I'm going
to call the management. You don't belong here, you're a menace, not
fit to be with normal people! I saw how you beat up that poor boy.
I'll call the police again, you wait and see! M'entends-tu? I'm going
to have you kicked out!"

Mina arched her eyebrows. Nobody was supposed to call her
retarded. When they did, she called Bruno and he told them. Except
she couldn't now because she wasn't talking to him. He was too
stupid.

She grinned, hearing how angry the neighbour was. If she had
to be upset, someone else should be too.

*

Gabriela was surprised when Mina didn't answer the phone. This
was their time to talk. Mina always picked up immediately — as if
she were sitting with the phone on her lap, watching the clock. When
the phone rang until the answering machine clicked on, Gabriela
hung up. She would call back in a few moments.

This time Mina answered, though her blunt, "Yeah?" sounded
annoyed.

"It's Gabriela. Were you in the bathroom?"

"No."

"Why didn't you answer?"

"D-d-don't know." It sounded like an accusation.

"Are you upset about something?"

"Yeah."

"You're not upset with me, are you?"

No words now, only slightly congested breathing, but the refusal to speak was stubborn and angry.

Shit, Gabriela thought. Had Bruno finally told her? Nice that he'd let her know. And quietly, "What did Bruno tell you?"

Still silence.

"I don't know what he said but we're not together anymore."

"Why?" More a reproach than a question.

"It doesn't affect how I feel about you. You know that, don't you? Bruno is just ..."

"Stupid!"

"He's not stupid. Don't say that about your brother."

"He is!"

"He loves you very much."

"No!"

"Yes, he does. You shouldn't—" Gabriela stopped. What Mina thought about Bruno was no longer her concern. "We're still good, aren't we? You and I?"

"You're supposed to b-b-be with Bruno!"

"Life sometimes works out differently from what we thought."

"Why didn't you?"

Gabriela waited but that seemed to be the whole question. "It can happen that two people realize they don't want the same thing— and it's a very important thing." She decided not to tell Mina about wanting a baby, because how would she explain if it didn't happen? "And then it no longer makes sense to stay together. Bruno ... I don't know what he wants."

"He's stupid." Pronounced with the full weight of Mina's experience and judgment.

Yeah, Gabriela thought to herself. Sometimes he is.

Carefully she guided the talk toward Mina's concerns. Was she still working at the church? Was the nun still taking her out for a muffin? Not always but sometimes. Anticipating when it would happen again was like predicting a horoscope.

*

Iris was crossing the park, boots crunching on the thin crusty snow. A week ago the path that cut from one corner to the other was bare, even though there was still snow under the trees. Then it had snowed, partly thawed, and frozen again. Welcome to winter à la climate change.

Yesterday evening when Bruno called, he said he'd told Mina he wasn't with his girlfriend anymore and she was angry with him. *Very* angry. He'd known she wouldn't like it but he wished it didn't make her so unhappy. Iris said she was coming to see Mina today and could put a good word in for him. No, he said, don't. Better not mention me or you'll get blamed too. Mina throws a wide net when she's upset. But I'm glad you're going to see her, so she's not all alone. She isn't going to want to see me for a few days and even then, I'll be in the doghouse.

The more Iris got to know Bruno, the more impressed she was by how he truly cared for Mina. He wasn't just making sure she got three meals a day and had a functioning TV. It genuinely hurt him when she was upset. And although he accepted that Mina blamed him for whatever was going wrong in her life, he couldn't have liked it.

Maybe she would try to say something in his defense. But would Mina listen? Bruno had warned her not to try. And now especially, she didn't want to alienate Mina.

She still didn't know how she was going to get more embroidery but somehow she had to. Mina was making art and it merited attention. Bruno might not realize that but she did. Hadn't she always sensed that she and Mina were meant to meet?

When Jenny had called her uncle, they'd invented a friend who painted and wanted to know how to go about getting her work in a gallery. He said gallery owners looked at photos. Artists didn't schlep huge tableaux about. But the photos needed to be very high quality. Iris understood what that entailed because she'd had a photographer take pics of her studio and some finished designs for her website. He'd come with cameras, stands, and flashes. Mina would never allow that inside her apartment.

She rang Mina's buzzer and heard the noise of the TV in the background when Mina answered. When she walked in, Mina was already back on the sofa with her embroidery hoop.

Excellent! Iris loved watching Mina when she embroidered. She stitched without pause until she came to the end of the thread on her needle. Then she peered hard at her tray of colours before snatching a new and unexpected colour. *Philomena in the heat of creation!* What a great video that would make! Iris would have to try to convince her to wear one of her funny hats even though she was indoors.

Iris had unbuttoned and eased off her coat, and settled herself in the armchair. From the TV in the corner a game show boomed honks and sirens. The same cacophony echoed from the bedroom. Even from where she sat, she could see how Mina had stitched gold and silver almond shapes, splicing the silver ovals with blue, mauve, and purple streaks. She was making larger stitches too, the way Iris had recommended. Did she remember that Iris had told her or had she come to the solution herself? Iris wished now she hadn't said anything and waited to see what Mina would do.

"Do you like using metal thread?"

No answer. Mina was focussed and working. Despite what Bruno said, she didn't seem unhappy.

When a horn blared from the TV, Mina stopped to watch a contestant who was jumping and screeching, fists clenched to her face.

"Must be nice to win money," Iris said.

Mina grumbled something Iris didn't catch and began stitching again.

Money, Iris thought. *That* was what Mina wanted! And without thinking whether it was good or bad, or even a doable idea, she said, "Bruno doesn't give you much money, does he?"

"Bruno!" A guttural noise of disgust.

"What if there was another way to get money?"

Mina looked up.

"You know how I love your knitting. Maybe ... I could buy one?"

Mina's expression didn't change.

Carefully Iris went on. She offered Mina twenty dollars per piece. That had to sound tempting. It effectively doubled her weekly income. The question was which Mina loved more: her embroidery or money.

"You could even decide which one you'll let me buy."

Mina still gave no sign. Had she understood?

"Or if twenty isn't enough, how about twenty-five? I could go up to twenty-five dollars."

Mina's rivetted, asymmetrical stare was making Iris nervous.

"For each, I mean. I would give you twenty-five dollars for each one. I'd like to buy a few, so that would be twenty-five dollars a few times."

Why wasn't Mina answering?

Desperate with impatience, Iris tried, "Thirty dollars?"

Mina's whole face winced with effort. "Th-th-thirty-five!"

"*What?* That's a lot of money!" Though it wasn't compared to what a work of art would sell for in a gallery. Not that she was trying to make money off Mina, but she had to think about what she could afford. And how would she explain commission to Mina? That would all have to come later. She hadn't thought this through. She should have waited.

Except now Mina was interested. "Th-th-thirty-five!" she repeated, thrusting her chin out.

Iris shook her head. But quickly, before Mina said forty, she agreed. "Okay, thirty-five."

Mina chortled.

"But for thirty-five, can I pick it myself?"

"No." Mina lay a protective hand on the stack of embroidery beside her.

"Okay, okay." Iris took her wallet from her bag, hoping she had enough cash on her before Mina changed her mind. "How about ... can I have more than one?"

"One today."

"Another tomorrow?"

Mina considered the calendar on the shelf next to her. "Friday."

Iris fanned the bills to show them to Mina, who made no move to take them. "Where should I ..." Mina nodded at the crowded end table. "You want me to put the money here?"

Mina waved a finger, gesturing, until Iris understood that the bills should be tucked under the Céline Dion CD with the ends of the bills still showing.

"And which embroidery can I have then?"

"Out." Mina tilted her head at the door to the hallway.

"Out? You mean ... you want me to go into the hallway?"

"Yeah."

Iris closed the door behind her and after a minute heard the lock click and the rattle of the chain. Moments passed. What if Mina left her in the hallway and pretended they had no deal?

Down the hallway a door opened and out came a man with a pug on a leash. There was plenty of room for them to pass, but he stopped and asked what she wanted. She said she was waiting for her friend to let her in. He asked if she'd knocked. Even the dog was eyeballing her with suspicion. She said her friend knew she was there. She didn't know what else to say and he wasn't leaving. He seemed the kind of upstanding citizen who might call the police.

Luckily, Mina's chain clanked, the lock clicked, and the door opened. Iris flicked a wave at the man and stepped inside.

The money she'd put under the CD was gone and an embroidery lay on the seat of the armchair. A swirling study in mauves and reds and browns. All curves, yet violent and menacing. Iris hadn't seen Mina make it. That meant she had more embroidery than Iris knew about.

Gently she lifted it. "This means a lot to me, thank you. You know I love your work."

Mina gave a smug sniff and picked up her hoop again.

Iris examined the embroidery more closely. The meld of colours, the design, the curved pathways of the stitching all added to the energy. And it was hers now, legitimately hers. She'd paid for it.

Still. As Jenny had said, people could be funny. "You know what? How about we keep this a secret between us for now? Let's not tell Bruno —"

"Bruno is bad!"

"He's not bad. He loves you and he does a lot of wonderful things for you. Look at that lamp he got so that you can see your knitting better."

Mina jutted her lips, refusing to look at it.

Iris realized she should stop talking about Bruno. "Do you have enough gold and silver thread or do you want me to get more?"

"Yeah."

Offering Mina more of anything always pleased her.

*

Gabriela was wheeling a patient from her office to the waiting room. She noticed a still figure, standing upright. A man facing her doorway. Someone who exercised, jogged, or hiked. Who had excellent posture. Only then she looked at his face. And felt herself flush. Had she conjured him with her late-night schemes to find him?

She turned to speak with the patient's daughter. "Oui, très important de faire les exercices, sinon la chirurgie ..."

She was on automatic pilot, her mind bounding. Why had he come? She knew why *she* wanted to see him again. To test if that spark she felt that one time was real. If his voice still reached inside, touching her.

"À la prochaine!" She squeezed her patient's shoulder, making more of a show of leave-taking than she usually did, not sure what to say to this man who could have no idea of the scaffolding of hope she carried.

"Hello, Gabriela?" He'd crossed to where she stood, holding out his hand to shake hers. "I don't know if you remember me, Daniel Lavoie? You saw my dad before Christmas. I'm sorry, I don't remember your family name." He looked at her name tag and nodded, as if committing it to memory.

Every woman of her acquaintance would probably advise her to mime blankness. To let him flatter and woo her. But she wasn't like that. "How's your dad? Still doing his exercises twice a day? He promised me he would."

"Most of the time, I think so. The intention is there. He doesn't want another bout of sciatica."

"So it's fear of pain that motivates him, not me? You've just burst my bubble of professional pride."

Who said what next? Did it matter? A few evenings later, they were in a quiet bar after having watched the movie that he thought would interest her because it was filmed in Guanajuato. She said she'd recognized him even before he said who he was. He said he'd been waiting for the right opportunity, not sure how he could tempt her — not even sure if she was single. She hesitated before admitting that she'd been in a relationship until very recently.

"But not anymore?"

"No."

*

Me! the blue clamoured. Here beside the silver. Me, me, me!

Mina was telling them the story about the man who had a magic word to make the mountain open. Magic words were supposed to be tricky and hard to remember because they were like keys. Inside the mountain there was so much gold heaped in chests that it spilled out. Gold was lots and lots of money — more than $35. But $35 was pretty good too! A twenty and a ten and a five. Every time Iris bought

a knitting, she would give her another $35. And if she took … Mina
stopped stitching to pay attention to the numbers in her head. If
she took two $5 to the bank, they would give her $10! If she took two
$10 … she would get $20! But she wouldn't leave that money at the
bank or Bruno would find out because he had a way of knowing what
was in the bank. She needed to hide it at home — like gold inside the
mountain.

The man said the magic word to make it open. He had a wagon
with a wheel in the front that you pushed. Mama had one like that for
the garden. The man in the story filled his wagon "… with g-g-gold."
He said another magic word so the mountain let him out again. He
wheeled the gold home and bought all kinds of wonderful things.

She'd stitched blue up the side of a silver leaf and was curling it
away now. Blues and mauves danced more than silver and gold did.
Silver and gold wanted to stay still.

The man went to the mountain with his wagon again. He could
keep doing that and keep getting gold, except —

What? the colours demanded. What could go wrong?

She held her needle poised. Bad luck! The man's brother followed
him to the mountain.

He heard the magic word so he could get in. He wanted gold too.
Except he … She couldn't remember what happened next but he was
stupid. That was the rule about this story. You had to be careful about
money and brothers. They were stupid.

Right now she wasn't talking to Bruno because of Gabriela. But
even when she talked to him again, she wasn't going to tell him
about the $35.

"Mine!" she told the colours and they said, Yeah, it was.

She would give Iris knitting that was already put away in bags
in her closet. So many bags she had, each filled with knitting — and
for every knitting she could get $35! So many things she would be
able to buy for herself without having to ask Bruno! Or maybe she
would keep the money for herself, keep it safe. She could do that too.

*

By the third transaction, Mina had devised a ritual. She folded the embroidery and left it on the armrest of the chair. With commanding gestures, she directed Iris to put the money on the kitchen table. There! she pointed. Under the plastic lemon. The bills should be fanned out, so Mina could see them, though she didn't touch them while Iris was there. Nor was Iris allowed to look at the embroidery while she was still in the apartment. She had to slide it, folded as it was, into her bag. Yes, like that, Mina nodded.

At first, Iris was amused by the ceremony but Mina gave her a hard look. This was serious. Smiles were not allowed. Nor was it funny, as Iris soon realized. She'd never before seen these embroideries. Were they all hidden in the apartment? That meant an untold treasury of artwork — and she was the one to discover it!

She hadn't yet told Jenny about the new arrangement because she'd gone to Vancouver with her boyfriend for the week. Iris knew Jenny was going to ask whether Mina understood she was selling her work. That question could only arise if a person didn't know Mina, who was so possessive about her embroidery that if she agreed to sell it, there could be no doubt about her intentions. And why shouldn't she have the right to sell what she made if that was what she wanted? Iris *wasn't* taking advantage of her. If there was more money to be realized, Iris would give her more.

Of course, she would eventually tell Bruno. But right now she couldn't risk him not understanding — which could happen since he'd never seen Mina's embroidery for what it was. Wouldn't he be more likely to understand if she had a gallery owner interested? That was when she would tell him, when she had everything in place.

He'd begun calling her most evenings when she hadn't come to the studio or to ask if she'd seen Mina, but that was only a pretext. They were getting to know each other, talking about themselves and sharing stories. Each detail felt like a peek into a new corner of their lives. He told her about losing his dad at seventeen and how he'd become the man of the family. That must have been tough, she said. No, he said, it was just the way it was. She described starting her business and the different obstacles she had to overcome. Sure, there were small business initiatives but try to get one when you were on your own and a woman. He said he used to hang out with his dad in the workshop and had learned enough carpentry to make him decide to go to technical college. She told him about taking the bus with a friend to Toronto when they were sixteen to see Madonna's Blond Ambition tour. They'd gone for the music but Iris was wowed by the costumes — the pink cone corset that gave Madonna warrior breasts. As much as any skills Iris had inherited from her grandmother, seeing how Madonna exulted in her body and how her clothes were designed to show it off, set Iris on her course in life.

Some days, when she was out for her walk, she stopped by the dance studio to watch them work. The way they stretched and leapt and careened and flipped had so much energy. She thought she knew bodies from dressing them, but with Tandi and Mathieu she saw what a well-conditioned body could do. Bruno might join her, standing beside her for a while, but even when he didn't, she knew he was aware of her — and she of him.

*

"Monsieur Corneau!" Faiza's desk was its usual I-Ching scatter of papers and folders around the island of her keyboard. Maybe for her, Bruno thought, solving problems was an act of divination.

He'd made an appointment to try to stop the annual absurdity of having to complete government papers to confirm Mina's status. Did the government believe that from one year to the next she might have lost the extra chromosome that gave her Down Syndrome? He pointed out that not only was it a waste of his time to fill out the papers, but the doctor's as well, since she also had to confirm that

Mina still had Down Syndrome. What was it about genetics the government did not understand?

Faiza said she empathized but could do nothing. Mina was categorized in a group, some of whose members could have a change in status. If he didn't complete the papers, her monthly support payments would be stopped while the government investigated — and then who knew how long it would take before she was reinstated?

"I suggest you simply accept this," she said. "There are things we can change, things we can't, and let's hope we have the wisdom to know the difference."

Wasn't that the AA prayer? He was Mina's guardian, not an alcoholic.

Faiza gave a little cough into her fist. "Has Mina said anything to you about her garbage?"

He hadn't heard from Mina since he'd told her about the breakup. She thought she was punishing him. He was having a vacation.

"You know the super retired?"

"The lobby looks messier."

"He used to take Mina's garbage to the basement for her. Now that he's gone, she leaves it in the hallway."

"Well, she shouldn't. And he shouldn't have been taking it down for her. She can do things like that herself."

"But she can't get to the basement. We have to —"

"Of course she can get to the basement. There's an elevator. That's where she does her laundry."

Faiza gaped at him. "There's an elevator?"

Lord help me, Bruno thought.

"Well!" She gave a stiff nod, gathering her forces anew. "Elevator or not, she's leaving her garbage in the hallway."

"Okay, I'll talk to her."

"It's not just garbage in garbage bags either. She's dropping teabags in the hallway. Eggshells and apple cores."

"Not apple cores."

"Yes! That's what they told me."

"Who's they?"

"The neighbour who lives next to her."

"Okay," he said as evenly as he could. "Mina doesn't eat apples. She hates them. If anyone is leaving apple cores, it most certainly isn't Mina."

"But then who ...?"

"Maybe the neighbour."

"Why would she do that?"

"How about you ask her? Is that the same neighbour who accused Mina of taking the Publisacs?"

"They're still disappearing, you know."

"Right," Bruno said. "So if Mina can't take her kitchen garbage downstairs, tell me how she drags a stack of flyers to her apartment? None of this makes sense — and no one has actually seen her do anything."

As he left the office, he swore under his breath. He had no choice but to see Mina. She might not have done everything Faiza suspected, but she'd done something. He knew she could be sneaky and vengeful. If she thought the neighbour looked forward to the weekly flyer, she might well make the whole stack disappear. She had a history of getting even. Once, a bus driver said she hadn't rung the bell in time and he wouldn't let her off until the next stop. Did he think he was teaching her a lesson? The next time she was on the bus when he was driving, she rang the bell, waited by the front door to get off, and snatched the keys to the bus as she did. He was so startled that he didn't react quickly. She was already off the bus. He yelled for her to bring them back, which she didn't. By the time he'd maneuvered out from behind the steering wheel, she'd lobbed them over a fence into a yard. If the neighbour in the apartment building thought she was making trouble for Mina by adding more garbage to what Mina was leaving in the hallway, she had better watch out.

When he buzzed Mina's intercom, she wouldn't let him in. "I d-d-don't —"

"Open up or I'll use my key."

There was a pause and the buzzer sounded. And look at this: in the hallway between her door and the neighbour's lay a yellow Cheerios box.

Mina had unlocked the door and was on her way back to the sofa, the sway of her walk bullish and stubborn.

He waggled the box. "What's this?"

Her eyes widened in a show of ignorance, her dramatics played out at time-lapse speed.

"Don't know."

"Really?" He leaned across her to grab the remote from the shelf next to her and lowered the volume on the TV. "You've been eating Cheerios since we were kids, remember? *Cheery-Cheery-Cheerios?*" Their mother used to give them a bowl of Cheerios for a snack. She told Mina they would make her feel cheery.

"I showed you where to find Cheerios in the store when you were doing your own groceries. I see the bill from your groceries now. You still eat them. And now you're telling me you don't recognize the box? Are you getting stupid?"

"No!"

"Then why are you pretending to be stupid?"

She crossed her arms high, tucking her fists in her armpits.

"I'm waiting, Mina. Tell me why there's an empty Cheerios box in the hallway in front of your door."

"Not my door!"

"Ah. So you know where it was. Is that because you put it there?"

As he spoke he surveyed the crowded room, the overstuffed shelves, the narrow path she'd left herself to walk from the kitchen to the sofa. In the bedroom even the bed was hidden under a welter of clothes, bags, cushions, and stuffed animals. There was no room for a mound of Publisacs — and each week a new mound. Though that didn't mean they weren't here. To look for them, he would have to dig and move things.

"You know very well that garbage goes into the garbage can, and that paper and plastic go into the bag I got you for recycling. And when they're full, you take them downstairs."

"Peux pas."

"Yes, you can. The garbage bags are small and they're not heavy. And if you can't carry the recycling bag, put it in your cart. You take the elevator exactly like you do for your laundry."

"Can't!" Arms still crossed high over her belly as if it was pouting at him too.

"Mina, there are things you have to keep doing for yourself or you won't be able to stay in your apartment."

"My apartment!"

"And in an apartment you have neighbours. They don't appreciate seeing your garbage in the hallway. We've discussed this ad nauseam. You know what ad nauseam means? It means I'm getting sick of it. You have to get along with your neighbours if you want to stay here. Do you understand? If I get another complaint about garbage in the hallway, I'll have to keep your spending money."

Her arms dropped to her lap. "It's mine! I need it!"

"If you can't figure out how to get your garbage downstairs where it belongs, then you don't have time to go to the store."

The intercom buzzed and Mina snatched the phone. She seemed happy to hear who it was. Maybe Iris? He'd be happy to see her too. "Who is it?" he asked but got no answer.

There was a tap on the door — and it was Iris as he'd hoped.

"Hi!" she said, drawing it out warmly. And to Mina, "Hey, you."

"We've been talking about Mina's garbage. She's leaving it in the hallway instead of taking it downstairs. I found this," he held up the Cheerios box, "outside her door."

"Mina!" Iris clucked her tongue. "You can't just throw your garbage out the door." But she sounded more amused than scolding. "Do you want me to take it downstairs for you when I come?"

"Yeah!" Mina beamed at her.

"No," he said quickly. "She has to keep doing things for herself. She already has services — someone who does her shopping and cleaning. If she can't do anything by herself anymore, she's going to be moved to a residence."

"I s-s-signed the lease!"

Social Services had felt that having Mina sign a lease would make her act more responsibly. However, at any time they could overrule the lease. They were the ones who decided who was still autonomous enough to live alone in a subsidized apartment and who needed to be placed.

"It's just her garbage," Iris said. "I don't mind."

"No, it's ..." Why was he always the odd one out, having to lay down the law?

"Don't worry, I'll take care of it. Mina and I will come to an arrangement."

He started shaking his head but then he sighed.

Iris had perched on the armrest of the sofa, one leg dangling. She was comfortable with Mina, which he appreciated because sometimes people weren't. Mina was comfortable with her too — which also wasn't always the case. Maybe if Mina had another woman to confide in, she wouldn't miss Gabriela so much.

Iris was leaning across to see Mina's tray of threads, asking if she needed more colours. Her legs were nicely moulded by her tight jeans. He was used to dancers' calves but Iris's were shapely too, her hips trim. She wasn't overtly sexy so much as easy in her body. More subtly attractive. Her hand, unknotting her scarf, bared her neck, her open collar, her skin. So fair she was. But not delicate, he could see that.

He suddenly realized he was sitting, watching Iris. Had she noticed? He cleared his throat. "I'll be on my way, okay?"

Mina said bye in a tone that sounded like good riddance. Iris winked at him in what he hoped was a signal that they would talk later.

Outside the door, on the carpet, was a cellophane tube. He nudged it with the toe of his running shoe. There were still crumbs inside. He picked it up. "Was this in front of the door when you came?" he asked Iris.

"Definitely not."

He turned to leave.

"Wait," Iris called. "Was that there just now? You know when —" She glanced at Mina, then back at him. "When what happened with Pierre? One of the neighbours said something to me about how Mina didn't belong in the building. She was pretty nasty."

"It's not up to her to decide who lives here."

"She might be trying to make trouble."

"Yeah," Mina chimed in, having understood enough of their exchange. "Cette Madame, I d-d-don't like her!"

"What kind of —" Iris began but he shook his head to stop her. Best not to fan any flames.

In the hallway he scanned the closed doors. He would have liked to pound on a few of them but he didn't trust what he would say. Nothing pleasant, that was for sure.

*

"Wow." Jenny stretched the word. She was leaning over the six pieces of embroidery Iris had placed side by side on the cutting table. Each was different in design and palette. A pink grid hazed with zigzags of red. Yellow, green, and red circles with blobby centres. Jenny bent closer to examine what Iris imagined as a group of emerald starfish with orange carbuncles, trailing blue seaweed. Mina's designs were abstract but the mind groped for definable images.

"And you didn't take these?" Jenny asked. "Mina let you have them?"

Iris rubbed her thumb and fingers in the universal money gesture. "As I told you. Once I found the key."

"You explained you want to take them to a gallery?"

"They're mine now, I can do what I want with them."

Jenny shifted her stance. "Not so sure about that. But you know what," she said more urgently, "you shouldn't lay them out side by side like this when you show them. They're each so different. They sort of... fight with each other. Better would be to show them one by one." She lifted one farther along the cutting table, moved another higher up.

Iris nodded, seeing what Jenny meant.

"Forget what my uncle said about photos. Pics wouldn't do justice to the texture. It's good you got these." Jenny brushed her fingers across the intricate terrain of stitched colour.

Iris saw how she traced a smooth glint, a mesh of layering, an island of knots. She wanted to shout Yes! and pump a fist like the kids who played basketball at the head of the street. She'd *known* Mina's work was extraordinary and Jenny's admiration confirmed it. The denizens of the art world had no idea what was about to hit them.

"Come." She hooked Jenny's arm to bring her to the computer. "Let me show you some websites of galleries."

4

Mina always came to Bruno's productions. He had to stay in the tech booth, but he'd been told that she sat riveted, eyes wide, forgetting even to close her mouth. There was no doubt she enjoyed watching dance, but with this performance Val had significantly stepped up the violence. For Mina, too, it had only been a couple of months since she'd been assaulted and almost raped. He decided not to tell her they were putting on a new dance — which would also solve the problem of Gabriela no longer being available to take her.

That evening when he stopped at Mina's, she banged her finger on the calendar and demanded to know when she was going to the dance. Iris had told her.

He hadn't thought to ask Iris not to, although they often enough talked about Mina — or used to. Now they mostly talked about themselves. When she came to the studio and they stood watching the dancers, he wondered if the strenuous physicality of their movements made her more conscious of their two bodies. Himself, he felt Iris's presence like a pulse down his side. When she touched him, as she sometimes did, was she only being friendly? Did she feel the tension growing like a forcefield between them? He was older by almost ten years but that wasn't so unusual. The loose bunches of her curls made him want to squeeze them. Run his fingers through the short hair on her nape.

But why had she told Mina about the dance? "I think it's better you don't come this time," he said. Mina's mouth quivered and she

began to sniffle. She promised to be good. He said he wasn't punishing her. He didn't think she should come because the dance might
upset her. She said it wouldn't.

That evening, when he and Iris talked, she said she'd told Mina
about the dance because she assumed Mina always went. Next
to birthdays, Bruno's dances were the social highlight of her year.
Bruno said he knew, but there was so much violence in this dance.
Iris pointed out how much violence Mina must see on TV and it didn't
seem to disturb her.

A live performance was more immediate and visceral than TV.
He knew that, but he let Iris convince him. She said she would make
all the arrangements. It was actually sweet that it meant so much to
her to bring Mina.

*

Mina waited, but none of the colours wanted to come. I know, she
told them. But we can't leave it like this.

Iris had made her a new dress. Having another new dress was
good, but not this dress. The neck scooped so low that everyone
would see her titties. She tried to tell Iris but Iris didn't understand.
Iris said the dress was to wear to the dance — a present for Mina and
a surprise for Bruno. Bruno didn't care about dresses!

She huffed at the crazy way Iris was acting. Talking too fast all
the time. Giggly when there was nothing to giggle about. Her silly
nose so high in the air that you could see up the holes.

The colours didn't want to come, but one of them was going to
have to. Come on! she thought. Help me. Fixing dresses wasn't the
kind of knitting she knew how to do.

She fiddled free a strand of green, wet it between her lips, and
took a needle from the pincushion. "D-d-do it." Even the needle
wasn't happy. She pinched the cloth. It was slippery and didn't want
to be knit. She pulled the stitches tight to close up the part that
showed off her titties, but now the top of the dress was bunched

and twisted. She stitched across where it was crooked but it still wouldn't lie flat.

She sniffed. Too many things that weren't the way they were supposed to be. Why was Iris taking her to the dance? Iris was okay but she wasn't her belle-coeur. Mina wanted Gabriela to come but Gabriela said she couldn't. She said Mina had to understand. What Mina understood was that nothing was right anymore because of Bruno. Always Bruno!

On TV a lady was trying to make a dog sit but the dog kept jumping around. Youpi, Mina and Bruno's dog when they were little, sat right away when you pointed your finger. Youpi was smarter than the dog on TV.

She reached for the remote to ... change the ... channel but ... her arm ... flopped ... the room ... blurred ... then ... nothing.

When she blinked awake again, she didn't know what the messed-up cloth on her lap was. Where had it come from? Everything was confused. She kept gazing around and slowly saw that the TV was on, and here was her pile of knitting beside her, and her pictures on the shelves, a kitten from the dollar store, the framed photo of a long-ago Christmas with Mama. Her tray of colours and her book of hidden word puzzles. All her favourite things exactly where she wanted them.

But what was that show? Not something she ever watched. Where was the remote? She poked her hand between the cushions where it sometimes hid. She finally had to wiggle off the sofa and look. Stupid remote! What was it doing on the floor?

She was getting back on the sofa again and remembered now that the twisted cloth she couldn't knit was the ugly dress Iris wanted her to wear to the dance. She couldn't throw it in the garbage or Iris would see it. She would hide it and one day when she went to the dollar store, she would shove it in the garbage can on the sidewalk.

*

Opening night. In the tech booth Bruno sat focussed, hands on the lighting and sound controls, attention alert for each cue. Even so, at the farthest edge of his galaxy of attention, he knew Mina was in the front row. She always wanted to sit as close to the dance as possible. She wouldn't listen when he said she would see better farther back.

On stage the dance was building to its climax. Mathieu, spurred on by the clamour of the cello, smashed the doll on the table. Tandi hovered, hands clenching and unclenching. The doll had been her only treasure, her only connection to home. When he swatted it to the floor and stomped on it, she swung at him. He made to whirl away, but she hooked him by the waist and threw him on the table.

The sawing of the cello was a tortured beast. Mathieu had twisted off the table and rolled across the floor, but Tandi leapt on him. He bucked and struggled but was unable to shake her off. Abruptly the cello stopped. Mathieu no longer moved. In the silence, Tandi crept around Mathieu's inert body. She squatted to peer at him, her face puzzled. Then ever more frenzied, she shoved and batted at his ragdoll limbs and sprang around him, desperate to dance him back to life.

Boogie gave an occasional hard slap with the flat of his hand on the cello. It sounded like a question. What now? What have you done?

She swung her head, scanning the stage, took in how truly alone she was now. Her body softening, she bent to Mathieu and began stroking his arms, his torso, his legs. Boogie plucked a low C string, signaling the change in mood. A new perception. She sat on the floor to gather Mathieu close and cradled him. As she held him, he slowly stirred awake. Stretched a foot, lifted his head. She curved his arm over her shoulders to help him upright and guide him to take a step. One, then another and another.

Bruno could feel how the audience was rapt. This was the *rise from the ashes* Val had envisioned. Still homeless, but they had each other — and wasn't that a deeper sense of home? At first unsteady and tentative, they began to dance together in a way that they hadn't

yet, one bracing the other to kick legs high, leaping, stretching, tipping. Tandi rotated Mathieu across her shoulders, him on his back,
legs straddled wide. This time, when she flipped him, she linked her
arms through his, keeping him by her.

When Bruno lowered the lights, people clapped and rose to their
feet. Tandi and Mathieu bowed and held their arms out to Val who
strode on stage. The dance critic for *Le Devoir*, who Bruno had spotted before the show, was still clapping. A good review in *Le Devoir*
would mean a full house for the rest of the run, an invitation to
Quebec City and Ottawa.

With everyone standing, Bruno could no longer spot Iris and
Mina. He craned his head to see past the people who were thronging
the aisles. Then Iris was waving and Mina was beside her, grinning.
He made his way to them. "Did you like it?" he asked Mina.

"Yeah! B-b-but ..." Her face puckered with objection. "Too loud."

"That's how I feel about the TV at your place."

"Pas comme ça," she said stiffly.

"She was okay?" he asked Iris.

"She just told you she liked it, didn't she?"

He knew Mina meant the spectacle, the movement, the lights,
the up-close wonder of coming to a live performance. She might
still have been disturbed by the violence. Gabriela had told him that
Mina sometimes used to grope for her hand.

He wondered about Mina but his attention was drawn by Iris
whose neck was bare except for a sparkle of jewellery. The deep blue
of her dress, her curls golden under the houselights. They'd already
agreed that she would take Mina home while he finished what he
had to do here, but they hadn't discussed what they would do then.

As they made their way to the lobby, he said there was an after-
party. Late dinner and drinks at a restaurant. Normally he went, but
this evening he wasn't interested in watching Val and the dancers
glory in a post-performance high. He wanted to be alone somewhere
with Iris, but did she want that? He couldn't gauge her mood with

all the people milling about and Mina, short yet very solid, between them.

On the sidewalk Mina was already making a beeline for one of the taxis at the curb. A taxi home belonged to the routine of coming to a dance performance.

"Did you want to go to the party?" he asked Iris.

"I'm not so big on parties, but I'd like a drink. There's a place in Verdun but the music will be too loud. We wouldn't be able to talk."

As he helped Mina get settled, his thoughts darted, trying to think of what to say. He knew what he wanted. That morning, after his shower, he'd stood naked before the mirror and gave himself a dispassionate once-over. He wasn't as slim as he used to be. Definitely thicker around the middle. He didn't have a big prick but he knew what to do with it. He did physical work and his arms had muscle. Tandi teased him about grey hair, but it still looked brown to him.

He closed the door of the taxi and said, "My place is quiet. I've got wine. Pinot Noir," he added, as if the vintage might be the deciding factor.

Iris reached into her purse. "What's your address?"

He told her and as she was tapping it in her phone, Mina knocked on the window and stuck her tongue out at them. She was waiting!

He nodded for Iris to head around the back of the car to the other side. Out of sight of the window, he handed her his clutch of keys. "The silver one's the front door. I won't be long, maybe forty-five minutes. The wine is —"

"Don't be silly," she said. "I'll wait for you."

As the taxi pulled away, he marvelled at how easily that had happened.

*

Iris woke to the smell of coffee, the angel looking down from the wall, its wings gleaming dully in the dim room. She rolled over and stretched, luxuriating in her body and the delicious soreness of sex.

She'd known it would happen, but not how or where — and hadn't expected that Bruno would simply hand her his keys. Yet she'd prepared yesterday as if they had a fixed date. High-cut lace panties, waxed legs, a dress that wrapped snug across her breasts, the barest glisten of lipstick, a come-hither pendant at her neck. Bodies and how to clothe them were her business. She understood how to show hers to advantage.

At his place she'd walked from room to room, noting the fixings of his domesticity. TV in the corner of the living room. A chintz armchair he must have gotten at an antique shop and had reupholstered. A small dining room with four chairs at the table. Bananas in a bowl. Half a baguette in a plastic bag. Washer and dryer. She didn't enter but stood in the doorway of his bedroom. On the wall hung an angel like Mina's. The bed was made, if hastily.

In the bathroom she saw the terrycloth robe on the hook and felt like getting undressed and waiting for him naked under his own robe, but that was a cheap stunt. Also: terrycloth? She could do better than that. Watching herself in the mirror, she undid the zipper of her dress, unhooked her bra, slid the straps down her arms. She zipped her dress up again and leaned forward, letting the V of the neckline open on her bare breasts. They were small, but she'd fit enough women with large breasts to know what a curse that was. For example, now. She could take off her bra and not ruin the dress's silhouette. Still watching herself in the mirror, she traced her nipples over the fabric. Come on, Bruno, get here!

The first time they fucked they were still on the sofa, her dress up to her waist, his shirt still on, the glasses of wine on the table hardly sipped. She liked that he was frank and hungry about sex, stopping only long enough to make sure his glasses were safe on a shelf.

When it was over and they both lay collapsed together, he gently unzipped her dress and slid it off her and she unbuttoned his shirt. For a while they were stretched naked on the sofa, sipping wine, speaking in murmurs, and only slowly began kissing again.

He'd been almost shy when he asked if she wanted to spend the night, because if she was going to, he would put fresh sheets on the bed. She offered to help but he said no. Alone in the living room, as she heard closet doors opening and closing, she reached for her purse where she'd stashed her phone and sent Jenny a text. *B is hot!!!!*

Now, even though she could smell coffee brewing, she didn't get up. She wanted coffee in bed and he would be a smart man if he would bring it. And here he came, wearing a T-shirt and boxers, carrying two mugs. Hairy legs, nice calves, elegant ankles.

"Sleep okay?" he asked.

"Until someone woke me around dawn."

"Yeah, same here." Still standing, he sipped his coffee.

She peeked at the mug he'd set on the night table and saw that he'd added milk. "I hope you didn't put sugar in."

"You don't take sugar."

"How do you know?"

Instead of answering, he went to the window where he parted the curtain only enough to let in a diffuse shaft of light — a lighting tech's control of ambience.

She lifted the sheet. "Getting in?"

He tilted his head as if to see what was underneath. "You want toast?"

"In a minute. I like to drink my coffee first."

"Good." He sat on the bed.

"Tell me about the angel. It's just like Mina's."

He looked up at it. "Not exactly alike. The expression is different and mine's blond. Hers has reddish-brown hair. But you're right, they're both Baroque angels."

"Baroque, you mean …?"

"I mean Baroque as in the 1600s. My mother's family in Austria work in church restoration."

"Statues and altars?"

"Frescoes, crucifixes, pillars, spires, arched ceilings, you name it.

The whole church. We went to visit them when I was seven."

"That must have been — hey, did Mina see all that too?"

"She wasn't born yet."

Dang, Iris thought. What an interesting chapter to Philomena's story that would have made. "Your family never went again?"

He rubbed his thumb along the handle of his mug as if testing its solidity. "There was some problem. My mother didn't want to tell me when I was younger and ... I don't know, time passed. We never talked about it and she never wanted to go back."

"But what about you? Have you never wanted to go? They're your family too."

He sipped his coffee. "I only went when I was seven. I don't feel any connection — or not to the people. Maybe only to that angel and my old book of Grimms' fairy tales."

"And it's a real Baroque angel?" She nudged her foot against him. "Isn't it risky for Mina to have a valuable antique in plain sight?"

"Who would think she had one? Better yet, who would even see it? Her apartment is so stuffed with clutter."

"I saw it right away, the first time I walked in."

"That's you, you're observant."

She liked how easily he could give a compliment. Not trying to flatter her or curry favour, simply making a statement.

"I think it's more important that she have the angel. She associates it with our mother, who used to hang them over our beds so they could watch our dreams."

"Why isn't Mina's in her bedroom then?"

"I put it where she wanted it. I'm not really concerned about her dreams either. It's during the day she needs watching."

"And you? I hope you don't associate your angel with your mother watching, because last night ..."

He set his mug on the night table. "A wooden carving," he said softly as he lifted the sheet and joined her. "That's all it is." Hand cupping her breast. "Wood." One kiss. "Paint." Another. "A bit of gold."

*

"P-p-pricked her finger." Sometimes Mina pricked her finger but only a little prick. The princess pricked herself so hard that she fell asleep and didn't wake again. Thorns started growing. Still she slept and slept. The drawing in the book showed roses and thorns all around. Inside them, the princess looked like a doll while she slept. So still and pretty.

Then one day a prince came. That was what was supposed to happen. "To kiss her." That was what princes did. They kissed the princess and woke her up and everyone was happy. Forever and ever.

Except! This prince grabbed the princess and ripped her dress. He had fur on his legs.

No no no! the colours moaned.

But that was what happened. He was a prince "... and a wolf!"

Mina sucked in her lips, not wanting to tell the story that was happening in her head. How he smashed the princess on the floor again and again till her head bounced and she broke.

No! the colours shouted. That wasn't the right story! Not about a princess who was a dead doll!

Mina turned up the sound on the TV but couldn't get it loud enough to stop the story in her head. She put her hoop on the shelf and pushed herself off the sofa. Elvis would keep the wolf away. Elvis in his blue sway shoes.

*

Val had convened an opening night post-mortem, which Iris thought sounded grim but Bruno said was standard. You don't have to come, he said. The costumes were perfect. I'll bet there were a few professionals in the audience who noticed. You'll get some enquiries, wait and see. Iris lifted crossed fingers. Hope so, she said.

She was coming to the dance again this evening, but sitting farther back this time so she could see the stage properly. She and Bruno were going to meet for pad thai before the show. He said that tonight they should join the gang for a drink. You know they'll guess about us, he said. Is it a secret? she asked. Not as far as I'm concerned, he said. But then he stroked a finger along her forearm. I hate to ask, but do you mind not telling Mina? She won't like you occupying what she considers to be Gabriela's place. It'll be easier if she doesn't know about us just yet. Iris said she understood he had to consider Mina's reaction. He gave her such a grateful look. Gabriela always minded, he said. She felt I put Mina's needs first. Then he shook his head. Sorry, our first morning together and I'm talking about my ex. Not true, Iris said. We're talking about Mina — and you don't have to apologize. What she heard between the lines was that he appreciated she wasn't like Gabriela.

Yesterday evening and this morning had been perfect. Practical, responsible Bruno had revealed himself to be a ready and attentive lover. She'd guessed they would click, but you never knew until you got naked together. And yeah, you bet that mattered. She'd never understood people who thought that sex was optional.

She was still smiling to herself when she remembered the false note from yesterday evening. When Mina took off her coat, she was wearing the dress Iris had made her to go to the wedding with Pierre. Where was the new dress? She'd shirred the waist, which took some time, so it would fit yet stretch. The wine-red fabric, streaked with cream, was a little flamboyant, but not too loud. She thought of it as the first in the Philomena line. But Mina hadn't worn it. When Iris asked why, she got a blank look. When she asked again in the taxi, taking her home, Mina turned her face to the window and ignored her. Iris knew her well enough by now to understand that something had happened. Bruno was probably the only one who would be able to puzzle it out, but what if Mina got in trouble then? Iris didn't want that. She couldn't have Mina upset with her now.

But what had happened with the dress? Iris was a first-class couturière. She'd designed and made a dress specifically for Mina, who had clearly chosen not to wear it. Iris couldn't help but feel snubbed.

*

Gabriela pressed the phone to her ear, but it didn't help her understand what Mina was saying. Something about a wolf? She wasn't even sure the word was wolf. And a doll? Mina was very upset about the doll.

Gabriela kept asking questions until she finally understood that Mina had gone to Bruno's new dance. After she hung up, she looked online for a review. The critic praised the haunting rendering of isolation and homelessness. Another review mentioned the brilliance of using a doll as object/symbol.

Gabriela scrolled and clicked. What had been done to the doll? She stopped at an image of two dancers seeming about to rip a doll apart. Had Bruno left Mina by herself in the front row where she liked to sit, so close to violence being enacted right in front of her? That didn't sound like something he would do.

She had patients waiting and couldn't think about this now. Lunch was a quick sandwich she'd made at home. She bought herself a drink and returned to her office. She wished Marie-Paule hadn't taken the day off. She needed advice. She reached for the phone. Put it down again. She did not want to talk to Bruno. But for Mina's sake, she had to.

"Allô?"

"It's Gabriela. I talked with Mina this morning."

"Is something—"

"Something upset her about the dance you took her to— something about a doll and maybe a wolf. I read the reviews, Bruno. They talk about the violence. Was that a good idea to bring Mina? Don't you remember how recently she was attacked?"

"There was no wolf—"

"There was violence, right?"

He didn't answer.

"I can't believe you took her."

"And why is this your concern?"

"Because it doesn't sound like you're concerned and she's upset."

"She told me she liked the dance."

"Don't be so simplistic. Emotional responses work at different levels. You need to pay more attention."

"According to you," his voice was cold, "I pay too much attention. You should make up your mind what you're accusing me of."

"Stop it. This isn't about you and me. I'm telling you Mina is upset."

"Fine, I'll talk to her. Are you finished now? I have things to do."

She hung up. Her cheeks were hot. She told him what she felt she had to, but that wasn't how she wanted the conversation to go.

*

Bruno let the phone clatter onto the coffee table. Gabriela had nerve! She'd wanted out of his life so why didn't she stay out? Where did she get off, calling to lecture him when it suited her?

He ground his teeth. Because he'd known Mina shouldn't come to this dance.

Back in the kitchen, he stared at the cutting board, trying to remember what he'd been about to do. Tonight was the first free night after the weekend run and he'd invited Iris for supper.

Damn! He strode back to the living room, grabbed the phone, and called Mina.

"Yeah?"

"It's me. How are you?"

"F-f-fine."

"You talked to Gabriela?"

"Yeah?" Always that hopeful inflection when Gabriela was mentioned.

"Did you tell her you didn't like the dance?"

"No."

"You liked it?"

"Yeah."

"Were you upset by anything?"

"La musique!"

"You told me. But maybe the dance was too rough for you? Did all the banging around and kicking upset you?"

"My p-p-program," she said.

He looked at the clock. Her soap operas. "Sorry, I didn't look at the time."

"D'okay. Bye."

She must have said something to Gabriela. Gabriela wouldn't have called otherwise. Wasn't that just perfect though? His sister was confiding in his ex, but not him.

5

Iris was stitching Mina's embroidery onto squares of linen. She'd considered raw silk for its rich look and feel, but it was heavy and she didn't want the border to compete with the texture of the embroidery. Cream linen was simple. She'd finished the edges of the squares with an overlock stitch, also in cream. By hand, of course. Everything by hand.

Mina was still only letting her have older work, even though Iris kept hinting that she would love certain pieces she'd seen Mina make and where she could legitimately say that she'd supplied her with the thread. Although even these older pieces made with dollar-store thread demonstrated Mina's astounding flair with colour and design.

As Iris stitched, she imagined talking to a gallery owner or a journalist about Mina. She'd been asking Bruno, who'd been telling her fabulous stories. One was the time he went to Mina's place and found her table full of fluffy plugs with a string attached that he finally realized were tampons. Mina had bent, mangled, and pulled them apart. She'd seen them on TV and wanted to know what they were. He told her she didn't need them because of the operation she'd had. That too, the operation. Doctors had actually said Mina should be sterilized. Bruno could still hardly believe it, though he admitted it was easier for him not to have to deal with periods and contraception. He told Iris about the time Mina snatched the bus driver's keys, how for a few months she wore a plastic stethoscope because she believed it made her look like a doctor, about the boyfriend

who got a black eye when he took a cigarette after Mina said not
to. The stories highlighted how she stood up for herself, her curios-
ity and inventiveness, her bold self-image. Iris toyed with trying to
find out more about the church restoration relatives in Austria, but
she decided they were best left in the shadows. Let Mina shine on
her own.

When Iris placed the square, framed in linen, on the stack she'd
already stitched, she saw how the layered rectangles resembled the
pages of a large book. What if she stitched them together along one
side like a binding? A person could leaf through the pages one by
one, appreciating each embroidery on its own — as Jenny had suggested. Iris could call it an art book. Not a book about art but made
with art. She liked that idea. She liked it a lot.

She'd scoured the internet for everything on Judith Scott she
could find. Over and over she watched the videos of Judith creating a textile sculpture. Iris would do the same with Mina: film
her enthroned on her sofa, surrounded by her tchotchkes, and
embroidering. There would be close-ups of her hand stitching and
the expectant stillness that came over her face when she chose a
new colour. Maybe they could even film a re-enactment of how she
and Mina had met. Iris walking through the park and from a distance seeing a woman who was sewing, getting closer and realizing
the woman held an embroidery hoop, and then even closer and
seeing what she was creating. Although for that video she would
have Mina stitching one of her abstracts, not a boyfriend's name.
The many decals embroidered with her ex-boyfriends' names were
a good story, but they weren't art.

Or … maybe they were. There seemed to be a lot included under
the umbrella of *outsider art* once a person was recognized as an artist.
The Down Syndrome angle couldn't be more timely. Get ready, world,
Iris thought, for Philomena Corneau!

*

Mina glared at the phone. Bruno never agreed to anything when she asked him on the phone, but he hadn't come to see her yesterday or the day before. He wasn't coming every day like he used to. Mama had said he would always, always, always be there for her. Mama should have told him too!

She punched in his numbers, saying each one out loud so it stayed where it was supposed to. That was another thing she wanted, a phone she could take with her everywhere. She tried it with this phone, putting it in her bag and going to the dollar store, but it didn't work when she tried to call Bruno from there. It needed to be a flat phone like Gabriela and Iris had.

When Bruno answered, she said what you were supposed to say to start talking. "S-s-something to tell you."

"Why else would you call?"

She didn't like when he used that voice. "I need blinds."

"Need isn't the same as want. We've had this discussion before. You don't need blinds because you have curtains."

"Blinds are b-b-better."

"Blinds are easier to break, so it's actually better for you to have curtains. We got you brand new curtains just last year. Have you forgotten?"

"Don't like them."

"You liked them when you picked them. We went to the store together and you chose the fabric. Besides, you don't have the money to buy curtains one year and blinds the next."

She couldn't say anything because Bruno wasn't supposed to know, but she *did* have money. Lots and lots of it now that Iris was giving her $35 every Tuesday and Friday. But that was her money, not Bruno's. He was supposed to buy what she needed for her apartment.

She started again. "Blinds—"

"No blinds."

"My windows—"

"Your windows are fine. You have curtains. There's nothing wrong with them. I have to go now, okay?"

It wasn't d'okay but he still hung up. She sat staring at her windows where she wanted to have blinds. The tops of the curtains were very high up. If she got on a chair, she might fall. She kept staring until she knew what to do.

Mouth set, she walked across to the windows. Grabbed a big handful of curtains and tugged. When she tugged again, even harder, things on the windowsill got knocked and fell to the floor. Something broke. Too bad. Tit for tat. It was Bruno's fault. She bunched her fists in the fabric and yanked as hard as she could.

*

Bruno lifted the lid of the pot. The rice was almost ready. Iris was sitting cross-legged on the chair she'd brought into the kitchen from the dining room. She had a glass of wine and he was telling her about the meeting with Val that afternoon. They would be taking the show to Quebec City and Sherbrooke in early June, but Val had gotten a booking in Ottawa next week, so they had to discuss furniture and props more quickly than planned. The dolls were obviously coming with them, but what about the table? They couldn't count on the venue having one the correct height and length for Tandi to roll across. He was quickly building one with folding legs and hinges that locked. Everything, as well as the four of them, had to fit in a van.

"I thought it would be fun for you to come too," he said, "but there won't be room."

"That's okay. I've got a few commissions with deadlines. It always happens like this. One client hears that another is having a dress made for a dinner and so she wants one too. I've got this other client who's just discovered gaucho pants and wants five pairs, but each with a variation."

"You mean those divided skirts? What can you do with that?"

"Slash pockets, knife pleats, flat front, basque waist, box pleats ... Is that five?" She flourished her wine glass.

The way Iris talked about her clients, he could understand why she wanted to take her talents elsewhere, but did she understand that dancers, actors, and performers would be even more entitled and demanding? The britches and little apron she'd made for them were great, but she was lucky that everyone approved of them. Val might have declared the strips of fur were too fussy or Mathieu might have decided the britches impossible to dance in.

"You're pretty busy then," he said.

"Why, what's up?"

He slid the turbot fillets under the broiler. "I wondered if you could look in on Mina while I'm gone."

"I see her every couple of days. You know that."

"This would be a little more involved. I need someone available if she thinks she's got an emergency — which doesn't mean that it will be an emergency, but she'll panic if she doesn't have someone to call."

"That's fine, Bruno. It's not a problem."

"Thanks. I really mean it. I'll only be gone for a couple of nights. I'll have to give your number to the social worker too — as a contact. She might call you but it won't be anything. She comes up with wacky stuff, wackier even than Mina sometimes. Her latest thing ..." He took a big swallow of wine as if needing to brace himself.

"Yeah?"

"Mina has started wearing two watches. I don't know if you noticed. I didn't. But the social worker is turning it into a crisis. She wants her to stop."

"But that's not her business."

"She says she wants Mina to look *normal.*"

Iris guffawed. "Whatever that is."

"Exactly." He appreciated that Iris understood about Mina — understood, too, how others often didn't understand. He liked that he could talk to her. Not just about Mina, but about work as well.

She was curious about the production aspect of dance and wanted to be more involved.

There were other gratifying surprises that he hadn't expected. Her small, lean body that looked boyish when clothed was compellingly seductive when naked. She was the most energetic lover he'd ever had, not just with her body. She used the whole bed — or wherever it was they happened to be. He'd obviously had sex in the shower before but never as with Iris. Yesterday he found her rifling through his closet. A belt, she muttered, a tie, something... That too was new for him.

Thinking about Iris and sex made him want to shuck his jeans on the spot. Fish under the broiler, be damned. But when she saw how he was looking at her, she wagged a finger. "Supper first. No dessert till you've eaten your vegetables."

"No bending the rules?"

"Nope. You're too good a cook. If you were just heating up a can of ravioli, I wouldn't care." And in another tone, "So you haven't told me yet, did Val say anything about the next dance you'll be doing?"

"She hasn't decided yet, but do you know Pied Gauche up on St. Laurent? They're hosting an evening of short pieces, max five minutes. We might do one. The thing is that short doesn't mean easy."

"Is it worth it then, for only five minutes?"

"Depends on who else they've got lined up. It could be a really interesting evening to be involved in. Val might not choreograph a new piece either. She could chop something from the repertoire."

"But you'll still need costumes, right?"

"Depends on what we do."

"Because when I said I was busy, I didn't mean I was too busy to design costumes. I'll always make time for that. For you or someone else — in case someone asks."

"Noted," he promised.

He opened the oven door to check the fish under the broiler. "Just about ready. How about you take our glasses to the table?"

*

Mina dragged the pink and green feathers along the railing. This was a stupid job. Wood that got dusty. Statues with dead eyes. One of her hands itched inside the glove. She'd shown the pharmacist who gave her a tube of what he called unguent to make the itching feel better, but she'd finished the tube and she couldn't see him behind the counter anymore. She told another pharmacist, saying the word as well as she could, but nobody knew what rongan was. She asked Bruno to get her rongan but he didn't know either. He asked what it was for but she didn't want to show him her hand. Rongan! she said. Why did no one understand?

Her hand itched too much. Her feet hurt. It was too hard standing up. Why was Bruno always making her work? Whenever a job ended, he found another one. Mama never made her work. Mama would have got her blinds. Mama loved her. She moaned out loud. She was too full of feeling upset. She hitched herself onto a pew and jutted out her bottom lip.

There were steps and Sister slid onto the pew and put her arm around her. "Qu'est-ce qu'il y a, ma chérie?" Sister held her so close that she could smell the soap in her clothes. "What's got you upset, my dear?"

"Feet hurt," she blurted. "My hand."

Sister stroked her head and brushed the hair from her face. Cupped her cheek and cuddled her close. "There, there. Don't be upset."

Close like this was nice. The squish of Sister's titties against her face. A small giggle rising in her throat.

"If the work is too much for you, my dear, you don't have to keep dusting. We'll get one of the parishioners. You don't have to come here to work, you can just visit the church. Any time, my dear. You know you can always come in here to tell God your thoughts."

Mina breathed in Sister's good smell. It was lovely sitting with her like this.

"You're such a sweet child. You know you belong to God, don't you?"

Sister's hand on her neck and down her back was giving her a shiver of pleasure. She would have climbed onto Sister's lap if she could, but she was too big! That made another giggle in her throat.

"God loves you. Don't ever forget that, my dear."

Mina put a hand on Sister's titty. It was soft like her own. She squeezed gently.

Sister yanked herself away. "What are you doing?"

"Titty."

"Ti—" Sister gaped. "You can't touch people like that, did no one ever tell you? It's a sin!" She was standing now, tugging her skirt straight, mouth a stern line.

Why was she angry? It had been so nice sitting together and being hugged.

"I'll call your social worker and tell her this work is too hard for you. I'm sure she'll be able to find something else for you to do. I have to get back to the vestry now. If you're finished, you can go. There won't be a muffin today. That probably wasn't such a good idea. Thank you for all you've done for the church. Goodbye, Philomena."

Not getting a muffin wasn't nice, but Mina was glad she didn't have to come to the church again. A big, boring, empty place that kept getting dusty.

*

The budding greenery on the trees was so fresh, the sky so blue, that Bruno took the longer route to Mina's place, walking past the community garden where he could see the winter garlic like rows of rabbit's ears pushing up through the soil. A woman in a turquoise sari was raking her plot. On a day like this his mother would have been in her boots in the garden, deciding what she would plant where.

Iris had wanted to come along. Why couldn't Bruno say that she was his friend the way she was Mina's? But Bruno knew Mina might

sense something and get upset — and could he please not have a
scene on his birthday. He told Iris that they would celebrate when he
got home. This, taking Mina out for supper, was how they did birthdays since their mother was gone. He took Mina out for her birthday
and he took her out for his. It wouldn't be a late night. He would be
home before eight.

Mina was waiting on the sidewalk, her red fleece snug around her
beach ball girth, her too-long sleeves rolled into bulky hems. Today
she wore a pink polka-dot sunhat. As soon as she saw him, she began
singing. "Bonne fête à Bruno! Bonne fête à Bruno! Bonne fête, bonne
fête! Bonne fête à Bruno!" And taking another huge breath, she
launched into English. "Happy birthday to you! Happy birthday to
you! Happy birthday to Bruno! Happy birthday to you!" Interesting,
he thought, how she didn't stammer when she sang.

He gave her shoulders a quick squeeze. "Thanks, Mina."

She handed him the plastic bag she was holding. "Your cadeau."

Inside the bag was a soft rectangle wrapped in Christmas paper.
And though he knew the answer, he still asked, because it was part
of the birthday routine. "Can I open it now?"

"No! The restaurant!"

Mina never used to give him presents, but after their mother
died, she started. It was never more than a gewgaw she'd bought at
the dollar store, but he was touched that she'd taken on what she
seemed to think a maternal duty.

"How old now?" she asked. Another ritual question. She wasn't
asking because she didn't know, but to check if he did.

"Let me see. I was forty-six last year, so now I must be ..."

"Forty-seven!"

"Getting old, aren't I?"

"In June I'm thirty-nine!"

"You're catching up to me." Every year she triumphed when she
was a number closer, except then he had another birthday and she
fell behind again.

"What do you think," he asked, "should we take a cab to the restaurant?"

She grinned up at him from under her brim. Today's button was the King of Rock 'n' Roll.

"Give me your keys and I'll run into your apartment to call a cab."

She started to unzip her purse and then stopped. "I locked the d-d-door."

"I hope you did. You're supposed to when you go out. That's why I'm asking for your keys."

She gripped her purse closer.

"What's in your apartment?"

"Nothing."

Obviously there was and it was something he wasn't going to like. He knew he should look, but it was his birthday.

They walked at a slow pace to Wellington where he flagged a cab. He held the back door open for her and sat in front with the cabby. "St. Henri," he said.

"You take care of her?" The man had a Caribbean accent.

"She's my sister."

"I see her all over the Pointe and in Verdun."

People often told Bruno that they'd seen her. She was hard to miss — the short, round fact of her, the bright clothes she wore, her unwavering conviction that she was important.

"We had one like that back home."

Bruno didn't ask *like what*. The man seemed to mean it kindly.

"Her, that one back home, she did okay." The cabby glanced in his rear-view mirror at Mina. More quietly he added, "But she didn't live long, maybe thirty."

"My sister's almost forty." His mother had told him the doctors said she wasn't likely to live past forty, but look at her, still healthy and making mischief.

"Bruno," she called from the back seat.

"Yeah?"

"What are you saying about me?"

"How old you are."

She gave a contented sniff.

The cabby smacked his palm on the steering wheel. "Nothing gets past her, does it?"

"The problem is what she tries to get past me."

Bruno had wondered if returning to the diner where he'd told her about Gabriela might upset her all over again. Maybe, maybe not. He chose a diner farther down the block. The same Arborite tables, the same greasy smells, the same lights bright enough to perform surgery. As they made their way to a booth, he saw a signed and framed poster of Céline Dion. Here? He doubted it, but he said, "Look who ate here." Mina wanted to sit facing it.

The menu was standard, and as always she would have a club sandwich with frîtes, but she still pored over the photos of spaghetti and hot chicken.

When the waitress came, she looked to him for Mina's order. "Ask her," he said. "How should I know what she wants?"

As they waited for their food, Mina recounted her goings-on. What she'd eaten lately that she liked. That cigarettes had gone up in price. That margarine was too hard to open. And as if challenging him to object, she said that Gabriela called her every Monday and Thursday at ten o'clock.

"Iris comes to see you too, doesn't she?"

Her expression twitched.

What did that mean? But he said only, "Aren't you lucky to have so many good friends?"

"Gabriela est ma belle-coeur!"

"And Iris? Will she ever be?"

"No." Prompt and decisive.

"She's really nice to you, Mina. She's been bringing you thread all this time. And she's taking down your garbage, which I don't think she should and she doesn't have to, but she is."

The chin again. Mouth clamped.

"Hey," he said. "Did you forget? It's my birthday."

She immediately beamed at him. No bad moods on birthdays! Birthdays were holy.

The waitress arrived with their heaped plates and he reached for the ketchup. Mina waited with a frîte in hand, eyes riveted on the bottle. He smacked and too much ketchup shot out, but she didn't mind. She would eat it all.

"What's this I hear about your job at the church? Faiza said the nun doesn't need you anymore. Did you get rid of the dust forever and ever?"

Mina grasped one of the tricky triangles of sandwich.

"I hope you didn't fight with the nun?"

No reaction. Food was more important.

"I guess it doesn't matter. That wasn't a good job for you. The only person you saw was the nun. You should be with a group so you can mingle. How else are you going to find a new boyfriend?"

She gave a muffled hmmph, eyebrows raised.

He waited for her to finish chewing and finally she said, "No more p-p-prince."

"Pierre was the only one who ever hurt you. You liked ..." He wasn't actually sure. Did she like the boyfriends or only having them? If she'd decided she no longer wanted one, why was he pushing it? Even if they didn't hurt her, they trailed other complications. The one who convinced her to dye her hair blond and she ended up with orange. How long had that taken to grow out? The one who began every sentence with D'ya know? until Mina started saying it too. The one who emptied her kitchen cupboards to reorganize them like at his mom's house, but then left the boxes and cans his mom didn't stock on the floor. The one — no, he stopped himself from remembering that one.

"Don't worry about the church," he said. "I'll talk to Faiza about finding another job."

"I don't w-w-want to work."

"And I don't want you being home all the time. It's not good for you. Mina —?" He'd just noticed her wrist. The flesh was puffy around the straps of her watches, the skin red. "What's wrong with your hand?"

She dropped her sandwich, letting it fall apart on her plate, and hid her hand under the table.

"Let me see." When she didn't, he insisted, "Show me."

Her wrist was so swollen that it looked throttled by her watches. "Doesn't that hurt?"

"Ça gratte."

"Itching is a kind of hurt. This looks like a rash, a very bad rash. You need to see the doctor. I don't think you should be wearing a watch."

"Two watches now!"

"I don't care if you wear three watches — but not right now. Not till the rash goes away. You don't want it spreading up your arm. Do you have it anywhere else?"

"No." She strategized another triangle of sandwich, clamping it so tightly that mayonnaise squeezed out and dripped over her fingers.

"Listen to me. You don't have to take your watches off this minute in the restaurant, but when you get home, you take them off until you've seen the doctor. And you don't wear them again till the doctor says it's okay." How could Faiza complain about Mina wearing two watches and not see her wrist looked like a sausage?

Mina didn't look at him. How could he convince her? "Do you … do you remember my book of fairy tales when we were kids? There was a story I used to read you about a girl with no hands." He couldn't remember why she'd lost her hands, but he remembered the ink drawing of a girl standing under a tree laden with pears. She'd tipped back her head to bite into one that hung within reach of her mouth. The sleeves of her gown hung empty because she had no hands.

Mina stopped chewing, staring before her.

"Do you remember the story?"

"… Yeah."

"How did it go?" He waited but she said nothing. It was as if the story was playing itself out in her mind and she assumed he could tune in.

He knocked on the table to recall her attention. "Just bear in mind it can happen that a person loses her hands, and that rash you've got looks nasty. I'll call Faiza to get you a doctor's appointment ASAP. In the meantime, no watches. Not even one." But until a doctor in a white lab coat said so, he knew she wouldn't listen.

He'd finished his meal. She always took longer, eating one fry at a time and only half her sandwich. She liked taking the other half home to have for lunch the next day.

"Can I open my present now?" he asked.

"After you s-s-sing."

It was absurd but for lack of family, he had to sing to himself. Softly he began, "Happy birthday to me! Happy birthday to me!"

Mina sang with him. A woman at a nearby table joined in, then two waitresses, and even two teenage girls having burgers with their boyfriends. The boyfriends lowered their heads, sliding exasperated, embarrassed looks at each other. Everyone smiled at Mina, and at the last moment a waitress scurried to their table, one hand protecting the flame of a candle on a piece of pie she set before Mina who blew it out.

"Bonne fête!" the waitress cried.

"Him!" Mina pointed at Bruno.

The waitress looked puzzled but he didn't explain.

"You can have the pie," he told Mina. She didn't object that she was dibète. On birthdays dibète was ignored.

He examined his gift from all sides to find a spot that hadn't been shellacked with tape. He finally found an edge and picked at it with a fingernail. She snuffled, delighted by the hard time he was having. A present was supposed to be hidden.

He finally freed enough paper that he could tear it. That too: a package was supposed to be eviscerated. Opening a present *should* be dramatic.

Out fell a rectangle of blue knitting. "Thank you." He squeezed it. "It's very nice. It's ... ah ... it's ..."

"A scarf!"

He slung it around his neck. The two ends only just met at his collarbone. She seemed not to notice that it was too short. "Great, Mina, I love it. I'll have it for next winter." She looked pleased. He kept it on but stuffed the paper in the bag. She'd never before given him knitting. Was she getting sentimental? The cabby had reminded him that in Down Syndrome years she was already getting old. But look at her, no grey hair, her appetite in no way diminished, as feisty as ever. The only sign that she was slowing down was her unwilling-ness to be on her feet too long—though that could also be laziness. She never had a problem getting to the dollar store.

With dainty deliberation Mina popped the last frite in her mouth. He asked the waitress to package the leftover sandwich and the pie.

On the sidewalk Mina looked up and down the street, curious about these new stores she wasn't familiar with. Second-hand furni-ture with wooden tables and dressers. A pet store with a kitten asleep on a cushion in the window. She knocked on the glass and cooed but it didn't wake. The lights of a pharmacy.

"Yeah!" Her face brightened.

"Yes?" He knew what was coming.

"La pharmacie."

"Let me guess, you need something?"

She blinked. She either didn't want to say or she didn't actually need anything but didn't want to miss the opportunity.

"I have an idea. Because you gave me a present, how about I give you one too. Does that sound fair?"

She beetled down the aisles ahead of him, shockingly fast when she wanted to be. What would she pick? In this respect, she wasn't calculating. She could want a trinket with as much fervour as a luxury foot massage bath. She slowed and snatched up a red toiletry kit.

"Do you know what that's for?" he asked.

"To p-p-put things."

"Okay, if that's what you want, it's your gift on my birthday."

In the taxi he held the box with her sandwich and pie. She was examining the many pockets of her new bag. He got out with her at her building and waited as she grabbed the railing to hoist herself up the steps. It didn't use to be so hard for her. What if she fell? Was this safe? Again he recalled the cabby's words.

In the entrance she flipped open her purse and with great panache pulled out her keys that dangled from a glittery fob he hadn't seen before.

"Is that new?"

She unlocked the lobby door and was heading down the hallway on autopilot, the key to her apartment door ready to shoot into the lock, when abruptly she stopped. "You c-c-can't come."

"Why can't I?"

Eyes lowered. Stubborn silence.

He'd forgotten how she hadn't wanted him to come in earlier. This was going to be bad. "Unlock the door, Mina."

She didn't move.

"I said unlock it. Now."

She jabbed her key into the lock and banged the door open. Over her head he saw the building across the street. The long large windows. The man who lived there watching TV. Why was he seeing a man watching TV? Shit. "Where are your curtains?"

"G-g-gone."

"They're not gone. You did something to them. Where are they?"

She pulled off her hat, pushed herself up onto the sofa, and ignored him.

"You might as well tell me. I'm going to find them." Though he'd never found anything she'd made disappear. Not when they were kids, not when they were older, not even within the small space of her apartment.

He dropped to his knees and peered under the sofa and then the bed. In the kitchen he opened the cupboards. He didn't normally look in her closets, but he was too pissed with her. Even on his birthday! Could he never get a break? He tried to shove aside hangers that were too packed together to shove aside. Was he going to have to dump out her bags?

She sat, scowling. She hated when he looked through her things. He didn't like doing it either. And to what end? They both knew he wasn't going to find those curtains.

*

Iris reached for the flat-tipped pointer to poke into the corners of the collar she'd turned inside-out. And though she knew the edges and the angles of the corners matched, she still lined them up to check. Because that was how you excelled at what you did.

Still. Collars. Not what she wanted to be doing for the rest of her life. But so far, no other dance or theatre groups had inquired about costumes. Mina too — what was going on with her? The last two pieces of embroidery she'd sold Iris were frankly mediocre. Iris couldn't include them in the art book, though of course she kept them. Mina had made them and if she became famous, anything would sell.

When the phone rang, she hoped it was Bruno. She could use some cheering up. But it was Jenny. "Hi." She put it on speaker so she could keep basting.

"What are you up to?"

"Sewing. What else?"

"Not hanging out with lover boy?"

"We're not a tandem bicycle."

"That's not what it sounds like when you talk about him. Bruno this, Bruno that ..."

"Don't exaggerate."

"You don't hear yourself. You are *smitten*."

"Stop it."

"What I don't understand is how much you like this guy and you're keeping secrets about his sister."

Iris clucked her tongue. "It isn't a secret. I'll tell him when I've arranged everything."

"And what if, when you finally tell him, he doesn't like it?"

"What's there not to like? I told you, as far as he's concerned, her embroidery is no different from her word puzzles or her soap operas. He thinks it's how she keeps busy, that's all."

"But this isn't about embroidery, Iris. You're planning to launch her into something that will change her life. He might not agree with that."

"*Maybe* change her life. We don't know that yet."

"You're hoping it will. And if it does, this won't just be between you and her anymore. What if when he finds out, he thinks you went behind his back — and then you can forget about you and him."

"He's not like that. He wants her to make her own decisions."

"Perfect. So tell him she's made a decision. But you have to tell him, Iris. If you're thinking about having any kind of relationship with him, you have to be straight from the start."

Iris rolled her eyes at her faithful group of tailors' dummies. Never much to say for themselves but at least they didn't criticize. "Did you call to lecture me?"

"I called because I wondered if you're spending every night with lover boy or if you might be available to go to a movie with your friend who only has your best interests at heart."

Iris smirked. "Sure."

They agreed where they would meet the next day. Iris knew she would get another speech on relationships, but Jenny was also the only person she could confide in.

*

Mina grabbed the plastic in both fists and ripped, upending the slide of pages. On the floor by her feet were the other Publisacs. She only had to open one. The others were exactly the same. When she first moved here, she used to take several bags and open each one. Finally she figured it out. The new Publisacs that were delivered on Thursday had specials that were different from last week — but they were all the same as this week. Bruno never explained that to her. She had to work it out herself. He only complained when she cut out all the pictures. You only have to show me one, he said. Look ... four, five, six, seven, eight footstools! You don't have to show me eight times. Since then, she knew she only needed one Publisac. The others were for the neighbours. *If* she wanted the neighbours to have them, which right now she didn't.

She kept the pictures of what she wanted Bruno to buy in a basket. Sometimes she stuck a shiny red heart on the picture to show she *really* wanted it. But that didn't mean he would get it. Shiny red hearts meant nothing to Bruno. When she showed him the picture of the blinds, he wouldn't even look. He said no was no, but then Faiza came and saw there was nothing on the windows, and that wasn't right because now people could see in.

Mina knew that! Go tell Bruno.

He was still asking what she'd done with the curtains. Too bad! Tit for tat. The curtains were gone.

She tapped her finger on the picture of a lamp. It would be perfect for knitting. Bruno would say he just bought her a lamp but this one was better. She snipped it out and added it to the basket.

And here ... a hammer! She needed a hammer but they didn't have one at the dollar store, the grocery store, or the pharmacy. Bruno had one in the toolbox but it was too high on the shelf in her closet. She'd jabbed at the toolbox with the broom handle but couldn't make it fall down. She cut out the picture of the hammer but didn't put it in the basket because Bruno couldn't know about the hammer.

She checked the time to see if it was when she used to go to the church to dust. She wore her watches on the other arm now. She didn't like them there but she had to put the cream the doctor gave her on her sick arm. The new arm had started to itch but she had to wear her watches.

She still had the number for the phone in the priest's room. On the other end it rang twice, then Sister answered. "Allô … Allô? Who is there? … Allô? Why do you keep calling?"

Mina closed her mouth tight so no noise escaped, but after Sister smashed down the phone, she laughed out loud. It was such fun to make people frightened.

*

Bruno and Iris lay head to toe on the bed, which was how they'd ended up. He stretched an arm like a wing, wondering how he could feel so replete and emptied at the same time.

Iris plumped a pillow behind her head and set her foot on his chest. "Massage."

"Please?" he prompted.

She jiggled her foot. "Massage."

He began to squeeze and rub it.

Lazily she said, "Why do you think Mina wants a hammer?"

He heard and didn't hear. Was she really talking about Mina? Gabriela had said he was too involved in Mina's life, but he'd never talked about her while floating on a postcoital high. But now that Iris had said it, it was in his head. "What about a hammer?"

"She showed me an ad for a hammer and asked me to buy it for her."

"Don't, okay?"

"I wasn't going to."

"She's probably got something broken she thinks she can fix. She won't ask me because we're at a standoff about the curtains."

"What are you going to do about that?"

"I don't have any choice. I have to get her blinds. Ah … why are we talking about Mina?" He squeezed her foot a little harder than he had to.

"Ow." She jerked her foot.

"Mm-mm. Nice view I've got from here …"

She let her knee fall open. Tilted her pelvis a little. Watched him.

He rubbed his thumb along her arch until she pulled her foot away and crawled up the length of his body to meet him.

*

The girl married a rabbit but the rabbit was a bad prince. He hit her! Mina didn't want to tell this story but it was in her head and it was making her remember the dance. And Pierre.

The rabbit was like a wolf. It did bad sex. "Bad," she told the colours. So bad that the shape they were making was full of teeth. Jagged ugly wolf teeth! When she touched the stitches, she could feel their terror shivering against her fingers.

"Wait," she said. Because in the story the girl wasn't alone. She had a doll who helped her. "A f-f-friend." Better than a friend. A doll was like Gabriela who was her belle-coeur.

Not like Iris who acted nice and did things for her, but was always looking. Her eyes were too hungry, her hands too greedy. But Iris brought her thread and now she gave her $35 every Tuesday and Friday. $35 and $35 was $70. With Bruno's $20 that was $90! She'd put the tens and the twenties and the fives on the table and counted them again and again, and every time she got $90. She was rich like people on TV and Bruno didn't even know!

The tail of her thread was short now and she needed another colour. She stared at the colours to see which wanted to come next — when her eye caught a movement on the wall. A spider! She stuck her needle in the pincushion and slid off the sofa fast-fast but already the spider was moving up the wall. She knew what to do, crashing to the kitchen no matter what she knocked over because she had to get that spider! Broom in the air swiping back and forth and back — and bang! Mama's angel flew, cracked against the other wall, and —

Mina gaped in shock. The angel lay on the floor against the wall. The curled flip of its golden wing broken off. Grief stabbed her chest. "Mama!" she bawled. "M-m-maaa-m-m-ma!"

She fumbled for the phone and dialled.

"Allô."

"Mama's a-a-a-angel!" she sobbed.

"What about the angel?"

"S-s-s-s —" She stopped. "Broken!"

"The angel is broken?"

"Mama!"

"Isn't it on the wall?"

"No!"

"I can't believe it. Mina, what the —"

"Brisé! C'est brisé! C'est b-b-b-b —"

"Okay, okay, stop crying. I'm coming."

6

The river was high, the water churned and brown, the footpath muddy. After squishing around one yawning puddle and then another, Iris climbed the slope to the bike path again. She wasn't in a meandering mood. She needed to walk. Walk fast.

She'd made a list of art galleries and marked the ones most likely to exhibit fibre and/or outsider art. She prepared a few sentences of introduction and would have called Jenny to rehearse them, but Jenny wouldn't stop being such a pain about Bruno. Bruno was going to be delighted. He always said people didn't do Mina justice. Well, wait till he heard that Iris had arranged for Mina to have an art show!

This morning, with her agenda open before her, Iris called the first gallery on the list. Aim high, she told herself. Think positive! The woman who answered the phone listened for a moment, then said she wasn't familiar with Philomena Corneau's work. Where had she exhibited? Iris said she hadn't yet. The woman said they might be interested at some point in the future, but at the moment they were booked two years in advance and weren't considering any new portfolios. Iris had persisted. The woman was firm. Thank you, no.

Iris called the next number. Then the next. Each time she was asked where the artist had exhibited, followed by the same pat, uncompromising response.

She'd thought the challenge had been getting her hands on Mina's embroideries. From there, she'd assumed she could get them into the world. She hadn't expected the world to be so hedged with obstacles. Ridiculous obstacles too. Wasn't the art world supposed to want innovative, cutting-edge material? She would never have been successful in her business if her first clients hadn't been willing to give her a try.

She sat at her table, tapping her pencil so hard that the tip broke. She swung off the stool and grabbed her raincoat.

Walk! She needed to walk. Face grim, step after step, until the fresh air cooled her cheeks. A red-winged blackbird twanged from the trees. Sumac cones, still soft and delicate, were pointing from among the spray of leaves.

What had she done to start her business — when all she had was her determination and her sewing machine at the kitchen table of her apartment? She hadn't been polite and shy. She hadn't asked permission. She'd *shown* people what she could do. She went to meetings with bank loan officers wearing a suit she'd designed and sewn herself. Those who knew suits could see the Milanese buttonholes and the pic stitching. She, the loan applicant, was dressed more elegantly than they were. She'd made Jenny's mom a dress to wear to a luncheon at the Mount Royal Tennis Club. The dress showed off the flattering drape of the bias cut design, the loop closings, the smooth edge of the round neckline.

Still stomping along, Iris imagined walking into an art gallery like an ordinary nobody. She would look at the work on the walls. Suss out the space. Then: unzip her portfolio bag and whip out the book of Mina's embroideries. Before anyone could drone on about previous exhibits or being booked years in advance, the gorgeous evidence of Mina's vibrant colours would hook them.

Except — oh! Why had she started with the top three choices on her list? She should have made a trial run with just any gallery to find out what the routine was. Or she should have talked with Jenny's uncle. In exasperation she swung up her arms. Now she'd already exhausted her best chances. Although ... would those galleries remember her phone call? She'd got the impression they hadn't really been listening so much as waiting for her to finish speaking so they could say no.

That was it! She had the goods. She only had to make people see.

She'd marched to where she could see the white line of the rapids. Closer to shore a heron stood on a rock. The sky was low, the underbellies of the clouds like tarnished silver. She felt the spatters of rain starting up again but didn't turn back, striding with a renewed sense of purpose.

*

Gabriela was walking past the brick row houses where she'd lived for five years. She'd wondered if returning to the Pointe would make her sad, reminding her of what she'd lost, but what did that matter now? The upswing of emotion she felt for Daniel was a tonic coursing through her veins. She'd told him she wanted a baby, and although he was taken aback, he hadn't said absolutely no and he hadn't run away. That alone, that openness — whether or not it came to pass — made her feel she could love this man.

Yesterday was her birthday and Mina had insisted on seeing her. It didn't have to be on the very day, but close to the day, definitely. For Mina, a person's birthday was the most important day of the year. Gabriela remembered how she used to call Bruno on their parents' birthdays, even though both had been dead for many years. Bruno said Mina knew they were dead. She'd grieved and wept, kissed their mother's urn and said goodbye. But being dead did not preclude continuing to have birthdays.

Mina was already waiting on the sidewalk. They were going to the little café close by that didn't have muffins, but the owner had always let Gabriela bring a muffin for Mina. Since they'd last come, though, the café had changed ownership. The new barista said that Gabriela couldn't bring baked goods from outside. Gabriela began to explain when Mina interrupted loudly to say *this* was a birthday!

And she could only eat *muffins* because she was dibète! People at the other tables were watching and the barista relented.

Mina had brought Gabriela a cadeau, a long, floppy package, and once she finished her muffin and tea, she said Gabriela could open it. She must have used half a roll of tape and swathes of wrapping paper. She groaned happily, watching Gabriela wrestle with the layers. There was a glimpse of brilliant colour. Something made with yarn. Gabriela finally managed to tear enough of a hole to pull it out. Mina had knit orange, pink, and lavender squares that she'd stitched into a patchwork with thick blue yarn. She'd sewn the patchwork into a ... knit sausage? Ah, a cushion.

"The colours are so you, Mina. I love it."

"T'es ma belle-coeur!"

"And you, my dear, are mine. And you know what? I think this cushion is going to be just what my new armchair needs to make it comfortable."

When they left the café, Mina tucked her hand inside Gabriela's arm and so they walked, Gabriela adjusting her steps to Mina's light-footed sway.

The cushion was the perfect fit for the armchair too, but it was lumpy, probably because Mina hadn't known how to stuff it. Gabriela bought a bag of polyester fibrefill and set about snipping through the tight coil of thick blue yarn that closed the end of the cushion. It wasn't easy. What Mina stitched together was meant to stay together. Gabriela had to be careful not to cut the loops of knitting that made up the outside of the cushion.

From inside she pulled out long, torn strips of thick flowered cotton. Pink roses on a cream background. Where had she seen this before? She and Bruno had taken Mina to choose fabric for curtains. Mina didn't understand how a bolt of fabric could become curtains that would hang in her windows. She told Bruno she didn't want cloth, she wanted curtains. Gabriela finally suggested they get a fabric that Mina liked that was also suitable for curtains.

Now, with a heap of strips on her carpet, she supposed these were the leftover bits.

*

Bruno was driving Mina home. He would drop her off, return the car, then come back to install her blinds. "Remember," he said, "you don't touch the boxes. You leave them alone."

She didn't answer. She was looking out the side window, hand fiddling with the strap on her bag. What was wrong now? She should be happy. She'd gotten the blinds she wanted.

"What is it?"

She muttered as if fed up with having to tolerate an incompetent vassal.

"Spit it out."

"Mama's angel."

"I told you it would take a while. I can't use crazy glue on a four-hundred-year-old carving. I'll have to go to an antique shop or a museum." Or send it to Austria, he thought. Dear Family Who Do Church Restoration! Can you please repair and return? Your Forgotten Relative in Canada. Oh, right, his mother had stolen the angel. Probably not a good idea.

"When?" Mina asked.

"I don't know. Do you want me to hang mine in your apartment till yours is fixed?"

She gaped at him, her expression matched by the orange googly-eyed button on the baseball cap she wore today. The button next to it was the Volkswagen logo.

"Does that mean you do or you don't want it?" he asked.

"I want m-m-mine!"

"So you have to wait for yours to be fixed."

He parked in front of her building and slid the long boxes from the back seat. Mina hoisted herself up the steps and held the door for him. Inside her apartment, as he looked for space to lean the boxes, he wondered why her bedroom door was closed. It was always open so that she could hear the second TV. Then he noticed that there was no doorknob.

"What happened to your doorknob?"

She tossed her baseball cap on the sofa. "Don't know."

"How can you not know? You're the only one who lives here."

He felt with his fingers inside the hole for the lever that worked the latch and pushed the door open. The bedroom looked as it always did. The bed heaped with clothes, pillows, and stuffed animals. The TV in the corner. The walls were such a mirage of photos, posters of Céline Dion, Elvis, and Walt Disney princesses that he didn't at first see the crater the size of a dinner plate smashed through to the concrete. On the floor lay a hammer and chunks of drywall.

"What the fuck, Mina! What are you doing in here?"

She had pushed herself up onto the sofa but refused to look at him. Her mouth trembled with injury. Yelling always made her clam up. He knew that but couldn't stop himself. "Can you give me one good reason why you made a hole? Is it for a drug stash? Is that where you stuffed the curtains? What are you thinking, wrecking the walls? *What* is the matter with you? You know you can't do that kind of thing! You know it's wrong!"

He needed to pace but there was no room in this small apartment that was jam-packed with junk. "I don't even know if I can fix that. If Faiza sees it, she'll have to report it." He wheeled an exasperated hand in the air. "I've told you and I've told you. If you don't behave responsibly, you're going to lose your apartment."

"It's mine!" She glared at him.

"So why are you making holes in the wall? Can you explain that?" He pinched the bridge of his nose and wiped his hand down his face. "I have to return the car. And you know what? I'm not coming back to install your blinds, because to be honest, at this moment, I don't want to do anything for you. I don't care who looks in your windows. If that bothers you so much, you should have left your curtains up."

He turned to go, remembered the hammer, and went to the bedroom to snatch it from the floor. Without saying goodbye, he left, closing the door firmly behind him.

*

Now that Bruno was gone, Mina let out the hurt that was shuddering up her throat, clotting into sobs. He wasn't supposed to shout at her! Mama had told him! It hurt too much when he shouted and his face turned into the wolf, the evil witch, the angry stone head, the bad man in the forest!

Why did he go in the bedroom? He knew that was the rule: you do not open closed doors. If it wasn't your door, stay out! But he always did what he wanted. Always telling her to do this and not that — except *he* did everything he wanted! He was so mean to her! It wasn't her fault, it was his! If he hadn't opened the door, he wouldn't have seen the hole and the hammer. He wasn't supposed to go in her bedroom when the door was closed.

And he'd said he was going to put up her blinds today! If he didn't … She would drag those boxes down to the garbage. Huh! That would serve him right.

It felt good thinking about it, seeing herself doing it in her head and feeling in her hands and arms how she would get rid of the blinds. Except she knew he was going to come back and put them up. He had to. Maybe not today, but tomorrow or the next day. He'd promised Mama he would always help her. That meant he had to.

And then: she had a really good idea — a better idea! So good that it made her stop crying. Because she'd already found out that the hammer didn't work. There was something inside the wall that wouldn't break.

She would have to go to the dollar store for her new idea. It was too late now but she would go tomorrow. She knew exactly which aisle.

*

Bruno had called Iris to ask if she could find out why Mina had made a hole in her wall. Iris thought it was a joke. What do you mean, a hole? A hole, he said, like a hole. In her bedroom wall. Big enough to put two fists through. Okay, don't shout at me, she said. He apologized. He said his patience had just about run out. He was doing some deliveries for one of his antique dealers in Verdun tomorrow and would stop by Iris's studio afterward. She said she'd find out.

The next day, one look at him in her doorway and she said a walk by the river would do him good.

"Did you find out?" he asked.

"Let's walk. I'll tell you."

"Because—" he began.

"How about we walk for a while. Nothing's going to change in the next fifteen minutes."

The footpath by the shore wasn't always wide enough to walk side by side, so they stayed on the bike path, overlooking the water. A light breeze rustled in the poplars.

Iris wondered if he could see the river as she did. "The river looks blue to you, right?"

"More or less, yes."

"Do you see the brown shadows? The current makes them ripple and it looks like otters swimming just under the surface."

After a moment he said, "Otters, yeah."

"I love the river. It's my favourite place to come."

"I'm embarrassed by how many years I've lived only a half-hour walk away and I never come."

"Anytime." She bumped her elbow against him. "Let me know. I'm always up for a walk."

"Okay," he said. "You might as well tell me what Mina's up to."

"To start, she doesn't think she did anything wrong."

"She never does."

"She seems to blame you because you weren't supposed to see

the hole. It's not the hole that's the problem but that you went into her bedroom."

"Of course, big bad me. What else is new? But why did she do it?"

"She wanted to break through to the neighbour's apartment —"

"What?" He stopped walking.

"— so she could shout at her."

Bruno tilted his head to the sky and let out a long groan. "What is it between those two?"

"You know that woman wants her out."

"Forget the neighbour. At this point, the way Mina is behaving, she's going to get herself kicked out all on her own. I can't even say she didn't mean to do it. She didn't just grab a hammer and attack the wall. She asked you to get her one. She must have asked someone else too. Think about it, if it was murder, that's proof of premeditation."

"A hole in the wall isn't murder, Bruno."

"If the neighbour was standing in front of her and Mina had a hammer?"

"Come on, you don't seriously think —"

"There's no telling what she'll do — or what she'll dream up next." He lifted both arms and dropped them. "She always did sneaky things, but this stunt with the hammer is beyond anything she's ever done."

Iris didn't like the way he was making Mina sound conniving or potentially dangerous. A little eccentric, okay, she was an artist. It came with the territory. But not vicious. It was because he was angry and he was exaggerating.

"You know," she said, "I'm amazed she got the doorknob apart. *I* wouldn't know how to do that."

"She would have needed a screwdriver — so she had to get that too."

"She's smart, Bruno. And determined."

"Yeah, well, I wish she would apply it differently. She's never as clever as when she wants to do something she isn't supposed to do."

He blew out air. "I don't have any choice. I'm going to have to with-hold her spending money. It's the only leverage I have. Except that, like every other time, she's not going to see why I'm doing it. She'll just be angry with me."

"So why do it?"

"I have to do something. I can't just let her smash a hole in the wall."

Iris hesitated, but what could she say? The money she was giving Mina was going to undermine Bruno's attempt to discipline her — but the money was also the only way she could get the embroidery.

"And what about her birthday now?" Bruno had gotten tickets to an acrobatic dance and circus troupe from Belgium. "I can hardly take her out to celebrate while she's being punished."

"Come on," Iris objected. "You keep telling me how important birthdays are to her. You can't not celebrate her birthday."

"You're right, I can't. I don't know what I'm going to do."

"Begin by withholding her spending money," Iris said gently. "I'll talk to her too. Maybe I can get her to understand that she has to get along with her neighbour."

A snort escaped him. "If you can get her to understand that she doesn't live on an island unto herself, it's more than I ever managed."

She leaned against him and he put an arm around her shoulder. "Are you still seeing those otters in the river?" he asked.

"I see gulls. And two herons."

"Ha-ha. Aren't you funny? I see them too. Pretty hard not to. Oh," he interrupted himself. "Guess what? I'm getting a cell phone."

"I thought you said you were never getting one."

"My antique guys complain they can't reach me and I'm losing work. Val too. She used to be reliable with emails, but now she's send-ing texts all the time. But listen, I absolutely do not want Mina to have the number. It would be like handing her a leash to strangle me."

"Understood. Zipped lips."

*

Me! cried the yellow. Mina loved this yellow because it made her think of the flowers Mama used to grow under the kitchen window. She licked her fingers to wet the thread and said, "D-d-do it," to make it poke through the needle. She was knitting on oatmeal-coloured cloth Iris called linen. Linen was good for knitting but why such a blah colour? She had to knit and knit and knit and knit to cover it. Blues and yellows, lighter and darker. Little pinholes of green.

She wasn't telling a story because she had to go through every step of the plan in her head to be ready. The spool of pink cord was on the kitchen table. Pink like bubble gum, only it didn't stretch like bubble gum. It would be tight!

Nobody was going to find out this time, not even Bruno. She wasn't happy with him at all right now. She didn't like him. He didn't put her blinds up yet and he wasn't giving her money this week or next week. That wasn't right! It was *her* money. But! She would let Iris buy an extra knitting on Tuesday, and $35 was better than $20 because $20 was only $20, but $35 was a $20 *and* a $10 *and* a $5. Bruno could go fart in the flowers!

Normally she went to bed at midnight, but tonight she stayed up waiting for everyone in the whole apartment building to be asleep. She hadn't even taken her Metamucil and orange juice yet. Both watches said 00:26. She was waiting till 00:35 because 35 was her new lucky number.

She'd tugged the pink cord between her fists as hard as she could and it didn't break — and she was stronger than that old lady next door. Her and her friend across the hall were always talking and making crooked eyes at her. Mama said no one was allowed to call her a retard. If they did, she was supposed to tell, but telling on people didn't always make them stop.

At 00:35 she stuck her needle in the pincushion and set her knitting aside. She dropped the spool of pink string and a pair of scissors in her pockets. At the door she considered the slippers on her feet and then went back to sit on the sofa to kick them off. Her slippers were quiet but socks were quieter. She'd shut off the TV at midnight the way she always did, so that anyone listening would think she was asleep.

She'd already slipped her key fob in her pocket and patted her hip to make sure it was still there. She wasn't going to lock the door going out because she was only going down the hallway, but Bruno had told her never to leave her apartment without her key.

Did she have everything she needed? Scissors, extra strong pink string, her key.

*

When Bruno got home, the answering machine was flashing with six messages. That would be Mina calling six times to harass him about putting up her blinds or to shout about her money. Ignoring the me-me-me! flash of the light, he went to the kitchen to put water on to boil for pasta, grabbed Parmesan, mushrooms, and the carton of eggs from the refrigerator.

But what if it was Iris? He walked back to the living room and jabbed the button on the machine. The first call, as he'd expected, was Mina. She seemed to be protesting her innocence, but he couldn't tell about what. Her stutter was worse than usual. Then Faiza's shrill voice.

"Monsieur Corneau, we need to speak immediately! This is urgent! Please call me immediately!" The next message was Faiza again, reiterating the urgency. Then Mina again. And again. Something about going to bed at night and sleeping? The last message was from Faiza, this time with her private number. It was absolutely important that he call, no matter the hour.

Shit. What had Mina done?

He picked up the phone, wondered which version to get first, and decided that Faiza's might be closer to consensual reality. As he listened to her, he dragged the back of his hand across his mouth. For once he didn't object that she had no proof. Who but Mina could have dreamt up such a simple yet wackily effective stunt?

"It's out of my hands," Faiza said, sounding unnaturally subdued. "With the hole in the wall and now this, your sister has shown she's a danger to others and needs more supervision."

"Which means?"

"She's been put on a list for a group home."

He dropped his head. A stone on his shoulders. Faiza was still talking. He couldn't take it in. And then lifting his head, interrupting her, "You know she'll fight it every step of the way. And she's capable of wreaking more havoc in a group home where she doesn't want to be than if she's left in her apartment where she wants to be."

"As I said, we have no choice. It's only a question of time before she does something more dangerous."

He didn't want to agree but he knew she was right. "Did you tell her?"

"We thought you might be able to explain it so she would understand."

A mirthless laugh. "*Understand?* She won't ever. But yes, it's probably better that I tell her."

He felt grim as he walked to Mina's. He'd known she wouldn't be able to stay in her apartment forever, but given her health, she should have been able to live there for a while yet.

When he pressed the intercom, she didn't answer. He pressed again, longer. She still didn't answer and he was about to use his key when he heard, "Yeah!" Defiant.

"It's me. Let me in." The door buzzed.

She was toddling back to the sofa. Green plaid pants stretched wide across her bum, striped yellow sweater drooped off her narrow shoulders. Exasperated as he was by what she'd done, he felt sorry for her. The world as she knew it was about to tip into an abyss and she would never understand that she was the one who'd tipped it.

She pointed an accusing finger at the boxes with the blinds that he hadn't put up yet, but didn't otherwise acknowledge him. MiNA was printed in heavy black marker across them.

He leaned to reach for the remote but she clamped her hand over it. "Turn it down," he said.

She didn't.

"No problem. I'll unplug the TV."

She pursed her mouth but turned the sound down.

He took a seat across from her in the armchair. This wasn't going to be easy however he did it. "I understand that the police were here this morning."

She arched her eyebrows but said nothing.

"I talked to Faiza. She told me."

"I d-d-didn't —"

"You did. Look at me, Mina."

She slit her eyes at him.

"You tied your neighbours' doorknobs together."

Her eyes shone for a triumphant millisecond before she remembered to set her face in denial.

"Your neighbours couldn't open their doors. They were trapped inside."

The thought didn't seem to trouble her, but empathy had never been her forte.

"Did you know they wouldn't be able to get out with their doorknobs tied together?"

Her mouth was softening to smug satisfaction.

"Of course you knew. You're not stupid."

"I'm not stupid!"

"But this is where you miscalculated. One of your neighbours has a cardiac condition — something wrong with her heart. If she'd tried to get out and she couldn't, she could have died."

Smugness was turning into not-listening and wanting him to stop talking. He looked around for the pink cord Faiza had described but he didn't see it. That meant nothing though. Mina knew to hide evidence.

"The problem is that you endangered someone's life." Whether or not Mina understood, he had to say it. For himself, if not for her.

"I've told you and I've told you and I've told you. You have to get along with the other people in the building if you want to stay here."

"I have my l-l-lease!"

"The lease can be ripped up when you do something really bad. You've done a few things that are really bad. This last one was beyond really bad."

"She —!" Mina jabbed a finger in the direction of the neighbour's apartment.

"I have no doubt that she provokes you. But she didn't make that hole in your wall and she didn't tie her doorknob to the doorknob across the hall."

"Yeah!" Mina shouted.

"No, Mina." How could he protect her if there was no telling what she would dream up next? "You're going to have to leave your apartment. You're going to be moved."

Whatever protest she wanted to blurt made her choke and she started coughing. He went to the kitchen and brought a glass of water. "Drink some."

She gasped. "M-m-m-my lease—"

"Forget the lease. The police want you out, Social Services want you out, the owner of the building wants you out. You can't live here anymore." Blunt words but they were simple and she understood. He could see it in the shock on her face.

"Mama said you had to!"

He opened his empty hands. "What you did has proven you can't live unsupervised. I'm sorry, Mina, but that's how it is."

"Mama said!" she bellowed.

"Mama had no idea what you would get up to."

"I w-w-won't go!"

"We don't have any choice. The things you've been doing lately … Even I can't argue that you should stay here."

"No!"

"Remember how you didn't want to move from your apartment

where you lived before? And look how comfortable you are now. Wherever you go next, you'll get comfortable there too. I'll still be watching out for you — and Faiza and Iris. I know you think losing your apartment is the end of the world but it isn't."

Again he lifted his empty hands. For him, this was a failure too. He'd done his best but it wasn't enough. "I'm going to leave you to think about it, okay? I know you don't understand but ..."

Mina had grown very still, eyes latched onto the TV. He wasn't sure what to do for her. Faiza hadn't said how soon there would be a place for her in a group home. If it was anything like the move from her last apartment, he would have months to talk to Mina and get her accustomed to the idea.

*

Iris walked as quickly as she could, breaking into a trot now and again. Bruno had called and told her what Mina had done. He sounded so defeated. Nothing was as important to Mina as her apartment, but not even he could argue that she should stay there if she was doing things that endangered other people. What if she tried to start a fire to burn down the neighbour's door without realizing the whole building would go up in flames? She'd basically proven that she couldn't be trusted to live by herself anymore.

He asked Iris if she could look in on her in the morning. Of course, Iris said. But as soon as she hung up, and even though it was already past nine when no one was allowed to call because Mina had a roster of TV characters to check up on, Iris called. No answer. Was Mina so absorbed in her programs or was she too upset? Upset, Iris decided. For Mina, her apartment wasn't only her home; it was who she was. Philomena Corneau, as she'd identified herself on her mailbox.

When Iris tried calling again and Mina still didn't answer, she shoved her feet into her shoes and grabbed a sweater. She would go see her and talk face-to-face. Try to comfort her. If nothing else, let her vent about Bruno.

The lamps that lit the path through the park turned the trees into stretched bodies with monstrous ghoulish heads. She would tell Mina that it wasn't her apartment that made her special. It was her creativity. *That* was Philomena. And she could do that anywhere. Nobody could take that from her. Iris would help her to understand that.

She'd never visited Mina this late and didn't know if she would answer the intercom. On the sidewalk she saw the light from Mina's lamp and the syncopated flashes from the TV. For days Mina had been complaining that people could see into her apartment because Bruno hadn't installed her blinds yet, but the ground floor of the building was high enough from the sidewalk that Iris could only see the upper half of the walls with the embroidered decals of names.

Iris pressed the intercom, waited, then pressed it again. She took out her phone and dialled. Still no answer. She didn't want to startle Mina, but from the sidewalk she reached up with her phone to rap against the window.

Nothing. Maybe Mina couldn't hear that over the noise of the TV.

Iris glanced along the sidewalk, then walked around the building. The side door was locked. In the alley she found an abandoned recycling box. It was cracked but it would hold her weight. She carried it to the window, where Mina's TV continued to flash its manic lightshow, and climbed onto it as lightly as she could, grasping the window ledge for balance.

In Mina's living room the sofa was empty, except for the usual mound of cushions and embroidery. Iris hopped off and carried the recycling box to the bedroom window. Mina wasn't there either.

Back to the living room window, fingers gripping the window ledge, Iris craned her neck to see into the kitchen, though its light wasn't on. She scanned the living room again. The cushions weren't usually in such a big pile on the sofa.

That was Mina slumped over! Iris jumped — nearly fell — off the recycling box, hand scrabbling into her pocket for her phone.

*

Bruno's eyes burned in the dry hospital air. It was imperative to think about nothing but Mina. He had to believe that he could bring her back from wherever unconsciousness had claimed her.

When Iris called, he'd run from his place, keys clenched in his hand. Breath ragged, he found her unresponsive and pale, sprawled over her cushions. He and Iris propped her upright and he was tapping her face and calling her name, when suddenly the paramedics were there, telling him to move aside. Did she have a heart attack? he demanded. Out of the way, sir, we need space. I can help carry, he said. She'll be heavy. We'll be fine, the attendant told him. And added, It's a good thing she's bottom-heavy. It kept her from tipping onto the floor. Oh Lord, Bruno thought, Mina *has* to live so that one day I can tell her she was saved by her big bum.

The ER doctor said she had most likely had a cerebral hemorrhage. They didn't yet know how severe. She was being taken for a CT scan and would be transferred to the ICU.

Bruno and Iris sat in the ICU waiting room. At first, he was glad she was there, squeezing his hand and trying to sit close, but she kept murmuring assurances until he asked her to stop.

As the hours passed, he felt ever more urgently that he should be alone, holding vigil. He leaned his head against the wall and closed his eyes, directing his thoughts to Mina. Get through this! You have to! There's still so much life to enjoy — so many frîtes to eat! Your embroidery and hidden word puzzles. TV and Elvis. The dollar store! You want to go back to the dollar store, don't you? And you can still do all that, even in a residence. I'll put the blinds up in your new place. I'll get you that new lamp you wanted. *I'll, I'll, I'll, I'll …*

Running running running running, panting and tripping across the tree roots in the forest, desperate to reach the mountain he had to find if he was to save his sister who lay unconscious, her face pale, head lolling on the cushions. Branches and thorns tore at his clothes and skin. It was unholy magic to try to subvert what had been decreed since before they were born, but to not attempt would leave him broken. He could not bear to think she would die. He staggered through the trees until he saw the mountain before him. He knew that at the top was the castle, but its turrets and pinnacles were concealed by veils of mist. Sheer walls of rock rose before him. His hands bled as he tried to climb. He couldn't find the way and he wept with frustration. I'm here! he called. I've come! Finally the raven, who saw how vainly he searched, took pity and showed him the hidden crevice that marked the path. He tried to hand the bird a gold coin in thanks. Keep your gold, he heard. Riches are of no use to me, nor to you in your quest. Go—if you still hope to save your sister! Legend held that there were untold riches in the towers of the castle. Iron-banded chests of jewels, lustrous, thick carpets that had been carried by camels across deserts, handblown goblets in colours that no longer existed. He cared for nothing of this. His steps did not slow. His errand was through the low arched doorway beneath the castle into the dungeon. Here, the air was dank and heavy. Fat candles fluttered atop casks. He walked on soft feet to the stone wall he could sense more than perceive in the gloom. Earthen bricks had been mortared to shape boxes where bottles were stacked, one atop the other. Each was filled, corked, and labelled, though the writing was faded and illegible, eaten by the powdery spread of mould. Many bottles were sealed with a hammered silver cap imprinted with the years the person had lived. Among all these bottles, he had to find his sister's and steal it. How else to stop it from being capped?

7

Iris had stayed with Bruno throughout the night, but in the morning, when she said she had to cancel an appointment with a client, he told her to go home, have a shower, and meet with her client. She protested but he insisted.

He had gone into the ICU often enough by now that the beehive of glass cubicles no longer looked like an extraterrestrial spaceship. Each cubicle housed a patient penned inside the high walls of a bed, flanked by beeping machines. Mina lay so immobile and unlike herself that he worried she might never wake. He was only allowed to see her for a few minutes at a time. When he was asked to leave, he returned to the waiting room, feeling disoriented, bereft, helpless. He was there. That was all he could do. He knew he had to be there.

Other family members in the waiting room dozed, sometimes snored, spoke in low murmurs, or sat huddled into themselves. One woman was camped in a corner with a crocheted blanket and cushions. Young men brought her containers of spicy food they heated in the microwave and urged her to eat. She motioned that the bag of samosas be passed around to everyone. Her husband had been in the ICU for three weeks already. The young men were her grandsons.

Outside the swinging door to the ICU was a sign in many languages that told people to use the red telephone to request permission to enter. French, English, Spanish, Arabic, Chinese, Portuguese, Italian, and Russian. But not German. Weren't there enough German speakers in Montreal? Sitting there, his mind both febrile and numb,

Bruno wondered how it would be worded. The red telephone would be … das rote Telefon. What was the word for use? He was too exhausted to think further. Then, from somewhere in his brain, a rhyme surfaced. *Berg Semsi, Berg Semsi, Tu dich auf!* Magic words that commanded the stone face of a mountain to open.

He kept his eyes fixed on the doors, thinking, Open up! Tu dich auf! — when suddenly the doors swung open and there was Mina's nurse. He leapt up with a bound that startled both of them.

"Sorry," he mumbled.

"Your sister's conscious. She's heavily sedated and she might not know you, but you can see her."

He followed the nurse. The ICU doctor had told him that individuals with Down Syndrome were at higher risk for cerebral bleeds. Why had no one ever told him? The doctor said there was nothing he could have done to prevent it. Your sister was lucky, she said. Her hemorrhage was not severe and you got her to the hospital quickly.

Mina's eyes were open. The anxiety that had gripped him in a fist since yesterday relaxed a little. Her gaze was unfocussed, but that meant nothing because she wasn't wearing her glasses and wouldn't be able to see him clearly. He bent over her. "Mina, it's me. It's Bruno."

She didn't react. The doctor had told him they wouldn't know how much damage there had been until the swelling in her brain receded.

He squeezed her hand. He had to believe she would be well again. He stooped close to her ear and said, "As soon as you're well, we'll go out for a large frîtes!"

Nothing happened and he had to blink away the stinging wetness in his eyes. "It's okay," he whispered. "You heard me, right?"

Her eyes had closed but already he could feel this was a different kind of absence from when he'd found her unresponsive in her apartment.

*

Once the client left, Iris called Jenny at work.

"Very busy here," Jenny said. "Make it quick."

"Mina had a cerebral bleed."

"*What?* What is that? Like a stroke?"

"Something like that, I think."

"Oh ... Wow. How's Bruno?"

"In a state of shock. He told me once that the doctors said she wouldn't live past forty, but he always said it like he didn't believe it. I think he hoped she would prove everyone wrong and live till she was eighty."

"I'm really sorry, Iris. Are you at the hospital with him?"

"I'm at the studio. I had to meet a client. I'm going back now."

"I hope Mina will be all right."

"Yeah, I do too." Obviously she wanted that. But not only for Mina and for Bruno. For her plans to work out, she needed Philomena. But that was an ugly thought that she wouldn't let herself think. All that mattered now was Mina.

Somebody else had started talking to Jenny, even though she was on the phone, and Iris said she had to get back to the hospital.

*

Bruno had asked the nurse for Mina's glasses. It seemed obvious to him that she wasn't likely to respond as long as everything around her was a blur. Maybe you had to be near-sighted yourself to know that. But even when he settled her glasses on her nose and ears, her expression remained placid. He'd never known her to be so undemanding. She always had expectations. Umpteen things she wanted him to do or buy for her.

"Iris is coming," he said. "She was here earlier, do you remember?"

Her expression didn't change.

"And," he pretended to shriek, "*Faiza wants to see you too.*"

An amused look seemed to touch her face. He couldn't be sure.

He turned to see who had approached the bed. The stiff fabric of the doctor's white coat contrasted with the lambent blue silk of her hijab. She clasped Mina's bedrail, leaning forward to address her. "You're doing very well today."

Was she? Bruno desperately hoped so. The last couple of days had stretched like an eternity with Mina at its unmoving centre.

The doctor looked at the nurse's notes on Mina's clipboard and then asked, "Did someone tell you that the CT shows she had a small ischemic event in the past?"

"She already had a cerebral bleed?" He was appalled.

"A small stroke. Hypodensity in the right cerebellum. You've never noticed any problems with her balance?"

"Her balance has always been precarious. She's got such tiny feet. I also don't know everything that happens to her. She doesn't always tell me."

"Don't blame yourself. You couldn't have predicted this."

He nodded but didn't believe her. He should have noticed something. "Is she still not talking because of the swelling on her brain?"

"Very likely, yes."

"So she will talk again."

"We hope so. Although there may be some loss. It will be hard for us to determine because we have no baseline for your sister. You'll be a better judge of that."

"Can this happen again?"

"A cerebral hemorrhage? It's likely, yes."

"Will we be able to tell when?"

"There isn't an answer for that. But now that it's happened once, we have a strong indication that she has amyloid deposits in the cerebral blood vessels. That's most likely what caused the bleed."

"Can't you find out for sure or give her something to prevent it?"

"Unfortunately, no. We can only confirm the diagnosis with an autopsy." She paused, letting him absorb that. "What this means for now is that your sister will have to be placed in a supervised setting."

"She's already on a list for a group home."

"More than a group home. She'll need to go into a residence with nursing care."

"She won't like that."

"Perhaps she won't mind so much."

He couldn't imagine Mina not demanding her independence and the dominion of her apartment. He couldn't imagine —

"It's her birthday on Saturday," he blurted. "Do you think she'll remember? It's the highlight of the year for her. I was going to …" He stopped, realizing that it didn't matter what plans he had. He was talking in circles.

"You'll have to help her remember. You can do more for her in that respect than we can." She smiled and backed up a step. She had other patients, other family members to see.

Mina's eyes were closed, but her glasses were still on. "Mina?" he asked softly.

She opened her eyes and seemed to be looking at him but he couldn't tell if she knew who he was. She was lost somewhere in the swollen corridors of her brain.

"I'm here," he said so she would know where to aim when she was ready.

*

The room had glass walls so the nurses could see her. The needle in her arm was attached to a tube and a machine. She had another tube between her legs for her pee to sneak into a bag. The nurses kept telling her how good she was for not pulling out the tube and the needle. Why would she do that? She knew tubes and needles from when Mama was in the hospital.

Hospitals were places where you lay in bed and waited for what was going to happen next. With Mama, Mina had pushed her chair close so she could put her head on the bed, and Mama stroked Mina's hair. Now Mina was in bed, and Bruno and Iris and Faiza came. They talked and held her hand and said they loved her. That was good but someone was missing. Mina longed for that someone to come but she couldn't remember who it was.

Words were missing. Other things too. A green stone on her finger. Something on her arm that was very important. She could almost *almost* remember but she couldn't.

She slept and woke again. The nurse was there with a man holding sheets and towels and blankets. "We're going to get you up for lunch. You remember? You sat in the chair last night."

Mina liked the big chair that was padded with blankets and pillows, but she couldn't get there by herself. The nurse put funny paper slippers on her feet. The man loomed beside her like a giant. He held her steady around her shoulders and pushed the machine attached to her needle. The nurse was on the other side with her arm around her waist.

The nurse tutted. "When you think of the fuss other people make about getting up and how they complain — and look at her, she's a fighter."

The man tucked blankets up and down her legs and across her lap. "Ça va?" he said. Gently he put her glasses on her nose and ears. "Now you can see me."

Mina could see him before. Did he think she couldn't? Only now, with her glasses, she could see more things about him. The drawing of a heart on his arm. His white hair shaved close to his head. He draped a towel like a bib across her chest and pushed the table over her lap.

The nurse carried in a tray of food. "Just wait a sec, honey. I'll help you."

Mina didn't need help to eat! The feeling was so strong that the word came. "M-m-m-me." She squeezed the spoon in her hand as well as she could.

"Look at you! It would be easier if you used your other hand without the IV. Do you want to use your other hand? No? Not even try? ... Hm, all right, you do it however works for you." The nurse pulled up a chair. "Do you want your crackers?"

Mina waited for the nurse to rip open the packet and crumble crackers into the bowl. Her spoon wasn't steady but she got some to her mouth.

There was a rush of movement and outdoor smells, and Iris was there. "Mina, you're up and eating all by yourself!"

Of course she was eating by herself. She knew how to eat. Even if the needle in her hand hurt and the peas kept rolling away.

Iris was talking to the nurse who left and then Iris sat on the chair. "What the — ? Who thinks up these meals? I mean, peas? Here, give me your fork."

Mina held it more tightly.

"Don't be silly, I'm not trying to steal your food." Iris took the knife to fold mashed potatoes over the peas. "There, that should be easier."

Mina jabbed her fork into the potatoes. Yeah, this was better.

"But don't eat everything because ..." Iris leaned forward to whisper. "Guess what I brought? A chocolate-chip banana muffin."

Mina held her breath with suspense, the supper on the tray forgotten.

"Fuck diabetes, Mina. You nearly died. And today I decree that you can have chocolate in your muffin." Iris snuck a hand into her knapsack and ever so slowly brought out a paper bag. She looked over her shoulder to make sure no one was watching through the glass, took out the muffin, and broke it into pieces over the napkin.

Mina grabbed the largest chunk and shoved it whole in her mouth.

"Hey, slow down! You don't want to choke. You'll get me into trouble."

She tried to slow down but this was too delicious.

"Tastes good, doesn't it? I'll bring you one again, okay? And ..." Iris bobbed her head. "When you get that needle out of your hand and you're feeling better, I'll bring you some thread and your hoop so you can knit if you want."

Iris kept talking, but Mina couldn't listen anymore. She was so tired. She'd had enough muffin too. She wanted the nurse to help her back to bed to sleep.

*

Gabriela was puzzled when Mina didn't answer the phone that morning. Something must have come up and Mina couldn't let her know since she didn't have Gabriela's number. Gabriela had told her it was a secret. Mina might not like it but she had unquestioning respect for secrets.

Gabriela didn't have time to call again until almost noon and still there was no answer. She hoped Mina was all right. On Sunday she was going to be seeing her for her birthday.

The afternoon was busy with patients. She didn't think of Mina again until she was home. She called and still there was no answer. This was unusual, even very unusual. Mina was never gone all day.

Or maybe it was the phone? Gabriela called the phone company who confirmed that the line was functional. They asked if it was possible that the phone was broken. With Mina, yes, that was possible, and by now Bruno would know and Mina would be harassing him for a new phone.

Gabriela didn't want to call Bruno but didn't know what else to do. Except he didn't answer either. She didn't leave a message, not sure what to say. The last time they spoke he more or less told her to butt out and mind her own business. She waited an hour and tried again. He still didn't answer. Neither Mina nor Bruno? She was starting to feel alarmed and this time she left a message.

When it was time to go to bed and he still hadn't returned her call, she was convinced that something must have happened. Bruno would be frantic. Or — what if something had happened to Bruno? What would Mina do? Where was she?

Gabriela dozed and jerked awake. When the night began to pale and Bruno still hadn't called, she knew with certainty that

COLOURS IN HER HANDS

something was wrong. But if no one told her, what could she do? She felt grim and helpless.

She showered and went to work where she had patients scheduled. She was on her hands and knees, demonstrating an exercise, when the phone on her desk rang. If the receptionist had put a call through while she had a patient, it was urgent. Gabriela sprang up with an apology, saying that she had to answer.

"Gabriela." Bruno's voice. He spoke all in a rush, telling her Mina was in the ICU — but no longer in danger. "I didn't think to call you, sorry. I'm sure she would want you to know. Not that I can tell what she wants or understands right now. She's not herself yet — if she ever will be again. The doctor says she might have lost some brain function."

Gabriela didn't dare interrupt. She was torn between being relieved to hear from him and upset by what she was hearing.

"I didn't call last night because I didn't get home till two and I was … I couldn't even think. I've been living in the ICU waiting room for four days. I'm going back to the hospital now but I have to get to a store first. It's Mina's birthday tomorrow."

"The poor dear," Gabriela breathed.

"I was going to take her to a circus performance at TOHU. That obviously isn't going to happen now, so I have to get something else, I don't know what. Assuming she even knows it's her birthday."

He was babbling. Even though he said he'd slept, he sounded exhausted. The last four days must have been a torment for him. She heard movement behind her and looked. The patient had started doing stretches on her own, pretending not to overhear.

"What hospital is she in?" Gabriela asked. "I can't come today because I'm babysitting the boys right after work until late but I'll come tomorrow."

"On her birthday would be great. It would mean so much to her."

She was taken aback by how grateful he sounded. Any memory of disagreement between them was forgotten. All that mattered now was his sister.

After she finished with the patient, she did a quick internet search on Down Syndrome and cerebral hemorrhage. There seemed to be a good chance that Mina would recover with not too much loss of function, but she would forever be at risk for another bleed. In healthcare terms, Gabriela knew that meant she would not be allowed to return to her apartment.

Oh Mina, she thought.

*

The last place Bruno wanted to be was trawling through stores looking for ... he had no idea what. But he had to bring Mina something. He wouldn't let himself believe she no longer cared about birthdays. Iris had suggested a necklace to match Mina's green ring. Would Mina like that? He didn't know.

At the hospital he loped up the stairs. He was a seasoned regular by now. The red phone etc. Das rote Telefon.

In the ICU, the doctor beckoned from the counter. "Mina's doing well. She doesn't need to be with us anymore, but we don't need the bed right now and the nurses love her. It's not often that we get the chance to sing 'Happy Birthday' to a conscious patient." She tilted her head as if she'd told a joke. "Even if she's not talking much yet, it doesn't mean her brain isn't working. It will help if you give her memory prompts."

"How well do you think she'll be next week? Well enough that I can leave the city for two days? It's for work. I can be back in Montreal within an hour." Val had insisted he only come if he was absolutely, one hundred percent sure that Mina was safe. His first thought was that she would never be safe again. Except, if anywhere, here she was at least already in the hospital. Iris had said she would come stay with her and maybe Gabriela would stop by too. There would be nurses and orderlies. Mina wouldn't be alone. The doctor said there was no reason why he couldn't go. Mina would only be staying in the hospital until a residence could be found for her.

Mina sat propped up in bed, eyes closed but with her glasses on. Every time he saw her, she looked more like herself: that confident air of rotund dignity. Even in a hospital gown.

As he pulled up a chair, her eyes opened. She said nothing but he saw she spotted the glittery bag stuffed with tissue paper he was carrying. "It's your birthday, Mina. The nurses and doctors already sang to you, right? You remember birthdays?"

She looked from him to the bag and back to him. He wasn't sure but he thought her expression was expectant. He set the bag next to her and softly, for just the two of them, sang, "Happy birthday to you, happy birthday to you, happy birthday dear Mina, happy birthday to you!"

He waited but she seemed not to know what to do with the bag, so he snatched out the tissue paper and showed her that inside the bag was a small jewellery box. Once upon a time she would have said, Wh-wh-what's that? But everything happened at a slower pace now. And in silence. The nurses told him she'd said a few words but he had yet to hear her speak.

He gave her the box. "It's for you."

The box was stiff to open but she seemed to want to struggle with it herself. Her grip had always been strong. When it finally clicked open, she only looked. She didn't react.

"It's a necklace," he said. "To match your ring with the green stone. Do you remember your ring?" The nurses wouldn't let her wear it yet so he touched her middle finger.

She lifted the other hand — the correct one, he realized — and he gasped a sob, suffused with relief at every sign, however small, that she was returning to who she was.

"Iris will be bringing you a present too. And guess who else is coming? Gabriela."

Mina's breath hitched and she began blinking rapidly. Oh no, he'd made her cry! He grabbed tissue from the box on the bedside table and dabbed her cheeks and around her glasses. "Don't get upset, sweetie, please don't. She didn't know you were here but now that she does, she's coming to see you."

"G-G-Gabriela!"

He sat back in the chair. "Well, well. So you *can* talk when you want to."

She was still sniffling but it sounded happier now. A contented sniffling.

"Gabriela means a lot to you, doesn't she?" Why did he even say that? He knew Mina loved her. "I'm sorry I didn't think to call her but all I was thinking about was you."

He lay a hand on her leg and squeezed through the layers of blanket. "I think even Faiza will be coming." He pitched his voice high. "*Because it's your birthday!*"

Mina didn't react. Was she tired? Did she understand? He used to feel frustrated because he couldn't tell what she was thinking, but all those times when he thought he didn't know, he'd always had an inkling. Because now he really couldn't tell.

"I'm wondering if it's all right with you if I'm gone for two days next week." He held up two fingers. "Only two. We're going to perform the dance in Ottawa. Do you remember the dance? There was —" He stopped, unable to think of a happy recollection from the dance.

Mina looked relaxed. She'd cupped her hands over the box with the necklace, which he took to mean that she liked it.

"Will you be okay for two days? You won't get into any mischief in here, will you?" He glanced around the room at the monitors and perfusion pumps. The old Mina would have had a heyday. This new quieter Mina ... He let out a long breath. He wasn't impatient. He knew she needed time. But how he wished she would say one word, only one, so that he knew she understood what he'd said. A magic word to release him.

"D'okay."

He lowered his forehead to the rumpled sheets on the mattress and whispered, "Thank you." And felt a hand, very light, touch his hair.

*

Iris let the studio door slam behind her and threw her knapsack on the stool. She'd gone to visit Mina and found her pink-cheeked and happy, because Gabriela had been there. What was *she* doing there? Who had told her?

Mina was decidedly more humdrum about seeing Iris. She didn't even react when Iris showed her the thread she'd brought — colours she'd chosen, thinking how they would tempt Mina. Earth-rich ochre, milky lavender, fresh lime green. But Mina's eyes skimmed across the slim bundles of colour as if they were limp dirty socks.

It made no sense. Embroidery was her passion. It was how she expressed herself. Iris hadn't expected her to start embroidering at that instant, but the doctor had said to bring her memory prompts. What could be more vital to an artist than the material she worked with?

When Iris urged her to look and to touch the rich colours, Mina turned her head and closed her eyes. Under her arm she had a pink heart-shaped cushion Iris had never seen before. She put the thread on the bedside table and said she would come again.

In her studio she filled the kettle. Grabbed the jar of coffee and spooned some into the French press. She hadn't realized Bruno was still in touch with his ex but how else had she found out Mina was in the hospital? The way he recounted it, they'd broken up because she wanted a baby and he didn't. When he talked about her, he sounded resentful. His ex had chosen an unknown future with a possible baby that might not even happen over a certain future with him. Iris knew how that could hurt. But even if a person hurt you, that didn't mean you stopped loving them.

She poured boiling water over the coffee and crossed the room to the cutting table where work waited. Chalk outlines of pattern pieces for a tunic that she'd traced on embossed silk. She still wasn't sure what she would do if she saw Renée again, but she knew she would feel weak-kneed. Did Bruno still feel like that about his ex?

She picked up the heavy tailor's shears to begin cutting, but her vision blurred with tears and she didn't trust her hand. Her life had been fine as it was. She didn't need this mess! Hadn't she already learned that lesson when Renée went back to her ex? "Idiot," she muttered.

Except that Bruno seemed so steady and serious. A man who did the utmost to ensure his sister's wellbeing, even if it meant turning his own life upside-down. Everyone at the dance studio trusted him. He'd given her the keys to his house that first night without any hesitation. He was the one who'd approached her to make costumes. The way he looked deep into her eyes. The generous, fabulous sex — because she'd had enough casual sex to know the difference between the sensory hygiene of a good fuck and having a partner who cared. Bruno cared. The way he'd noticed that she took milk but not sugar in her coffee. How they'd already been talking about plans for the summer. She'd said she was going to make him chino shorts to show off his nice legs and how he said, Me? Legs?

She walked to the counter to push down the plunger and pour herself a coffee. She nodded to herself and stood straighter.

*

Mina had her hands on a pillow that was covered with a towel.

"You wait and see," Gabriela said. "All the bruises from the needles will be gone soon and your nails will still be pink." She bent close to blow softly across the wet polish. Her dark hair was twisted up in a clip. "This isn't the first time I've done your nails, do you remember?"

"Yeah," Mina said, though she didn't. She was so happy Gabriela was there.

"You have to keep your hands still until the polish dries." Gabriela looked at the bedside table. "Where's your ring you always used to wear?"

"N-n-nurse." The nurse had it locked in a safe place.

Gabriela left the room and didn't come back for a while, but that was okay because she would. She always did. She was someone you could trust.

Mina didn't have glass walls around her bed anymore. She was in a room with a very old lady beside her. The nurse asked if they could keep the curtain between the beds open so the lady could see into the hallway. Then a man came to visit the lady and he closed the curtain. Behind the curtain he said that he didn't want to have to look at that. After he left, when the nurse wanted to open the curtain again, Mina said no. The nurse asked why not? Didn't she want the light from the window? Mina shook her head. No.

Here Gabriela was again, followed by a nurse carrying an envelope.

"Voilà!" The nurse ripped the envelope and out tumbled the winking, twinkling green ring that Mina hadn't seen for so long. She grinned, thinking hello hello hello hello hello!

"Wait," Gabriela said. "Your nails aren't dry yet. Let me ..." Carefully she slipped the ring on Mina's finger.

There was a loving word Mina wanted to say — a name that was only for Gabriela — but it was too far away. It wouldn't come. She could feel it though.

Bruno walked into the room but stopped when he saw Gabriela. "Oh, hi. Don't let me disturb you. I'll have a coffee and come back in a while."

"No, that's all right, I have to get to work." Gabriela dropped the bottle of polish in her bag and stood to leave. She leaned over to kiss Mina. "I'll come again soon, I promise. The polish should be dry now. You can move your hands. Look how pretty they are." She took away the towel and pillow, and gave her another kiss on the cheek. "I love you, Mina."

Mina wished Gabriela wouldn't go but she felt hugged by her words.

Bruno watched her leave like he wished he could follow her. So why didn't he? But he turned back to Mina, opened his knapsack, and took out a square kit he set on her bedside table. "Do you know what this is?" He unzipped it and took out a little brush, a little bowl with soap, and a razor. "Let me get a basin and a towel."

Was Bruno going to shave here in the hospital? Her eyes got big when he walked back into the room holding a basin with a couple of towels slung over his shoulder. He arranged the bedside table and draped the towels *across her*. Then he sat on the bed next to her hip.

"There's not much room but you're going to have to scootch closer to me. Glasses off too." He lifted them away, wrung a facecloth in the water, and wiped her cheeks and jaw.

"Wh-wh-what are you doing?"

"What do you think? Doesn't look like anyone else is going to."

He wet the brush and rubbed it on the soap in the bowl, making a thick lather. "This is how I shave. I don't use an electric shaver like you do."

Someone else used to shave like this. Someone who made her heart fill with love. But she couldn't remember who ... and didn't have the words to ask Bruno, except that she could feel inside herself that Bruno knew.

He was brushing foam onto her cheeks and under her chin. It tickled a little but it felt lovely too. He dipped the razor in the water and ran it down the foam on her cheeks. He made a face to show her to stretch her upper lip so he could shave her moustache. From the hallway she could hear the sounds of the hospital, but close up only the swish of the razor in the water and when he gave it a sharp tap on the edge of the basin.

"I'm being careful, don't worry."

She wanted to say d'okay but wasn't sure if she could move her mouth. An orderly, who'd stopped in the doorway, watched for a few seconds and gave her a thumbs up.

When Bruno finished, he wiped her face with a warm, wet cloth, and then dried it with a towel. "Now you're ready for the world. New pink nails, fresh new face."

But when he reached to open the curtain between the two beds, she said, "No."

"What do you mean, no? You're not fighting with your neighbour here too, are you? That has to stop, Mina." He sat on the chair. "You're going to be living with other people now. You'll still have your own room, but you'll be eating in a dining room and there'll be a common living room too." He looked at her and waited. "You know you're going to a new place?"

The pretty doctor who always wore a scarf had told her. She said if something happened to her again, it was too dangerous for her to be alone. She could get sick again. Mina didn't want to be sick again. Faiza had come too and talked and talked and talked about going to a new place.

"And you're all right with that?"

"Yeah."

"Okay. I guess ..." He picked up a magazine that was on the night table. "Have you had a look at this yet? You used to love doing word puzzles."

She'd opened the pages. They were filled with letters. She could say some of them, but she didn't know why they were in rows or what to do with the grids.

"Don't worry," Bruno said. "It'll come back to you. Do you remember when your birthday is?"

She just had her birthday! Did he already forget?

"Do you remember?" he asked again. "I'm not asking for me, I'm asking you."

"June."

"When in June? What day?"

"Quat'!"

"And mine?"

She watched him hard but it didn't come.

"May ...?" he trailed off.

"Ten!"

"Excellent, Mina! You always remember birthdays. Next — not today, maybe tomorrow — we'll do money. I'll let you keep whatever you identify correctly. How's that for incentive?"

Money was important. Money was like … In her mind she saw a drawing of a chest heaped with shining … "Gold!"

He laughed. "Sorry, no gold. I was thinking dimes and quarters."

"One!"

"One what? Do you mean loonies? You obviously remember what they are so there's no point testing you."

"Yeah!"

He barked a soft laugh. "Sounds to me like you're getting better. The doctor said you'll remember more every day." He reached for his knapsack that he'd hooked on the back of the chair. "I wonder if you'll remember this." He lifted out a box, holding it gently. "This is very old, Mina. You have to be careful."

Inside the box were layers of tissue paper, but she'd already spied the booted feet. As Bruno folded back the layers, she saw the blue dress, the painted face, the braided crown of hair, the little teeth. Remembering was like a slow dream becoming real.

"This was Mama's doll," Bruno said. "From when she was little. It belonged to someone she loved very much who was called Philomena. That's why you're called Philomena."

Mina opened her hands.

"Careful," he said.

She meant to hold the doll carefully, but the feeling that it was Mama's was too strong and she hugged it tightly to her heart.

*

Downsizing Mina's belongings to fit into a single room was a mammoth task Bruno was dreading. It wouldn't help to ask what she wanted to keep, because she would want everything. She had always been so fierce about her home and all the treasures in it.

He decided that the most important possession — the constant that would help her feel at home — was their mother's angel. He needed to get it repaired. He enquired among his antique dealers who recommended a Madame Durig who worked with historical statuary. Originally from Switzerland, she had been living in Montreal for forty years. She didn't normally take private commissions but had agreed to look at the angel when he said it was four hundred years old and Austrian.

Her studio was in a stone building on a cul-de-sac off rue de la Commune. Bruno climbed the stairs. An unsmiling woman with round, black-rimmed glasses and grey hair gelled close to her skull answered the door. Without a word she held out her hand — not to shake but for the package. Was he supposed to follow her? She didn't say but he wanted to.

She took the package to a scarred wooden work table. There were several. The clutter of jars, stained sponges, spray bottles, old yogurt containers, matted rags, and cans of brushes took him back to his childhood memories of his uncle's workshops in Austria.

She unwrapped the paper and considered the angel. Without looking, she reached for the magnifying lamp and swung the head toward her, though she seemed to use her fingers as much as her eyes to examine the broken edge of the wing. On another table lay a Christ who'd been detached from his crucifix.

She murmured.

He waited, not sure if she was speaking to herself or to him.

"The style of carving," she said more distinctly. "Probably from the late 1600s. How does it come to be in your possession?"

"My mother's family in Austria work in church restoration." He wasn't going to tell her his mother had bundled the angel in their dirty underwear to smuggle to Canada.

"Who are your family? What is their name?"

When he told her, she looked at him with seeming interest for the first time. "What relation are you to Berndt?"

"He's my uncle. But I only met him once when I was seven."

"I only met him once too." Her eyebrows arched above the black circles of her glasses. He didn't know if that was good or bad. His uncle had a forceful personality that could charm people but also offend them. Even as a child, he'd noticed.

She was examining the tip of wing that had cracked off. He'd found it after searching on his hands and knees, feeling along the baseboard, fingers combing the carpet under the furniture.

"I'll repair this," she said. "As a courtesy to your family."

Should he say he wasn't in contact with them? She hadn't asked. He was curious to know how she would do the repair. "What kind of glue will you use?"

She pointed to the bottles along the back of the table where he recognized the same carpenter's wood glue he would have used.

"Oh, I thought..." He'd assumed there was a special brand of his-torical artefact glue.

"Reattaching the tip isn't the issue. To do this properly, I'll have to regild over the join." She went to a cupboard she unlocked. Inside the cupboard she unlocked another door. He wished Mina could see. She would approve of the keys and doors and locks.

Madame Durig returned with a booklet of purple tissue paper. She gently fanned the edge of the booklet with her thumb so he could see the micro-thin squares of gold that glimmered between the pages. "You must have seen gold leafing done at your uncle's."

"I was young." But with his hand he mimed how his aunt had swiped a wide brush back and forth across her cheek before touch-ing it to the gold leaf.

Madame During nodded. "That's right. For the body fat. It makes the gold leaf adhere to the brush. We use the forearm now because people wear face cream and makeup."

"My aunt also had a tool. She said it was a ... wild boar's tooth?" He looked at her questioningly because he'd always wondered if that was really true.

"To polish the gold leaf. We can use agate too. It has the same hardness as tooth enamel." From a drawer she took two long wooden handles attached to hard, L-shaped tips. "These are agate." She gave him one so he could feel the stone. "But polishing is only at the end, the very last step of gilding."

"And before that?"

"Before that we prepare the surface." She frowned at him. "Did no one ever explain that to you?"

"I —" Was only a kid, he was about to say, making excuses for what she seemed to think was a failure of protocol or duty, he wasn't sure what.

But she was already speaking. "Preparing the surface is why gilding is such a time-consuming process. We need to build up layers of gesso to make a cushion, so that the gold leaf doesn't tear when you rub it with —" She pointed at the agate tip he still held. "We paint as many as twenty layers of gesso and each layer has to dry completely before we sand it — with rough paper and then with fine paper — until the surface is completely smooth. And we do that with each and every layer. If we don't do it properly, the gold leaf will tear when we're polishing, and then we have to remove everything and start over. We don't take chances. I even make my own gesso with ground chalk from Bologna."

Bruno recalled watching his aunt when she worked. "You're saying gesso, but gesso is white. My aunt was putting gold leaf on a red ground."

"Exactly. After the last layer of gesso we paint bole, which is volcanic earth mixed with olive oil soap and …" She pushed a dirty jar that was closed across the table. "Smell it."

He started to unscrew the lid but stopped at the first pungent whiff, tightening it again.

She crimped her mouth in what he guessed was her version of a smile. "Aged egg white. I make my own bole too."

His nose still stung. She could just tell people, he thought, not make them smell it.

"Do you know why we paint red bole before applying gold leaf?"

"Because the gold is so thin that the red shows through just enough to warm it?" he guessed.

"You see, you're a natural. It's in your blood."

No, he thought, he had experience from painting stage sets. Though he had to admit he felt a kinship with this workshop, the cabalistic ingredients and tools. Volcanic earth, olive oil soap, and sulphurous egg whites. Chalk from Bologna and agate — or boar's teeth, if they could be found. The little purple booklet with its hidden leaves of gold.

"Did your family tell you that we use the same technique for gilding that the Egyptians used 5000 years ago? The same, the same, the same." With each repetition the soft thump of her palm on the table.

He thought of time unfolding. Gestures repeated across millennia.

She gave another of her crimped smiles. "Do you know what the Egyptians called gold leaf? The skin of the gods."

"Did they think gold made you a god?"

"Gold," she intoned. "There is nothing so powerful, so rich, so sexy." She strode across the room to where a figure about a metre tall was draped in cloth. Arching her arm high, she plucked away the sheet, unveiling a Madonna. Over her painted blue dress her cloak was freshly gilt. It hung down her back, gleaming and rippling with light.

"Do you feel how the gold pulls your eyes like a magnet? Remember, when these statues were made, there was no electricity. All you had was candlelight and shadows. And then, this Madonna — on a pedestal. Think how she would look in a room that's only lit by candles. What else would you look at but this gorgeous, shining gold?"

He imagined a dark, stone church with this Madonna in an alcove. The flickering light of the candles at her feet and shoulders. Her cloak a glimmering aura of gold.

*

Mina's living room, always crowded, was impassable with boxes and garbage bags shoved wherever they would fit on the sofa, the armchair, and the floor. Bruno was considering each item before dropping it in a garbage bag, a charity bag, or a box to keep. Iris did the same, asking him when she wasn't sure. Progress was slow. The apartment was crammed with a surfeit of everything and nothing — precious to Mina, of dubious value to anyone else.

They'd been packing in sober silence for a while. Iris said, "Should I put on some music? There's all this Elvis —"

"No," Bruno said sharply. "Elvis was her favourite. It wouldn't feel right."

Iris straightened from where she'd been bent, emptying a shelf. "This isn't her grave, Bruno. She hasn't died, she's only moving."

"But we're dismantling her home."

Bruno had told her last night that although he hadn't wanted Mina to die young, he'd sometimes thought it would be kinder for her to go before she lost her apartment. Having her own apartment was so important to her. Remember the dance, he'd said, about having and not having a home? That was how fiercely Mina felt about her apartment. Being in her own apartment was how she proved to the world and herself that she was who she was. Iris had almost told him then that what was truly special about Mina was her creativity, and how she had plans for Mina that were going to open new horizons — and once Mina's days were filled with things happening for Philomena, she would no longer miss her apartment.

Bruno had begun sorting more quickly, deciding at a glance. Yes, to pictures of their parents and their childhood dog. No, to the innumerable photos of sidewalks or faces Mina had cut off across their forehead or chin. No, to the trinkets and figurines. "Look at this." He dangled a bag of chocolate caramels. "It's amazing she never put herself in a diabetic coma."

Although packing up Mina's home was disheartening, Iris couldn't help feeling a small thrill of excitement. This was her best chance of finding the embroidery she was convinced was hidden in the apartment. She'd been making a separate cache of everything she was finding related to needlework: embroidery and knitting needles, pincushions, balls of yarn, crochet hooks. She was surprised to find more than a dozen embroidery hoops, since she'd only ever seen Mina use the same plastic yellow hoop.

"You know," she said, "I took her a ball of wool and knitting needles but she didn't even look at them."

"She's not doing her hidden word puzzles either."

Iris nearly rolled her eyes. Hidden word puzzles didn't matter. Embroidery and knitting did. "What about all these cushions?" she asked. "One, two, three, four, five, six, seven—" Cushions in all shapes and colours tumbled across the sofa.

"Only keep two. That'll have to do. She won't have a sofa in her new place."

"No *sofa?* But that's where she embroiders."

"What do you want me to do?" he snapped. "She's only allowed to take her bed, an armchair, and one dresser. Everything has to be able to fit in one room and one closet."

"Hey! Don't bite my head off. I'm here to help, right?"

"Sorry. I ... I didn't mean ... I just can't help thinking how she'll react when she sees how much less she has. She might have accepted that she's moving—which I still don't understand—but she has no notion of what downsizing means." He opened a drawer and groaned.

From where Iris stood she could see that the drawer was filled to the top with erasers. She gaped at Bruno. "What was she doing? That's enough to stock a whole school for a year."

"She didn't want to run out. And," he added drily, "I'll bet she didn't buy a single one."

"What do you mean?"

"You know she steals, don't you?"

"Mina?"

"She never took anything of yours? Then you're the only one. She swipes something every time she goes to a store or comes over. That's how I lost my favourite paring knife. She's been doing it since we were kids."

"You're exaggerating."

He waved a hand across the drawer he'd just opened. Filled level to the top with notebooks.

"She's a hoarder," Iris said.

"All stolen. I guarantee it."

He was flipping through the notebooks, putting the ones that were blank in the charity box, ripping out the few pages here and there with only one word painstakingly printed across it.

"Hydrasense," he read. "What's that?"

"A skin moisturizer."

"Here's a phone number. Maybe I should call and see who answers. It could—" He stopped mid-sentence and she looked up from a stash of crewel needles she'd found. He was shaking notebooks upside-down over the seat of the armchair. Not from each, but from some, money fluttered out. He already had a few tens and twenties — enough that he reached for the notebooks he'd already put in a box to shake them too.

"Where did she get all this? I only gave her twenty bucks a week. I know she hides things, but this isn't even statistically possible — unless she was stealing money too."

Iris had never asked herself what Mina did with the money she gave her. All that had mattered to her was that Mina wanted it.

Bruno began looking into the green garbage bags that were partly full. "Where did you put the cushions?" He found one and squeezed his fingers around the seams.

"You think she hid money in the cushions too?"

"An old trick of hers." He'd grabbed a pair of scissors and was trying to cut through a seam that had been densely zigzagged with thread.

Iris stepped around the boxes and took the scissors from him. "Let me." She peered at the stitching. "She didn't mean for this to be opened. I have to …" She began to snip through the fabric where she felt a lump and groped in the hole with her fingers. "It's not money." She fished out a green suede glove, squeezed the whole cushion, and looked around. "Where's the other glove? These are mine! I thought I lost them."

"Told ya," he taunted.

"It's not funny." Iris grabbed another cushion and squeezed it. She'd asked Mina if she'd seen her gloves. She'd told her they were her favourite, a gift from her best friend. That Mina had not only taken them, but hidden them inside a cushion where they were of no use to anyone — all the while that Iris was asking her if she'd seen them and was probably even leaning against the cushion where they were hidden — was not only secretive; it was willfully hurtful. But Bruno seemed to think it was a joke.

"How long has she been stealing?" Iris demanded.

"Ah, so you believe it now that you're a victim too."

"Hasn't anyone ever tried to stop her?"

"How?"

"By—" Iris had no idea.

The next drawer was filled with rolls of toilet paper. They didn't seem to come from the same package either. Had Mina stolen these too? Bruno examined each tube before putting it in a charity box. Some had things stashed inside. A screw, a comb …

Then Iris remembered the interviews with art curators who'd talked about the objects Judith Scott wrapped with fibre and how x-rays revealed that smaller objects were also hidden inside. Surreptitiously she slipped her phone from her pocket and took a few pics of the notebooks, the rolls of toilet paper, the messy heap of money on the armchair.

"I think I'll get started in the bedroom," she said. It would be easier to look through the closet when Bruno wasn't in the same room.

"I have an idea." He'd followed her.

"Why don't you finish in the living room?"

"I will. But you'll have more room to maneuver in here if I prop the bed on its side."

"Oh, right." She moved to help, sweeping the cushions and teddy bears that were on the bed to the floor.

They lifted the mattress, with the sheets and comforter still hanging from it, to prop against the wall. On the bare box spring were more hidden items. He stooped to reach for a cheque book. "That's where that went to."

Iris unfolded a tea towel. "Look, your paring knife."

"Actually, no." He smirked. "Someone else's. Mine had a wooden handle."

He snatched up a flat cushion embroidered with blue fleurs-de-lys and gold and silver swirls. "Any idea where this might have come from?"

She held out her hand, looking closely at the embroidery, and softly rubbed it. "The flowers are silk. The embellishment is gold and silver thread."

"You mean real gold and silver?"

"It could be. It looks real to me." Mina had asked her for gold and silver thread. Iris wondered now if she'd gotten the idea from this cushion — wherever it had come from.

"I wasn't aware she knew people who had things like this." Bruno shook his head. "I don't even know who to ask if it's theirs."

"Just keep it for now."

He tossed it in a box and returned to the living room. She waited until she heard him rummaging again. She eased open the closet doors and stooped under the hanging clothes to reach past the vacuum cleaner and the boots to where she spied green garbage bags. She tugged one forward. The top wasn't fastened and she reached inside. Hats and hats and — ouch! She'd pricked herself on one of the buttons pinned to a hat.

She wiped the bead of blood on her jeans and reached for the next bag. More hats. Were all these bags filled with hats?

She snatched at another bag that felt more blockish and heavy. Without pulling it forward, she felt inside. Smooth and nubbled ridges. This was it! She tilted the bag to see inside and nearly fell onto the vacuum cleaner when Bruno spoke behind her.

"I just saw the time. I'm supposed to — Are you all right?"

She'd shoved away the bag and got to her feet but knew she looked flustered. "You can't believe how many bags of hats she's got."

"These are only the spare ones. She keeps her main hats in the front closet."

"More bags of hats?"

"She likes hats."

"Yeah … um … What were you saying?"

"I didn't see how late it was. I have an appointment to go look at another residence with the social worker."

"That's okay. I'll stay and get some more packing done."

"You don't have to. You shouldn't have to be here alone."

"I know I don't have to. I don't mind, Bruno. Truly, I don't. I want to help."

His eyes were sad, but he smiled. "You're too good. I appreciate it, really." He unhooked Mina's keys from his keyring and handed them to her. "See you at my place then. I'll pick up Thai, okay? I'll probably have to come back here in the evening."

"I'll come with you."

"I don't expect it, you know. She's my sister."

"Stop that." Iris leaned forward and gripped his shoulders. "We're a team, right? And she's my friend."

Again that deep, sad look and smile. He bent his head and they kissed. "I've got to go."

"Don't forget to ask for extra coriander," she called after him.

She heard the door close but still stepped around bags and boxes to watch from the window. He walked away, not looking back.

In the bedroom she heaved all the bags from the closet until they filled the floor space where the bed had been. She didn't have time to look beyond the first few pieces at the top of each bag, but she plunged her hands down the sides and felt the layers of stitched fabric.

She had to get the bags to her place before Bruno threw them in the garbage. He would say Mina had only kept them because she kept everything. Iris was the only one who understood how precious the embroidery was.

But even though she'd guessed that Mina had embroidery hidden, this wealth was beyond anything she'd expected. Years and years of textile art, a body of work — an oeuvre!

*

The hospital social worker had booked a conference room where they sat around a long table. Bruno and Mina, Faiza, the hospital social worker, one of Mina's nurses, the owner of the residence, and one of her employees. Faiza was more than usually shrill, insisting how much Mina would benefit from living in a group environment.

Would she? Bruno wondered. He still didn't trust Mina's strange passivity about leaving her apartment. She'd had a cerebral bleed, not a lobotomy.

Mina was in a good mood, hair freshly washed, a blue terrycloth robe Bruno had never before seen belted over her hospital gown, a Montreal Canadiens button pinned to the lapel. At her neck hung the pendant he'd given her for her birthday. It wasn't the same green as her ring, but she didn't seem to mind. She beamed, aware that she was the centre of attention.

He hadn't yet told her that he was packing her belongings. He'd decided not to ask about the money. He would never get a direct answer — and wasn't sure that he wanted to know.

The owner of the residence asked Mina if she liked playing bingo. Mina said she did, though as far as Bruno knew, she never had. She could learn though, certainly at the geriatric speed of the other residents.

He'd visited the place and been impressed by the airiness of the room she'd been assigned. It was at the corner of the building with windows on two sides. Her laundry would be done for her, the room vacuumed once a week, her sheets changed, her meals cooked. The shared bathroom was directly across the hall. He'd been less impressed by the meal being served in the dining room. Macaroni with a lurid orange sauce that suggested food colouring more than cheese. Baskets of sliced white bread on the table. No vegetables in evidence. Small dishes of chocolate pudding for dessert. Mina would love such a meal but would it be good for her weight and diabetes? For that matter, was it good for anyone?

The other residents were in their final years. Mina might be too, but she was thirty-nine, not eighty-nine. Except for noisy chewing, grumbling and gumming, silence reigned in the dining room. Hair was a variation on grey, white, dyed, or non-existent. Hands trembled. There were walkers next to the tables and against the walls. Bruno watched a man grasp his walker, struggle upright, and lean on it to creep-roll toward the elevator. It must take him the whole time between meals to travel from his room to the dining room and back again.

Mina was no athlete but she could still move. Her conversation had always been idiosyncratic, but she could have one. Faiza's plans to jumpstart Mina's social life in a group environment weren't likely to amount to much here.

Bruno watched the owner of the residence deciding that Mina was a darling. Indeed, she was on her best behaviour, agreeing to all conditions, claiming to eat all foods.

The woman who'd come with the owner introduced herself as Madame Bingham. She had a jaw so remarkably cleft that she seemed to have two joined chins. She told Mina that they would be seeing a lot of each other. "Will you like that?"

"Yeah."

"If you want to have breakfast with me, you'll have to get up at 6:30."

"D'okay."

Bruno said nothing, careful to hide his incredulity. Mina never rose before 9:00.

"Do you drink coffee or tea in the morning? We have both. I'll bring it to you myself."

"C-c-coffee!" Mina grinned as if she'd landed in paradise.

Bruno guessed that Madame Bingham was his age. Her manner toward Mina was overseeing and maternal. Maybe even a little bossy? Good luck with that, he thought.

The meeting ended with everyone looking pleased. He wasn't about to burst their complacent expectations. Let Mina move there. Let her get settled. Let Madame Bingham wait for her to show up for breakfast at 6:30. He had to remember to ask Faiza if the home could evict Mina once they discovered she wasn't as good-natured as she appeared. He wondered if they'd been told the story of the doorknobs. Did they know not to leave string, hammers, money, or toilet paper lying around? Or Publisacs. When packing up Mina's things, he'd found a heap of Publisacs disguised under a sheet to look like a pouffe in the bedroom.

He walked with Mina down the broad hallway to her hospital room. Despite her girth, her steps had always been light. A graceful waddle.

"Do you want to come with me to the cafeteria for a coffee?"

"Thé," she reminded him.

"Right," he said. Coffee for breakfast, tea throughout the day. He crooked his elbow for her to take. "Mina, Mina, where do you come from?"

She gave an amused, exasperated groan. He squeezed her hand against his ribs. She was his sister. He wasn't ready to lose her yet.

In the cafeteria she tackled the muffin he set in front of her with such avidity that he asked if she was getting enough to eat.

She considered. "Soup. Patates. Meatloaf."

"No dessert?"

"I'm dibète," she said proudly.

He remembered the chocolate caramels he'd found in her apartment. She wouldn't be able to cheat in the residence. That would be good for her, but it was also sad to rob her of her little rebellions.

"I know you're starting to remember things and I wondered ... Do you remember the stories I used to read to you?"

She didn't answer but she watched him.

"There was one about a princess who lost her golden ball when it fell into a well." Mina always used to trace her fingers across the drawing of the young woman with a tiny crown on her head who stared forlornly into the well. "Do you remember what happened with her ball?"

"A prince!"

"Not so fast. That wouldn't make much of a story if the prince happened to be right there. Besides, a well is deep and full of water. What would a prince be doing down there?"

Mina's eyes were unfocussed, as if she were watching the story at a distance.

"There was a ..." He waited.

"F-f-frog!"

"Exactly. The frog rescued her ball. But then she had to be his friend, and he started sitting by her plate at the table and sleeping on her pillow. And she didn't like that. So she—"

Mina raised an arm and flung the imaginary frog in a splat against the cafeteria wall.

Bruno nodded. "And *then* he turned into a prince."

"Yeah!"

He wondered if it was the drama that appealed to her, or if she liked how the princess's bad temper was ultimately rewarded.

"What about Hansel and Gretel? The brother and sister who got lost in the forest." Not lost, he remembered. That would have been a later, romanticized version. In his book, the parents didn't have enough food to feed the family, so they took the children into the forest and abandoned them. Authority figures were often corrupt and self-serving. The heroes were the children, the animals, the naïve, and the so-called idiots — a narrative Mina could identify with, even if she hadn't understood it as such.

"House," she said now. "With c-c-cookies."

"That's it. A house made of gingerbread cookies, and Hansel and Gretel were hungry. But the problem was that the house belonged to a ..."

"Hexe."

"You know the German word?" Though why was he surprised? Their mother used to talk to her in German and the stories he'd read to her were in German.

He was surprised by how happy he felt that she remembered following him into that magic world of riddles that solved mysteries, conniving wolves, straw that could be spun into gold, and fish that granted wishes. How often had they sat together, him reading out loud and her listening, leaning over the pages to see the drawings?

"There you are, Mina!" A nurse with a tray stopped at their table. "The social worker is looking for you upstairs," she told Bruno.

He gave Mina his arm again, but her grip was heavier, her gait not as steady. When he saw an orderly rolling a clutch of empty wheelchairs down the hallway, he asked for one.

Pushing the wheelchair, looking down on Mina, he saw how she arranged her hands on her lap, making sure that the birthstone on her ring was centered and visible. She gazed along the hallway as if upon crowds from a palanquin. Her hair was black with not a glint of grey yet. She was frailer but still so very much herself. She would have supervision and be safer in a residence. He wouldn't have to be on constant alert for whatever might happen next. That should have been a relief, but for the moment it felt complicated and unknown.

*

Iris wore a dress and a matching boxy jacket with wide lapels and cloth-covered buttons. First impressions were everything. She was determined to feel upbeat, even though the two art galleries she'd already visited had been failures. Not complete failures but still. The person she would have to see to discuss an exhibit wasn't there. Did she want to make an appointment? No, she declined politely. She would return again. *If* she returned again. She had five galleries on her list today. She crossed her fingers, wished for three times lucky, unzipped the portfolio she carried, and swung open the door.

An elegantly dressed individual behind a large bare desk gave Iris a cool once-over. Look all you want, Iris thought. She knew that her clothes passed muster.

She hadn't yet reached the desk when a woman in jeans and an untucked white shirt walked out from a well-lit back room that seemed to be an office. Iris made a split-second decision that she must be the owner. She had to be in order to get away with dressing so casually when she expected her employee with the movie star eyes and square shoulders to look impeccably smart.

Iris stepped forward, held out her hand, and introduced herself.

The gallerist — as she seemed to be — shook her hand but with no warmth. "Do we …?"

Iris reached into her portfolio for the embroidery with a cream linen matting she'd had mounted under plexiglass. She'd practised the move so often that it was swift and confident: herself under a blazing sun, the hour high noon, the portfolio a holster, the framed embroidery a gun, its effect a bullet. She didn't speak. Mina's embroidery spoke best for itself.

The gallerist flicked an automatic glance, her face already set in refusal, but her eyes stayed locked. She didn't move, then took the frame from Iris, and carried it toward a light.

Not waiting for permission, Iris lifted out the heavier book of embroideries she'd bound. The assistant, noting the owner's acute silence, flourished a bangled wrist for Iris to place the weighted fabric pages on the desk.

The gallerist had soft, fleshy features with intent, narrow-set eyes. She swivelled her head at the soft thump and walked to the desk. Slowly Iris folded back pages. A fat paisley bubble in yellow and cream tones with a subtle orange shimmer. Emerald swirls compressed in a squat turquoise onion.

"The irregular stitching. What's your rationale?"

Fantastic! Iris thought. She's interested and she doesn't even know the best part. "I don't make these," she said, trying to keep her voice even, though her pulse pounded in her temples. "I represent the artist, Philomena Corneau." She paused. "Who has Down Syndrome."

The woman's stance shifted. Out of the corner of her eye, Iris caught the complicit widening of lashes from the other side of the desk.

"Philomena is entirely self-taught. No one tells her what colours to choose or how to stitch them. I don't know if you've seen the work of Judith Scott, the internationally —"

The gallerist raised a hand for silence as she turned the pages. She stopped for a very long time, considering the vortex of jade and forest green exploding into pink that was Iris's favourite. This was the one that would convince her!

"Who are you in relation to the artist?" The voice was cold, but Iris knew that was only a strategy. She could sense the excitement.

"Her agent."

"How much work does she have?"

"Bags full."

"Bags?" A moue of disgust. "Is that how you store them?"

"She kept them in bags. I'm putting them in boxes."

"And how are they being stored?"

"I only recently discovered she had so much work. I'll get it stored properly." What did that entail, Iris wondered. Humidity and air control?

"Where are her family?"

"Philomena has full legal capacity." Hadn't Bruno often told her that Mina's signature was binding? "But since you ask, her parents have passed away. She only has her brother and he has no interest in her textile art." She didn't like making Bruno sound like a boor, but in this case it was true. She wasn't misrepresenting.

She described finding Philomena embroidering in the park and how she was immediately struck by her intuitive mastery and skill with colour. She began to visit Philomena, who created this amazing art with no seeming foresight or planning. And — so funny! — even though she was embroidering, she insisted on calling it knitting. Iris had decided not to mention the cerebral bleed. It had no bearing on her art. Philomena, the artist, was vibrant and alive.

"Who else has seen these?"

"I have several appointments," Iris lied. "But as yet —"

"Cancel them. You will deal with me, please. I'm Ruth. My assistant is Françoise. Give her my card, Françoise."

"Philomena hasn't had a show yet," Iris said.

"If she does work like this? That's not a problem. But as I said, you deal with me. You came to me and I'm interested — very interested — but my interest is exclusive. This is between us and only us. I want that understood."

"Agreed," Iris said.

Jenny had told her to consider several offers before making a decision, but Ruth's unequivocal response to Mina's embroidery was too compelling. Iris wanted to shriek like on one of Mina's game shows but she forced herself to stay calm and business-like.

*

When Gabriela stepped off the elevator on Mina's floor, Bruno was coming down the hallway. They'd seen each other a few times now and were able to talk more easily, though so far only about Mina. She knew he'd been packing up her apartment and asked how it was going.

"Pretty well done. For better or worse. I know she'll blame me for every single pin I didn't keep, the dollar-store junk and clothes that didn't even fit anymore."

He called it junk but she heard the regret in his voice. The accumulated jumble of trinkets, figurines, stuffed animals, and cushions was Mina's heyday — and he'd had to dismantle it.

"Oh," she said, remembering the vivid needlework draped over her furniture and tacked to the walls. "I hope you didn't throw away her embroidery."

"I took most of that, even the boyfriends' names."

"Her princes."

"Her princes," he repeated. And with a grimace, "Would you believe it, she even embroidered Pierre's name, that creep."

"That's —"

"I know. I threw his away."

They said nothing for a minute. How, in Mina's scheme of life, did a man who had assaulted her sexually rate a place on the wall? And what did that imply about the other names?

"I should go see her." Gabriela nodded in the direction of Mina's room. "Do you know, she knit me a cushion for my birthday? It's gorgeous — like her embroidery — the colours so wild and deliberate."

"A Mina special."

"I love it. But it was odd. She stuffed it with ..." Gabriela hesitated, unsure about mentioning things she and Bruno had done together.

He was watching her, waiting.

"Do you remember when we took her fabric shopping for curtains? Did you give her the leftover fabric because —"

"No!" he said far too loudly for a hospital corridor and an orderly pushing a trolley gave him a stern look. He told Gabriela about the disappeared curtains. Stuffing the cushion with them must have seemed the ideal solution.

"She used me!"

"Not completely. You got a cushion out of the deal."

"I guess ..."

ALICE ZORN

"It's all in the past now," he said. Again that tone of regret. And with a sigh, "I should let you go see her. You're her favourite person."

He couldn't mean that, Gabriela thought as he walked away. Surely he knew he was Mina's favourite person, even if she complained about him and called him names.

*

There were only three steps — like at her apartment. Three was lucky! Mina grabbed the railing and hoisted herself up. One step, then the next and the next.

"Are you okay?" Bruno asked.

She knew how to do this! Even though she was puffing at the top. This was the new place she was coming to after the hospital. First, the hospital where she had been sick, and now this place until she got better, and then she could go home again.

"What do you think?" Bruno asked.

She liked that there was a carpet in the hall, but the living room they walked past was full of old people. Very old people who couldn't do anything anymore.

A nurse walked toward them. "Hello, bonjour! How are you? En français? In English?"

Mina didn't answer. How was she supposed to know what the nurse wanted to talk?

"She understands both," Bruno said.

"No kidding! That's great!"

Mina didn't like how loud the nurse was. She didn't like the old people sitting and doing nothing. She didn't like the smell.

But here was Madame Bingham, bustling down the hallway, and she grasped Mina's shoulders and gave her two big smackeroo kisses. "My new friend!" She sounded so happy that it made Mina feel happy too. "But listen, my little Minnie Mouse, I'm making a cake, so I have to get back to the kitchen. Your brother can show you your room."

"Here's the elevator," Bruno said.

She knew what a levoluva was. Daddy used to fix broken levo-
luvas. That was his job. Why did Bruno think that he had to tell her
what it was?

"You're on the third floor. Number 3." He pressed the button.
"You'll like it here, you have a nice room. Wait until you see."

The levoluva was slow. The slowest she'd ever taken. The whole
while Bruno kept talking. Too many words, too fast. What was wrong
with him?

She followed him down a hallway of closed doors. Some had
pictures or things on them. Dried flowers, words on plaques. There
was still that smell she didn't like. He stopped before a door with a
poster of Elvis — exactly like the one she had on her wall at home!

"Are you ready?" He opened the door and waved her in.

Then nothing made any sense — because there was her green
bedspread and cushions, her armchair, the shelves where she kept
her notebooks and knitting. Even her TV? Her princes' names on the
walls? Mama's angel over the bed?

"Wh-wh-wh —"

"You don't have as much space here, so we couldn't keep everything."

"What d-d-d-d —"

"This is where you'll be living now. I'll come to see you here. Iris
will come, maybe Gabriela, and Faiza too. She's still going to be your
social worker."

The words wouldn't come out, her throat was too choked with
fury. She balled her fist to clobber him and he backed away.

"You knew you were moving, Mina. I told you, we all told you.
You can't live by yourself anymore. We —"

"My apartment!" she bellowed.

"It's not your apartment anymore. I'm sorry, Mina, I'm sorry."

"My lease!"

"The lease is gone. We've explained it to you over and over. You
can't live by yourself anymore. Shit, I knew you didn't understand!
You'll fall down again and no one will find you till it's too late."

"My th-th-things!" she shrieked with so much force that her voice cracked.

"We kept what we could. Look, here's your TV, your CD player, your cushions —"

He was pointing around the room but she didn't *want to see!* They weren't her things if they were here! Her things were in her apartment!

"I even got Mama's angel fixed, did you see?"

She began to bawl with rage and sorrow, her heart rent with betrayal.

"Please, Mina, please stop! We had no choice. We told you —"

Madame Bingham flung open the door. "What's all this shouting? What's going on? Don't you like how your brother arranged your room? It doesn't matter. We can fix it up however you want." Madame Bingham pulled her close in a hug. "You're my Minnie Mouse. I'll help you, you'll see." And to Bruno, "You can go. I'll take care of her."

"But she's —"

"Go. I think it's better that you leave us alone. We're fine here."

From where Mina had her head tucked, she could see that Bruno didn't want to go, and although part of her didn't want him to leave her in this strange place, it wasn't as strange with Madame Bingham holding her. And she was so upside-down in her head — and angry about what he'd done, putting her things here where they didn't belong, that she didn't want to see him!

"Will you be all right?" He was stooping to get her to look at him, but she turned her face into Madame Bingham's neck.

"Of course, my little Minnie Mouse will be all right with me, won't you?"

"Her name is Mina."

"All my darlings have special names," Madame Bingham said in a voice so soft that Mina felt comforting specialness seep into her.

Bruno still wouldn't leave but Mina refused to look at him.

"Go," Madame Bingham said again and that felt good. That she was telling Bruno what to do.

"I'll call later, okay, Mina?"

He waited but she wasn't going to say d'okay or bye. He didn't deserve it.

He shuffled his feet, finally moving to the door. "You'll be all right here. I know you don't think so, but you will."

Then he did go, and she almost called out that he couldn't leave her here, but Madame Bingham was walking with her to the bed.

"I see you've got Elvis on your door. You like Elvis?"

"Blue Sway Shoes," Mina said.

"That's one of my favourites too." Madame Bingham started to hum it as she stroked Mina's shoulders and back. Humming wasn't as good as when Daddy used to sing it but it was nice to sit close like this.

"Now, you tell me where you want everything. I think the bed is fine here in this corner, but we can move the armchair and the TV if you want. And look at that lovely angel. Who gave you that?"

"Mama."

"Of course she did. Because she loves you like I still love my little girl, even though she isn't with me anymore. The love stays. The love is forever. You know that, don't you? That's how it is with mothers and their little girls."

Mina could feel the truth of the words. The way Madame Bingham said them made the room feel less strange.

Except that she was still angry with Bruno for moving her things here. Very angry.

*

Mina's phone wasn't installed yet, so Bruno had to call the residence. The attendant who answered said that Mina had had supper in the dining room with the others and was doing very well. Bruno doubted that she was doing *very well*, but maybe Madame Bingham had convinced her to behave. Or perhaps the attendant had no idea who Bruno was asking about. He said he wanted to speak with his sister but the attendant said he couldn't expect her to come all the way downstairs. Don't you have a cordless phone? Bruno asked. Apparently not.

In the morning he was again told that Mina couldn't come to the phone. He asked to speak with Madame Bingham. He had to wait so long that he'd finished his coffee before she picked up the receiver.

"Hello?" And then, "Yes, yes, yes," when he said who he was.

"Did my sister get up to have breakfast with you at 6:30 this morning?"

"Of course."

"*Really?*" He didn't try to hide that he didn't believe her.

"She had one piece of toast with peanut butter and another with Cheez Whiz."

That had to be Mina. "Will someone please tell her I'll come later today?"

"We think it's best you don't."

"What did you say?"

"It will be easier for her to adjust if she accepts that she has to."

He didn't agree. He also wasn't letting this woman dictate when he saw Mina. He would have marched to the residence at that moment if it weren't that Val had called a meeting.

Not yet nine o'clock, but the air was already humid, the sun brilliant. That these same sidewalks were rutted with snow a few months ago was hard to imagine. At least this winter he wouldn't have to worry about Mina slipping on ice in her stubbornness to get to the dollar store. He would come and take her out though. He'd kept her purple parka, as well as one bag of hats. One bag was more than she would ever need, but who would Mina be without her hats?

At the studio Tandi was chatting with Liliane from across the hallway.

"You," Liliane said when she saw Bruno. "I made apricot cake."

"My mother used to —"

"That is what you always say! You don't say, thank you, Liliane, how sweet you are to bring us apricot cake. You say, my mother made cake like this."

"But she did."

Liliane rolled her eyes.

"Thank you," he said. "How sweet you are to bring us apricot cake." Full stop. But she was watching him suspiciously and he couldn't resist. "My mother used to make apricot cake."

Tandi laughed. "This isn't about cake, Liliane. This is about nostalgia."

Val and Mathieu were coming up the metal stairs with a great reverberation of talk and steps. Liliane said she would bring them cake later.

Val must have an important lunch meeting because she wore a chic, pale green tunic over wide-legged trousers. Bruno asked if they were recording and she said, Let's. Everyone got settled on a chair, on the floor, against a wall as Bruno opened the tripod and attached the camera.

Val wanted to discuss the short piece for the performance at Pied Gauche. "Five minutes max. The question is whether we whip up something new or chop something from the repertoire."

"What about that sequence with the hula hoops?" Tandi sat on a mat, knees bent and the bottoms of her feet pressed together.

"Kid stuff," Mathieu said. "If we're performing with other dancers, we're competing, and hula hoops aren't going to make headline news."

Tandi looked at Val. "It's not a competition, is it?"

"Not officially, but he's got a point. There will be some vying to outdo each other."

Tandi grimaced. "Sometimes I just wish ..."

"Listen, I might have an idea." Val held up her hands, clasped tight, fingers laced to form a single tight fist. "This is you." She looked at Mathieu and Tandi. "A knot that has to break apart because if it doesn't—" She waved her clenched hands before her, straining the muscles of her bare arms, but couldn't tug them apart. Even when one finger lifted, the other fingers held fast. "Joined like this, they strangle each other."

"If that's supposed to be us," Mathieu said, "it's a total, two-body, clove hitch. That's intense."

"We have to break apart," Tandi said. "Either that or we die."

Val dropped her hands, slack now. She leaned back in her chair and crossed her legs. "Three to four minutes in a knot..."

"Lots we can do," Tandi said. "Roll around the floor, crawl up a wall. Almost break free but not—"

"But finally we will," Mathieu said. "Because otherwise, like you said..."

The sandal that hung off Val's foot bobbed. "Could be people. A relationship. An idea. Anything that's too rigidly stuck."

"What about staging?" Bruno asked.

"Like Tandi said. The floor and the walls. We keep it simple. Leotards and skin."

"How about..." He was trying to follow the idea he'd just had, wondering how to do it.

"Yes?"

"If their hands were gold."

"You mean gold gloves?" Tandi asked. "I hate dancing with gloves on."

"I was thinking gold skin but makeup wouldn't last. Probably paint."

"Gold hands and feet!" Mathieu said.

Tandi swished her hands through the air. "Very abracadabra."

"Maybe," Val said. "Gold is precious. It could symbolize striving."

Bruno was thinking about the visuals. The two-bodied knot struggling to break apart would be tense, but the flash of gold would intrigue. He remembered how the gold leafer said that gold pulled the eyes.

Tandi held out a hand and Mathieu pulled her up.

"Gently," Val said, staying seated in her fine clothes.

They rolled their shoulders, stretched on their toes, Mathieu dropping into knee squats. Bruno saw, though, how each eyed the other's body like the corresponding half of a knot.

*

Mina woke to an orderly standing by her bed talking.

"I thought you were already up. Didn't I see you downstairs having breakfast?" The woman walked around the room, opening the blinds and straightening the toiletries by the sink. "Aren't you a strange one, going back to bed after breakfast? The others are all downstairs, dressed and watching TV."

At that, Mina struggled up in bed and put on her glasses to check that her TV was still in the corner where it had been when she fell asleep last night.

"You don't have much to say in the morning, do you? I think it's time for you to get up and brush your teeth and wash your face. You can wash on your own, can't you?"

Mina was shocked into saying, "Yeah." Of course she could! But she got dressed earlier that morning to have breakfast with Madame Bingham, and washing came before dressing. Too late now.

"Do you remember where the bathroom is across the hallway? You let me know when you want to take a bath and I'll help set you up."

Mina had no intention of having a bath where other people did. A toilet was okay. A toilet was like when you were in a store and had to use the washroom. But bathtubs were … She didn't know the word but the feeling was strong.

"I can't make your bed if you're still in it. How about you get up? I'll be back in a few minutes." She closed the door behind her but then opened it again. "That wasn't a suggestion. You get up now."

Mina didn't like her tone. Also how she opened the door without knocking. Who said she could come in—while Mina was sleeping!

People kept doing that here. Walking in to see what she was doing. Looking around. She didn't like that at all!

She decided to stay in bed. She didn't have to get up. She didn't have to do anything she didn't want to. If that orderly tried to make her, she would give her a good shove.

Except that lying here while she was awake was boring. She squinted at her new watch. 10:38. Her old watches had disappeared when she was in the hospital. This new watch had a cloth strap she couldn't fasten tight like the old ones. She would have to get to a store to buy a better one. She would have to...

She looked around. Where was her money? Madame Bingham said Bruno had brought her things but so far all she could see were Mama's angel, her TV, her armchair, the shelf with some of her notebooks and little animals, the cushion with the silver and gold knitting—which was supposed to be hidden! It was too confusing to think about all that was hers that *wasn't* here.

And now her door opened again! She was about to shout *get out*—and felt only a little mollified to see Madame Bingham.

"What's this I hear? You went back to bed after breakfast? How about you get up and brush your teeth." Madame Bingham perched on the bed, pressing her lips tight to show that she meant business, but Mina could see the smile in her eyes when she leaned forward to stroke Mina's hair from her face. The feeling was so delicious that Mina wished she could grow small and curl up in Madame Bingham's lap.

"Out of bed now, okay? And I'll make you a cup of tea."

"I d-d-don't—" Mina flung an exasperated hand at the sink. There was water, a new kettle, and a box of teabags, but—! "Pas d'lait."

"You'll have to come have your tea downstairs where there's milk. If you want milk in your room, you'll have to get a little fridge. That's something you can tell your brother. He called this morning to ask how you were. As if there was a problem! Why would there be a problem? Of course you're fine. You're with us now. You're our Minnie Mouse."

Mina was still very angry with Bruno because he'd brought her things here where they weren't supposed to be, but she had to talk to him. "I need Bruno."

"You don't have a phone, ma chère. I hear you're having one installed but you don't have one yet. I'm not even sure that's a good idea." Madame Bingham flung back the duvet and was waving her out of bed.

"I n-n-need Bruno!"

"But there's no phone." Madame Bingham shrugged as if there was nothing she could do, but she'd just said that Bruno called, so there had to be a phone somewhere.

There was a knock on the door. Madame Bingham called, "Yes?"

Iris peeked in. "Hey, Mina! I came to see how you're doing."

"I need Bruno!"

"He'll be here this afternoon, he told me."

"I don't think so," Madame Bingham said. "She needs to get settled. We advised him not to come."

"Maybe you advised him but you can't stop him. And besides, she wants to see him."

"It's better that he stays away. We have experience with these situations."

"I don't doubt your experience, but I know Mina and you don't." Iris took her phone from her pocket. "Let's see if I can reach him."

Madame Bingham screwed her mouth. Was Iris calling Bruno? That was good, but Mina could tell Madame Bingham didn't like it. And didn't like Iris.

Iris was listening to her phone and now lifted a finger. "Hi Bruno ... Yes, I know, I'm at the residence ... She's fine and she wants to talk to you. Hang on."

The phone was flat like a calculator except Bruno's voice was coming from it. "Mina, are you there?"

"S-s-something to tell you."

"I'm listening."

"I need a key! The door!"

"Sorry, Mina, but you can't have a lock on your door."

"I want one!"

"I'm sure you do, but that's the whole point of you being there. So they can check on you in case you fall over again."

"Won't!"

"I hope you won't but the doctor said you might."

"I n-n-need a key."

"Let me think what to do, okay? I'll try to come up with something. Tell me, how was your first night? Did you sleep?"

"Yeah. But I need …"

"I'm all ears."

"A frigo for milk! For t-t-tea."

Madame Bingham said, "A mini fridge."

"A mini frigo!"

"I pretty well exhausted your bank account getting you set up there. I don't know how much a mini fridge costs. I guess you want cold Pepsi in your room too."

"Yeah!"

"Let me see, okay? Maybe I'll have to give you a present for being so good while you were in the hospital and moving into your new place."

She liked presents and she wanted milk and Pepsi in her room, but that didn't mean she had to agree to be good in this new place.

*

Two days earlier Iris had brought her laptop to Bruno's to show him videos of Judith Scott and a few other sites she'd bookmarked. She would start by introducing him to the idea of Down Syndrome artists in general. Then she would tell him what she had planned for Mina. If he expressed doubt as to whether Mina's embroidery was art, guess what? She already had a gallery eager to exhibit Mina's work. Fait accompli. She couldn't make it any easier or more obvious. Mina *was* an artist.

But when she got to his place, he was so miserable about Mina's reaction to the residence. I knew it, he kept saying. I knew she didn't understand when we told her she was moving. You should have seen how angry she was. She took a swing at me. She'll adapt, Iris said. Didn't you tell me how she screamed blue murder when you moved her from Park Ex to the Pointe, and look how that turned out. It'll take some time, that's all. You'll go see her and I'll take her out for frîtes and she'll adjust. I bet she'll love not having to fix her meals anymore.

Still Bruno sighed, worried, and she rubbed his tense neck muscles and slid her hands down to his shirt buttons. It wasn't the right time to talk to him about Judith Scott.

The next morning when Jenny called to find out what happened, Iris admitted she hadn't told Bruno yet. Jenny said she was crazy. The timing would have been perfect — telling him that Mina was about to become a star just when it looked like all her doors were closing. You can't wait, Jenny insisted. You already waited too long. Iris told Jenny to stop nagging. She knew what she was doing.

But that evening Bruno said not to come over. He was spending it with Mina. How about tomorrow she come over for supper?

Again she packed her laptop. On the way to Bruno's she bought salad fixings. Leaf lettuce, radicchio, fennel, avocado. He'd said he would get a baguette, pâté, and cheese. At his house she placed the laptop like a guest, silent yet visible, at one end of the table.

Bruno was in a better mood because Mina was talking to him again. Or rather, he added, she had demands. Her cable had been installed — which she didn't acknowledge, of course — but what about her phone? And *where* was the mini fridge?

"She sounds like her old self," Iris said.

"We'll see ..." And then, as if he'd only just thought of it, he mentioned that the troupe had started work on a new dance.

Iris was about to scoop a carrot stick through hummus. "You never told me."

"The show at Pied Gauche. Sure, I did. A whole bunch of us, five minutes max, remember?"

"But not what dance you were doing."

"Sorry, my head's full of Mina just now. And I didn't see you yesterday."

He started to explain the dance, gripping his hands in a fist over his plate of salad, pretending he couldn't tug them apart. "It'll be short but intense."

Iris was watching him. Why didn't he say anything about costumes?

He nudged the salad bowl. "Do you want more?" She shook her head and he emptied the rest of the salad on his plate and began forking up leaves. "The set will be simple. Probably only the floor. Val has to go look at the space where we'll be performing. If the back wall is solid — not just a backdrop but a real wall — she'll use that too. She basically wants to work with surfaces. No furniture, no props."

"And costumes?" Iris said stiffly.

"No costumes for this. Val wants leotards."

"What about a straitjacket? Not a real one, obviously, just the idea. Long sleeves wrapped around the torso, something like that?"

He kept smoothing his knife across the Gorgonzola he'd spread on a chunk of baguette. "Val already said. Leotards and skin."

"That's because she hasn't heard my idea yet."

"There aren't always costumes, Iris. Dance is about movement and the body. Everything else — the lights, sound, props, costumes — serve the movement and the dance. Val doesn't introduce extra-dance elements unless she decides they're necessary."

"She liked my costumes in the last dance. She liked them a lot."

"That was the last dance. This is a new dance."

"Fine. So I should talk with her about costumes, not you."

He cleared his throat. "Sure, of course you can talk to Val if you want to."

She was about to retort that she didn't need his permission to talk to Val, but he was already talking again. "Can we not argue about this? My nerves are on edge with everything that's going on with Mina."

"I don't want to argue." And she didn't. But her idea was good and he wasn't listening. She didn't like how he was putting her off. Why had he told her they would get her to design costumes, only to block her? She didn't like his Bruno-knows-best tone that might work with Mina, but not with her.

He asked if she'd heard about a new Iranian film. Tandi said it was good. Did Iris want to go? Maybe, she said. He tapped his forehead and said he had to remember to call the phone company again about Mina's phone.

At the other end of the table the laptop gleamed dully, but Iris no longer wanted to talk to him about Down Syndrome artists. Not this evening.

Bruno began stacking plates and stood to clear the table. She said she had to return to the studio to work for a couple of hours. Up until now, when she came for supper, she spent the night. She thought he might say something but he didn't. He saw her slide her laptop into her knapsack but didn't ask why she'd brought it.

They said bye and kissed but didn't move closer. "Don't work too late," he said.

*

Mina liked breakfast and lunch because Madame Bingham was there. The margarine tub was already open on the table and if you needed someone to spread it on your toast, they would. But in the afternoon Madame Bingham went home. She came to Mina's room to kiss her bye-bye and promised she would see her for breakfast in the morning.

Once Madame Bingham left, everything started to go wrong. At 4:30, when Mina was supposed to go downstairs for supper, she couldn't because the levoluva didn't come. She waited and said câlisse at it, but it still didn't come, even though she could hear it moving and creaking.

When the door finally opened, the levoluva was full with a woman in a wheelchair and two old men with walkers. They stared at her but didn't move aside. The door started to close. She jabbed the button and it opened again. Still no one moved to let her on.

She kept pressing the button and the levoluva stayed there. Then one of the men called her a bad word. People weren't supposed to do that.

Behind her in the hallway, a door banged open and an orderly called her. He said he would show her how to take the stairs. She didn't want to walk down the stairs but the orderly said supper was getting cold. He said Madame Bingham told him to make sure she came to supper. Step by step he walked down the stairs with her.

In the dining room he brought her to the table where the man who'd said the bad word sat. No! She was not sitting there! The orderly said she had to. She knew she didn't. He started to argue, but she kept saying no — and no was no! Finally they fixed a place at another table, but now she was sitting beside a man who wore a watch with a very loud tick. She couldn't eat with that tick-tick-tick-tick-tick. Why was there no radio or TV? Tick-tick-tick-tick-tick-tick-tick-tick. She liked noodles and tomato sauce, so she ate. But it was hard to eat while she was angry. She didn't want to be here — not in this chair, not at this table, not in this room, not in this place! Tick-tick-tick-tick-tick-tick-tick. When they put a bowl of chocolate pudding before her, she ate it, even though she wasn't supposed to. It wasn't her fault that they gave her pudding. Tick-tick-tick-tick-tick-tick! That watch was making her crazy!

She shoved out of her chair to go back to her room, but one of the old people hollered when she used her big belly and bum to push past the walkers to get on the levoluva before them. The orderly said she had to wait in line. Those were the rules. Too bad! Tit for tat!

In her room, even with the TV on loud, she could still hear tick-tick-tick-tick-tick in her ears. Her head was hurting with it. She wanted a cup of tea but didn't have any milk. If she was at home, there would be milk. Everything that was happening was wrong. She needed to tell Bruno — only she had no phone. If she still had no phone tomorrow, how was Gabriela going to call her at 10:00? She needed a phone!

Her door opened and she glared. The orderly said Madame Bingham had told him to bring her a cup of tea. She relaxed a little when she heard Madame Bingham's name. He set the tea next to her and sat on the bed. "She's going to explain to you tomorrow about the elevator."

He cocked his head at the TV. "What's that show about?"

She looked at him sideways. Everyone knew this show.

"It's good you have your own TV if you watch English shows. Downstairs it's French."

He kept talking. Why didn't he go so she could watch her program?

There was a knock on the door and it opened slowly. "Mina?"

Bruno! How she had wished he would come! Then she remembered how upset she was and how all this was his fault and she glared at him.

"Are you her brother?" the orderly asked.

"I am. You can go."

"She's —"

"You can go," Bruno said with an angry stone voice. She hated it when he used it with her, but she liked him saying it to the orderly, who sidled out past Bruno so fast that she grinned.

"How are you settling in?" Bruno asked. "How was supper?"

She remembered she was angry because he'd left her here and she stopped grinning.

"I asked them on the way up and they said you ate everything."

"There's a m-m-man with a watch!"

"Since when do you have a problem with watches?"

"Tick! Tick! Tick! Tick!" With each tick she smashed her finger on the armrest.

Bruno groaned. "You're not complaining because a man's watch is too loud, are you? You're not, right? I mean, you're really not. Tell me you're not?"

"Yeah!"

"Why did you sit there then?"

"Ils m'ont mis là."

"Fine. I'll ask them to put you at another table — though it might not be a bad idea for you to get used to this man's watch, because once you're at another table, you'll find something else to complain about."

She crossed her arms, not interested in his blah-blah-blah.

"So tell me, where are you going to put this mini fridge?"

That was a good question! She considered the room. A frigo belonged in the kitchen and the closest she had to a kitchen was her sink. She pointed under it.

"The P-trap will be in the way under the sink, but I think you're right. It's going to have to be on the floor. Will you be able to get down there?"

She remembered a movie where a naked man reached from his bed into a mini frigo on the floor beside the bed for a beer. He handed it to the naked woman with him. She peered now at the floor beside her bed, wondering if that would be a better place.

Bruno had sat on the bed and was looking at the hidden word puzzle she had open on the table. "You're doing puzzles again. Are you finding them harder than they used to be?"

What did he mean? She did what she could and what she couldn't, she didn't.

"What about your stitching? Iris says you're not doing it anymore."

Mina puffed out her cheeks. Iris was bothering her! Always bringing her thread! She waved it around and pointed at the walls, and even put cloth on a hoop and left it on the table. Mina threw the hoop in the garbage. She didn't need anyone to do that for her. She could do it herself. But she didn't want to!

"You've always stitched, Mina. From way back when we were kids, remember? That was what you did all day while I was at school learning about Robespierre and dissecting frogs. I came home and you were in your corner of the sofa with your needle and thread." He looked around the room. "Where is your tray of threads?"

The tray was too big for the small garbage can in her room, so she'd hidden it. She didn't want to see it anymore. The colours didn't dance for her like they used to. They were dead now. She couldn't knit dead colours.

"Don't you want to stitch anymore?"

"No."

"Not at all?"

"No!"

"Don't get upset. That's okay. If you don't want to, you don't want to. How you spend your time is entirely up to you — as long as you're not bored." He nodded at the TV. "You've got your constant companion there. And ... do you think you'll make friends here?"

"Madame Bingham!"

"She works here. That's different. What about your neighbours?"

The old people? She arched her eyebrows at how very stupid that was.

"Let me show you what I brought." He went to the door, opened it, and reached into the hallway. "Ta-da!" He flourished a roll of bright orange cardboard, slipped off the rubber band, and let it unfurl. It had a large black X with words across the top. "The X is to make people stop. The words say that they have to knock before opening your door."

She liked making people stop. But an X wasn't a key. "I n-n-need a key."

"I told you, Mina, you can't have a key. In case you fall down again. You were lucky last time. I don't want you to be unlucky if it happens again."

"I won't fall."

"It's not in your control."

"A key is better."

"For some things, yes. For some things, no. This time, it's no. That's just how it is. No key."

He taped the X on her door below Elvis and made her come out into the hallway to see what it looked like when her door was closed. It was okay. She liked the X. But Bruno was wrong. A key was always better.

*

Iris strode quickly, glimpsing the river, grey and flat, through breaks in the marsh grass. The path was beaten bare with tree roots humped and buckled across it.

Bruno had tried to warn her but she hadn't wanted to listen. Big mistake. Telling Val about an idea that didn't interest her was like asking for a bucket of ice water in the face. Iris would gladly have told Bruno he was right about Val, but he hadn't called last night. Why not? She didn't need all this uncertainty and negativity now when she wanted to be psyched up about bringing Ruth to see Mina.

Ruth had been pushing for a meeting and Iris finally told her that Mina had been ill. Ruth had the arrogant impatience of people used to getting what they wanted. But that was good, no? A sign of how interested and committed she was. Iris remembered how long and hard Ruth had looked at Mina's embroidery. The unmistakable stillness of genuine awe.

Except that Iris could also feel the predatory quality beneath the privileged chic. She sometimes sensed it with her clients. The aristocracy of money could be heartless and that made her anxious.

And Mina. What was going on with her? Iris hadn't seen her embroidering once since the bleed. She didn't even look at the thread Iris brought. It was like she didn't know what it was for.

Iris ground her teeth. Why hadn't she taken a single video of Mina embroidering when she was ensconced on the sofa in her apartment? Who needed a professional photographer? Idiot! She had a phone. She'd wanted everything to be perfect — and now ...

What if Mina never embroidered again? The possibility made Iris slow to a halt. She had bags of Mina's work, but this wasn't only about the embroidery, gorgeous as it was, but the marvel of Philomena — who had to *be* Philomena for everything to happen.

Iris pushed through the fronds of marsh grass to the edge of the river. The water, glimmering and sepia under an overcast sky, betrayed nothing. Gave her no answers.

*

Bruno had pulled over the van to let Pascal out. Pascal was the nephew of one of the antique store dealers. A young fellow, stocky, he often helped when Bruno did deliveries.

Today they'd brought a bird's-eye maple dresser to a condo in Ahuntsic. The building was a sleek metal and glass tower, but the unit was furnished with antiques in dark wood, leaded glass, and brocade that gave the rooms a weighted feel, especially facing the bright, floor-to-ceiling view onto the city. Bruno filed the atmospheric disconnect in his mental archive. An idea that might one day work in a dance. Or not.

That was what Iris didn't understand. Straitjacket sleeves wrapped around the torso might look interesting, but that wasn't reason enough to use it. They all floated ideas, talked about them, waited to see what gelled — and what didn't. That was the process. He hadn't meant to sound so dismissive, but he also hadn't expected that she would take it so personally. If she was going to continue making costumes, she was going to have to learn.

He firmly believed that, but after a day had passed and he still hadn't heard from her, he began to question whether he should be the one to teach her. As her boyfriend — if that was what he was becoming — he could have listened and let her keep talking. In the performance milieu there were enough other people ready to knock you down a notch.

He liked Iris. He liked her a lot. She had so much energy and excitement. She'd been so happy about the britches. She'd always been kind to Mina. The way she spread her arms wide to the river. The freckles across her cheeks and nose. Her blond curls like cork-screws of light. Her mouth on his body. Her mouth, her body ... She was lively and bold in a way Gabriela hadn't been. He was lucky to have met her, he knew he was. When he told her that he and Gabriela had broken up because she wanted a baby, Iris assured him she didn't and never had.

He flexed his hands on the steering wheel as he waited for traffic to move. How could he and Iris have fought over a straitjacket? He wanted Iris in his life. He didn't want to lose her. So what, she had an idea for a costume that he didn't think Val would like? He didn't have to be the one to tell her. Breaking into costume design was so important to her.

He glanced into the rear-view mirror where cars were snaked behind him. He wasn't moving anyhow. He turned into a side street and parked. Wasn't that what cell phones were for?

"Hello." Her voice was reserved.

"Iris, I'm sorry."

"Val told you."

"Val? I haven't talked to her. I wanted to say I'm sorry for the other night. I should have explained better about not needing costumes for this dance. That's why I didn't tell you about it before. Believe me, if Val ever says she wants costumes, I guarantee you'll be the first to hear."

"You mean, *if* Val ever wants to see me again."

"What do you mean?"

"You tried to warn me not to call her."

"No, you can call her. I wasn't trying to stop you. It's just that I knew she already decided what she wanted and she can be —"

"Dictatorial?"

"Oh. Yeah, she can," Bruno said. "We can all tell you stories. But you know she loved the britches you made and next time we need costumes, she'll be asking for you."

"Do you really think so?"

"Definitely. Listen, I'm at the other end of the city and traffic isn't moving, but when I get home, do you want to meet me for supper in Verdun? Everything seems quiet at the residence and for one evening I think Mina can do without me."

"I'd like that, Bruno, I would. But can I take a rain check? I have to be somewhere tomorrow and I still need to prepare."

"You're really busy, eh?"

"A couple of things, yes. I'll tell you all about it when I see you."

"So how about tomorrow?"

"That would be great."

When he eased back into traffic, it was still only stop-and-start creeping, but he was smiling.

*

Iris met Ruth at the gallery so they could drive to the residence together. She explained that after Philomena's recent illness, the hospital had wanted her to spend a few weeks in a convalescent facility. She was fudging some details, but why would where Mina lived have any bearing on her embroidery?

Iris didn't know cars but she knew design and material. Ruth's car was expensive. Seats in real leather. She and Ruth made disconnected small talk about weather, traffic downtown, the incessant road construction that plagued Montreal. Iris told herself to relax. She made her hands curl loosely in her lap. But it was hard not to feel nervous. So much was at stake. She had to direct Ruth along the streets below the Lachine Canal.

"Left here … Next right … This is it." She nodded at the greystone building with rows of windows.

"Shouldn't she be in a larger facility with an occupational therapy department that has an arts component?"

"Everything I showed you was made on her sofa. That's where she creates."

"True," Ruth murmured. "We want the autodidact, outsider angle." But she narrowed her eyes at the locked front door.

"For the Alzheimer's patients," Iris said quickly.

"Does Philomena ... ?"

"Down Syndrome." Iris hadn't meant to snap but why was Ruth so suspicious? Iris rushed her past the large common room where the geriatric residents slouched on the sofas. Luckily, the elevator was there.

But Ruth had still seen. Frowning, she asked, "How old is Philomena?"

"Thirty-nine. She was transferred here after the hospital because there was a room available. You know, unless you go private, you can't choose where they send you." A woman like Ruth might not know that.

When the elevator doors opened on the third floor, Iris saw how the corridor of closed doors looked like a residence, not a health-care facility. This was all so wrong. So *not* how she had envisioned introducing Philomena. And — shit! The Elvis poster on the door was probably okay, but she'd forgotten about Bruno's orange sign with an X.

Ignoring it, she made a show of looking at her watch. "Excellent! Two o'clock on the dot. Philomena is very particular about time." She knocked firmly but when she heard only the TV, she opened the door. "Philomena? Here's the person I said I was going to bring to meet you."

She almost didn't step inside when she saw Mina, sitting low in her armchair that was even lower because Bruno had taken the legs off so that her feet could reach the floor, but the impetus of all that she'd set in motion was underway and Ruth was close behind her. Mina's hair was raked aside and needed a wash. Her hands rested possessively on her belly. She wore stretch pants that might also have been pyjamas.

Iris had told Mina she was going to bring someone important and had assumed she would wear nice clothes. Why, why, *why* hadn't she come earlier to check?

Stop it, she told herself. Mina's clothes didn't matter. The art she created was the treasure. Ruth should be used to artists and their irregular habits. She should be able to see past discount stretch pants. Bedhead should be okay too.

Fortunately Mina was in a good mood, responding affably to questions about how her day was going and how she was feeling. Ruth's questions were polite, yet Iris could feel how she was probing.

"So, Philomena, you must be looking forward to being well and in your own home again."

"Yeah."

"Do you miss it?"

"Yeah."

"Let's hope you get back soon then."

Mina began to describe her apartment, listing her sofa, her kitchen, her own bathroom, her many things that were hers — but that weren't h-h-here!

Iris doubted Ruth understood every word, but she acted as if she did. She darted looks around the room, lingering at the large pieces of embroidery Iris had tacked to the walls. She lifted a questioning eyebrow at the decals of names and Iris nodded. She would explain later.

But then, without warning, Ruth touched the thickly stitched runner in variegated blues that covered the table next to Mina's chair. "This is lovely. Do you mind if I move these things to see it better?" Instead of waiting for an answer, she picked up the holder of pens and markers.

"N-no!"

"Ruth," Iris said.

"I'm being careful. Look, I'll put it right here." Ruth moved it to the window ledge.

"No!" Mina glared.

"She doesn't like people handling her things," Iris said.

Ruth hesitated but returned the holder. "I'm sorry, Philomena. I didn't mean to upset you."

But the apology sounded fake. Iris could hear it and guessed that Mina could too. She realized she'd made a huge error in not calculating how Mina might react. Stationary and harmless as she appeared, she was unpredictable and potentially volatile.

And hoping to placate her, Iris said, "I've told Ruth about your knitting. I showed her the pieces I have — you know, the ones you gave me."

Lips jutted. Not a good sign.

"Ruth is very interested in your knitting. Like I am. You know I've always loved your knitting — since we met in the park, remember? She would like to hang your knitting on walls that many people would come to look at. These people would love to see your knitting."

Mina kept staring at the TV.

"Ruth would pay you," Iris said.

Mina didn't look at Iris but she blinked. She'd heard. Good!

Except that Ruth didn't understand this slow game of helping Mina understand. She pressed her index finger on the blue runner and asked, "Did you make this, Philomena?"

Iris froze. Hadn't she just told Ruth not to touch?

Mina fixed the trespassing finger with such a dark look that Ruth took it away. But again she asked, "Did you make it?"

"Of course she did," Iris said.

But Mina didn't answer, and although Iris knew it wasn't a good idea to push her if she didn't want to talk, she tried coaxing her. "Come on, Mina, you know you made it. And that, and that, and that." She pointed at the embroidery on the walls. "Where's your tray of threads? Where's your hoop? You always have them beside you."

She looked around but couldn't even recall when she'd last seen them. She was beginning to feel disoriented by how different everything seemed. She crouched before the armchair, trying to get Mina to look at her. "You know I only want what's best for you. I believe in you and what you can do. I think the world should see what you create. Mina — Philomena — you're an artist! That's why I brought my friend Ruth to see your gorgeous knitting. She just wants to talk to you about it. You know how you love to knit. You do it all the time."

Mina was staring past Iris's head at the TV, her mouth a stubborn bud of silence.

"Philomena," Ruth said now, "do you know how to embroider?"

"I told you she calls it knitting," Iris said. She squeezed Mina's knee. "Ruth means your knitting."

Mina picked up the remote and raised the volume.

Iris stood. "We should go. You upset her when you touched her things." She would come back later to talk to Mina. "Bye, Mina, I'll see you in a while." But Mina ignored her.

She and Ruth had to wait a long time for the creaking elevator to come. Its confined cube of lighting made even Ruth's smooth tan look jaundiced. The whole time Iris talked. She was desperate to explain. The meeting hadn't gone well, but Philomena wasn't always in a sociable mood. Artists sometimes weren't, right? What mattered was the artwork. Being a recluse belonged to the artistic temperament, didn't it? Philomena had been ill too, seriously ill in the ICU. She was still recuperating. Once she was well again, Iris would film her. She had so many stories about her too — she'd been writing them down.

Ruth still hadn't said what she thought. Between her silence and Mina's, Iris wanted to howl. The common room looked even more like a dismal shoreline where sad, depleted remnants of humanity had washed up. Near the door an elderly man tried to snatch Ruth's arm, pleading to know where his wife was, and they had to wait for an orderly to lead him away before they could escape.

In the parking lot Ruth stopped and said, "No."

"What do you mean, no?"

"The person you presented to me could not have produced that artwork."

"But she made it! I saw her with my own eyes!"

"I seriously doubt that."

"Didn't you see how possessive she was? She didn't want you to touch it because it was *hers*, because she *made*—"

"That poor woman," Ruth spoke across her. "I don't know where her family are that they don't protect her from an unscrupulous person like yourself, but they should be alerted."

"But the embroidery! You called it art!"

"Without provenance?" Ruth said haughtily. "No one reputable will handle it." She beeped her car door and opened it. The engine was already purring.

Iris followed to the passenger door but Ruth was already backing up, ignoring Iris, and drove off.

Iris stood in the parking lot, arms hanging. What had just happened? Until she'd heard Ruth asking Mina if she could embroider, she hadn't realized that Ruth might doubt her claims. For that matter, how could she prove Mina had done the embroidery if she wouldn't say she had?

*

Gabriela was about to knock on Mina's door when she heard a voice inside, louder than it should be. Was Mina being scolded? She opened the door and recognized the woman she'd seen last winter leaving Mina's place. She remembered the thin, coldly pretty face and the deliberate way she'd looked at her. When Gabriela told Bruno, he said that was the person who brought Mina thread. She made clothes and liked encouraging Mina with her stitching. Where was the harm?

Today the woman's cheeks were flushed and Mina was scowling. There was too much emotion in the air for this to be about thread. Without a word, the woman snatched her knapsack off the bed, and with ostentatious care to step around Gabriela, strode from the room.

"What's going on here?" Gabriela called after her, but she'd already pushed through the stairwell door.

Back in the room, Gabriela asked Mina what had happened.

Mina pursed her mouth.

"She sounded upset with you."

"Don't know."

"Did she bring you thread?"

"No."

"So why did she come?"

Nothing.

"What's going on, Mina?"

Nothing.

"Why would she be upset with you?"

Still nothing.

Gabriela held up the small paper bag she was carrying.

Mina's face brightened. "Wh-wh-what's that?"

"It smells like something baked. With banana?"

She made tea as Mina recounted a circuitous story that Gabriela slowly divined was about mac and cheese for lunch. The unpleasant visit seemed to have been forgotten.

She was walking to the métro, wondering why this woman would be scolding or badgering Mina. No one should be talking to her like that. She took out her phone and called Bruno.

"Allô?"

"Hi, I was just with Mina."

"How is she? Is there a problem?"

"Do you remember the woman you told me once brought Mina thread?"

"Iris. What about her?"

"She was with Mina when I got there and I think she was ... I don't know. Talking to her in a pretty hard tone. That's what it sounded like through the door."

"Through the door?"

"I hadn't opened it yet."

"It must have been the TV."

"It wasn't."

"But you don't know her voice so how would you recognize it?"

"When I walked in, she looked upset and so did Mina. And she walked out as soon as she saw me. Why did she take off like that? She didn't even wait for the elevator. She took the stairs."

"Her visit was over. She didn't want to intrude on yours. Seems to me that was considerate. And I take the stairs too. That elevator is more geriatric than the patients."

"It's not funny, Bruno. There was something going on."

"Fine, I'll ask her. I have to go now. I'm supposed to be somewhere."

Gabriela shoved her phone in her pocket. Usually Bruno took up arms to defend the slightest slight against Mina. Why was he so ready to make excuses for this Iris?

Her stride slowed. *Really?* Already someone new?

Except that hadn't she already found someone too? She picked up her pace again.

In January the possibility of a baby was an evaporating hope, but now she'd stopped taking the pill and was having regular periods again. She and Daniel were talking — and he told her he was game. He'd never been in a relationship where children felt necessary. He spent his days working with kids. But he was getting older too and a child with Gabriela was a whole new prospect. If it felt precipitous to be making a life-changing decision while they were still getting to know each other, there was also a sense of destiny — as if they'd been waiting to meet each other for this to happen. Or, as Daniel said, they weren't teenagers, still figuring out what they wanted. There had to be some advantages to being more mature. Or, in another tone: who cares what people think?

*

Witches with their cookie houses and sweet words. That was how they tricked you. Oh, you pretty child, can you knit gold? It's so lovely and rich, what you do! Smiling with their mouths but looking down their long noses with hard wolf eyes. The wolf knew how to make his voice soft too. That was how he fooled the little animals.and gobbled them. And now the wolves and witches and evil queens could get at Mina because she didn't have a key! Bruno with his stupid X on the door!

She grabbed her phone and punched in his numbers. "Two … two … four …" But he didn't answer and why, if he wasn't home, did it ring so many times?

Finally his answering machine came on. "S-s-something to tell you." She paused. "I need a key!" But she didn't know how to explain about the wolf Iris had brought right into her room to stand before her. "A key," she repeated. "I need a key!" She paused again because you had to when you talked on the phone. She finished with an angry, "Bye."

There was a knock on the door and the man who collected her garbage came in. "Minnie Mouse, ça va?"

She didn't answer because everything wasn't all right.

"Hey, what's that sad face?"

She could smell he'd just smoked a cigarette. That was another thing that was wrong here. No cigarettes! Bruno said he couldn't bring everything, but he'd brought her important things. Well! He forgot her cigarettes in the freezer! "Pas d'cigarettes."

He tilted his head, didn't seem sure, but then pulled his pack from his shirt pocket. "You know you can't smoke in your room, right? Do you know where to go?"

"Yeah."

He put two cigarettes next to her phone. "You tell your brother or one of your friends to bring you some." He emptied her small garbage can into his large bag. "Hang in there, okay?"

Two cigarettes! It had been so long, she had to have one right away. But — another thing Bruno forgot — her lighter! She knew what to do though. Anyone who smoked could ask anyone else who smoked for a light.

She heaved herself out of the armchair, hid one cigarette in her underwear drawer, and took the other with her down the hallway to the room with the circle of dried flowers on the door. She'd been in all the rooms to look through the dressers in case there was anything interesting that wanted to be hers, and in this room everything smelled of cigarettes.

No one called when she knocked, but she still opened the door. The old woman was sitting in a chair doing nothing. She didn't even look surprised to see her.

Mina held up her cigarette. "Du feu?" As polite as in a fancy café in a movie.

"On the ... windowsill." The old woman pointed with her bony hand. "But you can't ... smoke ... in your room ... They'll take your ... cigarettes ... away."

Mina snorted at how stupid that was. She had no cigarettes to take away. She clicked the lighter and sucked in that first delicious drag. Oh, how she'd missed it!

She wanted to pocket the lighter but the old woman was watching her. That was okay. Mina could come back later to take it. She put it back on the windowsill and shuffled from the room, closing the door behind her.

Only out in the hallway again did she remember to say, "Merci."

*

Iris and Jenny sat in a booth in the small pub. Iris could have spit when she thought of how Ruth talked to her. *An unscrupulous person like yourself,* she mimicked prissily. As if Ruth hadn't expected to cash in big on Mina herself. She took another swallow of beer. She was more than a little pissed at Mina too. Obviously Mina did the damn embroidery! Why wouldn't she say so? Jenny tried to interject now and then. Mina hadn't known what was happening. Ruth was a stranger. So what, Iris snapped. But she had to admit that she'd miscalculated. She'd thought explaining would come later. That Mina would understand once she saw her embroidery framed and hung and people were telling her they loved it.

"What about other galleries?" Jenny asked. "Just because this stuck-up bitch —"

"No one will believe Mina did the embroidery if she won't admit it."

"But you said this woman was interested before you told her the artist had Down Syndrome. You know the work is good — it's great!"

"So who do I say did it? Apparently I need *provenance*."

"What if you say you found the bags?"

Iris scoffed. "Hidden treasure in a dumpster?"

"Doesn't have to be a dumpster. The bags could have been in a cellar or a closet. People are always finding art in weird places."

"No. You should have heard this Ruth person. If she finds out about a show like this anywhere near Montreal, she'll go after me."

"You mean like legally go after you?"

"You should have seen how she drove off. Spinning her tires on a moral high horse."

"So what are you going to do?"

"I don't know. I don't know if there's anything I even *can* do if Mina won't admit she made the embroidery. I don't have any proof." Iris tipped her head back, asking the heavens beyond the pressed tin ceiling, "Why didn't I film her when I could have?"

"I'm sorry, Iris."

"Yeah, me too. You know ... she's not even embroidering anymore. I haven't seen her with a needle and thread since before her bleed."

"She doesn't want to?"

"I don't know ..." Iris twisted her glass one way, then the other. For a few moments both sat without speaking.

Then Jenny said, "I guess it's just as well that you never told Bruno."

Iris let out a shaky breath. She'd sent Bruno a text that she wouldn't be able to see him for supper this evening. She couldn't, not with Ruth's contempt fresh in her ears. Although she wished she could curl up with him and tell him how awful Ruth had been. He would be the only one to understand how exasperating Mina could be when she didn't want to listen.

Except that telling Bruno was always supposed to include the amazing news that Mina was going to have an exhibition of her embroidery — and now Iris didn't have a gallery, didn't know how to proceed, or even if she could with Mina being so stubborn.

She slid her arms across the table and dropped her head onto them.

Then Jenny's fingernails were stroking the back of her neck. "Oh, baby. You always want too much."

"Nothing's too much," Iris mumbled into her elbow. She'd planned it so well and it should have worked.

*

The door at the bottom of the stairs wasn't locked like the big front door. Mina had pushed it now and then to check. It opened onto a parking lot. Parking lots were good because they led to streets and where there were streets, there were stores and restaurants and banks. In her wallet she still had her banking card. She remembered her PIN because it was the year Daddy was born.

The door in the stairwell was a way of getting out and today she had to. Madame Bingham wasn't there at breakfast and the orderly finished serving coffee to everyone at another table before he brought hers! When she finally got her coffee, the platter of toast was too far away to reach. Madame Bingham always dropped two toasts on her plate. My toast! she called but the orderly walked away. There was no use asking the woman next to her because she couldn't hear. She told the man who had the toast in front of him to push it closer but he just kept chewing. He didn't like her and she didn't like him. She'd told Madame Bingham she didn't want to sit with that man anymore, but she'd already sat at every other table. The man with the too-loud watch, the woman who burped while she ate, the one who drooled, the one who made noises like the food was going into his nose, not his mouth. Madame Bingham said Mina couldn't have a table to herself like she wanted, because those were the rules. Mina understood about rules but a rule like that was stupid!

When nobody gave her any toast, she thumped her fist by her plate and the orderly told her to go to her room if she was going to behave like that. Well, how was she supposed to behave if nobody was going to give her toast? She didn't have to stay here!

In her room she opened her dresser drawer and pulled out the hoodie with the zippered pockets. In one pocket were tightly folded ten-dollar bills — one of her secret places from before the hospital. Bruno had found a lot of them, but not all of them. She had to keep them even more secret now because he didn't give her money anymore. He said that when there was a shopping trip he would give her some. Until then, she didn't need to go to the bank machine.

But she did! It was her money and she wanted it.

The sun was shining but she still put on a sweater, because it might be cold when she went into the diner to have frîtes. Oh boy, was she going to have a big plate of frîtes! But which hat should she wear? Hats were lucky. They made things happen. She picked a red and blue beret with a yellow fat cat button.

She kept hold of the railing going down the stairs. She wanted to hurry but she had to be careful too. Stairs were dangerous. She got out the door to the parking lot, no problem. Because she was good at this! She knew to stay close to the wall like on TV, so that no one looking out the windows could see. But when she reached the street, it didn't look like any street she knew. There weren't any stores.

She walked to the next street but it was all houses and apartments. Not even a dép where you could buy a bag of chips.

She walked and walked. What crazy place was this where there weren't any stores or restaurants? She walked all the way up to the door of a building that looked like a bank, but there was no bank machine and no one getting money at the counter. A man behind a desk called, "Do you need help?"

She turned and left, even though he kept calling. It might be a trick.

She wanted a Pepsi and frîtes. She had never walked so far and still not arrived anywhere. She was so tired. Finally there was a bench where she could rest.

A bus pulled to the curb. "Are you getting on?" the driver called.

She didn't know where the bus was going. Of course she wasn't getting on!

"Are you lost?"

She didn't answer.

He got off the bus to ask again. "I can call the police to help you but I can't wait. My bus is full. Will you stay here on the bench? I'll tell the police that's where you are."

Long ago, when she was little, she was in a police car and it was fun. "D'okay."

The police who came helped her into the back seat of their car. They wanted to know where she lived and was there someone they could call? She gave them her address and soon they were driving on streets she knew. There! The diner with the good frîtes where Iris always took her. Here! The park where she liked to sit. Brick houses all in a row. And here, her building with the three steps up.

"H-h-here!" she shouted as they stopped. She wanted to barrel out of the car and up the steps and down the hallway to her apart-ment, but suddenly discovered she was stuck! There was no handle on the car door.

The police opened it from the outside. "Do you need help?"

She was panting with excitement. Finally finally finally home again! She saw the man from down the hall with the funny little dog but she didn't have time to say hello. She yanked herself up the three steps by the railing.

One of the police was reaching around her. "Let me get the door for you. Is this where you live? Do you have family here?"

She jabbed her finger at her name on the mailbox — except? She stared. Where her name had always been, there was someone else's. She swayed a little and the police held her elbow. She shoved his hand away.

"Hey, calm down. What's wrong?"

Who had taken her name away? "M-m-m-m —"

The police was trying to talk to her but she didn't want to hear. "Ici c'est à moi!" she cried.

"This man says you don't live here anymore. He says —"

"Go fart in the flowers!"

"I think we need to — Oh!" He buckled. She'd punched him as hard as she could.

*

The studio was empty today so Bruno had come to do noisy drill and sander work. He was building a small ramp to add spatial variation to the otherwise bare planes of the set.

Last night again Iris had had to work and couldn't come over. He understood she had a business to run and he respected that, but he wished that seeing him was important too. He hadn't said anything though. She sounded so tired on the phone. Tomorrow, she said, for sure tomorrow. She had to do a house call in Outremont. Maybe they could meet at that little pizzeria downtown that he'd told her about.

When his phone rang, he hoped it was her but he didn't recognize the caller. It was a social worker — not Faiza — who unfortunately needed to inform him that his sister had escaped her residence.

Before he could react, she assured him his sister was fine. She was being returned to the residence by the police.

The police? *Fine?* There was no way Mina was fine if she'd tried to escape.

He abandoned his tools and jogged to St. Patrick where he flagged a cab and arrived at the residence in time to see Mina refusing to budge from the back seat of the police car. She did not live here! No! She bellowed with rage, called the police names, swore at the orderlies with language Bruno hadn't known she knew, screamed that she hated him because it was all his fault. She wouldn't calm down and the doctor on call for the residence prescribed a sedative.

Bruno stayed with her until she fell asleep. He didn't mind that she blamed him. She needed someone to blame. But it grieved him how desperately she clung to a past that was forever gone, never to be found again. That she was being protected for her own good was too abstract a concept. Poor, inconsolable Mina. Even asleep, her breath heaved as if she were sobbing in her dreams.

He hadn't wanted to interrupt Iris when she was with a client and now he'd left it too late to call and change their plans. He still wanted to see her, but he'd meant to go home to shower first. He didn't have time now. She wouldn't mind a bit of sawdust, would she? After they ate, maybe they could stop at the residence to check on Mina.

The subway ride downtown was only a few stops and a short walk. Iris hadn't arrived yet and he took a table beside one of the long windows. The restaurant was on the ground floor of a renovated factory that had once processed beaver pelts. The industrial air ducts that ran along the high ceiling were still in place, their metal construction amplifying the clank of dishes and the hiss of milk being steamed. Huge ferns hung over the tables that were built from repurposed wood. Out the window he had a view onto the back of a stone church with stained glass windows. A couple of blocks away, stores sold electronics, running shoes, perfume, books. This was how a city evolved: cafés and bars in the old fur district, afternoon concerts in a Protestant church, the changing trends of commerce.

Iris walked in, looking pale and preoccupied. It was because she never said no to a commission, even when she had more than enough work to fill her day. She was going to have to learn to say no, if she wanted to be available to design costumes.

She shrugged off her suit jacket and dropped its shoulders on the back of the chair. He enjoyed seeing how she handled clothes — like a chef with food or a musician with an instrument. But her mood seemed heavy as she sat.

"Difficult client?" he asked. He would wait until she had some wine before telling her about Mina.

"More like depressing. I spend a ridiculous amount of time convincing women that they aren't too fat or too short or their legs aren't terrible or their waists too high or their necks too long. Some appointments feel more like therapy sessions."

"You're here now. Relax." He nodded at the space around them, thinking she might comment on the post-industrial spaciousness, the high ceiling, the hanging ferns.

The waiter approached to take their order for drinks. After he left, Iris wrinkled her brow at the long thin menu on her plate. She still hadn't looked up when the waiter set their glasses on the table. She sipped her Merlot but seemed restless.

Bruno tried to make the story of Mina's escape amusing — not that it was funny the way Mina roared and flailed, and that it had taken five people to force her into the residence she refused to call home.

But Iris only watched him. It was like she hadn't heard.

"Are you all right?" he asked.

"Mina," she said flatly.

"Yes, I'm talking about Mina."

"I didn't tell you before because ... well, I just didn't. But you know, I had such plans for her. It would have been amazing. She would have loved every moment of it — and it would have made her feel better about living in a residence, because she still would have gotten out to see the world."

That Bruno didn't have even the least hunch of what Iris was talking about was giving him prickles. "What are you saying?"

"I'll tell you." She nodded. "I'll tell you."

He pushed up his glasses. "I'm listening."

They were interrupted by the waiter setting their pizzas before them. Iris looked at hers as if she'd never seen goat cheese and arugula before.

"Iris," he said sharply. "Tell me."

"Well, you know she embroiders."

"That's why you brought her thread." Then something clicked — what Gabriela said about Iris scolding Mina and he hadn't believed it. "What have you been doing to Mina?"

"To her?" Iris tossed her head as if he were being ridiculous. "*For her*, you should say. I brought her thread because the embroidery she makes is stupendous. I was helping her."

"She didn't need you to bring her thread. She was happy enough with the thread she got at the dollar store." He'd picked up his knife and fork but only held them.

"She's creating art, Bruno."

"*Art?*"

"How she mixes her colours. How she chooses them. She knows exactly what she's doing. She doesn't even trace her designs. They're entirely freeform and so intricate —"

"What do you think you're telling me? I've seen her embroider since we were kids. I grew up with her."

She sat back hard in her chair. "I knew that would be your attitude. That's why I never told you."

"Told me what?"

"You never saw that what she does — what she *creates* — is special.

You know what I've realized about you?" She began sawing her pizza as savagely as if it were a haunch of meat. "You're so concerned about Mina's best interests and protecting her and making sure she's comfortable, but you don't even see what she can do. I had an art gallery interested in —"

"*What?*"

"A reputable art gallery who were ready to have an exhibition of Mina's embroidery."

"You can't do that!"

"If Mina agrees, why not? You told me yourself that her signature is legal and binding."

"Iris!"

"It's because you think she needs you to oversee everything. You act like it's some kind of power trip. *Bruno to the rescue!* But the one thing you've never seen is that she's an artist — all on her own, nothing to do with you! And —" She jabbed her knife to point out the window. "There are people out there who agree with me!"

Bruno's mouth went dry. Who was this woman? What was she saying? How had he let her get so close to Mina? What had she done? "How —" he began, stopped, and tried again. "How did anyone from an art gallery see Mina's embroidery?"

Iris looked down at her pizza.

"*How*, Iris? You'd better tell me fast. Because it wasn't Mina who walked into an art gallery on her way to the dollar store."

Iris glanced at the window and then at him. "I showed them the pieces I have."

"Have? How? Mina doesn't give things away."

"She sold them to me."

He would never have thought it possible, but the instant she said it, he realized it was.

"They're mine, fair and square. I bought them."

"And who decided on the price?"

"She did."

"And she knows how much a supposed piece of art costs?"

"I wasn't trying to take advantage of her, so don't make it sound like that! I'd have given her more money when I got it. To start with, I needed to have embroidery to show and we agreed on a price. And let me tell you, it's not easy approaching an art gallery for an unknown artist. Even with a portfolio and working up a presentation. Just trying to get an appointment is impossible."

"But you did it." He tried to keep his voice even. "You took her embroidery to an art gallery —"

"Because I knew it was art!"

"— without telling me."

"She doesn't need permission from you. She has rights. She's her own person. That's what you're always saying."

"I'm her legal guardian. It's not like you don't know how to contact me."

"Whether or not she wants to be known as an artist is a decision she should be able to make herself."

"But she doesn't understand what that means, Iris. How did you explain that to her?"

"Stop it! You're getting angry for no reason. I already told you that nothing's happening — because now all of a sudden Mina won't say she did the embroidery. She acts like she has no idea what I'm talking about. And so this gallery person doesn't believe me."

Everything Iris was saying and her attitude — practically bragging about what she'd done — sickened him. The deceit, the hiding, the pretense, the lies. And all the while playing at being Mina's friend.— and his lover!

"You can't believe how much work I put into this."

"Right! And all behind my back."

"No no no no no! Don't twist this into something it isn't. I did this because you didn't see what Mina could do, and I knew you wouldn't want me to do it until I could prove —"

"I wouldn't have wanted you to do it because people would only be interested because she has Down Syndrome. That's not fair to her."

"That's not true! What she creates is art! Like I said, you don't get it."

"No, *you* don't get it. I don't care if what she makes is art. She's not a clown to be put on display. I don't want people gawking at her."

"She does make art, I'm telling you! This gallery owner —"

The waiter was at their table. "We need to ask you to pay and take your discussion outside."

Bruno reached for his wallet, Iris for her purse. He had to pay with a card but Iris had cash and was able to snatch up her jacket.

She'd already stomped halfway down the block but he ran after her. "I thought you were seeing Mina because you cared about her. I cannot believe —"

"Yeah, well, guess what? Maybe I care more about her than you do, because I see more happening for her!"

"You call that wacky idea —"

"Only wacky to you because you can't —"

"I'm her brother, I'm —"

"— see who she is. She would have loved being fêted as an artist."

"— her only family she's got left, I —"

"She was going to be called Philomena. She loves being called Philomena."

"— see her every day."

"I would have made her dresses and got her —"

"She likes her privacy, she likes being by herself and keeping to her routines."

"— some really funky hats."

They shouted and flung out their arms, marching past pedestrians who veered from their path.

"You make clothes, Iris! You don't know anything about —"

"You are such a —"

"— the demands of being an artist."

"—control freak!"

"I'm her brother. I know her better than anyone."

"You think you know her, but you can't. Nobody can get inside Mina's head!"

He stopped dead, not wanting to take another step with her.

She spun around, head high, facing him. "The world should know what people like Mina can do!"

"People like Mina," he sneered. "That's exactly what I said. You want to turn her into a clown."

"How dare you say that?" she shrieked. "I was doing this for Mina!"

Saliva pooled in his mouth and he had to walk away before he spit at her. This woman he thought he was starting to love. He'd trusted her and she'd tried to take advantage of Mina. What kind of person did that?

He cut past people and crossed against a red light, striding as quickly as he could to get away. He ground his teeth and muttered. Iris and her grandiose ideas. She had no sense of perspective. Like imagining she was going to catapult from a pair of britches to designing period costumes for the opera.

Then he gave a triumphant if bitter laugh, because this much he'd understood in that mess of crazy nonsense Iris spouted. Mina hadn't agreed. She'd nixed Iris's plans. Scorched them to the ground.

8

Blue Sway Shoes was Mina's favourite song and Madame Bingham hummed along with it, making her feel even happier. They were lying on the bed, facing each other, and had to snuggle close or they would fall off. Mina had her hand inside Madame Bingham's blouse, one finger stroking her large, squishy titty. Looking up, Mina could see Madame Bingham's chin. The little notch where the tip of her finger fit exactly. She liked doing that but titties were better.

When Madame Bingham wasn't humming, she talked. "You liked the birthday party last week, didn't you? We have one every two months — for everyone whose birthday it's been. It's fun, isn't it? Makes a little change. Some singing, some dancing."

Mina nestled her head closer, excited to think about dancing and birthday parties that would keep happening — until it was time for hers! She could wear her dress that swished around her. And a shiny, pointed hat! At the party they were all given hats and for the rest of the week she'd worn hers when she went to the dining room, until yesterday when Madame Bingham said it wouldn't be a birthday hat anymore if she wore it every day. That was okay, she had her own hats to wear. She should have had lots more hats too, but Bruno had brought only one bag. He was so stupid!

"What's that big sigh for? What's wrong, my sweet?"

"N-n-nothing." How could anything be wrong while they were cuddling?

Madame Bingham pulled her closer and hummed again for a while. She was as good a hummer as Daddy was a singer.

Mina was almost bursting with her surprise, but she wasn't going to tell Madame Bingham yet. Surprises got better when you kept them secret for longer. Last week Bruno took her shopping and they'd walked through the dollar store to find a new puppy mug to replace the one that he forgot to bring from her apartment. She walked behind him, watching the shelves to see what wanted to be hers. Her hands were still fast-fast. A bottle of perfume, a pair of black nylons, a pad of colour for putting around eyes. The surprise was that ... they were all gifts for Madame Bingham who was her grand amour!

"What are you giggling about now?"

"A secret."

"You like having your little secrets, don't you?"

"Yeah." Secrets were magic no one else knew about. Titties were a secret too. Madame Bingham said she could touch, but she must never never never tell. When you had a grand amour, there were always secrets. She knew that from TV.

Madame Bingham looked at her watch. "I have to get back downstairs, little Minnie."

Mina burrowed her head and held tighter, not wanting to let her go.

"Ow! Why are you hurting me? You know I have things to do. Be reasonable. You're a smart girl, I know you are." Madame Bingham sat up and straightened her blouse, closing the buttons. "We'll cuddle again tomorrow. I always come see you, don't I? You're my favourite girl, just like my little girl I lost. I don't love anyone the way I love you." She leaned close and tickled the end of Mina's nose until Mina couldn't help but smile. "But now I have to go. I still have baking to do."

Mina jutted her lips again.

"Mais voyons. What's wrong? You don't usually carry on like this."

"Baking!"

"Ah, because you can't have dessert ..."

"Yeah."

"You can't expect the others not to have dessert just because you can't."

Mina did. But it wasn't only dessert. She was sad because of the long hours she was going to have to wait for Madame Bingham to come hold her again. Sorrow began to seep from her eyes.

Madame Bingham smoothed the tears off her face and bent to kiss her cheeks. "It doesn't seem fair to you, does it? So much that's not fair," she murmured.

Mina felt the lovely kisses on her cheeks, her nose, and finally the softest brush of lips on her mouth that made her part her lips and wish the kiss were longer.

*

They'd used body paint before, but Bruno wanted to test a new brand that the salesperson claimed wouldn't transfer and was safe even for children.

When he got to the studio, Tandi was on the floor, her hips locked in the scissored grip of Mathieu's legs as he arched backwards. "Farther," Val urged. "Farther! And you, Tandi, lever yourself—" Mathieu collapsed.

"Okay." Val circled an arm in the air. "Let's go back." But she'd seen Bruno in the mirrored wall and pivoted. "You have something?"

"I wanted to try this in action." He held up the tube of gold paint. "See if it's really as non-transferrable and sweat-resistant as it claims."

"When we take a break in a few moments, okay?"

"You know where to find me."

Bruno had little to do for this production until the choreography was in place and Val was ready to discuss lighting. He unlocked the tool cupboard for his whetstone and the tied leather roll where he kept his chisels. Sharpening them was quiet work, and methodically sliding a blade along stone again and again was the physical equivalent of a chant to restore order.

Slowly order was being restored too. Mina was complaining less and seemed to be adjusting to life at the residence. Iris still left messages on his answering machine, but he deleted them as soon as he heard her voice. She had betrayed him, but fortunately he'd found out. He refused to let himself miss her and for the most part was succeeding.

He'd finished one chisel and taken up another when Val called, "Okay, Bruno!"

He'd expected Tandi to be the guinea pig, but Mathieu was waiting. He held out his palm and Bruno squirted a dollop of paint, thick as toothpaste. "Feet first," Bruno said. "Before it dries on your hands."

Mathieu sat, propping one calf on his knee, smoothing paint around his instep, heel, and toes. Bruno looked around for paper where Mathieu could set his feet while they dried.

"How long will this stay on?"

"Long enough, I think. We'll see."

"No, I *mean* if I keep it on. Will I still have gold feet by tonight?"

Bruno didn't want to know why. "It's water soluble, so if you don't take a shower ..."

"Don't you think," Tandi said, "it's getting a bit cold to show up at a bar in bare feet?"

"Don't worry," Mathieu said. "I'll manage." He waggled his feet where the paint was drying to a semi-matte finish. "I thought the gold would be shinier."

"It looks velvety," Tandi said.

"No, he's right," Bruno said. "It should be shinier. We won't use this brand."

"Let me still do my hands." Mathieu reached for the tube.

"Water soluble," Bruno reminded him.

Val was still on the other side of the room, deep in a phone conversation. Bruno returned to his chisels. He didn't realize Tandi had followed him until she said, "What happened with Iris?"

He kept his eyes on his hands and the blade. "She did something with Mina."

"What do you mean?" Tandi stepped closer. "Is Mina all right?"

"She's fine."

"But what did Iris do?"

"Mina likes to stitch — not sewing, more like embroidery. Iris decided to take some to an art gallery where everyone was amazed that a person with Down Syndrome can use a needle and thread." As he spoke, he stopped sliding the chisel. "I don't want Mina turned into a performing clown for a freak show."

"Hold it," Tandi said over his last words. "There was a gallery interested? That's a big deal, Bruno. Galleries aren't in the charity business. I've got friends who can't get into galleries and are begging cafés to hang their paintings."

"That's neither here nor there," he said shortly. He turned the whetstone around to the fine side, added a drop of oil from the bottle, and began to slide the blade again.

"But nothing's happening now?"

He shook his head.

"So then why are you upset with Iris? I mean, I think it would have been amazing, but if it's not happening, what does it matter?"

"She did it without telling me."

"Eventually she would have told you, right? All she did was take a chance. Honestly, I don't think that's a reason to condemn her."

He didn't answer.

"You know, we all liked her here. She felt like part of the team. And you were happier, Bruno. You wouldn't—"

"Tandi!" Val sang out so loudly that she must already have called a few times. "Thandiwe Nangolo! Can we get back to work?"

With a wide look of mock-alarm, Tandi skipped off.

Bruno focussed on the slicing hiss of the blade. Val's prompts and cajoling. The percussive thump of feet. He tried to will away Tandi's words, not wanting to test their truth. But he couldn't unhear them.

*

Jenny stood in Iris's studio, hands fisted on her hips. It wasn't good to stay cooped up like this. Iris said she had to work. Since knock-off Dior was her lot in life, she might as well buckle down. Come on, Jenny said more gently. Let's go for a walk.

They left the streets and buildings, walking toward where the sky was more open and there were trees. A few were already tufted scarlet. And past the trees, the river. Slate grey today, beneath grey clouds. The surface barely rippled but a gull, perched on a piece of debris, floated past swiftly.

Iris had already told Jenny about the scene at the restaurant. How Bruno hadn't understood, hadn't even tried to, and how he'd accused her. Jenny hadn't said anything, but she didn't have to. Iris remembered how she'd warned her.

Not that first day or the next, but after a few days, Iris began to think about Bruno's reaction. He worried about everything to do with Mina, and these last months — with the hospital, having to pack Mina's things, the move, how unhappy Mina was about living at the residence — must have been especially trying.

She decided to call him in the evening when they normally talked. She would explain more calmly. Surely he couldn't think she had ever meant to harm Mina. But he didn't answer, even though she knew that he had to be home at that hour.

"He doesn't want to hear anything I have to say," she told Jenny. "There's not much I can do if he just wants to accuse me and blame me. I've called and left messages — and how many messages can I leave and still keep my self-respect?"

"You have to talk to him," Jenny insisted.

"How — if he won't listen?" Iris's throat tightened. Only a week ago she'd let herself start to believe that they were becoming a couple. Having meals together. Her toothbrush at his place. Falling asleep with his hand on her hip.

"Let's think," Jenny said, "We'll come up with something. You like this guy. It's not like you to give up."

*

Mina sat on the floor, taking each can of Pepsi from the frigo. It was hard work and she groaned as she stretched, but she needed to see the cans in front of her to count them properly. On the wall by the sink was the calendar where she marked how many she had. Every day when she took one, she subtracted that from the previous day's number. Last week the number of cans didn't match the number on the calendar, but maybe the cans were playing tricks.

And today again. On the calendar it said ten, but when she looked into the frigo to count the cans, she only got eight. "... cinq, six, sept, huit." She started over again. "... cinq, six, sept, huit." Eight wasn't ten!

She had no choice but to take all the cans out of the frigo and line them up on the floor where they couldn't hide.

Slowly she counted them in front of her. There were only eight! Someone was taking her cans! Bruno was so stupid with his big X that he thought would keep people out. An X wouldn't stop her. She'd been into every room in the hallway, but everything she found looked old and almost dead. Only the brooch with the swirly shape and shiny stones wanted to come with her. She'd shoved it into the toe of her yellow and brown sock that she hid at the back of a drawer.

To stand again, she had to push her bum across the floor to the bed and haul herself up. It was a struggle and a few times she nearly tipped. The bedspread got messy again but that wasn't her problem. The orderly was supposed to make it look nice.

Saying them out loud, she punched Bruno's numbers into the phone.

"Allô?"

"S-s-something to tell you."

"I'm listening."

"My Pepsi."

"Isn't the orderly bringing you cans? I thought that was settled. I gave him the money."

She told Bruno about the numbers on the calendar and how
many cans were in the fridge. He didn't understand right away.
She had to tell him again.

Then he said, "Are you sure?" And quickly, "Forget it, I know
you're sure."

"I n-n-need a key!"

"I've explained this. You can't have a lock on your door."

She had another idea but didn't know how to explain it. On TV
she'd seen how people could watch movies of someone going in their
door when they weren't home. If she couldn't have a lock and a key,
she wanted one of those movies.

"I'll look into the Pepsi," Bruno said. "But everything else is okay,
isn't it? Your TV works, you have a phone, your room is warm, there's
lots of food?"

That was all true but she didn't want to agree. Then she remembered the other thing. "A man. Between my legs!"

"... Are you saying there's a man trying to have sex with you?"

"Yeah."

"Where does this happen, in your room?"

"In the l-l-levoluva." It had always been a hard word, especially
when she was little and wanted to tell people that her daddy fixed
them.

"In the elevator? How does he —"

"Pushes his thing!"

"Is he one of the residents or someone who works there?"

"Old man," she said with disgust.

"And when does this happen?"

"Tout le temps."

"Since when?"

"Long time!"

"And you've never told Madame Bingham?"

She couldn't tell Madame Bingham because the old man was
one of her special friends. She made him coffee in the morning and

flirted with him. Madame Bingham wasn't supposed to have other special friends.

"I can't come today because I'll be at work till late, but I'm thinking this can't be too serious if it's been happening for a while and you're only telling me now. I'll come tomorrow, okay? In the meantime, you give that old fellow a shove. He's got no right touching you if you don't want him to. And we'll figure out what's happening with the Pepsi too, okay?"

"S-s-something ..."

"There's something else?"

"Yeah." But she couldn't think of anything else. She just wanted to keep him on the phone.

*

Bruno was bent over, tying his running shoes, when he spied a small object against the skirting board. A tube of lip balm. He recalled Iris moistening her lips, saying she had to keep them ready for kissing. And they were: always ready.

More gently than he'd snatched it up, he set the tube on the shelf where he usually left his keys.

It was recycling day and in the street he saw a man with a large garbage bag rattling the bins along the sidewalk, looking for cans. A few neighbours, like Bruno, left their cans on the sidewalk, next to the bins.

He didn't usually go to the residence so early in the day, but if Mina was having problems with her Pepsi and there was a man harassing her, then he had to see Madame Bingham, who was only there in the morning. He still didn't care for her manner — too familiar with Mina, too offhand with him — but he'd realized that dealing directly with her was the most effective way of getting things done.

He took the stairs to the third floor where he found Mina in her armchair watching TV. "Bonjour, m'lady. Did we have a good breakfast today?"

Mina did. One piece of toast with Cheez Whiz and another with peanut butter.

"Good. So all's well in your world." He wasn't being glib. For Mina, having breakfast as she liked it didn't guarantee that she would be in a good mood, but *not* having breakfast as she liked it meant that she would definitely *not* be in a good mood. "So what's this about Pepsi?"

Doggedly she told him. There were a lot of details about counting.

He tried to decipher her calendar that was dotted with numbers in different colours. "Which colour is Pepsi?"

"Yellow!" As if how could he even ask.

He stooped to the fridge to count the cans. She was right, some were missing.

"I'll talk to Madame Bingham."

"I n-n-need a lock!"

"You know the answer to that."

"A TV."

"You have a TV."

"Pas comme ça."

"Sorry, Mina, I have no idea what you're trying to tell me."

"In my apartment—"

"You're not in your apartment."

She hmmphed and wouldn't look at him.

"Come on, admit it, Mina. Your life's a lot easier now. You get your meals cooked, Madame Bingham makes you coffee in the morning, your garbage gets emptied every day, no laundry to do …" He looked around the room for more examples and saw her towel. "Have you started taking your bath every week?"

He'd noticed one day that her hair looked lank and greasy. He asked if she washed it and she said she did. When she took a bath. But her hair stayed dirty and he finally asked her to show him how she took a bath, at which point he discovered that she didn't know how the tub worked. She didn't even have shampoo when he looked for it. He brought her shampoo and bubble bath and said she had no excuse now not to have a bath. Two days later the bottles still sat unopened like prize trophies on her windowsill. The orderlies at the residence were responsible for washing the sheets and the laundry. They scrubbed the sink in the room, emptied the garbage, and swept the floor. But the residents? The orderly Bruno spoke to said that old people didn't sweat, so what was the problem? Bruno had made a complaint.

There was less shampoo and bubble bath in the bottles now, and Mina's hair was clean. Someone had been telling her to change her clothes more regularly too.

"Explain to me about the man in the elevator."

"Between my legs!"

"Show me what he does."

She sighed.

"There are different ways of getting between legs, Mina. You need to show me."

Grimacing, she slapped at her thighs and belly.

The residents he'd seen could barely shuffle from their rooms. How had one of them mustered the energy to be aggressive with Mina? "Do you know which room is his? Let's go hear his side of the story."

She tightened her lips in a manner reminiscent of their mother when she was being righteous, heaved herself up, and walked to the door. Back straight, face grim in pursuit of justice.

Bruno waved at an orderly who was pushing a hamper down the hallway. "Can you come with us? I need to talk with one of the residents and I want a witness."

"It shouldn't be me. I'll go get —"

"It's not to notarize a will, only to listen. You can do that."

Mina stopped at a door. "Ici."

Bruno knocked. From inside he heard a feeble call.

"Just go in," the orderly said.

A grey-skinned man sat hunched in an armchair. He looked at them placidly until he saw Mina and he scowled.

"Bonjour, Monsieur. I see you know who my sister is."

"She has no manners," the man muttered.

"She says she has problems with you in the elevator."

"*She's* the problem! She pushes ahead to get on the elevator and doesn't leave room for us with our walkers." He lifted a crooked finger at his walker at the same time that Mina pointed, both looking triumphant.

"Th-th-that!"

"That's what he shoves at you?"

"Yeah."

"Okay, Mina, come on." And over his shoulder, "I apologize for having troubled you. I'll talk to her. That's fine," he said to the orderly.

Mina looked smug, even swaying a little as she returned to her room. She touched a door decorated with a wreath of dried flowers. "Pretty."

"I thought you liked Elvis on your door. Do you want flowers like that?"

Her eyes opened wide. "No!"

In her room again, he sat on the bed. "Do you remember how people used to yell at you when you went to the head of the line in the bank instead of waiting?"

"I d-d-don't have time!"

"You have just as much time as everyone else does. You have to wait your turn. That's just the way it is. When you go ahead of people who are waiting, they don't like it, and this man needs more room than you do because of his walker. He shouldn't be shoving it at you, but maybe you're not moving aside either. He's old, Mina."

She pouted.

"I have to get to work. I'll see if there's someone downstairs I can talk to about your Pepsi. And how about when you see that man with the walker, you stay away. That's the best way to protect between your legs."

Downstairs he asked for Madame Bingham. He was directed to the kitchen where he found her rolling out dough on the counter.

"Someone is taking Mina's Pepsi," he said. Her eyes flashed but before she could object, he lifted his hands. "Or let's put it this way: she has Pepsi missing. Maybe it walked out on its own. But she counts everything, and if she says she has Pepsi missing, then it's missing."

"She made a mistake."

"With counting? I doubt it. It's her special mania."

"You know how people like her distort things."

"What do you mean, *people like her?*"

She flapped a hand at him. "Don't get excited. I know all about Down Syndrome. My little girl had it. That's why my heart opens right up when I see your sister. That's why I —"

"I'm sorry about your daughter but she was your daughter, and Mina is Mina. She's her own person with her own likes, dislikes, and habits — and she doesn't make mistakes with numbers. If she says she has Pepsi missing, then she does. Maybe to you it's only a couple of cans, so who cares? But she's got little enough left that she can call her own, and I don't want anyone taking even one can of Pepsi that belongs to her."

Madame Bingham had drawn herself up, her deeply cleft chin adding to her pugnacious look. "What are you saying?"

"Not much," he said quietly. "You say you care about her. How about you act like it? Find out who's taking her Pepsi and tell them to stop. Because someone is taking it."

He stretched a smile that he didn't feel and turned away. Behind him he heard how she smacked the rolling pin on the dough.

*

Mina wanted her green hat but couldn't find it. Something else Bruno had thrown away! How could today be special if she didn't have the right hat? She huffed and pulled a yellow toque on her head. A toque was stupid for now when there were still leaves on the trees.

She sat in her armchair to wait because she couldn't wait outside. They wouldn't let her outside by herself anymore. Her bag was on her lap. She'd turned off the TV so she would be ready. She'd already decided she was going to have a club sandwich with frîtes. Her new doll was beside her, helping her wait, but she wasn't going to come along.

Mina checked her watch. 11:24. Soon but not yet. Gabriela was always on time when she wasn't at work. Where Gabriela worked sounded like the dining room downstairs, or the bank where people stood in long lineups and nothing happened the way it should.

Now she listened because there was talking in the hallway. She checked her watch again. 11:26. Still too early. She could hear Gabriela's voice and a man's. Gabriela's new prince had better be nice or she would tell him to go away. She was tired of princes and didn't want one anymore, but Gabriela had told her about needing one to be a daddy for a baby. *That* was different. Very different — and good! Gabriela even promised that if she had a baby, Mina could hold her. The way she said it made Mina remember Mama holding her close.

Gabriela didn't know yet if or when the baby would come, only that she had to be ready. Mina knew about that kind of magic. Like the good things that happened in stories. Not the first time and not the second. You had to wait for number three. Three was the lucky time.

Now there was a tap on the door and Mina checked her watch. Exactly 11:30.

"Yeah?" she called.

The door opened and there was her belle-coeur! Her darling face. Her black hair on her shoulders. Gabriela was as beautiful as an actress on TV.

"Mina," she said gently, "I want to introduce my friend, Daniel."

He didn't look like Bruno, which surprised her because she still thought of Gabriela with Bruno. This man had a funny short beard on his chin that she wasn't sure she liked. But he was smiling and saying it was a pleasure to meet her. Gabriela had told him all about her. He looked around the room and said, "A mini fridge. That's handy." Which was very smart because the orderly who cleaned the floor said it was in the way and she didn't need one. She did.

"A phone too." She put her hand on it to show him.

"So you can call your brother — and Gabriela can call you."

He knew about Bruno and didn't mind? Her princes had always been jealous, not liking the names on her wall. But she told them too bad. Tit for tat.

"Are you ready?" Gabriela asked. "Is that the hat you want to wear? Because it's warm out today and that's wool."

"I d-d-d-don't —" She stopped in frustration.

"We can stop at a store and buy you a new hat," Gabriela said.

"And lunch?" She wanted to be sure.

"We're going out for lunch, yes. That's the plan, isn't it? But we want you to be comfortable and that hat's too warm for now."

A new hat and lunch in a restaurant! This new prince seemed okay. His name was too fancy for every day. Like hers, Philomena. She was going to call him Danny, which was already a good name because of her social worker from long ago, Danny Plourde.

*

Tandi asked Bruno whether he'd talked to Iris yet. He looked at her but didn't answer. Later, rethinking the question, he heard again how she'd said *yet*. As if he would talk to Iris. He only hadn't yet.

That evening when he stopped to check on Mina, she was full with the news of having seen Gabriela. Gabriela had called a few days earlier to tell him she was going to take Mina out for lunch. Was that all right? That was perfect. Mina would be delighted.

Now Bruno heard about the club sandwich and frîtes. A new hat! Mina pointed at the sunhat hanging off her closet doorknob. She smoothed her hand down the new flowered shirt she was wearing. Her words rushed and stumbled over each other, but he saw the slide of her eyes and knew there was something she wasn't telling him about the afternoon. A secret between her and Gabriela? Mina always had secrets.

And if he were being honest with himself, it wasn't only Iris who had maneuvered behind his back. Mina had too.

"Listen," he said. "I need to know what happened between you and Iris."

Mina blinked. Her excitement died. He hadn't meant to cut her off but they could talk about club sandwiches again. He needed to ask this now. "Did you give Iris some of your stitching?"

Mina looked at the TV.

"Did she give you money for them?"

The magic word got her attention. "My money!"

"I think I found it," he said slowly. "I wondered where it came from."

"It's m-m-mine!"

"And you gave her stitching for the money she gave you."

"Yeah."

"You decided it was yours to sell because you made it."

"Yeah."

She didn't sound puzzled or confused or ambivalent. She clearly understood the nature of the transaction, if not all it entailed.

"Okay," he said. "I've got the money and we'll work out something. I know it's yours, but I don't think it's a good idea to keep it here because it might disappear like your Pepsi."

From her expression — and because she didn't protest — he knew she understood.

"If you want, I can bring it so you can count it, and then I'll keep it for you and you can tell me when you want it."

"D'okay," she said grandly.

*

"Me!" Mina shouted before remembering the correct word. "B-b-b-bingo!" She laughed with glee, but the woman next to her was still staring at her card.

The orderly walked over to look. "Hm. How many times in a row now?"

"Four!" Mina was good at bingo and she knew why. Because she separated her yellow, red, and blue chips. The others had their chips all in a heap.

"She cheated," someone grumbled. That old man again. She would get him yet.

"That was a fast game," the orderly said. "Will we play again?"

But the old man had fumbled upright and was knocking into the chairs and tables with his walker.

"Aren't you staying, Charles? You love bingo."

He kept shoving his walker. Someone said, "Ow!" And now everyone was shuffling away and the orderly began walking along the tables, collecting the chips in a Christmas cookie tin. Mina had had social workers like that. They only did what they had to. Not like Madame Bingham who loved her!

The orderly said, "Why don't you go watch TV with the others?" She didn't see how Mina flattened her hand over a few chips and squeezed them in her fist.

"T-T-TV in my room."

"Maybe that's not so good for you."

Mina arched her eyebrows. What a stupid thing to say!

The orderly put the cookie tin and bingo cards in the cupboard and left.

Mina sighed. From down the hallway she could hear the TV in the common room. Why was today so blah? Gabriela should come more often. She sat for a while, feeling stubborn. Hand clenched, she felt the chips pressed into her palm.

That gave her an idea. She could put them in the old man's room and get him into trouble. Now was a good time too because every-one was watching TV.

But in the hallway the levoluva didn't come! And didn't come! When it finally did, the doors didn't close! When they finally shut, the levoluva stayed nowhere, not moving. "Go!" she said. "Move!" She wanted to kick it but that could be dangerous because she was inside. When it finally opened on her floor, she told the levoluva it was stupid.

She waited till it closed again before *not* going to her room, but the other way down the hallway to the old man's room. While she walked, she counted the doors. Twelve of them like in a story, and each one of them unlocked.

*

Bruno was washing the dishes. When the bell rang, he dried his hands on his jeans and walked down the hallway. Iris looked up at him from the sidewalk. He felt himself leap across the three steps to hold her, but his legs didn't move.

"I still have this." She held up the house key he'd given her.

But she didn't hand it up to him and he didn't want to reach down for it. His decades of designing and building sets told him the staging was all wrong. There was no coming together like this. But he didn't ask her to come in, even though his eyes traced the line of her jaw, her shoulders, her hair, the way she stood.

Still holding the key, she gestured at a flat, wrapped package leaning against her legs. "I wanted Mina to have this."

Without even thinking, he shook his head. "No." He still had to protect Mina from her.

"I think you should let her decide." She stooped to pick up the package and carried it up the steps, not pausing when she reached him so that he had to move aside. She set it on the floor in the hall-way and turned to face him. They were level now and he could have stepped closer. But he didn't. Even as he saw her soft mouth. Her sad expression.

"I miss you, Bruno."

He missed her too. But how could he trust her again?

She cleared her throat. "Remember how you told me about your mother breaking off from her family and you didn't even know why? What struck me is that nobody ever reached out, not your mother, not them. You come from a long line of people who hold to their idea of what's right, as if that's all that matters. You told me that the very first morning I was here. I guess I should've listened."

She set the key on the wall shelf and moved past him and down the steps.

He wanted to call, Don't go! Give me a moment! But already his boxed view onto the sidewalk was empty and she was gone.

He closed the door and regarded the package. Even before picking it up, he guessed it was a frame. But he wasn't giving Mina anything from Iris without first seeing what it was. He carried it to the dining room table and peeled off the tape. Folded back the brown paper and saw the frame he'd expected.

Wary but curious, he turned it around — and gaped at the exuberant yodel of colour. Threads crisscrossed and shot in riotous paths of depth and texture. A design of unpredictable energy. Intricate, yet raw too. And so vivid.

Was Iris saying Mina had made this? He could hardly believe it, except ... wasn't Mina always sitting in her corner of the sofa stitching? Their mother had taught her how to thread a needle, but no one had shown her how to create this intriguing meld of colour. That was — that had to be, he realized — pure Mina.

Had their mother understood? He didn't think so. Only Iris had seen what Mina could do.

*

Iris was folding and pinning pleats on the hip of a skirt. Three on each side, each pleat four centimetres deep. Her eye was usually accurate to the half-millimetre, but she was making herself measure each pleat. That morning she'd found a pattern piece on the cutting table and couldn't account for how or when she'd put it there. It didn't belong to this skirt — not even to this client as she immediately saw from the pencilled measurements on the paper. What had she been doing? She couldn't make mistakes like this. If she'd cut out the wrong pattern piece on sixty dollar a metre fabric?

But the scolding voice in her head was dull. So what? Who cared? Bottom lip sucked in, making herself measure the pleats with a small metal ruler before she started basting.

When the phone rang, her head jerked. But it wasn't Bruno.

"Hi," she said dully.

"That bad?" Jenny asked.

"He let me stand on the sidewalk."

"I hope you didn't try to explain yourself." Jenny had told her to stop trying to explain because it put her on the defensive. Iris should move ahead to now.

"I asked him to give Mina the embroidery. I had it all wrapped up."

"He didn't ask what it was?"

"Didn't move a muscle."

"Did you tell him you missed him?" Jenny had suggested that too.

Iris bit her lips to control her hurt, but when she finally said, "Yes," it still came out choked.

"Oh, Iris. I'm sorry."

"Yeah, I am too."

"I don't know." Jenny blew out air. "He sounds like one hard bastard. Maybe —"

"Don't," Iris said. "It's not going to make me feel better to trash him."

*

A lady spun a wheel and fuzzy, coloured mice rolled along a track while people shouted and bells dinged. The lady clapped her hands to her face and shrieked, "A car, a car!"

Mina wrinkled her nose because that didn't mean the lady won a car. In a minute the coloured mice would do something else and the lady would be sobbing and someone would lead her away.

The knock on the door was formal and loud. That was how Bruno always knocked to try to fool her into thinking the X on her door was like a key. It wasn't.

"Hello Mina!" He came in holding a large flat package.

"Wh-wh-what's that? For me?"

"No, I'm schlepping this around the city for my own amusement. Building up my muscles, you know?"

Now he was being stupid. If he brought a package here, then it was for her! Since she was in this new place with the boring old people, he kept bringing her things. That was good, except it didn't make up for all the things he'd thrown away that weren't his to throw away.

He said the package was too heavy for her lap and he put it on the bed. She had to get up out of her chair. It wasn't wrapped properly and she made a disgusted noise so he knew. Ugly brown paper! And only a few pieces of tape! That wasn't how you were supposed to give things.

She ripped the paper and there was a knitting under glass, but it wasn't a good one. None of them were good anymore. The colours didn't throb and shiver and pulse the way they used to.

"You made this. You remember, don't you?"

She remembered how the colours used to call her to make shapes while she told them the stories in her head. The stories were still in her head but the colours didn't call her anymore. They used to dance and leap and twist, and she could feel the movement in her hands. But that didn't happen anymore. The knitting was dead.

"I'll put it up on the wall for you."

"No."

"Why not?"

This wasn't a good present. Pictures of kittens and puppies were better. She shuffled back to her chair and dropped into its comfort.

Bruno stood with his hands on his hips, looking at the knitting on her walls. She didn't put them there and didn't want them there. If she had a broom, she would knock them all down and put them in the garbage.

"You did all this, Mina."

"Before."

He turned around to look at her. "You don't want to do it anymore?"

So many stupid questions. If she wanted to, she would. But she didn't!

"Don't you miss it? Because you did it all the time, Mina. You must have enjoyed it."

On TV a new lady was shrieking. This one had orange hair.

Bruno sat on the bed. "Iris asked me to bring this to you. She thought you would like it."

"No."

"No, you don't like it or no, you don't want it because it's from Iris."

She kept her eyes on the TV.

"What do you want me to do with it?"

"Take it."

"And what about Iris?"

Iris used to take her out for frîtes but she hadn't for a long time. The other thing Iris did was bring the wolf into her room where she lived now. She'd felt the gobbling eyes and heard the sneaky questions. That was very bad. Maybe if Iris took her out for frîtes again, it might be okay again. She wasn't sure. Iris was tricky.

"Did she upset you, Mina?"

Bruno was talking too much and for too long. She stared at the TV, thinking, Go! Stop talking! Get out!

Finally he folded the ugly brown paper over the frame again. "So you want me to take this? I'll put it on my wall and if you ever want it, just tell me."

She wanted him to go! That was what she wanted.

"I don't understand how you did this all the time — since you were little — and now you don't even seem to miss it."

He waited, but she didn't look at him.

"Okay, bye, Mina."

She was glad when he closed the door. She didn't like when he stayed too long or said too much. She knew she used to knit. She didn't now. There was nothing to miss.

Missing was how she felt about Mama. Her apartment. Her things that were hers and were gone now. How she used to be able to walk out the door if she wanted. Get on the bus and go to the dollar store by herself. *That* was missing and it hurt. She didn't like it but Madame Bingham said it was good to hurt like that. It meant you had love in your heart. When she felt too much missing and it made her cry, Madame Bingham held her and it didn't hurt as much.

*

Iris was coming down the sidewalk when the tabby cat from next door bounded from between the bars of the gate to waylay her.

"You want me to scratch behind your ears? That's the spot, eh? Hard for you to reach. You just ask me any time." She felt energized and calm after a long tromp by the river. The vista of open water, the never-still reflection of the sky.

Crouched as she was, she didn't notice the man approaching, until his running shoes stopped in her lowered field of vision. She knew those running shoes. She gave the cat a last head to tail stroke and whispered, "Bruno's come." Then she stood.

"Iris."

But that was all he said. If she looked at him too long, she didn't know what she would do, so she looked past him. She could feel his eyes probing her, but as long as he didn't say why he'd come, she wouldn't speak.

But then she had to ask, "Did you give Mina the embroidery?"

A muscle in his cheek flinched. "I tried and I'm sorry, Iris. She wouldn't take it."

"Did she tell you why?"

He shook his head, and she turned away to hide her hurt that Mina wouldn't accept her gesture.

"Were you heading out for your walk? Can I come?"

"I've just—" She was about to say she was returning, but she was too surprised that he wanted to come.

They didn't speak as they strode down the street, but the silence didn't feel uncomfortable. Walking together was a kind of talking.

They crossed to the embankment where Iris took a trail between the trees to the footpath. Here they had to walk single file. The marsh grasses had grown all summer until they were taller than she was. The willow tree drooped leafy branches to the water.

She was thinking that Bruno wouldn't have come to the river to accuse her. She turned around to face him but hadn't realized how close he was. He nearly bumped into her, drew back, and then didn't.

"You were right," he said. "Mina's embroidery is ..." He widened his eyes. "I don't know why I never saw it, but I didn't."

She cupped both hands to his stubborn head and pulled it to her.

*

Bruno was explaining to Mina that the performance was going to be several short pieces. Each would be unique—different music, different styles of dancing, different dancers. But he could tell she wasn't listening. She was impatient to say something herself. "What is it?" he asked.

"To go with Gabriela!"

"Gabriela? Oh ... Okay, well, ask if she wants to come with you."

"You ask."

"But this is for you." Mina's skewed eyes stayed on him. "You want me to make the arrangements."

"C'est ça."

"I can ask but you know, she might not do it for me. She's not my girlfriend anymore."

"No," Mina said more agreeably than he'd expected. "She has a n-n-new prince."

He'd guessed Gabriela might but he hadn't known that for a fact. "I'm just explaining why she might not say yes."

"Pour moi!" Mina flattened a hand on her chest.

"For you, maybe."

"Yeah!" As far as Mina was concerned, it was happening. And then with a grin, "A better prince!"

"Gabriela has a … better prince than me?"

"He's giving her—" She stopped. He knew that eyes-ears-mouth shut expression.

"He's giving her a ring? You should be happy. Isn't that what you wanted for her?"

Mina's mouth mumbled but she managed to keep the words to herself. He marvelled at the hold Gabriela had on her. And why would it be a secret?

"I don't know if she'll take you to the dance, but I'll ask. Tell me, what's up with your Pepsi? Any more of them missing?"

"No."

"But I'll bet the ones that were missing didn't happen to walk back, did they? And what about the elevator? Any new problems?"

She gave him one of her bland innocent looks. That old man with the walker had better watch out.

Her room was becoming ever more crowded with trinkets and cushions, word puzzle notebooks, pens and markers, perfumed soaps—not to use, just to have—pictures of kittens, the dresser drawers decorated with shiny stars and Donald Duck stickers. She didn't knit or embroider anymore, but Iris had tacked several embroideries on the walls. The expression and movement of colour in the designs were so wildly creative and lively. He couldn't account for how he hadn't seen it before. Because he was too close to Mina? Too beset by all she needed to keep her comfortable, dreading every new *something to tell you?*

Iris had shown him the videos of Judith Scott and perhaps, maybe, the art world wasn't the freak show he'd imagined. Judith Scott seemed to be respected for who she was. Although he still believed that Mina wouldn't have liked the fanfare of going public. She'd always preferred to be private in her apartment. She didn't like to have her routines disturbed. Her tolerance for people was limited. She'd stitched obsessively, but had she ever shown it to anyone before Iris? Even that must have been Iris's idea, not Mina's. He remembered the stack of embroidery she'd kept next to her on the sofa like a darling pet. Her embroidery wasn't meant for anyone but her. What she loved best, she always kept to herself.

Even when — ha! — it didn't belong to her. He stretched across the bed to snatch up the cushion embroidered with gold and silver swirls. He knew she wouldn't tell him but still he asked, "Where did you get this?"

"It's m-m-mine."

"Yours because you've got it now, but whose was it before?"

She ignored the question. A firm adherent of the finders keepers school, she'd long ago learned how to find what she wanted to keep.

"And that —" He nodded at the doll propped on the windowsill. It looked like the dolls he'd beheaded and painted because they were too peach-coloured and cute. "Since when have you started playing with dolls?"

Cross-eyed indignation. "Not to p-p-play!"

"What else do you do with a doll?"

"She's my friend."

He was about to say that a doll couldn't be a friend, but he remembered how important it had been to their mother to have her grandmother's doll with her in Canada. "So what you're telling me is that this doll wandered in one day and hopped up on your windowsill."

Mina patted inside her armrest where there would have been room if she didn't fill the chair so completely. "She s-s-sits with me."

"I'm asking how she got here."

A proud tilt of the head. "A cadeau."

"Who's giving you presents?"

Her clapped-shut face again. Maybe Gabriela gave her the doll. Except Mina would happily have boasted if she had. And Iris hadn't been here. Who else then? Confined to a residence, her dominion no larger than a room, and still Mina conjured secrets.

*

One patient after another, each individual, each also the same. The man at 9:45 had been doing the exercises Gabriela had given him two weeks earlier, but with unnecessary force. She coached him through them all over again. "Just press, don't shove. Pull slowly, don't swing. Stop before you feel pain." How did people get so dissociated from their bodies?

She kept an eye on the clock so as to phone Mina more or less on time. Yesterday Bruno had called to say that Mina absolutely wanted Gabriela to bring her to a dance. Gabriela said she was happy to go with Mina. She always used to enjoy the dances. He surprised her then by asking if she wanted an extra ticket for her new friend to come as well. Had there been a hint of sarcasm or was he trying in his clumsy Bruno way to be gracious? What else had Mina told him? That wasn't necessary, she said, Mina would be her date. She said she was glad that Mina was adjusting to life in the residence. He said he wasn't sure if adjusting was the right word — though she was settling in. In spite of perils, hazards, and pitfalls, Mina continued. She was like a character in his old book of fairy tales.

Gabriela glanced at her watch. 10:03. Mina would be waiting. "That's good," she told the patient. "Keep doing these, twice a day — but gently. Remember, you're stretching, not forcing."

Mina answered on the first ring. She was always happy to get a call, but today she sounded more than usually excited.

"What's up with you?" Gabriela asked.

"La danse!"

"So you know I'm coming with you."

"Avec ma grand amour!"

"What's that?"

"With my grand amour."

"I thought I was your belle-coeur. Am I your grand amour too?"

"No! Ma grand amour!"

"This is someone new?"

"Yeah!"

"Someone you met at the residence?"

"Yeah."

Gabriela hadn't expected that Mina would be attracted to any of the elderly residents, but she'd also never heard her call anyone her amour, much less her grand amour. Whoever it was had shot an arrow deep into Mina's heart. "That's great, Mina. I guess that's why you're so happy these days."

"Yeah!"

"Just like me then. You've got a new prince too."

"Not a p-p-prince!"

"But you just said you met someone."

"A princess!"

After an instant of surprise, Gabriela realized she wasn't surprised at all. Mina had always been more affectionate with women. At best, boyfriends were social accessories. Names to embroider and post on the wall to show she'd had them. Easy come, easy go, never all that important in themselves.

"My grand amour ..."

Gabriela had never heard her sound so dreamy. "You seem very happy."

"My grand amour is coming to the dance!"

"Did you tell Bruno?"

"... No."

"I'll talk with Bruno. We'll bring your grand amour."

*

"I thought you'd be over the moon about your big reunion. Makeup sex and all that." Jenny's tone was saucy but she held herself as still as the tailors' dummies beside her. She wore only her bra, camisole, and a skirt turned inside out. She bought clothes to fit her hips and brought them to Iris to make the waistline smaller. Clothes off the rack were made for skinny or blob-shaped people. *She* had a proper figure with curves.

Iris was on her knees, tucking and pinning the skirt. "I'm deliriously happy. Bruno's the real deal and I'm not letting him go. We talked all night and explained everything. Why I did what I did, and he ..." She winced. "... he explained why he did what he did. And he sees now that Mina is an artist and I ..." She exhaled with annoyance. "... I understand that he takes his responsibilities as her guardian very seriously." She sat back on her feet, scowling. "We've forgiven each other and everything's great."

"Then why are you making such a face?"

"The construction of this skirt is below par, even for clothes off the rack."

"What do you mean? It cost $250!"

"There should be a facing here, not just material folded over and top-stitched."

"Nothing's ever up to your standards," Jenny said. "Except for the amazing Bruno from the sounds of it." She sucked in her tummy as Iris unzipped the pin-studded skirt and eased it down her hips.

"You can get dressed again. I'm not working on this now." Iris held the skirt under a lamp and scraped her fingernail across the slipshod excuse for a waistband. What a mess — and at such an inflated price. She lay the skirt on the ironing board, a small nightmare to deal with later.

"And Mina, what about her? Have you seen her yet?"

"Not since the last time when she wouldn't talk to me. But Bruno said not to worry. He said she'll forgive most anything if you buy her a plate of frîtes. One of these days he'll tell her about us and we'll take her out for lunch. There's no rush."

"You don't sound too interested, considering how you were ready to champion her."

Iris opened her hands as if to show they were empty. "She doesn't want to be championed. And anyhow, what choice do I have? As far as I can tell, the cerebral bleed she had killed Philomena. It's like she doesn't even remember what she used to be able to do. Bruno said when he gave her the framed embroidery, she acted like she'd never seen it before."

As she spoke, she walked across to the embroidery book that lay on the sewing table. She'd shown it to Bruno, who was once again impressed by what Mina had created and how handsomely Iris had presented it. She asked if he minded her keeping it in her studio as a display. Textile art complemented her work. Clients who came for fittings might leaf through the book. He said he would make a pedestal table for it.

The embroidery book was open on an energetic composition of shimmying jellyfish splashes in lime green, lavender, silver and black. Iris squinted, so the outlines blurred and she only made out the colours.

Jenny traced her fingers along a curve of thick stitches. "Her work always makes me want to touch it."

Iris gave a long, shuddering breath. "That she doesn't remember how she used to embroider hurts me. Mina was so gifted — and just like that, it's gone."

*

Bruno walked past the living room where residents slouched on the sofas, faces turned to the TV — the only sun that still lit their failing minds. Not one among them, male or female, looked like a possible heartthrob for Mina.

Gabriela had called to ask if he'd noticed whether Mina had a particular friend at the residence. Hardly, he said. If anything, she was fighting with everyone. Not everyone, Gabriela said. There was someone she was calling her grand amour. Really? Mina was always alone when he came. He couldn't even guess who the new Romeo was. Rome*a*, Gabriela said. Oh. He paused. That was new. Though maybe Mina wasn't explaining herself well — like the man getting between her legs with his walker. Mina was pretty clear, Gabriela said. She called her grand amour a princess. I think she's in love, Bruno. I mean really and truly. *Mina?* Bruno said. He was glad if she met someone — he didn't care who it was — but for Mina nobody was ever as important as Mina. Did she tell you who? he asked. No. Neither spoke for a moment. She's an adult, he said then. She makes her own choices. But after what happened with Pierre, I think I'll check.

He knocked on Mina's door, waited until he heard her call, "Yeah?" and opened it cautiously. She was alone, watching TV. Her face was placid, her hands folded across her belly.

At times he missed how she used to begin every conversation with a resounding *s-s-something to tell you*. Was it age, was it living here where everything was done for her, or had she suffered damage from her cerebral bleed? She seemed to be more content — and he hoped she was. As she made fewer demands, his life had become easier too. But it still gave him a little ache to see how quietly she sat, her once-busy hands at rest.

"How are you?" he asked.

"F-f-fine."

"No complaints?"

Her expression didn't change.

"What about if I gave you five dollars?"

"Yeah!"

"So money still matters."

She held out her hand.

"I didn't mean that I was giving you five dollars. I said *if*."

She banged her open hand on the armrest. "Cinq dollars."

He pulled out his wallet. "I suppose I asked for this. Hm ... all I have is a ten."

"D'okay."

"I'll bet it's d'okay."

She folded it into a tiny square, and though he was watching, he didn't see where she put it. But it was gone. Disappeared.

"Gabriela was telling me you've got a new romance in your life."

She raised her chin. "My grand amour."

"Are you going to tell me who it is?"

"To take her to the dance!"

"It is a her then."

"Yeah."

"So who is it?"

She kept her eyes on him but wouldn't say. That was odd. Her boyfriends had never been a secret.

"I need a name for the ticket for the dance." Not true but Mina didn't know that.

Nothing.

"I can't get a ticket for her if I don't have a name." Still Mina said nothing.

"I know who it is," he sing-songed. "It's the lady with the flowers on her door."

"No!" And then proudly, "C'est Madame Bingham."

He took his elbows off his knees and sat upright. Mina must have misunderstood. Madame Bingham was always eager to show off that she could win Mina's confidence, but this time she'd clearly overdone it. "It's because she takes such good care of you. That's why you call her your grand amour."

"She loves me," Mina said with stately calm.

"There's love and there's love, Mina. It's not like when you had boyfriends."

"Better."

"What do you mean, better?"

"B-b-better."

"But you don't … there's nothing going on, is there?"

"L'amour!"

"You don't have sex with Madame Bingham."

Mina scrunched her mouth, disgusted. "No white stuff!"

"No, Madame Bingham wouldn't have that. But …" He hated prying but he had to protect Mina. "Do you take your clothes off?"

"I love her!"

He got up from the bed and walked to the corner windows where he had a view onto grey sky, the last tattered leaves on the trees, an empty parking lot. He didn't believe anything sexual had happened. It sounded more like emotional intimacy — and what if Mina had only imagined what she thought was happening? Like the man with the walker.

Even so, that she expressed love was unusual. She'd been stubborn about some of her boyfriends, but never emotional. She was usually too focussed on her own interests to get attached. But when she did, the bond was deep and loyal. She would always love Gabriela. She still mourned their parents. He had to be careful never to mention their childhood dog, Youpi, or she would cry as if she'd just lost him.

He turned away from the window. Mina sat with her arms hugged across her chest. Tears wet her face.

"Madame Bingham works here, Mina. She's responsible for taking care of you. You're not supposed to feel like that about her. She's not supposed to let that happen."

"I love her! Je l'aime!"

He'd never seen her like this. He wished he knew what to do. He grabbed a few tissues from the box and handed them to her. "Blow your nose. Calm down. Let me think, okay?"

He tried to lighten the mood while making her a cup of tea, saying how lucky she was to have a fridge with milk in her room. If not, just think, he would have to go all the way downstairs for milk, and by the time he got back — after waiting for that elevator that *never* came — her tea would be cold.

Mina agreed that the levoluva was stupid. Her attention was caught by some clowning on TV. From over the bed, the angel watched with a benign expression. Head nestled within the flutter of freshly gilt wings. He wondered what their mother would do.

He was used to Mina's anger, her resentment, even when she hated him because he didn't do what she wanted. But she'd never before professed love and it disarmed him.

*

Iris had pinned pattern pieces for a shirt onto pinwale corduroy, traced their outline with chalk, and was cutting them out. Her hands moved like the skilled appendages they were, but a few times she stopped, eyes narrowed at the scissors.

When she and Bruno had their long marathon talk, she'd forgotten about the bags she'd taken from Mina's apartment. No, not taken. *Rescued.* If she hadn't, Bruno would have thrown them out. He wouldn't now, but he would have then.

When she remembered the bags, she realized they would be harder to explain. What if she told Bruno and he thought she'd stolen them?

Taken, rescued, stolen: each word carried its own moral weight. And when it came to Mina, there was never any telling how Bruno would react. Could Iris take that risk?

Obviously the embroideries belonged to Mina, who'd made them, but if she no longer wanted them, why couldn't Iris have them? She was the one who'd discovered them. She knew their story. She was taking good care of them too. She had them neatly stored in boxes now, individually layered between acid-free paper. She had no clear sense of why she was keeping them safe, only that she had to. For their sake, if not for Mina.

Iris wanted everything to be open and honest with Bruno, but why introduce new complications? Why mention the bags, if no one knew about them?

For now, they were safe. And if one day it happened that some-one asked if there was more of this fabulous textile art ...

She would deal with it then.

*

Since Mina had told him who her grand amour was, Bruno had been trying to see Madame Bingham. First it was her day off and the next two days she was already gone when he arrived.

Mina persisted in saying that she loved Madame Bingham, who loved her too. He talked to Iris, who said he needed to get Madame Bingham's side of the story. Gabriela agreed with him that Mina shouldn't be so attached to someone who worked there. However, she also pointed out that Mina was happier about living in the resi-dence—happier than she'd ever been with her many boyfriends. If Bruno accused Madame Bingham of being too affectionate and she then stopped, where would that leave Mina? When he asked Tandi, she said she thought Mina's happiness was what mattered most. Who cared if Madame Bingham worked there? Bruno wanted to do what was right, but what was right in this case?

This morning he'd come even earlier and gone directly to the kitchen where he said he needed to speak with Madame Bingham on an urgent matter. As he waited, he watched an orderly smear beige paste across rows of sliced white bread. The paste could have been chicken or tuna or pulverized newsprint. The bread was slapped together, cut in half, and heaped on plates. Bruno was daring him-self to ask if that was going to be served for lunch when he heard a flurry of movement and rapid steps.

"Monsieur Corneau." Madame Bingham and her two chins.

"I wanted to speak with you about my sister."

"That's where I was just now. We spend a little time together every morning."

"When you say together—"

"Well, of course! The poor dear needs a cuddle. There's no warmth in this place. Don't you think I know that? And you, you come when you can, but do you give her a good hug and hold her?" She paused but didn't seem to expect an answer.

He pushed up his glasses. At most he patted Mina on the back or squeezed her shoulders.

"Who does then, eh? You're her only family—and if you don't?" She opened a cupboard and took out a couple of jumbo bags of potato chips and bowls.

"The problem," he said, "is that Mina feels more than affection. She says she loves you."

"I love her too. You should be glad she gets some love and warmth in this place." She wrinkled her nose at the plates of sandwiches on the counter. "You think I don't know that's not a proper meal? But it's all we've got the budget for. We do our best, but the owner—"

"My sister doesn't usually say she loves people."

"Well! I *hope* I'm more than people!"

"I'm concerned about her misunderstanding and being hurt—"

"I would never hurt her." She tore open the bags and upended chips into the bowls.

"She's a resident and you work here. That's an abuse of—"

"Don't give me that mumbo-jumbo," she said curtly. "I take care of everyone here. But your sister, yes, she has a special place in my heart. I told you that already. What I don't understand is why you're complaining. I'm here every morning, making sure she wakes up with a smile. You should be happy!"

"But if you become too important to her—"

"How can anyone ever be too important? She's very important to me too."

Madame Bingham was so defiant. She would hardly let him talk. "I'm concerned for my sister."

"Good, good, good." Madame Bingham bobbed her head up and

down. "You be concerned." She crumpled the bags and stuffed them in the garbage.

"I'm responsible for her so I have to ask."

"Ask then — ask!" She snatched a rag from the sink to wipe up the crumbs on the counter.

"The doll in her room — did you give it to her?"

She rolled her eyes. "She isn't allowed to get presents now?"

"She's an adult, not a child. A doll —"

"She's an adult who gets lonely. She used to go out into the city and now she's cooped up in a room. If a doll makes her feel she has company, why can't she have one?"

It was true, whenever he came lately, she had the doll squished beside her in the armchair.

Madame Bingham dropped the folded rag over the tap and turned to him. "Off you go to your busy life then. And don't worry, we're taking good care of your sister."

He opened his mouth to protest but then didn't. To her, that must be how it seemed. How, he realized, it was.

"I have things to do," Madame Bingham muttered. And not waiting for him to leave, she walked from the kitchen.

*

Once upon a time, when Mina lived in her apartment, she had a floppy pink top hat. She never wore it because the day never felt right. She kept it in one of her many bags, waiting for the right day.

Today, after breakfast, she pulled the only hat bag she had left from her closet, rooted around inside, and finally had to upend all the hats on the floor.

There! She plucked up the pink top hat that had escaped Bruno throwing it away! She shoved the other hats back in the bag that she stuffed in the closet again. She was panting by the time she was finished — but nothing was too much effort for her grand amour!

In the mirror she fixed the angle and brim, and then sat to wait.

The doll waited with her. "Bientôt," she told her. "She'll come soon." She didn't make tea because Madame Bingham would do that for her. The TV was on but she kept her eyes on the door.

Madame Bingham never knocked. She didn't have to. There was only silence and suddenly the door opened like magic and there she was. "Look at you! Aren't you a darling in that adorable hat?"

Madame Bingham's delight suffused Mina with delight. "My f-f-funny hat!"

"Funny because you want me to laugh at you?" Madame Bingham bustled around the room, picking up things and putting them away.

"For having fun."

"You should wear it when we have a dance downstairs and we all get together. You should have fun with the others too."

Mina pouted. Not the old man, not him!

Madame Bingham sat on the bed, shaking her head at her. "Come here, you."

Mina heaved herself up as quickly as she could because she wanted to lie down and cuddle, but Madame Bingham stayed upright and made her sit beside her. "Listen to me, Minnie. You have to stop with that attitude. We all live here together and we have to get along."

"Don't like the old man."

"Can't you try to be nice to him?"

"No."

"Not even for me?" Madame Bingham slid her arm around Mina's shoulders. The funny hat got pushed back but it didn't matter. Their faces were together and Mina felt happy.

"Hm?" Madame Bingham coaxed. "Will you try?"

Mina waited for the kiss that should have come, but Madame Bingham was waiting too. Finally Mina sighed. "D'okay."

"That's my Minnie Mouse. I knew you would agree." Madame Bingham kissed her on the nose. "And," with her own big sigh, "your brother, there."

Mina groaned softly. Not Bruno, not now.

"He came to see me yesterday, asking all kinds of questions. As if I don't know that my little Minnie Mouse loves me."

"Yeah!" Mina lifted her head. "I l-l-love you!"

"I know you do, my pet." Madame Bingham kissed her on the forehead. "I love you too. You are my very own, my dearest Minnie."

Mina nestled her head under Madame Bingham's chin again, but just thinking about Bruno, who was always doing the wrong things, made her breath go fast. "Bruno —" she began angrily.

"Don't get upset now. He's your brother."

Mama used to say that too. But a brother was supposed to take care of you, not keep being stupid! If he didn't watch out, he was going to ... end up a big black bird! The idea made her snort. Bruno as a big black bird!

But she didn't want to think about Bruno now with Madame Bingham's arm around her. She wanted to breathe in the warm smell of soap and cooking. Wiggle her finger between the buttons on Madame Bingham's blouse. Revel in being held safe and loved by her grand amour.

*

Entwined limbs, torsos snaked, a head jutted between thighs, a glittery gold foot wiggled high. The dancers were helplessly, hopelessly joined. A back arched until it seemed it would break at the hips. Did the dancers want to tear from each other to the point of tearing themselves apart? They rolled against the wall, strained to climb it, crab-crawled up the ramp.

Boogie, who sat with his cello left centre, made sounds. A pinging scrape across strings. A sonorous pluck. The stick of his bow tapped on the wood. As the bodies continued to fight to escape their knot, he began to bow fierce strains to encourage them.

Flinging each other about, upside-down, stretching, arms wheeling, torsos wrenching away from twisted legs — only to snap into a contorted ball again. Still the cello thrummed, urging them to keep trying. Again they churned their limbs, determined to break free.

Bruno had seen the choreography being developed and been present with his notebook for several run-throughs as he and Val discussed lighting. He always admired dance for the geometry of movement and bodies, and there was no doubt this was a short but very intense piece.

But today, sitting on a prop box, watching, he was mesmerized by the desperate tension of their togetherness. The bonds of emotion, history, obligation, love, and memory. The fierceness of their knot.

When — as if jolted from within — the dancers lurched apart into separateness and silence. They stumbled, unsure how to balance on only two legs with only one torso, one head, two arms. They experimented with this new relationship to gravity, the floor, the wall, the air. All that could be heard was the thud of their steps, the percussive beat of flesh and bone on the planks.

They could move? They could! Like gleeful, freshly escaped thieves they crept and leapt to diagonally opposed corners, about to flee, when Boogie drew his bow across the strings. Their heads swung around to gaze upon the emptiness where they had been joined — crippled — together. With their golden hands they tapped and touched their bodies, assuring themselves they were single and whole. Independent! They stamped their golden feet.

Another long tone from the cello. Fear? The menace of loss?

Bruno felt his breath catch, his throat thicken.

When Boogie drew his bow again, the magic of the third time compelled the dancers to take a step toward centre stage. Both were wary, one crouched, the other taut to spring away. They moved like cats with golden paws.

Shrinking but brave, fierce to stay separate, yet they faced each other. She opened her arms, bent a knee, and lifted a golden foot. He set gentle hands on her waist and she dipped her head to the floor, leg swung high behind her for that instant of balance — a movement they could only do together — and she straightened again. The briefest pas de deux but it had taken all their daring.

And look! They were still whole and separate! Twinkling hands and feet, they scampered off, no longer in terror to escape. Free now to leap into the future.

There was silence and then Val said, "Excellent! Good work, people."

Boogie straightened in his chair. Mathieu stood with his legs apart, forehead glistening. Tandi was still bent, hands on her knees. Lifting her head she said, "That knot is harder than cartwheeling circles around the stage for three minutes."

"You're on top of each other constantly," Val said. "You're not just balancing your own weight but his too."

"She's no feather either," Mathieu said.

"My love," Tandi crooned. "You always give me the sweetest compliments."

Bruno still felt the haunting tone of the cello. The tension of the knot. The clamped limbs. He too, once Mina was gone, was going to have to find a new balance.

Someone sat next to him. Tandi, he thought, but it was Val who said, "Are you okay?"

He didn't know how to explain. Except that day in and day out he worked with these people. If anyone knew him, they should. "Mina," he said. "My sister and me."

"Is that what you felt?" Val's arm on his back tightened. Boogie plucked a string. Tandi lifted onto her gold toes, arms out to Mathieu who gracefully dipped her again. A gift for Bruno.

Later that evening, when Bruno was telling Iris about this last rehearsal before they moved to the venue, he said that when Val first talked about the dance, he'd assumed the goal was escape and that was how it would end. But this ending — with the dancers coming together for a single, delicate pas de deux — was more powerful. That moment when trust was stronger than fear or loss.

9

Gabriela was walking from the métro to the residence where she would collect Mina and Madame Bingham. The three of them would take a cab.

Her dress swished around her legs. She'd spritzed a little perfume on her neck. She was looking forward to the evening with Mina, finally meeting the famous Madame Bingham, and of course to the performance.

Daniel had hinted that he might be sitting incognito a few rows behind them. You don't have to come incognito, she said. Bruno would have gotten you a ticket. He's not like that — or he shouldn't be, because he's already got a new girlfriend. Also, you won't be incognito if Mina sees you. Incognito serves its purpose, he said. Mina would get it. Anyhow, she likes me. How can you be so sure? she asked. He gave a soft laugh. She would have let us know if she didn't.

*

The first number of the evening was a solo dancer crumping to mechanized sounds. Bruno knew Mina wouldn't like the music — though she might not remember it after the snappy bebop of the second number, which she would like. Two dancers strutted in connecting circles, bumping hips and buttocks when they met. The moves got more acrobatic and clownish. The audience laughed.

As Bruno waited for his turn in the tech booth, he watched Mina,

Gabriela, and Madame Bingham in the front row as per Mina's dictates. He'd gone to see them before the start of the show. Mina had a green hat jammed on the side of her head, but instead of a button, she had a brooch pinned to it. It looked genuine — a purple stone set in silver? He started to wonder where she'd gotten it, but quickly shut down the thought. He didn't want to know.

Madame Bingham had donned what he guessed was her finest polyester pantsuit. She sat with her shoulders squared and cleft chin powdered. She informed him that she had been to many spectacles before. He said he hoped she would enjoy this one.

Beside her, Mina beamed. Madame Bingham would never be his favourite person, but for the time that Mina still had left in this world, he wanted her to be happy.

He greeted Gabriela and she smiled at him. A beautiful woman with a kind heart. Her kind heart had kept her with him. She should have left sooner. He hoped she would have her baby.

People were thronging in and he had to step past and around them to get back to the tech booth. As he moved, he scanned the crowd until he spotted Iris. Her curly hair and bright eyes. She fluttered her fingers in a wave. Beside her sat her friend. He hadn't met her yet but after the show they were all going out for sushi.

*

Even absorbed in the pulse of the bodies, the lights, the colours, and the music, Mina never forgot that she had her grand amour on one side and her belle-coeur on the other. Being with her two great loves filled her with joy.

On stage the bodies tugged and pulled. Light bled across them, winking reflections off their gold hands and feet. The gold burst and waved at her, pulled at her eyes.

She knew the knot of bodies had to break so they could leap apart. She knew that as surely as when she used to knit and the colours told her how to make shapes.

The lovely swoops and punches of movement shivered pleasure through her. This was how music swayed and twisted in her belly when she danced. Once upon a time she could feel with her hands how colours swayed and twisted. How they strove, quivered, looped, buckled, and swivelled. The colours used to dance with her hands. They didn't anymore, but the dancing of the bodies under the lights made her remember.

Her heart flew with the marvellous soar of movement. She was so happy that she laughed aloud.

ACKNOWLEDGEMENTS

I could not have written this novel nor created the character Mina without having known my sister-in-law Joann Aubé. She was fiercely independent, inventive, smart, and stubborn. She had never been taught to read and had no interest in books. Yet when I told her that I wanted to write about someone like her, she admitted that it could be a good story. Merci, ma belle-coeur! I did my best.

I am ever grateful to Elise Moser for suggesting that I write this novel. She believed in it before I did.

I appreciate those who read early drafts and encouraged me. Heartfelt thanks to Anita Lahey for her always thoughtful, sensitive, and incisive feedback. Shaun Bradley of Transatlantic Agency offered invaluable insight and advice on re-envisioning the novel. Suzette Mayr kindly responded to an urgent request for editorial assessment, which helped me make crucial decisions. Thank you.

Deep acknowledgement to those who shared their knowledge and experience, which helped me better imagine the worlds of my characters. Clara Congdon graciously invited me to her studio to talk about textile art and embroidery. Susana Vera unstintingly shared her expertise in the design and construction of beautiful clothing. Monika Kapeller gave me a detailed demonstration of the many steps in gold-leafing. Stephen Morgan, Chris Plunkett, and countless backstage crew members spoke with me about set design, building sets, lights, sound, and stage management. Rob Clutton was generous with his musical smarts. Werner Campidell brought me to Burg Frauenstein where, years later, Bruno had a dream about a castle cellar. Randi Helmers helped me think through possible titles. My kinesiologist, Lucy Pereira, set the example for the work Gabriela does. Any errors, misunderstandings, or inventions are mine.

I am delighted to live in Montreal where contemporary dance is so spellbinding that I was compelled to write about it. Thank you to Gaby Agis for commenting on early pages. Susi Lovell offered later guidance, movement exercises, and a suggestion that was perfect. Any errors in understanding or description of dance are mine.

My Campidell Opa gave me the book of Grimms' fairy tales, so hauntingly illustrated by Fritz Fischer, that explains the world to Mina. When I told Carin Makuz about my fascination with Judith Scott, she sent me Betsy Bayha's movie, *Outsider: The Life and Art of Judith Scott*. And what luck! In 2016 the World of Threads Festival in Oakville, Ontario, hosted an exhibition of Judith Scott's fibre sculptures that we visited.

I am thankful for the generous support of the Canada Council for the Arts and the Conseil des arts et des lettres du Québec during the writing of this book. I am also fortunate in having the moral support of the community and resources offered by the wonderful Quebec Writers' Federation.

The team at Freehand Books have been a delight to work with. Deborah Willis's insightful questions and sense of nuance helped me find the current shape of the novel. It has been a learning experience and a joy to work with her as an editor. Especial thanks to Kelsey Attard for her enthusiasm and deft attention to details. Thank you Colby Clair Stolson for the marketing wizardry that's beyond my ken. A happy thumbs-up to Natalie Olsen for yet another fabulous book design.

Where would I be without my friends to discuss the what-ifs and hows of writing? I am blessed to count you among my circle.

As ever, my deepest love and gratitude to Robert Aubé for sharing my life and being with me. Always.

Alice Zorn has published two novels, *Arrhythmia* and *Five Roses*, and a book of short fiction, *Ruins & Relics*. *Five Roses* was a finalist for the 2017 Ontario Library Association Evergreen Award and translated into French. *Ruins & Relics* was shortlisted for the 2009 Quebec Writers' Federation First Book Award. A new book of short stories will be forthcoming with NeWest Press in 2026. Originally from Ontario, she now lives in Montreal.